Praise for
The Accidental Werewolf

"Cassidy, a prolific author of erotica, has ventured into MaryJanice Davidson territory with a humorous, sexy tale." —*Booklist*

"If Bridget Jones became a lycanthrope, she might be Marty. Fun and flirty humor is cleverly interspersed with dramatic mystery and action. It's hard to know which character to love best, though: Keegan or Muffin, the toy poodle that steals more than one scene." —*The Eternal Night*

"A riot! Marty's internal dialogue will have you howling, and her antics will keep the laughs coming. If you love paranormal with a comedic twist, you'll love this book." —*Romance Junkies*

"A lighthearted romp . . . [An] entertaining tale with an alpha twist." —*Midwest Book Review*

More Praise for
The Novels of Dakota Cassidy

"The fictional equivalent of the little black dress . . . funny, sexy, and a must-have accessory for every reader." —Michele Bardsley, national bestselling author of *Because Your Vampire Said So*

"Serious, laugh-out-loud humor with heart, the kind of love story that leaves you rooting for the heroine, sighing for the hero, and looking for your own significant other at the same time." —Kate Douglas, author of *Wolf Tales*

"Dakota Cassidy is going on my must-read list!" —*Joyfully Reviewed*

"If you're looking for some steamy romance with something that will have you smiling, you have to read [Dakota Cassidy]." —*The Best Reviews*

"Ditsy and daring . . . pure escapist fun." —*Romance Reviews Today*

THE
ACCIDENTAL
HUMAN

DAKOTA CASSIDY

B

BERKLEY SENSATION, NEW YORK

THE BERKLEY PUBLISHING GROUP
Published by the Penguin Group
Penguin Group (USA) Inc.
375 Hudson Street, New York, New York 10014, USA

Penguin Group (Canada), 90 Eglinton Avenue East, Suite 700, Toronto, Ontario M4P 2Y3, Canada
(a division of Pearson Penguin Canada Inc.)
Penguin Books Ltd., 80 Strand, London WC2R 0RL, England
Penguin Group Ireland, 25 St. Stephen's Green, Dublin 2, Ireland (a division of Penguin Books Ltd.)
Penguin Group (Australia), 250 Camberwell Road, Camberwell, Victoria 3124, Australia
(a division of Pearson Australia Group Pty. Ltd.)
Penguin Books India Pvt. Ltd., 11 Community Centre, Panchsheel Park, New Delhi—110 017, India
Penguin Group (NZ), 67 Apollo Drive, Rosedale, North Shore 0632, New Zealand
(a division of Pearson New Zealand Ltd.)
Penguin Books (South Africa) (Pty.) Ltd., 24 Sturdee Avenue, Rosebank, Johannesburg 2196,
South Africa

Penguin Books Ltd., Registered Offices: 80 Strand, London WC2R 0RL, England

This book is an original publication of The Berkley Publishing Group.

This is a work of fiction. Names, characters, places, and incidents either are the product of the author's imagination or are used fictitiously, and any resemblance to actual persons, living or dead, business establishments, events, or locales is entirely coincidental. The publisher does not have any control over and does not assume any responsibility for author or third-party websites or their content.

PRINTING HISTORY
Berkley Sensation trade paperback edition / March 2009

Library of Congress Cataloging-in-Publication Data

Cassidy, Dakota.
    The accidental human / Dakota Cassidy.—Berkley sensation trade pbk. ed.
      p. cm.
    ISBN 978-0-425-22595-0
    1. Women sales personnel—Fiction. 2. Selling—Cosmetics—Fiction. 3. Vampires—Fiction. I. Title.

    PS3603.A8685A64 2009
    813'.6—dc22   2008049049

PRINTED IN THE UNITED STATES OF AMERICA

10 9 8 7 6 5 4 3 2 1

DEDICATION

For my friends who love my craziness like a red-blooded male loves a good Victoria's Secret catalogue: Diane Whiteside, Sheri Fogarty, Kira Stone, Michelle Hoppe, Angela Knight, Erin, Jaynie Ritchie, Vicki Burklund, and Kim Castillo.

A very special thanks to Terri Smythe, Michele Bardsley, and Renee George because—suuunnnschineeeee on my schoulders makes me haaaaapppyyyy. They'll know what that means—I hope they know what they mean to me.

As always, The Babes and my Yahoo! group of "Accidental Fans"—you guys rule! Some fans that flew from parts near and far to come to my crazy book launch party—Amy, Kaz, Ali, and Alana—dudes, you da coolest.

My poor mother, Eleanor, who does everything for me but brush my teeth, and even then, she leaves a sticky note on my desk to remind me it's a no-discussion rule.

My sons, Travis and Cameron, who've found deep meaning (and dinner) in the middle of two pieces of stale bread and a slice of pasteurized American cheese. Thanks for making due when I don't have time to cook. Mommy loves ya.

My editor, Cindy Hwang, who so gets me and offered me the opportunity to finish this series that is so close to my heart. Leis Pederson, her assistant, who's brilliantly organized and crazy awesome.

My agent, Deidre Knight, without whom none of this would be possible.

Nina Bangs, who, when I began writing just four years ago after reading so many of her books, inspired me to take paranormal romance to the place I call zany and made me feel like it was crazy cool, but above all, okay.

And always, Rob, who smiles fondly while the swirling cloud that can sometimes be me and my personality flits from place to place, but also because he's taught me what it is to be loved by the real definition of a man. He cheers my successes, soothes my fears, and knows nothin' says lovin' like a Starbucks white chocolate mocha.

A very special thanks to Elaine Smythe. Here's to a woman well loved, a battle well fought, a friendship forever remembered and cherished.

ACKNOWLEDGMENTS

To Wikipedia, Diane Whiteside (brilliant writer), whose knowledge of all things historical left me shamefaced and very grateful she's my friend. To Gerianne Bliss, MD, who answered many of my medical-symptom-type questions. Also, to the Johns Hopkins website, and Iamtransgendered.com. And to all the women who may read this—*please, please*, see your gynecologist for regular checkups and pay it forward by hassling the crap out of the women in your lives to make sure they do, too.

CHAPTER 1

"Wanda?"

Damn. Not Nina. Not now. "Hey, Nina. What's up?"

"What's up? Did you just ask me what's up all casual-like? Have you lost your fucking mind? How could you ask *me* what's up? What the hell's up with *you?"*

Wanda ran a shaky finger down her list of things to prepare for tonight's Bobbie-Sue in-home party and answered distractedly, "I don't know what you mean." She braced the phone against her shoulder and put her pen behind her ear. Darn, had she made enough vegetable dip? Oh, God—vegetable dip was crucial to any in-home party. A clammy sweat accumulated on her palms as she grabbed her pen and searched her list of things to do for the amount of vegetable dip she'd made.

"What do you mean you don't know what I mean? Were you up reading those stupid romance novels into the wee hours again? What'd I tell you about reading that shit? It's bad for your eyes, it leaves you with unrealistic expectations of a man, and it keeps you up too late. Then you don't get enough sleep, and lately, you really look like you could use some shut-eye."

Running a finger over her throbbing temple, Wanda struggled to stay focused and ignore Nina's gibe about her appearance. She had a damned-good reason why she looked so tired. Like the biggest reason ever.

A sob welled in Wanda's chest, begging to be set free. Breathing. She was breathing. At least for the moment, anyway. Next week? Maybe not so much. "Look, lay off the romance novels, okay? They're my escape and I'm not going to defend them to you for the millionth time. Besides, don't make me break out the 'alpha male' card. You have one, and so does Marty. So again, I say, those romance authors can't be far off the mark. Now, I'm lost, Nina, and I have tons to do before tonight's Bobbie-Sue extravaganza. So what are you talking about and hurry up, you cranky night dweller. I have a Bobbie-Sue in-home party this evening, and I haven't even begun to make my cheese log yet. Do explain and please, by all means, do it with your potty mouth. I learn new words to add to my truck driver's vocabulary every day being friends with you."

If Nina were still a breather, Wanda just knew she'd screech a frustrated sigh. Instead she huffed into the phone. "Oh, the fuck you don't know what I mean, Ms. Schwartz. Where were you today?"

"Today?" *Today* . . . had there been anything else before today? Would there ever be anything else again?

Nina's words hissed in her ear, screeching her perpetual infuriation. "Yes, today! You were supposed to meet Marty and me to do some shopping and have lunch, remember? You know, the 'drag poor Nina down to the fucking fashion district and make her look at knock-off designer shit until her eyes bleed' date we had *today*. I put on a ton of friggin' sunscreen for this stupid shopping thing, Wanda. You so know what it's like for me to be out in the sun during daylight hours, and you couldn't even call to tell us you wouldn't be there? I'm a vampire, for Christ's sake, Wanda. A day trip is a lot of work for me. It's an *event*. And I don't even eat lunch anymore. Besides, do you know the hell I suffer when Marty drags me around, yapping constantly about my color wheels when you're not there to shut her trap up?"

She'd totally forgotten about their lunch date. But Nina was still talking about Marty in the present tense. Which meant she'd graciously allowed her to live another day. Verrry generous.

Crap, how could she have forgotten something as important as lunch and shopping?

Because your life just came to a screeching halt this afternoon and the blue-plate special at Hogan's with fries on the side are, in the scheme of life things, falling just a little short after today.

If she didn't think of some excuse for why she hadn't shown up, Nina'd drive her out of her mind with guilt, because Nina was a vampire, and it was a big risk to go out in the "fucking sun," not to mention, it fried her like so much bacon. And Nina never let them forget the sacrifices she made for her friends—never.

She did, however, let them know in the way of the most colorfully foul language. Wanda had to admire Nina's way of letting off steam, though—even if it made her cringe when they were in public. If only she could swear openly the way Nina did.

If there was ever a day to cuss up a blue streak—today was the day.

Today.

Her heart hammered in her chest with a rhythm so loud she could hear it in her ears. Where she'd been today had an easy enough explanation—but it had taken a turn down Complication Road quite suddenly and rather drastically. Wanda scrunched her eyes shut, forcing the darkest moment of her life to the back of her mind, and focused on Nina's voice.

The one that was all filled with sarcastic guilt meant especially to make her feel like crap.

And Nina was good at it, too, because guilt settled in like a newly constructed house settles into its foundation. Wanda scrambled to make up something—anything to get Nina off her back. She had, after all, been the one to suggest they meet, have lunch, and then do what she and Marty did best. Shop. While they dragged a pissy, crabby, non-fashion-loving Nina behind them. But she was the crappiest liar evah, and how she was going to keep where she'd been today from her two best friends in the world, escaped her. It wasn't like she could hide what had happened—eventually she'd have to spill. But she just wasn't ready yet. "Uh—I—I had a Bobbie-Sue emergency."

Brilliant. Because really, eye shadow emergencies happen hourly in the world of cosmetic sales.

What multilevel cosmetics saleswoman had emergencies so severe in nature they had to skip lunch and shopping with their two best friends?

It was makeup—not world peace, as Nina had so lovingly once reminded both Wanda and Marty, when they'd all been active recruits for Bobbie-Sue. Well, active was subjective for Nina. Nina had hated selling Bobbie-Sue, and, truly, if honesty sometimes went hand in hand with brutality, she'd blown at it. Major suckage. Nina's sometimes bully-like nature didn't make for many customers. Actually, that wasn't true in retrospect. It had made for one, and that was only because Nina had scared the shit out of her, and while sobbing in fear for her life, she'd bought some foundation or something. Out of luck, and out of her stenographer's job resulting from downsizing, no one had heard Nina kvetch more than she and Marty.

Finally, Nina had found a government-funded job-retraining program, and she'd willingly given up selling Bobbie-Sue to go off to college and become a hygienist. Which hadn't worked out so well, seeing as on her first day she ended up accidentally bitten by her very first patient—who'd turned her into a vampire and then into his life mate.

Oh, the crises they'd seen each other through this past year or so.

"Wanda, are you paying attention?" Nina cut rudely into her thoughts.

She shook her dark head no, but said, "Uh-huh."

"So what was the emergency?"

God, the suspicion she heard in Nina's tone. What was this, the frickin' Spanish Inquisition? Did she have to explain everything? "Just an emergency." She allowed her voice to become vague.

Nina snorted into the phone. Wanda envisioned her tugging at her long, dark ponytail in irritation while her lips thinned. "Oh, reeeeaally? What happened? Did someone have a color wheel crisis? Lose their favorite lip gloss? Gouge out an eye with a mascara wand?"

Wanda's face flushed with instant anger, and she had to grip the edge of her table to keep from telling one of her best friends in the world to shut the ef up.

She took a deep breath and rose from her chair to peek into her fridge at the festive canapés she'd picked up for the party. "Oh, knock it off, Nina. You're always poking fun at my job, but it pays the bills. And I hate to be a braggart, but I do have a sky blue convertible from sales to those in color crisis. So stop snarking on me for selling cosmetics at Bobbie-Sue for a living and accept my deepest apologies for not showing up today." *Wench.*

Nina tapped on the phone with what Wanda figured was her unpainted fingernail. "Yeahhh, sure, Wanda. Okay, and now, the

truth, and don't goddamn lie to me again. Not for one second do
I believe you'd miss lunch and fucking shopping, Wanda—we *are*
talking clothes here—because you had some Bobbie-Sue crisis. So
spew," she demanded in the way Nina was so gifted at. When Nina
wanted something, she'd beat you up for it. If not physically, then
with her potty mouth.

Wanda ran a hand over her grainy eyes. She did have a good
reason. Just not one she was willing to share right now. She fought
the sudden rush of tears and the lump in her throat. If she played
up the fact that Nina was right—which Nina liked nothing more
than to be—that'd shut her up. At least temporarily.

Appease, appease, appease. That was how to deal with Nina
Blackman-Statleon. In fact, if appeasing were a qualification for
a job, between Marty and Nina, Wanda'd have a Swiss chalet and
a yacht. All she ever did with the two of them was appease them.
Buffer their arguments—make nice. Stand between them when
Nina threatened to rip Marty's head off and shit down her neck. It
was exhausting.

How the three of them had become friends should be on the
list of the world's greatest mysteries. Right up there with Stone-
henge and crop circles.

But she loved them regardless, and if they had even the slightest sense of what was going on with her and why she'd missed
their lunch/shopping date, they'd roll over her like a pair of Mack
trucks and she just wasn't up to that right now.

Not today.

So she gave in. "Hookay, you win. See me fly my white flag
in defeat. You're right, Nina. I'm a putz. A total a-hole for missing our date. It's definitely the crappiest thing I've ever done.
In fact, the friend police should come and haul my bad-friend
butt away and throw me into the pokey. Happy?" Taking a deep
breath, Wanda waited. She could mentally see Nina cocking

her head, then absorbing Wanda's statement, smiling with glib satisfaction.

Nina's tone lightened instantly, even if her harsh words implied differently. "Damn right they should."

Voilà. One cranky vampire pacified. "Okay, consider it done. I promise to turn myself in after my Bobbie-Sue party tonight. So is there anything else you want to rag on me for, or are we good to go for today?"

"Hey, hey, hey! Don't you make me sound like some nagging fishwife for giving a rat's ass about you, Wanda. Don't even. If it weren't for you and Marty, I wouldn't be doing all this sappy-crappy shit like caring or worrying or being BFFs."

"If it weren't for me and Marty, Nina, you'd have no BFFs," she reminded her caustically. "And, yes, I know. We've dragged you kicking and screaming into the world of the sensitive, the courteous. We should hang our heads in shame. What were we thinking? Now mind your manners, you—you—meanie butt."

"Oh, c'mon now. You can do better than that. Go on and call me something really shitty. Like a bitch. You know you want to," she taunted back.

"I do not."

"Do."

"Nina?"

"Wanda?"

"Stop goading me. Jesus! You call me a nag? I don't want to call you the *B* word. I'll just sinisterly think it when I'm alone late at night, plotting your demise. And don't think for one second I don't *think* the words you throw around like you're flinging mud. I do. I just don't say them out loud, because it's crass and un-Bobbie-Sue-like. Now, I do want to go back to what I was doing, which was trying to make a living, if that's okay with you and the gestapo."

Nina's voice suddenly softened, something that had occurred

more and more lately since she'd met her life mate, Greg. "Look,
I'm sorry, okay? Marty and I were just worried is all. I mean, Jesus
Christ, Wanda. We couldn't reach you by cell, you weren't at
home, and I can't remember a time when we couldn't get in touch
with you. It *was* shopping . . ."

Which seemed utterly insignificant and meaningless compared
to what she'd found out today. Who needed a discounted pair of
Cole Haan's when . . . Wanda halted her thoughts with a sharp
tug.

No. No efin' way was she going to linger. She didn't have time
to linger. She had a business to run and desperate housewives to
offer color wheel hope to. "Yes, it was shopping, and I blew it, and
I'm going to have to chalk it up to my busy schedule as of late. The
Bobbie-Sue ads in the paper have exploded, and I've been booking
in-home parties left and right."

"Do you still put those bullshit ads in the *Register*, Wanda? You
know, the cryptic ones that say you can earn a buttload of money
part-time, but really mean you have to sell your fucking soul and
join the cult known as Bobbie-Sue?"

She'd get angry with Nina for mocking the multilevel sales
techniques of Bobbie-Sue, but she was too damned wrung out.
"Nina, sometimes you really can be the biggest of *B* words. It's
not cryptic, it's enticing, and it's written that way so people won't
miss the opportunity of a lifetime, you naysayer. Now, I really have
to go, because I haven't even begun my weenies in a blanket, not
to mention my cheese log. Still love me?"

Nina snorted again, that derisive, skeptical sound she made
when anyone broached the subject of a deep emotion. "Love
schmove. What-ever. Just don't do that to me again, got it? I hate
to worry, and you made me worry. It pissed me off. The world
just isn't right if you aren't hounding us about being on time to get
somewhere or organizing our every breath."

A brief smile flitted across Wanda's lips, but her gut clenched and her skin grew clammy again. Who would keep her friends on track if she didn't? "You're eternally pissed off, and right now, it's because you love me and you were worried, Queen of the Night. Now, go call Marty and tell her to stop the search party. I'm fine. Just busy. I'll see if I can't get my hands on some AB neg to make it up to you." Being the rarest form of blood, AB negative was a treat for vampires, because it was so hard to come by, and Nina loved her some AB neg.

Nina cackled, her laughter crisp in Wanda's ear. "You're a real smart-ass these days, Wanda. I've been trying to figure out what's been going on with you for months. You're all fiery and mouthy, and under normal circumstances, I'd totally dig that in a fellow chick. But there can only be one mouthy woman in this trio from hell. *I'm* the mouthy one in this relationship, and don't you forget it."

Nothing had been going on for months—she'd learned to speak up, hanging out with Nina and Marty, but that was just personal growth.

Today, well, her mouthyness had a whole different motivation.

Wanda blew a strand of hair out of her face and glanced at her list. "Well, just get used to it. After hanging around you and Marty, I guess I got myself a spine. They were on sale at Wal-Mart. It was a two-fer deal. Buy a set of balls and get a spine for free. I needed one so I could stand upright between you two when you go at each other like mud wrestlers, now didn't I? Besides, you only live once, right?" She slapped a hand over her mouth. Had she just said that? *Shutupshutupshutup, you twit.*

"No, Wanda. I don't know. Remember? Eternal life here," Nina joked.

Tracing a pattern over her small kitchen dinette table, Wanda felt that tightening in her throat again. Yeah. Eternal life. She knew.

Okay, she had to go or she'd lose her focus and turn into a total pile of poo. "I remember. How could I forget that I'm the only one in this threesome that's of the human persuasion—especially after paranormal-palooza?"

Nina's sardonic laughter rang in her ears. "Yeah, we've had some shit fly, haven't we?"

Indeed. The three of them had had more shit fly than a horse farm. Mucho shit. "We have, and now I'm going to go make stuff you can't eat anymore, because blood is your beverage of choice. Byyyeeeeee, vampire." Wanda clicked the phone off before Nina could find another reason to chew her a new one.

The moment she put the phone down, it rang again to the tune of "Love Story."

Her caller ID said it was the other person she'd stood up today—Marty. Marty the werewolf. The person who was responsible for them all becoming friends, and Wanda's first ever paranormal experience—first only to Nina the vampire, that is. Ironically, Marty, too, had been accidentally bitten by Keegan, her now husband, another one of those life mates that seemed to float all over the place completely unnoticed. If she were less secure, she might feel left out because she was so average, and she couldn't fly like Nina or shift into a shag rug like Marty. Or for that matter, live forever . . . But life wasn't meant to be eternal, not on purpose anyway.

But it could be . . . a voice, desperate and filled with fear whispered in her head.

Oh, shut the ef up already, she mentally warned her subconscious. It could not. What was meant to be was meant to be. Accidents happened, but you didn't purposely seek immortality.

You didn't.

Her phone kept chirping. Damn. If she took the call, she'd only get more of what Nina had given her—it'd just be minus the cranky and involve much less swearing. If she didn't take the call, Marty would stalk her until she answered, and she couldn't have that in the midst of a Bobbie-Sue event. It was unseemly.

With a heavy, reluctant hand, Wanda flipped open her phone and prepared for her next blast of shit. "Yes, Marty?"

Marty's breathing was rapid when she spat her words out. "Where have you been, Wanda Schwartz? Do you have any idea how worried Nina and I have been about you? I know I'm going to basically live forever, but eventually, wrinkles will ensue, and I think I'm getting some around the sides of my mouth. Know why?"

Wanda put Marty on speakerphone and popped open her fridge, looking for the crescent rolls and mini weenies. "Why, Marty?"

Marty's sigh crackled throughout Wanda's kitchen, leaving a pinging, irritated reverberation. "Because you didn't show up today! And we were shopping, Wanda. *Shop-pppiiing*," her voice rose an octave, dragging out the word with an accentuation on the letter *P*. "Remember—discounted designer clothes? You're the most predictable woman I know, and all of a sudden, out of the blue, no one can find you. It was like you fell off the face of the planet or something, and that's so not like you. You don't do unavailable. That's Nina's thing. Now, I want answers, and I want them this instant."

Cracking open the tube of crescent rolls with a thwack against her countertop, Wanda sighed, too. She was too tired to take issue with Marty's demanding tone. Though less abrasive than Nina, Marty could be just as much of an incessant nag. "I already explained this to Nina, Marty. I'm sorry about missing our lunch date and, yes, I know all about the sacrifices Nina makes when we do a day trip. God knows she reminded me using her favorite swear word of the day, but something came up, and I forgot all about it."

Marty's tongue clucked into the phone, admonishing her. "You *never* forget, Wanda."

Sweet fancy Moses, was she really that predictable? Okay, so she liked things to run smoothly. Often.

All right, *always*.

Was it a crime to like things to come off without a hitch? Was she a bad person because she liked order and harmony in her world? Wasn't the world a better place because of nitpicky whack jobs like her who didn't know how to do anything without a list and a stopwatch? Would it even matter after today? "Well, today I did. Oy and vey, just shoot me for having a lot on my plate, would ya?" Clearly, the task of keeping this afternoon's issue to herself wasn't going to be simple.

"No. Nuh-uh, Wanda, you don't get off that easy."

"Easy? This being read the riot act is easy? You'd think I missed you and Nina curing cancer." She fought a gasp. *Keep yon trap shut, Schwartz—you're the suckiest of liars. Don't get in too deep. Keep it simple, mouth.*

"Wanda, honey? Again, I say. You never forget. If there's a detail to be had, you're on it like Vaseline on a beauty queen, Ms. OCD. You're the one who's always fifteen minutes early to a party—the one out of all three of us who coordinates everything and makes a big ole stink if we're even two minutes late. Wasn't it you who almost pitched a hissy in front of the House of Hwang when me and Nina were five minutes late—because of traffic, I might add—on buy-one-get-one-free mai tai night? I believe it was. So I'm not buying this 'I'm busy, and I forgot' gig. Now, what's going on?"

Wanda shrugged her shoulders as if Marty were in the room with her, averting her eyes to her carefully planned weenies in a blanket. "What if I told you I was off wonking my next door neighbor Harry Stein all afternoon, and we got so jiggy—because, as you know, it's been a long dry season for me since my divorce— that I blew you guys off for some white-hot sex?" Take that from good old, predictable, list-making Wanda, why don't ya?

Marty's laughter tinkled, bouncing off the pristine white walls of Wanda's kitchen. "I'd laugh and laugh, and then I'd tell you to cut the delusional crap and tell me what's going on."

No one was going to make this easy, were they? She needed to buy herself some time, so she could talk to Nina and Marty at her own speed. "Why couldn't it have been that I was having freaky, sweaty, hot sex? I like sex just as much as you and Nina, and you guys are always having sex since you hooked up with Keegan and Greg. All I hear about is the incredible sex you crazy paranormals have. Well, maybe today I was having average old human sex. Whaddya think about that? Sex is good. Well, maybe not as good as it could have been had I had it with someone who knew what he was doing with his man-tool for half my adult life. My ex *is* a podiatrist, but I just know having sex, any kind of sex, is good. So how do you know that's not what I was doing?"

Marty coughed on a chuckle. "Because you don't have sex, Wanda, except for whatever you read in those romance novels. If you were having sex, you'd have told us, because both Nina and I know that eye roll you give us whenever we talk about our sex lives. It means you're not having any, and hearing about ours makes you want to puke."

Wanda scoffed. "I don't either want to puke, and maybe that's all changed due to the hotness of Harry Stein."

"Harry Stein is eighty if he's a day, Wanda."

"So, maybe we use Viagra. *A lot* of it."

"Yeah, and maybe those white socks he wears with his sandals are an über turn-on, too."

A giggle spilled from her throat at the image Marty evoked. Yeah, okay, so Harry had been a stretch, but she'd diverted Marty successfully. "Jeez o' Pete. Look, I swear nothing's going on. I've been booking a lot of in-home parties lately, and I have one to-night. I got my dates mixed up is all. I thought we were meeting tomorrow. I'm sorry. Even us OCs falter, and you pointing that out to me only makes my OCD worse. You don't want me to spend a month obsessively berating myself, do you? So, I already apologized to Nina, and now I'll do the same for you. I'm sorry, Marty Flaherty, and if that's not good enough, would you consider my humble offering of a live organ?"

Finally Marty laughed, and Wanda's deer-in-the-headlights moment passed. "Okay, okay. We've just been worried lately. You always look so tired these days. Are you feeling okay?"

She felt fabulous. Grand. Dope, as Nina would say—even if she really shouldn't. "I'm fine, really, Marty. I'm just tired because I've been working long hours. I totally want that new pension plan Bobbie-Sue is offering, and I can't get it if I don't put in the extra hours." Marty knew what ambition and Bobbie-Sue were like. At one time, Marty had sold Bobbie-Sue, too, and that's how they'd all met—because Marty had recruited both Wanda and Nina.

"Fine. You're off the hook for now, but don't forget karaoke next week. If you think Nina bitched at you for missing our lunch date today, imagine what she'll do if we miss a night of her caterwauling Barry Manilow at the top of her lungs."

Rolling her eyes at the phone on the countertop, Wanda nodded her head. "I'd rather be dead than suffer the wrath of a Barryless night." She gulped hard. *Dead* . . . Oh, Jesus, Mary, and Joseph. Wasn't it funny how often that word was so carelessly bandied about in causal conversation? Her heart picked back up to that rapid pace. She absolutely had to shut her piehole. Breathing deeper still, she closed her eyes and fought to concentrate. "Am I grounded now? Can I go, or is there more?"

Marty cleared her throat. "Don't you get snippy with me, Wanda. Because you know I can—"

"Yeah, I know." She began to drone the words Marty had used more than once with Nina since she'd been turned into a werewolf.

"You're a werewolf. You can take me. Nina's a vampire. She can take me, too. I'm just a plain old human with no superpowers."

"That's right, and don't think I won't kick your getting-skinnier-by-the-second ass if you give me shit," Marty barked.

"Marty!"

"What, honey?"

"I'm fine, but I really, really have to go. I've got a houseful of women coming over tonight, and if I'm going to have weenies in a blanket on the menu, I need to get my tuchis in gear."

Marty paused, her voice giving way to a warmer tone. "You go charm the socks off of more Bobbie-Sue recruits with your infamous cheese log, and I'll call ya later this week. 'K?"

"Deal. Bye now." Wanda clicked her phone off and blindly reached for a chair, sinking into it. Marty and Nina were right. She was tired, and today it seeped into her bones, settling in her muscles at an alarming rate.

She wanted to climb into her bed, burrow under the covers, drag them up over her head, and wait . . .

For the inevitable.

But it didn't have to be the inevitable, did it? She did have friends. Friends who could help her, but if she did something that drastic—that life-altering—there was no going back. God only knew, no one knew that better than Wanda after this past year.

Her mind raced with what to do next.

Her phone chirped once more, thwarting further dilemma-wallowing. If it was Nina, calling back to give her hell again, she'd scream. Maybe she'd even swear. Yeah. Lots and lots of swearing—very unlike the banal non-wonking Wanda Schwartz everyone was so sure they knew so well, eh? But when she picked up the phone, she didn't recognize the number. It could be one of the women she'd recruited via her newspaper ad, and she couldn't take a chance she'd miss someone. Swallowing her worry, she summoned her Bobbie-Sue spirit. "This is Wanda Schwartz, your Bobbie-Sue regional color advisor. How may I help you?"

Someone coughed, then cleared their throat. "Um, hello. I'm calling about the ad you placed in the *Register*." It was a man someone. A man someone with a liquid silk voice. A man someone who'd just sent a shiver up her spine with said liquid silk voice.

She shifted in her seat, crossing her nylon-clad legs. A man? Answering her ad? The hell? "Uh, yeah. I mean, yes. That was my ad. How can I help you?"

There was a slight pause, as if this man on the other end was struggling to put a sentence together, but when he spoke, though his words were far from remarkable, they commanded her attention. "I'd like to know how I can earn two to five thousand extra dollars per month working only part-time."

Calling her astonished that a man had answered her ad was an understatement. A man. A real live one. Shut. Up. "Really?"

"*Really.*"

Wanda's brow furrowed, her freshly plucked eyebrows raised. "Why?" Maybe he was some kind of perv. And then she remembered he had no clue what the ad was about. Yet it was so odd for a man to answer her ad. Even though the ad was designed to be cryptic, for whatever reason, she mostly got calls from women.

"Uh, because I need a job, and who wouldn't want to know how to earn an extra two to five thousand dollars part time per month?"

Indeed. Who? But a *man*-who? "But . . . you're a *man*." Shite. She bit her lip to stop herself from blurting out anything else. When had a little ole thing like a man stopped her from using her best sales techniques? Bobbie-Sue had men's products—they just didn't sell them as actively as they did cosmetics. Oh, wasn't she a sorry, sorry sales rep tonight for even questioning his gender. A recruit was a recruit.

"I am," his voice assured her with a seductive ripple in her ear, making the hair on the back of her neck stand on end. "Is that a problem?"

Problem? Oh, no. No problems on her end. Not even one. If she got lucky, she'd snare the first ever male Bobbie-Sue color consultant. A rare bird indeed. But there might be a problem for him once he found out he'd be hawking things like Berry-Berry Blush and Wild Watermelon Lipstick. "The ad I placed is to sell Bobbie-Sue *Cosmetics*. Um, you know, makeup. The stuff *women* wear, but men, not so much?"

His answer wasn't fazed—not even a little. "And?"

"And I don't want to state the obvious, but you're a *man*." There. She'd said it again. A man. He was a man. He had dangly bits—that made him a man—not a woman.

"Does Bobbie-Sue have some rule against men selling their cosmetics?"

"Well, no—"

"So just by virtue of my gender, you've decided I can't sell cosmetics." His words were clipped and kinda huffy.

A flush of heat shot to her cheeks. "No! No, I would never say that. I just mean—"

"You just mean, that because I'm a man, I wouldn't be any good at selling cosmetics, right, Ms. Schwartz?"

Ohhhhhhh, the way he said her name, all stern and reprimanding, made her stomach flutter with an odd jolt. Like a flock of freshly released butterflies had just been let loose in her intestines. "Well, let's be honest. What do you, a man, know about makeup?" Wanda shoved a fist into her mouth. Where had her Bobbie-Sue spirit gone? What if he was a drag queen and she'd just insulted the snot out of all drag queens across the land?

"Who says I can't learn?"

Again. Point for the man. The. Man. "No one said you couldn't learn. I'm just saying—"

"That I'm a man, and men don't know anything about the goop women put on their faces."

She'd been this close to swearing at Nina earlier. This wannabe cosmetics selling *man* was bringing her that much closer. Keeping in mind her emotions were seesawing wildly after a god-awful day, she bit her tongue before speaking. "Um, look, Mr.—"

"Jefferson. Heath Jefferson."

Heath . . . . Dreamy . . . Niiiice name—sexy—very *Wuthering Heights*. "Okay, Heath. First of all, *goop* is hardly a very flattering word, now is it? And secondly, all I'm saying is, it might be harder to sell you selling cosmetics than it would be for you to actually sell the cosmetics, you see what I mean?"

His husky voice bristled. "No. I haven't the foggiest what you mean. I think I got lost somewhere between my name and goop. But I believe I detect gender discrimination from this place called Bobbie-Sue."

Oh, no. He did not. That was just what she needed. Some man screaming discrimination in relation to Bobbie-Sue. "No. Not at all. Anyone can sell Bobbie-Sue . . . I guess you just caught me off guard. Usually only women answer my ad."

She heard a rustle and then a weary response. "Well, I'm a man who needs a job. Look, can I sell cosmetics in the world according to you, or not? My time at the pay phone is running out."

Wanda was incredulous, and it showed in her response. "You don't have a phone?"

"Um, no. So could we make this quick? I'm running low on quarters."

"O-okay. Um, I'm having an in-home party tonight to introduce potential recruits to the Bobbie-Sue way of life."

His sharp bark of laughter cut her off. "Way of life? Are there drugs involved?"

Wanda was aghast. Wasn't he the one who needed a freakin' job? How crude and insulting. "Drugs? Of course not! Don't be ridiculous. I don't even like to take aspirin unless I have to. It's just that when you commit to Bobbie-Sue as a sales recruit, you commit to making the world a better place by sharing your knowledge of color auras with everyone around you."

"Color auras . . ." Heath trailed off.

Glancing at her microwave clock, she realized time was of the essence. "Yes, color auras. Just one of the many things you'll learn as a part of tonight's in-home party. Now, if you'd like to join us, man or not, I'd be delighted to have you. Here's my address." She rattled off her home address and followed up with a cheerful, "The party begins at eight sharp. Bring your party shoes." Clicking off the phone, she plunked it down on the table and set about finishing up her weenies in a blanket.

A man . . .

She shook her head. This Heath would probably never show up. No man on Earth would have the courage to come to a party where a gaggle of women were going to gather and slap goop on each other's faces. But what a coup that'd be. The first ever male color consultant at Bobbie-Sue, and Wanda would be the one who nabbed him.

Weee doggie.

She scrambled to find her list—the one she'd made to prepare for the party—and ticked off the words *cheese log* and *weenies in a blanket*, to signify they were complete. Lists comforted her—they gave her a sense of accomplishment—they meant she had control of something.

For all the good her control would do her now.

The sinking feeling in the pit of her belly had fled while she'd been talking to Heath, but it returned with a slam to her gut when she remembered that none of this, not her perfectly rolled weenies in a blanket, her carefully planned vegetable dip, her famous cheese log, or even her man-coup would matter after today.

Wanda gripped the edge of her table, white-knuckled and fighting the shakes that wracked her body.

Seriously, what did anything matter when you were diagnosed with a terminal illness?

Like *dying*.

So in the spirit of her good friend Nina, Wanda thought, *Well, fuck.*

The next list she made—was going to be a doozy.

CHAPTER
2

Well, okay.

Nice.

She'd been owned.

Wanda narrowed her gaze in Mr. Heath Jefferson's direction as yet another woman swooned at his color recommendation, and to really top things off, not only was he crazy cute, he was flippin' spot-on. It was like he'd been doing this all his life—like he was born to create color auras.

Frankly, Wanda didn't even know why she'd bothered to hang around.

At her own party.

In her own house.

Because it would seem this Heath had commandeered not just the party, but the women attending. How had this happened? He'd waltzed in, giving her but the slightest of acknowledgments by nodding his windblown, sinfully male dark blond head. And obviously he didn't need much acknowledging, he *was* the first ever male Bobbie-Sue potential recruit. Then he'd popped some weenies in a blanket into his mouth, savoring them like they were the finest caviar while she'd done her Bobbie-Sue spiel, and just to really unnerve her, he'd watched her every move with eyes that could melt steel. And then, he'd taken over.

Completely.

He'd looked at the samples, had apparently absorbed the basic literature at the Evelyn Wood version of the speed of light, and began telling the other attendees exactly what was in their color wheels. But not before he'd captivated every female in the room with the notion that he wasn't anyone's husband or even a boyfriend of one of the partygoers. He wanted to *sell* Bobbie-Sue.

Seriously.

And all the ho's in Ho-ville had latched onto him like he was their first french fry after the Cleanse, all doe-eyed and gushing.

As if that weren't enough—as if watching this gaggle of women turn to so much melted butter beneath Heath Jefferson's mere gaze wasn't crazy pathetic—her cat, Menusha, fluffy, faithless slut that she was, was sitting at his feet, staring up at him with big green cat eyes, like he was one of those fancy kitty condos with the plush carpeting.

Heathen.

One of her attendees, a well-dressed redhead with flowing, curly hair, moved in for the kill, placing her long, lean fingers on the arm of Heath's immaculate navy blue suit. She'd spent the better part of the evening eyeballing him with a seductive stare. The kind of stare that upon re-creation would make Wanda look like she had an eye tic. Yet when the vixen here gave him that demure but sultry stare, it stole the breath from Wanda's mere mortal lungs.

Wanda watched as the woman scooted closer to Heath on the

couch, her ice blue, almond-shaped eyes sending arrows dipped in lust at him. She held up a sample lipstick, totally not in her color wheel—and undoubtedly, judging from her personal style, she darn well knew it wasn't—then asked breathily, "Is *this* in my color wheel, Heath?" She smiled flirtatiously, wetting her collagen-injected lips.

Each head of every bloody woman in the room turned their eyes expectantly, looking to Heath, waiting with bated breath for his answer. Wanda rolled her eyes from her fold-up chair at the back of her small living room and attempted to maintain a professional facade for the sake of her Bobbie-Sue reputation. She cleared her throat, waiting for him to answer—because he had them all. Answers, that is.

Heath tilted his freshly shaven jaw and appeared to ponder for a moment, then shook his blond head, making the wisps of hair that just touched the crisp collar of his white shirt rasp against it. "Nope. It has too much orange in it. You need a blue base, if you're going to wear red lipstick." He reached out to the table that held the samples Wanda had laid out before her guests had arrived and picked up another lipstick to show Mindy, or Mippy, or whoever the hell this tart was, what he meant. His broad shoulders didn't budge an inch, the slight tilt of his lips, ultra confident. "This one is more appropriate for your color wheel." He said it with such authority and all while being so—so completely male, he left absolutely no doubt he knew what he was talking about and that he was all man while he was doing it.

In-freakin'-credible.

There was a small hush while the others looked at their color wheel charts for verification, and then with wide eyes filled with adulation, they all squealed their approval. A couple of them even clapped their hands. Like he'd just given them detailed directions to the Fountain of Youth. Heath's eyes met hers above the fifteen or so heads, his gaze held smug satisfaction. His firm lips fell into a line of quiet superiority.

And as hard as it was for her to admit it, this Heath was dead-on. The vixen that almost couldn't contain the spill of her über-hooters from her charcoal gray silk shirt should definitely never wear anything with an orange base to it.

Bastard.

Why his grasp of color concepts and the fact that women were falling at his feet like dead flies after a shot of Raid was leaving her so unsettled, escaped her. If nothing else, she should be excited that she'd found a recruit who could potentially earn her some serious moolah. And he would, if the way he was working these women over was any indication. And he was a man. *Male*—maybe even a heterosexual man. It was the Bobbie-Sue coup of the century. Except, what good was moolah and coups when you were . . . Wanda snapped her thoughts to a screeching halt.

Hookay. This was so over, and she was so over his showing her up. The damned show-off. Wherever he'd learned to whip a color wheel into a frothy frenzy was one of those unsolved mysteries, but this was *her* party and these were *her* recruits. It was time to take charge like any good regional color supervisor would. That she wanted to do it while she stuck her tongue out at him was another story.

Wanda rose, feeling the niggle of pain in her abdomen that had become so familiar to her as of late as she did. She placed a hand where the indentation of her waist met her hips and said with a smile, "So, ladies, I think you can see Bobbie-Sue speaks for itself, and I hope you'll all agree. Sign-up sheets for the starter kit are in the kitchen. If you'll follow me, we'll get down to the boring paperwork," she joked, smiling, then began to make her way to the kitchen.

While everyone else stayed exactly where they were.

As close to Heath as they could possibly get.

The excited hum of voices rose and fell as each woman dawdled in the living room, coming up with one excuse after another to stay with Heath. She popped her head around the corner and gave the Pied Piper of Color a pointed gaze. "Mr. Jefferson? Why don't you be the first to fill out the paperwork that will mark the beginning of your new future as a Bobbie-Sue Cosmetics consultant? Seeing as you're so obviously attuned to color wheels and all," she added, flashing him a fake smile. She didn't know what his gig was, or why he'd decided to crash a party clearly designed for chicks, but she was ready to call him on it.

If he thought her weenies in a blanket and some makeup were going to be his vessel to pick up broads, he'd thought wrong. Maybe this was some weird fetish of his? She'd seen plenty since she'd found the Internet and read all those romance novels, and if this were some bizarre kink he indulged in, he wouldn't be getting his kink on at her house with her potential clients.

No kinking on her watch.

But Heath shot her another confident smile and popped off the couch, rising to his full height, leading the way to Wanda's kitchen, his pack of newly acquired drooling flunkies on their feet and at the ready. "Just say where." He smiled down just inches from her face, his hazel eyes glittering, then slid past her, his hand brushing her hip as he did.

A shiver raced along her spine, and she wasn't sure if it was from the touch of his broad hand or the smell of his cologne settling in her nostrils. Which was yummy, but whatevah.

Bodies filled her kitchen, and as Wanda supervised the paperwork, she lost track of the pens she handed out, the applications for starter kits that were signed, and Heath, who'd apparently not been as serious as his game face had claimed. He'd disappeared shortly after the redhead had asked if *Heath* could be her color supervisor. Yeah, a color supervisor was exactly what came to mind when Wanda thought about positions Ms. Wonder Boobs needed to fill.

An excruciating hour later, as the last of the women filed out of her front door, she leaned forward on it, resting her forehead against the cool, painted surface, breathing a sigh of exhaustion. Her hand shook when she ran it along her hair.

The clatter of dishes in her kitchen made her jump.

"I assumed you might need some help cleaning up." The deep rumble of Heath's voice washed over her, and she found a disturbing tingle settled in her belly just hearing it. Then it freaked her out. She was *alone* with a strange man in her house. A man who could still create color wheels even if he were blind. A man who'd make Bobbie-Sue herself shed tears of envy with his gift for wooing an audience of women into signing up to become a rep.

Wanda turned around and flattened herself against the door, her hand on the knob, ready to flee if he was like an ax murderer. "I think I've got it, but thanks." Her ears perked to the weak tone of her reply, and if she didn't feel like she was going to fall flat on her ass, she'd care more. Right now, she just wanted him to go away so she could go to bed and forget today.

And do it without him killing her in cold blood.

He popped a fistful of mini Ritz crackers in his mouth and closed his eyes, very clearly savoring them, before directing another one of those steel-melting gazes at her. "You look pretty tired, Wanda, and I don't mind helping. It's a mess. Those women sure could eat, huh?"

And fawn. And gush. And make goo-goo eyes at Heath. A giggle slipped from her lips. She nodded her head. "Yeah, eat they can. Among other things." Her living room was a sea of paper cups, crumbs, and platters with very few remains of her carefully planned appetizers left. It was a friggin' disaster area. Her energy level sank to a new low just contemplating straightening it up.

"C'mon," he said over his wide shoulder. "I'll wash, you dry."

Wanda blew out a raspy sigh. Uh, no. The best thing for this man to do was leave. He could be some nut, or worse, a hardened criminal, or—in favor of thinking the worst—a serial killer. Ted Bundy had an eye for the ladies, too, didn't he? Handsome . . . charming . . . hookay, she was only freaking herself out. She was in no mood to be someone's victim tonight. She had nuthin' to lose after today. Yet, still she chose to pacify him for fear of stirring his serial-killer juices up. "I've done this a hundred times. Really, it's okay. I'm good."

"Not if those dark circles under your eyes are any indication. I'd highly recommend you hit the Bobbie-Sue concealer—in dark ivory, judging from your skin tone, right?"

There was a lot of nerve going on in this here room, and even if he was right about the color her concealer should be—it took hella guts to point it out. It was unsettling her to no end and thus, tweaking her for reasons she had no explanations for. But again, the role she'd played most of her life kicked into overdrive. Peace-maker. Pacifier. If money could be made making nice—she'd be a superstah. "Uh, right. Seriously, I can't ask you to clean up a party I invited you to. I've got it." But Heath wasn't listening, he was back in the kitchen, his jacket on the back of one of her chairs, his perfect white shirt rolled to his elbows, and his forearms, sprinkled with light brown hair, deep in her sink.

Wanda zipped in behind him, grabbing a towel and moving with caution to stand beside him, taking the dish he handed her while giving her one of his congenial smiles. When her shoulder brushed against Heath's bicep, she moved farther to the right, locking her hips in place by pressing them to the edge of the counter. Her pencil-slim black skirt rustled in the silence.

"So, this Bobbie-Sue thing . . ."

Yeah, this Bobbie-Sue thing he seemed to think he could

conquer all in one breathtaking leap of hotness and man charm. "Hmmmm?"

"The starter kit's pretty expensive."

Her Bobbie-Sue-ness, reserved for those who might experience skepticism, immediately kicked in, and there was nothing she could do to stop it. It had become second nature to shoot down a cynic with a smile on her face and perseverance in her heart. "Expensive is a matter of perspective, if you ask me. If making ten times what the starter kit costs is expensive, then I guess it's expensive. But if you look at it as an investment in your future—"

Heath held up a soapy hand, the bubbles from the dish detergent fizzing along his lightly tanned fingers. "Save the spiel. I get it. I just don't have that kind of money right now."

Wanda waited for more, hoping he'd give her just a little more information on exactly why in the hell he, a man, wanted to sell makeup, but his lips returned to that stoic position and his profile held a cockiness she was growing tired of.

"We do take credit cards."

"Don't have one of those either."

No credit card? Who the frig didn't have a credit card in this day and age? Only men who lived in their mother's basements, that's who, and men like that were prime pickin's for serial killers in the making.

Now she was becoming crazy suspicious, and it left her edgy—but once more, she worried, if his intent was anything but innocent, he'd react—maybe badly. Definitely not so fly. So she kept her Bobbie-Sue persona in place. Light, airy, and noncommittal—just like the manual told all good reps to. As if she had something he wanted, and if he didn't want it—someone else would.

Wanda took the last dish from him and gave him a smile of sympathy while she dried the plate and put it into the cupboard above her head. She didn't want to rile him if he was some kind of lunatic grooming her for the kill by making himself useful and doing the dishes.

Clearing her throat, her plan was to keep her voice even and drama free. "I understand, but unfortunately, in order to become a representative, you have to purchase the starter kit. So I guess this is where we say good-bye." She smiled placidly—though her stomach dived as she watched the shift of the hard plane of his jaw—and waited for him to make a hasty exit, which was a typical reaction for those who didn't truly want to invest in making color auras their profession of choice. The starter kit *was* expensive, but for Wanda, it'd been an investment she'd never regret.

Her start with Bobbie-Sue had been rocky at best, but she'd worked her tail end off, and it'd finally paid off. So, buh-bye now. Mentally, even if he was cute and had a ba-donk-a-donk to rival all others, she'd dismissed him, hoping he'd leave with less attention than he'd come.

But alas, no. That'd be too easy.

Heath remained where he was, taking the dish towel from her and drying his hands on it. He folded it and buffed her silver faucet before placing it exactly where she put it when she was done cleaning her kitchen. Rolling his sleeves down, he buttoned each cuff. Then he did the stare thing again, cutting into her line of vision, grabbing onto her eyeballs, and refusing to let them go. "How about we make a deal?"

Like Monty? Lord. "A deal?"

"Yep."

Okay, she couldn't take it anymore. She was alternately ooked by the idea that all he wanted to do was snag a woman and intrigued as all hell about why he wanted to sell makeup—and maybe a little afraid he had some diabolical plan to whack her. But seeing as the spine she'd acquired dealing with Marty and Nina was in its rightful upright position, she asked, "Can I just interject something here?"

He nodded. "You can." His words were straightforward, but it was almost as if he were *allowing* her to speak, giving her permission, and it pissed her off. Which made the path she took next way easier.

"Don't you find this just a liiiittle creepy?" She held her thumb and forefinger together to emphasize her point.

His eyebrows, a dark brown in contrast to his hair, mushed together. "Creepy?"

Onward ho. "Uh, yeahhhh. I mean, I don't want to state the obvious again, but you're a *man*. A man who wants to sell *cosmetics*. Forgive me for being so brash, but if you were, say me, a woman, wouldn't you find that a little creepy?"

He suddenly grinned, further maddening her because it was so unguarded and, well, fabulous. "Maybe, but I can assure you I'm anything but creepy. Jobless maybe, but not even a little creepy."

Again, Wanda waited to see if he'd offer up a viable reason for just why he was jobless and not so creepy, but he kept his lips sealed. What did a guy, who was well dressed, well mannered, and so well spoken want to sell makeup for? He looked like he was Harvard-educated and spent his days sunning off the coast of some Caribbean island, smoking expensive cigars and dating women named Bipsy, ten years his junior. Not to mention, his suit wasn't cheap. Wanda knew her designers like the Pope knew a good sermon in Latin, and his jacket alone cost more than her new bedroom set. "And that's all you have to say?"

"I didn't realize when I came to this party that divulging my personal life was part of applying to Bobbie-Sue." His jaw clenched upon finishing his statement, his stance growing more rigid.

Again with the arrogant, overconfident jazz. Though honestly, she might have gone just a smidge too far. Crap. Next he'd be screaming that discrimination thing, and above all else, although Bobbie-Sue herself wasn't exactly beyond reproach after what'd happened with Marty, the company's reps were expected to behave accordingly. So Heath had effectively shut her down. Fine. She had a buttload of stuff to clean up before she could even consider going to bed, and she was tired of pussyfooting around.

Although she'd learned a thing or two about confrontation from Nina, she still sucked at it, unless pushed. She was much better at pacifying everyone and everything. Her sigh held resignation. "Okay, then tell me what kind of deal you want to make. I'm all ears."

Heath folded his arms over his wide chest and stared at her dead on. "If I get, say, twenty people to sign up for the starter kit in a week, which will, if my calculations are right, make you a helluva lot of money due to the percentage you rake in, you take a portion of *your* percentage and buy the starter kit for me."

Wanda's mouth dropped open. Twenty starter kits in a friggin' week? That was impossible. They were five hundred bucks apiece. Both she and Marty, on their best *months* had only sold six or seven, and that was so rare it was like actually still owning your original set of boobs these days.

No way could he sell twenty starter kits, and even if he did, most likely more than half of the women who bought them would back out within a couple of days. Bobbie-Sue had a five-business-day grace period. More often than not, once the hype ended after a meeting, giving the potential rep time to think about how tough it could be to sell door-to-door, they backed out. She didn't need a psychic to tell her that—it was statistically pretty sound.

He clearly read her disbelief. "All I'm asking for is seven days of your time. If it doesn't work out, you'll never hear from me again. Promise." He crossed his finger over his heart and paused for a moment, expressing a strange look of irony, then directed his steely gaze at her once more.

Woooooow. He had nice eyes. They looked like they could swallow you up and consume you just by a mere glance. He had dark lashes that fringed them, thick and long, and a thin scar by his left eye.

Wanda found herself holding her breath. This was ridiculous. She didn't have the kind of time it would take to drag his ass around on cold calls, door-to-door, while she trained him for what would essentially be for free. She had a business to run and customers to deal with and . . . and well, stuff. Yeah, she had stuff.

Oh, you've got stuff, all right. You've got some big stuff.

Right. There was *that* stuff. Stuff she didn't want to think about right now, because it made her stomach dive and her heart throb with anxious beats against her ribs.

Think of the Bobbie-Sue legacy you'll leave in your wake if you manage to tame Neanderthal Man, Wanda. You'll make Bobbie-Sue history.

On the other hand, it was definitely a challenge, and a diversion she could use right now, because facing the truth was just too much for her to wrap her head around. But still . . .

"Wanda?"

She regained her focus and found herself mesmerized by the fullness of his bottom lip. "Yes?"

"Whaddya say?"

No matter how delish he was—her patience was waning, worn thin by his persistence. A persistence she just couldn't figure out. This made no sense. Why would a strapping, healthy male, especially one as good looking as he was, want to sell makeup? "But you don't have any idea what's proper protocol, and there are a million techniques to learn that you have to be certified in. We have rules at Bobbie-Sue. You can't do that in just a week. It took me a month to really grasp the Bobbie-Sue concept, and even then, I struggled." Christ, how she'd struggled. "Most reps don't hit the streets for at least that long, and even then, they're raw at best."

He rocked back on his heels, jamming his hands into his pockets. "I think I've proven I'm a pretty fast learner. I mean, was it me, or wasn't I right about the redhead's color junk—"

She rolled her tongue inside her cheek before saying, "It's wheel. *Color wheel* or color aura, and that's exactly what I mean. You can't use words like *goop* and *junk* when referring to Bobbie-Sue! It's degrading to call it goop. Bobbie-Sue'd have a chicken if she could hear you."

He emitted a sigh with an edge of irritation to it. "Whatever. Look, I'll call it whatever you want me to, but I don't think you can deny I was right about that woman's *color aura*, and she was definitely paying very close attention."

So close they could have become one entity. The trollop. "Okay, I won't deny you have mad color skills, but it isn't just about picking the right color for your clients. It's about nurturing their inner goddesses, knowing when a woman's feeling Pristinely Peachy or maybe she's more in a Whipped Bittersweet Dark Chocolate mood. It's about answering phone calls when a client has a big event and she's stumped on what color dress to wear with her new Iced Cotton Candy Lipstick."

Heath didn't falter. "I can do that."

Cheerist, he was tenacious, and if his arrogant attitude was meant to test her—good on him. He'd get an *A*. "No, you can't. You don't even have a phone! Wasn't that you dumping quarters into the pay phone earlier today? How do you expect to be able to help those in color crisis if you don't even have a way to communicate with your clients? Bobbie-Sue is very hands-on. We're very committed to making sure our clientele are nothing less than one hundred percent satisfied. You can't satisfy a client if you're punching quarters into a pay phone."

"*Color crisis?* Are you serious?" His face fell for just a moment. Now she had him by the short hairs.

"As a diehard Cubs fan."

"Women actually experience what you call a *crisis* because of makeup? Isn't that a little—how can I put this without insulting you? *Extreme?*"

Wanda clucked her tongue in disdain. "And there it is again. Do you really expect me to donate my time to you when in your small, male mind, you can't imagine a woman might have a problem crop up that has to do with her appearance? How we feel about ourselves, how we look, sometimes hinges on just the right pair of shoes—or the right shade of lipstick. It can make or break you. And I'm just going to throw this out there—men don't seem to mind that so much, do they? It's what attracts you Neanderthals to us most of the time. You know, the chase, the hunt—the inevitable capture? Most of you wouldn't be chasing us if we were perusing bars in our footed jammies and curlers, now would you?" God, he was infuriating. How could he possibly sell something as intimate as makeup to women with his attitude? It was untoward.

And she'd called him a Neanderthal.

Very Bobbie-Sue-ish.

Heath shrugged his wide shoulders with indifference. "I dunno. I like footed pajamas."

Wanda's eyes narrowed with disgust for his attitude. "You know what I mean."

"I know what you mean, and I swear on your curlers, I'll keep my knuckles off the ground."

God, what a fucknut. She was fragile today, and although this debate might be what some would call invigorating—she'd plumb had enough. "I just don't—"

But clearly, there was just no deterring him. "Look, I'll take the literature home and read it. I'll read all the rules and Bobbie-Sue regulations, absorb them like a sponge, and sell, sell, sell. Doesn't the sound of change clinking around in your pockets make your Bobbie-Sue heart do a backflip?"

Wow, he got cockier by the nanosecond. Yet there was a tone in his voice, an urgent one, if she was hearing correctly, that couldn't be dismissed. And Jesus H., she was tired. She got the distinct impression that if she kept lobbing roadblocks at him, he'd find a way to pick them up and hurl them back at her. Wanda pinched her temples, running a soothing finger over the throbbing pulse at the side of her head. "Okay. Fine. Deal. But if I give you the signal, you shut up."

"The signal?"

She slapped a hand against her thigh in exasperation. "See? You don't even know there's a signal. It's for when you need to shut up and let me take over the pitch. You think you've got this all in the bag, but there's a whole lot you know absolutely nothing about." And it gave her great satisfaction to point that out to him. So neener, neener, neener. But he wiped her smug smile right off her face with his next words.

First, he grinned. Deliciously, decadently grinned. Then he waved a verbal white flag. "I promise to learn the signal and shut up when I'm supposed to. So deal?" He held out his large hand to her, waiting for her to take it.

This was nucking futs, but she stuck her hand in his anyway, biting the inside of her cheek when the warmth of it made her forearm tingle. "Deal."

Obviously, that was all the confirmation he needed. Heath pivoted on his heel, dragging his suit jacket from the chair, then stopping to grab a cracker from the tray that was still on the kitchen table. He smeared a healthy dollop of her cheese log on it and popped it into his mouth, crunching the cracker with relish. "You make one helluva cheese log," he said before brushing his fingers off and heading for her door, letting it close behind him with a soft thud.

Wanda cocked her head, confusion disjointing her thoughts, leaving them half finished and scattered, while she stared at her living room door. She'd just agreed to help pay for his starter kit if he pulled off what would amount to turning water into wine.

Her lips became a thin line, but she shook it off and moved to the drawer where she kept a tablet of paper. She ripped a piece off and wrote "Things To Do Tomorrow" on it. Number one on that list was submitting Heath's application to Bobbie-Sue, for all the good it would do her. Number two was to look into a starter kit for Heath. Number three was . . . She threw the pen down. Her entire list consisted of things that had to do with Heath.

Heath, Heath, Heath.

He'd never be able to pull it off. Hell, he probably wouldn't even show up—which was just as well, because if this had been some batshit way to have a group of women at his mercy, he could forget it. Maybe he was one of those guys who liked to paint women's toenails or secretly liked to wear women's clothes and makeup?

Relief flooded her. She was being silly. He'd go home, realize that his success tonight was just a fluke, and go look for another venue to pick up women, forgetting all about Bobbie-Sue Cosmetics.

Game over.

HOLDING the Bobbie-Sue book balanced on his thigh, Heath Jefferson sat on the edge of a cot that was made for efficiency, not comfort. "So, my man, Archibald, I think we have this job-search thing in the bag, if you'll just hold still so I can practice. Jesus, Arch. Quit making faces." Heath had decided practice made perfect, and in order to make this makeover deal perfect—makeovers being what the Bobbie-Sue women used as a staple to woo new clients—he'd use Archibald as his guinea pig all night long if he had to in order to get it right. He'd be the makeover queen, er, king before this was over.

A derisive snort came from the cot adjacent to his own. "Oh, sir, I believe you're sorely mistaken if you think the path to earning an income even close to the one you once possessed will be had by selling"—he chuckled with unabashed, maniacal glee—"*cosmetics.* Certainly you could have found something more, how should I say this? Never mind, I'll just say it—manly. Perhaps next you'll find yourself the head of women's lingerie, eh, Heathcliff?"

Heath grunted back at him, cupping his jaw to take another swipe with the sponge applicator at the dark line of Archibald's five o'clock shadow, then working to minimize the sag in his old friend's chin. "Stop moving your face. It's all in the shading, but if you keep moving the hell around, I'll never get the right coverage. Now, do you have a better solution to our dilemma, Archibald? It's not like jobs are falling out of trees and landing in our laps, buddy. We don't have degrees or educations worthy of making more than minimum wage. Need I remind you? We're in dire straits here."

Archibald let out a sigh of revulsion, his shoulders slumping while he fought to stay still. "Indeed, I need no reminder of our straits. I do, however, question the sanity of this latest venture of yours. Need I remind you, you have absolutely no experience in the sale of anything, let alone, ah, womanly things?"

"No, you don't need to remind me, Arch. I know where we stand. We're fucked." Heath heard the rustle of Archibald's jacket, a jacket he staunchly refused to take off for fear it'd be stolen and sold for hooch. It was the distinct sound of disapproval at the fact that he'd used profanity, which was strictly frowned upon by his longtime manservant as evidenced by the firm, thin line his lips became. "Look, friend, we need jobs—soon. I don't care what kind of job it is, so long as we can get our hands on some cash. It's not like we've got offers coming out of our asses."

"There is the car, sir . . ."

Heath held up his hand to stop Archibald from going down that road. "The car wouldn't buy us a Slurpee at the 7-Eleven, and the watch, before you mention it again, was given to me by someone who was a good friend, not to mention, it's old. So it's not up for discussion—ever. Any money we'd make from them wouldn't last long anyway. We'd still need jobs. So end of story. Now, really, Arch, do you want to live like *this* forever? And if you keep yakking, I'll never get the application of lipstick, which, by the way, is the bow and crowning glory on your Bobbie-Sue package, right."

Archibald frowned, the wrinkles on his forehead standing out against the dim light pouring in from the small window across the vast room. "I daresay, no, sir. In fact, I'm certain I don't wish to live like this for the remainder of my years. The stench here is just dreadful." He reached into his jacket pocket and took out the perfectly folded handkerchief he always carried with him. Pushing Heath away, he placed it over his nose and inhaled deeply.

Heath chuckled. The stench *was* dreadful. There wasn't much about this situation that wasn't dreadful. But tonight had given him hope their luck might have taken a turn for the better. Okay, so he had to sell goop, er, makeup to do it, but the promise of some money, any money, was well worth the potential for humiliation. Desperate times and all. It also didn't hurt that this Wanda woman, who'd be his regional color supervisor, wasn't hard on the eyes. No matter how he'd tried to ignore it, because he was definitely in no position to be lusting after a woman, she had this appeal he couldn't take his eyes from. Not to mention, her cheese log was kick-ass.

And so was her ass.

She was a little thinner than what he'd found himself typically attracted to, but the round shape of her back end when she'd bent over to pick up the napkins from the floor had left him with his mouth hanging open. She was sort of snippy and defensive about this makeup gig, but he'd never met a woman who could resist him for long, and he wanted in on this Bobbie-Sue gig.

Heath assessed Archibald's jawline, scrutinizing his work before it was "lights out." "You know, I'm not half bad at this color wheel thing. It seemed pretty easy to me."

"I applaud your gift for making a woman's complexion sing." Archibald pulled away from Heath again, his dark eyes glittering. "However, mine has had quite enough. If this weren't our last hope, sir, I'd tell you to stuff it. That we've sunk this low, Heathcliff, that I'm allowing the application of cosmetics on my person, is—well, it's disturbing."

Heath slapped his friend on the back, shoving the liquid foundation and sponge applicator back into the gift bag he'd snared at Wanda's party. "Ah, you mock, but I'm telling you, it could be much worse. We could be flipping burgers or giving out samples of food at the mall."

Archibald expelled another breath, long and suffering, pushing off and settling on his cot for the night. "If only we could have mastered the fine art of wearing those ridiculous hats at Chick-fil-A, we'd be employed."

Heath smiled in the semidarkness of the room. "Doesn't matter. That hat wasn't in your color wheel anyway."

"Oh, sir . . ."

"Don't 'oh, sir' me like this is beneath us, Arch. We have to do what we have to do to survive, and if it means me mastering a color wheel and offering color consultations or whatever the hell they call it, that's how I'll roll. You read the ad, too. You saw the kind of cash we could make in a month. I don't know about you, but I'm willing to give it a shot, because our options right now are shit at best. What do we know about a nine-to-five? Not a damned thing, that's what." Heath rolled to his side, taking in Archibald's full length, cramped and too long for his assigned cot. "Now, speaking of jobs at the mall, how'd you make out today at that job interview? Short-order cook, wasn't it?"

Highlighted by the perfectly blended line of Lively Lavender Eye Shadow Heath had so carefully applied, Archibald's white eyebrow rose with haughty disdain. "They told me I didn't have enough experience for Chili's. I've cooked for kings and queens in my time, and they had the audacity to declare I wasn't worthy of making baby back ribs? And this from the manager. A boy no older than a pair of my best trousers. It was demeaning, to say the least."

Heath put the top of his fist over his mouth to keep from barking another chuckle. Archibald had taken his duties as Heath's manservant very seriously over the years. Any perceived slight to his work was considered high on his list of insults. "Don't you worry, Arch, brighter days are just over the horizon."

"Oh, indisputably, sir. Unquestionably you'll find yourself on the road to cosmetic prominence in no time, and we'll once more rule the kingdom known as Jefferson with you at the helm, making color charts for all the fair maidens in the land." He snickered.

"*Wheels.* It's color wheels, and can the sarcasm, funny man. You can't even get a job at Chili's. And after being turned down at not one, but three of the major fast food joints, plus Wal-Mart, we have a trend going on that isn't exactly what I'd label upwardly mobile. I'm the only shot we've got right now, and if what that ad says is true, we just might get the hell out of this hole. So knock off the pessimism and show a little team spirit."

Archibald clucked his tongue and offered blandly, "Of course. Hoorah, sir. Go team Jefferson."

Heath cradled his head in the palms of his hands. "I know I'm probably the last person you'd think would even consider selling makeup, considering our lifestyle up till now, and if I could find work anywhere else, I'd do it, but we need cash, Arch. *Soon*."

"I will say, Heathcliff, I must give you credit. You've definitely gone the longest mile. But it is *makeup* . . . Do tell, was this woman as surprised as I was by your foray into all things womanly?"

"To say the least, but you shoulda seen me, Arch, I worked us a deal. I wore her down. Just be glad I did, because we have no other resources at this point."

"Shall I be the first to point this out, sir?"

"What?"

"I would venture she thinks you enjoy the company of men. It's only natural, as most men aren't the least bit interested in selling makeup—nor would one expect them to be as adept as you at it. And do forgive my blunt assessment."

Now that would be awkward, considering women had once been his favorite sport. But it didn't matter—his ego wasn't so big he couldn't live with the idea that she thought he was gay. He didn't care about anything but getting them out of here. "Not all gay men know about makeup. That's just a little inflammatory in this day and age, Arch."

"Ah, but society does have their stereotypes firmly in place."

Heath gave him a ragged sigh. "I don't care what she thinks as long as cash is involved. Now go to sleep. Tomorrow's a new day."

"Filled with brightly hued color *wheels* . . ."

"Shaddup."

"Good night, Heathcliff."

"Night, Arch."

Heath rolled over, tucking his too-long body onto the cot, and closed his eyes. Tomorrow was definitely a new day. If it had to include eyeliner and whatever the hell that shit was in a bottle he'd seen on Wanda's coffee table, then so be it.

It was game on.

CHAPTER 3

"Ms. Schwartz?"

Wanda held the phone to her ear, snuggling farther under her blanket. "Speaking," she answered, sleep still lacing her voice. For the love of a good facial she was tired. Her dreams had been fragmented flashes of Heath's face and the days left of her mortality written on a big chalkboard, each day gone crossed off with an invisible hand holding a white piece of chalk the size of a tree stump.

"This is Heath Jefferson."

Wanda popped up, settling the phone on her shoulder. No. Way. "Uh, yes?"

"Are you ready?"

"Ready . . ." *For?*

"Remember our deal?"

She pressed the heel of her hand to her forehead. She remembered the deal, all right—in all its craptacularness. How he'd gotten her to agree to something so asinine would have to be excused by her weakened state of mind. But now it was time to stop the foolishness. "Look, Mr. Jefferson——"

"You're not reneging, are you?" His deep voice rumbled the question, making her stomach wobble, and the memory of his big, muscled body come to mind. "Because if I'm hearing right, I'm hearing hesitation in your voice. That can only mean you're re-neging. Any good Bobbie-Sue rep wouldn't do that, would she? I mean, if I'm not mistaken, and take this quote loosely, because I'm a little fuzzy after all the Bobbie-Sue literature I've consumed, but it does state on page thirty-eight, paragraph two of the Bobbie-Sue creed, honesty is the *only* policy, and as you're such a fine repre-sentative of the Bobbie-Sue corporation, I'm going to assume you consider a handshake—which we did—*your word*. Am I right?"

Oh, stop. He'd actually read the Bobbie-Sue creed? Even she'd just skimmed the creed. It'd said some shit about always keep-ing your Bobbie-Sue persona in check, keeping in mind you rep-resented one of the largest cosmetics corporations in the world, and then there'd been crap like color wheel integrity and the ten color commandments, but even she—as Nina called her, a fucking Bobbie-Sue juice drinker—hadn't read the *entire* manual.

Wanda groaned and swung her legs over the edge of her bed, grimacing at the tug in her belly. She shoved the covers off and shrugged into her open-toed slippers, heading for the Bobbie-Sue manual on her dresser. She flipped to page thirty-eight and skimmed paragraph two.

Christ on a cracker. He was right.

"Ms. Schwartz? You still there?"

"I am." *Stunned, but still here.*

"So you're not reneging, right? Because that would just be bad Bobbie-Sue form."

Her tongue felt thick, and her mouth was dry. Exactly whom

did he think he was even hinting she'd renege on a deal. How insulting. But she fought to keep her voice on an even, calm Bobbie-Sue-like keel. "I said no such thing. I'd never do that."

"Great," was his congenial reply. "Then I'll be right over."

"Over?" *Here? Now?*

"Yep. I'm at the pay phone across the street, and I'm swiftly running out of quarters."

Her eyes bulged as she went to her bedroom window overlooking the street, pushing the filmy bronze fabric away and pressing her hand to the chilled glass. Oh. My. God. Indeed, Heath Jefferson was in the phone booth at Wartson and Son's Bakery, cradling the phone to his ear, still in what looked like the navy blue suit he'd worn last night.

He turned suddenly, looking right at her.

Her heart pounded like a jackhammer in her chest when he lifted his hand and waved. If he had nothing else, he had a set of cajones being so friggin' cheerful when she looked so damned bad.

Immediately her eyes went to her old, worn nightgown. Pink, and displaying a fuzzy white bunny with googly eyes that wobbled when you walked.

Fabulous.

Sheeit.

"Wanda? Did I mention I'm running out of quarters?"

"But I'm not even dressed!" She glanced at the clock, noting it was just eight-thirty. "And it's not even nine o' clock yet!"

"Well, I figured the early bird and the worm theory."

Wanda traipsed to her bedroom and glanced in the mirror. Every hair on the left side of her head was mashed upward, and she had pillow marks on her face. For the love of all things decorous, she couldn't let him see her like this. "What was that about a worm?"

"The early bird gets the worm, Ms. Schwartz. I have twenty

starter kits to sell in seven days. I can't afford to waste time if I'm
going to keep my end of our bargain. You know the one. The one
where you supervise me while I sell, sell, sell. Color wheels, that
is. And the one where you give me the signal to shut up if I go too
far with a potential client. That signal being two winks of your
right eye and one with your left. Which seemed like it would look
like a serious eye tic to anyone who didn't know what you meant,
but that's what it said in the *Bobbie-Sue Manual*, so it must work. I
did my homework just as promised. Now it's time for you to keep
your end of our deal."

Wanda turned the taps on her sink and lined her toothbrush
with a perfect ribbon of white toothpaste. "You know, I have to
tell you, and forgive my brutal honesty here, but you're pretty
presump—"

"Aha! You *are* reneging. I gotta tell ya, that's not very Bobbie-
Sue-like," he admonished, though his overly cheerful tone didn't
change.

Her face burned, and her cheeks turned bright red. Damn him
for reading the fucking manual. And how dare he call her on her
ethics. "I'm am *not* reneging. I'm just thinking you might want to
renegotiate. Here's a little heads-up from me to you. No one, and
I do mean *no one*, not in the history of Bobbie-Sue, has ever sold
more than maybe—maybe five, six tops, starter kits. I'm only trying to think of you and the degree of difficulty you'll experience."
There. She was only trying to be realistic and in her realism, thus
helpful. Any reputable Bobbie-Sue rep worth her salt would do
the same. "I mean, you don't want your dreams of Bobbie-Sue
greatness to be crushed, do you?" She fought a snicker and ran
her toothbrush under the water, jamming it into her mouth, then
swishing it over her top teeth.

His response was to chuckle, low and deep with an almost
growl. "I think I've got this in the bag. So don't you worry about

me and my feelings. I have to hang up now because my time is almost up. I'll be right over."

He hung up before she had the chance to sputter that she hadn't even showered. Just as she was spitting toothpaste out of her mouth, her doorbell rang. She ran a hand through her messy hair, giving one last attempt at looking presentable. That she should care whether she looked pretty bugged the living shit out of her.

Grabbing her robe, she threw it on and ran for the door.

And there he was. In the same suit. Smiling. Maybe even hotter in the daylight than he'd been last night under the fluorescent lights of her kitchen. Her legs grew wobbly, and her heart began that slam dance in her chest again. He'd make this hella easier if he'd just not be so male. So supremely male. So—so, what was the word Nina used when referring to a man who was hot?

Fucktacular.

Yeah, Heath Jefferson was fucktacularly fucktacular.

Hell to the yeah.

He smelled good. He looked even better, and at this point in her life, she couldn't even believe she'd taken note of anything other than what was now, what some would consider, her tragic fate.

Oy.

Her hands self-consciously ran along the sides of her hair, still kinda sticking out everywhere.

"You're not ready." He said it like she was some huge Bobbie-Sue failure. A real slacker. Who was helping whom here?

Ingrate.

Wanda held the door open, sweeping her hand wide to allow Heath entry. "Well, of course I'm not ready. I just woke up ten minutes ago." The nerve of this pushy, overconfident man, shoving his way into her house and demanding she tutor him.

He grinned, and this time Wanda was granted the full, white, shiny perfection of his smile, minus the all-knowing arrogance. "But according to Bobbie-Sue, if what the manual says is true, in order to achieve the fresh, glowing Bobbie-Sue look, you should need no longer than ten minutes in front of a mirror." He pointed to his watch. A Rolex, mind you. Go figure. Yet another piece of the strange puzzle that was Heath Jefferson. "It's been almost fifteen."

Wanda tightened the lapels of her bathrobe over her chest and grunted. "Yeah, most of which I spent on the phone with you. Now quit trying to impress me with your enthusiasm, and let me at least have some coffee before you start reciting chapter and verse from the Bobbie-Sue creed."

His steps were sure when he strode past her, heading for the kitchen. The broad width of his shoulders filled out the suit, which fit him to perfection. His white shirt against his lightly tanned face had a healthy glow to it that even Bobbie-Sue makeup couldn't achieve. He stopped in the doorway and paused, glancing over his shoulder. "I'll tell you what. I'll make you another deal." The glitter in Heath's hazel eyes made her pause.

And tingle.

Bow-chick-a-wow-wow.

She rolled her eyes at him, trying to keep from pulling her bathrobe up over her matted hair and pillow-marked face. "What now? Maybe a case of free moisturizer, if you pull this off? A percentage of my stock in Bobbie-Sue?"

"You hold stock in Bobbie-Sue?"

"Yeah, and it's not up for grabs, buddy."

"Here's the deal. I'll make breakfast if you make haste."

Wanda heard the imaginary hiss of the air leaving her protective bubble. He was making it damned difficult not to like him—punk-assed attitude and all. No man had ever made her breakfast. Her ex-husband sure as hell had never made her anything. But miserable, if one were to split hairs. "I don't normally have much more than coffee in the mornings." Her protest was feeble. Just the idea that someone else was doing the cooking sounded good. Living alone, she didn't cook much anymore. That this someone was so hot he made her eyeballs feel like they were singed *and* he was offering to cook her breakfast, had a decadent, almost sinful feel to it.

"Everyone should start their day with a good breakfast under their belts. It's the most important meal of the day. It does the body good."

Her brows knit together while she fought her naughty thoughts about him. "I thought that was milk."

"Then I'll make something with milk."

"There really is no winning with you, is there?"

He wiggled his eyebrows at her. "Not when I want something. Besides, you'll need your energy for where we're going. Now go get ready."

She lingered for a moment, rooted to the spot, crazy bed hair and all. "Hold on one second. About where you seem to think we're going . . . call me crazy, you wouldn't be the first, but exactly *where* are we going? I mean, a girl can't be too careful these days, and while I don't want to sound repetitive—you're a man. Bigger, stronger, faster. You have what some would call the upper hand."

Heath slid a hand into the pocket of his pants and gave her that fed up look. "Not the man card again. I thought we'd sailed over that hurdle and moved on to a more prosperous beginning to our working relationship."

Wanda rolled her tongue over her dry lips and tried to find a sensitive, diplomatic way to express her misgivings. And then, in the spirit of Nina, and with a little nudge from the Grim Reaper, she thought *fuck that*. Life was too short, and in her case, a lot shorter than she'd planned, to take a risk that might end her time here on the planet before she was abruptly taken. She'd far prefer it was from her illness—not some whack job who'd bury her body in his backyard, or maybe his deteriorating great-aunt Ethel's basement.

So there was going to be no more scamming her, if that's what this was. Because if it wasn't, nothing made sense anymore. "Look, again I'm going to refer to our very strange circumstances, and while I don't want to insult you, before we go any further, you *are* a man who wants to sell cosmetics. That happens like never, and I've been doing this for almost two years now. I'm a woman who's beginning to wonder if this is some nutty scheme of yours to pick up women. Believe me when I tell you, I've heard about far crazier, much more elaborate schemes to meet women. Or worse still—maybe you have some fetish for all things girl-like." There. No more word mincing or beating around the bush.

"Uh, fetish?"

If he was faking that perplexed look, he was damned good. And still yummy while he did it. Wanda waved a hand at him. He knew damned well what she was talking about. "Yes, *fetish*. You know, like some men like to wear women's clothing even though they're perfectly straight. And others like to wear diapers and have their girlfriends bring them bottles. It's called infantilism, if I remember correctly, and while I fully support whatever gets your freak on as long as it's safe, sane, and consensually indulged in by two—or even ten—adults you can't use me and Bobbie-Sue as your freak vehicle. Got that?"

Heath's sharply edged jaw shifted, then popped while his eyebrow arched upward. "Diapers . . . Okay. I think I just achieved a new level of awareness I could have lived another two hundred . . . er, lifetime without. Here's the thing, I have absolutely no desire to wear diapers or drink anything from a bottle that isn't labeled

Heineken or better still, *Jack Daniels*. I applied for a job, and don't think I don't get how unusual this is—a man selling a product women primarily sell. But I need a job, and if that means help- ing women achieve what that manual calls color success by selling makeup, then I'm all about it. For the last time, I don't want to pick up women. Though I think I see how you might think that's what I'm up to. I don't have any fetishes—especially involving women's clothing and makeup, or any that I know of that even re- semble what you just mentioned. Which now has *me* freaked out. So thanks for that. I have no criminal record, and I'm not some serial killer. I'm here because I want a *job*. Period." His confused expression was replaced by a harder, colder determination.

And it was fierce.

Delectably so.

Wanda shivered, but plowed ahead. If he was this serious, then he wouldn't mind if she prodded some more. "Are you gay?"

Heath's eyes narrowed, and his posture stiffened. "That matters how?"

Eek. He was right. If this were another woman, she wouldn't be asking such a sensitive, incredibly personal question. In fact, on a personal level, she knew very little about her recruits. His sexu- ality shouldn't matter one iota to her. But for whatever reason, she found herself hoping he wasn't gay. Which made her a horrible person.

Ah, but then again, her life was short, and if he was gay, the possibility of his wanting to use this supposed need for a job to pick up women declined radically as did the idea she might end up some case for a New Jersey CSI investigator. And that made her feel safer. So she'd poked at him with her imaginary stick. Which, again, made her a shitty person, but whatever. "It doesn't matter—but it would make more sense."

His fantastically sexy mouth became a thin line of pissed off.

"So what you're saying is, if I'm a gay man, I'd be more likely to want to sell makeup? I'm missing your point."

Apparently, so was she. Remorse for her insensitivity set in, and it trampled all over her resolve to nip this craziness in the bud. "Sorry. That was really insensitive of me, and it's totally none of my business. I guess I just thought if you were gay, the chances you just want to pick up women, or maybe kill them and stuff them in some wood chipper, would be less likely, you know?" Omigod. That was so not why she wanted to know if he was gay, and she'd just lied about it—blatantly. But dayum—it'd sounded soooo convincing she felt momentary pride. Even Nina would have patted her on the back at how convincing she was. But her proud moment faded. She'd broken a cardinal rule of the new millennium, and it was unforgivable. Don't ask, don't tell, and all that political correctness shit.

Cue awkward moment.

But Heath surprised her, barking a laugh that was sharp. "A wood chipper? Messy, don't you think?"

Wanda expelled a tension-filled breath and laughed, too. "Definitely."

Heath didn't say anything else as he leaned against her door frame, filling it with his rugged, well-muscled maleness, but his eyes held hers with that gaze that left her feeling like she was bucknaked and he was an X-ray machine.

Wanda clucked her tongue, refusing to squirm under his hard glare. She couldn't stop her skepticism from oozing out in her tone, and she wasn't going to let him think this was easy because he'd wooed all those women last night. "I was just trying to be honest with you. If you can't tell how crazy this idea of yours is, then I guess you'll just have to see firsthand. Women relate to other women about things of a personal nature far easier than they ever will a man. Makeup, despite the belief that it's frivolous and

silly, is personal—*very personal*. In fact, I'd dare you to tell any of
my clients that it isn't. And I can't help but get the impression that
the very idea is joke-worthy in your mind. I think the luck you had
last night was just that—luck. To do this day in and day out takes a
certain level of *commitment*. It takes a true desire to see your fellow
sister shine—be the best she can be. I realize it isn't like curing
cancer, but for some women, women who never understood the
difference it could make in their lives and how good it can ulti-
mately make them feel—it can be."

His look was pensive, his face serious. "Wow, that's deep. You
have to admit, though, the analogy to curing cancer is kinda dramatic and big."

God, if that wasn't just a shade shy of Nina and her pessimism.
Okay, so it was a little dramatic, but each woman she'd made over,
some who actually were in a hospital she visited once a month and
really did have cancer, who felt like shit, who'd lost their hair—
made the comparison startlingly close. "And this is where your
trouble will lie—you're not a woman. You can't possibly understand what a little blusher can do for you, because you're a man."

But Heath wasn't whipping out his white flag. "Yep. I am,
and I say you let me worry about whether I can relate to these
women."

"I'd do that if it wasn't something that's so crucial to creating
a client-to-representative relationship and imperative to my good
reputation with Bobbie-Sue."

His face fell as he mock-pouted. "Boy, you're determined to
crush my color wheel dreams, aren't you? First it was picking up
women and fetishes that made even a Neanderthal like me cringe,
and now it's color crises and the possibility that I'm gay. If I were
less of a man, I'd have handed you my man-parts by now and taken
my toys home." His grin was teasing, but again, there was that
dogged look in his eyes.

Wanda couldn't help the snort that escaped her lips. Alrighty then. He won—this round anyway. He was in for a serious color walloping, and the only way to let him see that for himself was to let him fall flat on that hot, overconfident ass of his. But she could admit she'd been out of line. She had no right to question his sexuality. "I'm sorry I even suggested you share your sexual preferences with me—it was totally out of line. So I'm just going to skulk off and take that shower now, but not before I saw off my wildly flapping tongue with my nail scissors or something. You go ahead and make breakfast, and when I come back, we'll pretend I have manners and start over, okay?"

His dark blond head nodded affirmation.

Satisfied, she turned away to hide her flaming cheeks.

"Wanda?"

Her feet stopped at the threshold of her bedroom doorway, sparing him a meek glance over her shoulder. "Yeah?"

Heath grinned again, self-assured and cocky, flashing his teeth. "I'm not gay. But if it makes you feel any better, I think Home Depot had a sale on wood chippers this past week—I bet they're all out." He winked before heading to her kitchen without saying another word.

Wanda threw her head back and laughed, scuffling off to her bedroom and heading for her closet. Heath wasn't gay.

Yippee and skippee. Totally rad.

Or bad because she had no business fending off butterflies in her belly and the hot rush of excitement she'd experienced over this small piece of clue cake. He was, for all intents and purposes, her employee, and if that wasn't enough of a mood dampener, she might consider her shortening mortality one.

Her throat clenched, tightening with anxious fear. Wanda gripped the rack she'd just cleared last week of clothes she'd given to Goodwill. Her knuckles turned white, but then her eye caught her favorite teal sweater, and she reached for it. Clinging to it because it was tangible, and just touching the sweater, running her fingers over it, meant she was still in the here and now.

Living in the here and now meant she not only had purpose—and an avoidance tactic—but it also meant she had something to keep her busy.

Heath and his notion he could sell makeup because he'd gotten lucky last night. Whether she liked it or not—they now had an employee-employer relationship. Even if it was an unconventional one.

Or what some might call really fucking weird.

But whatever.

Hopping into the shower, letting the hot spray soothe the dull ache of her belly, it occurred to her that she was now naked in her house with a strange man who was in her kitchen making breakfast for her. How naughty. How risqué, or was that risky? How un-Wanda-ish. That she hadn't begun a background check the moment Heath'd said he wanted to sell Bobbie-Sue should have been testament enough to how hinky her world had become after just one doctor's appointment.

And she didn't even care. Again, not Wanda-like at all. Had there ever been a time she wasn't cautious about her own safety? Sometimes even paranoid to the point of looking people up on the *America's Most Wanted* website?

Instead she was in her shower stomping all over her OCD-edness with soapy feet and thrilled to itsy-bitsy bits that Heath didn't play shortstop for the other team.

She mentally stuck her tongue out at Nina and Marty. How was that for predictability, eh?

She wasn't feeling at all threatened by him in her kitchen either—which could be an incredibly stupid emotion to continue to entertain if he were say, an ax murderer. But the vibe she got from him was anything but malicious. Annoying, persistent like no one she'd known before him, and oddly urgent, but not malicious or threatening.

Turning the taps off, she grabbed a towel and scrubbed her skin dry, then popped open the medicine cabinet and took out her bottle of aspirin, hoping it would quell the building ache in her gut.

She caught sight of her reflection in the mirror as she swung it open, focusing on the ugly truth. Aspirin wouldn't keep at bay what she had forever. The prescription for pain meds poked its frayed, finger-worried edge out at her from the cabinet shelf, just to give her a healthy dose of the here and now. Wanda shoved it to the back of the cabinet, hoping she'd be able to stall filling it.

She firmly shut the cabinet door and took one last look at her blue eyes in the mirror, devoid of makeup, full of fear. She saw this for what it was. What she was really doing was avoiding the inevitable. *If you close your eyes, no one can see you* . . .

She'd played that game when she was little, when she was embarrassed—uncomfortable—when she wanted to be invisible. Although what she'd been diagnosed with was invisible to the naked eye, she couldn't hide it by closing hers.

A rap on the bathroom door startled her. "Wanda? Maybe we could speed things along? Your eggs'll get cold if you don't pick up the pace."

Heath's voice reminded her, her hair was wet and she still wasn't dressed.

And breakfast was waiting. Breakfast.

And they were going *somewhere*.

Together.

Alone.

Niiiiice.

*   *   *

"You have a Yugo."

"Yep."

"It's—it's nice." Which sounded like the biggest lie ever. But there it was. Nice was reserved for a Hyundai, maybe a Saturn, but that was all she could summon—*nice*.

Wanda stood astounded, unable to make sense of Heath and his fancy suit, with his shiny Rolex watch and now—a Yugo. Did they even exist anymore? When he'd offered to drive, she'd hesitated, but then decided she was tired—she didn't want to have to fight traffic, but if he was willing, what the hell. She was feeling content after a breakfast of scrambled eggs, toast, and rich, black coffee. She'd lost her edge and maybe even her will to continue the war of words with him. He always won, because he always had an answer, anyway.

But this—this car, him, everything about this—was just, well, wonky.

"It's a classic now. From 1986—the first year they came out," he said, running a proud hand along the gleaming white fender before guiding her to the passenger side door.

Like she'd know anything about what year it was, other than it was a Yugo.

A *Yugo*.

No matter how immaculately maintained.

"Wanda?"

"Huh?"

"In—get *in* the car, or we'll be late."

Her head bobbed upward, narrowly missing his as they stood at eye level. Crap, she so wanted to ask a million questions. Instead, she slid silently into the passenger seat, shivering from the feel of cold vinyl beneath her nylon-clad legs.

"Ready?" he asked, turning the key in the ignition.

"I don't know. Why don't you tell me where we're going, then I'll tell you if I'm ready."

He grinned, making her heart thump with an irregular skip to it. "To a place where you can see color wheels for miles and miles and I can sell those starter kits, as promised."

Wanda folded her hands in her lap, fighting her schoolgirl reaction to him. "If I were a smart woman, I'd make you stop this car right now and let me out. I'm in a car with a man I've known less than twenty-four hours who could still turn out to be a nut—with no knowledge of our destination. Oh, and I have Mace, in case you were thinking of going all killing spree on me." Yeah. She did have Mace, too. Mace and pepper spray *and* a whistle. There'd be no whacking Wanda Schwartz today. No siree. She'd learned from the master—Nina—and Marty had taught her a thing or two about not ending up in the county morgue.

He shook his head, resting his arm on the ledge of the driver's side window. "No, if you're a smart woman you'll let me make you some money, and for the final time, I don't want to kill you. At least not until I've sucked you dry of every last ounce of your Bobbie-Sue knowledge. After that, I make no promises you won't find me in the Home Depot with some cold, hard cash." He winked, his chiseled profile relaxing into yet another one of those wolfish grins that screamed he was mocking her while he looked ridiculously comfortable in a car where his head nearly grazed the roof.

Turning on the seat, she repositioned herself to face him and began to speak, then stopped. He was hell-bent. Who was she to try and stop him? If he made money, she did, too—which wouldn't mean squat for her in the end, but maybe she could leave it to her mother. It was just that dude was way into this. Typically, new recruits were nervous and awkward, worried they'd look foolish, but not Heath. He threw off the kind of vibe that hollered anticipation—a lust for the Bobbie-Sue kill.

Omigod, she'd been wrong. He wasn't Nina. He was Marty, only with dangly bits. And hotter.

Wanda stifled a chuckle. Marty had had much the same thrill of the hunt in her eyes when they'd first all met and gone on cold calls door-to-door. Marty could sell a subscription of *Modern Day Mercenary* to an Amish woman. She was that good when she'd been a Bobbie-Sue rep. Wanda's approach was a little less rabid than Marty's, but she loved selling Bobbie-Sue.

She loved Marty.

She loved her life.

Whoa. Maudlin alert.

The car came to an abrupt stop, forcing her to turn her whiny thoughts off.

"Welcome to Hoboken," Heath said, casting a sidelong glance of amusement in the direction of the crowd forming in front of a large window with dark glass.

Wanda's gaze was too caught up with the people on the sidewalk, milling about the establishment they'd pulled up in front of, to pay much attention to where they were.

A long, lanky woman with fishnet stockings and the hottest pair of six-inch-heeled thigh-high boots Wanda'd ever seen turned, flipped her luscious, waist-length curls over her shoulder, and winked, right at Heath. Did women wear thigh-high boots in broad daylight?

A woman who had an Adam's apple?

Huh.

Wanda pursed her lips, staring with a fixed gaze at some trash that blew along the curb. "Um, where are we again?"

"Hoboken."

"No, not the town—the establishment."

"Oh, right. Dirty Petey's."

"Dirty who?"

"Petey's."

"Right."

"So you ready?"

"For?"

"To sell cosmetics."

"To?"

"The Miss New Jersey TransAmerica contestants."

Holy feces.

CHAPTER
4

"I dunno, Wanda, whaddya think about the Yuck-It-Up Yukon for my under the brow highlighter? I mean, do you think it picks up the gold foil wraps I had Leland do on my wig? Or do you think it makes me look pasty?" Miss Egg Harbor, er, Joe, tilted his head from left to right, catching the light of the big bulbs surrounding his mirror.

Wanda smiled, placing her hands on the back of his chair, trying valiantly to forget the caaa-raziest sales pitch she'd ever watched go like so much helium from a balloon in favor of keeping a straight face. "I think Heath's right on target and the Yuck-It-Up-Yukon is soooo in your color wheel, it's almost scary. You look—well, you look better than I ever could. You're gorgeous."

And he, uh, *she* was. The colors Heath'd chosen were—much like last night with the vixen—spot on. His work was impeccable, too. He'd wielded the square sponge applicator like it was the equivalent of a remote to a big screen TV. His lean, tanned fingers had whisked over the planes of one contestant's face as though Bobbie-Sue herself had taken over his body in some kind of kooky Linda Blair possession.

And Wanda had thought more than once, *What the bloody fuck?* Where Heath had learned to apply makeup with such expertise remained another mystery. He'd also proven her wrong. She felt a smug attack from Heath coming on, and it left her unsure whether she should clap him on the back for being right, or deitz him in the head with two fingers for being right.

Miss Egg Harbor waved a dismissive, bawdily bejeweled hand at her, tapping Wanda's nose with a red Lee Press On nail. "Guuuurrrlll, if I had your skin, I wouldn't need foundation. And those lips. I'd kill you for them if you weren't so damned nice." She reached up and pinched Wanda's cheek. "Skinny, but nice, and I think I owe you my left testicle for introducing me to the joys of Bobbie-Sue foundation. God saves rooms in Heaven for women like you, sugarplum."

It was all she could do not to let her mouth fall to the floor the entire time they'd been with the contestants. Heath had not only charmed his way backstage to the dressing room of Miss Trans-America, but he'd sold twenty-two starter kits. Twenty-flippin'-*two*. He was like the color king or something.

"This is faaaaabulous, Heath," Miss Brick cooed, flicking the finishing powder over her face with a wide brush to set her makeup. "I cannot believe the coverage I'm getting from this foundation. It even hides my five o'clock shadow, but feels light as a fluffy feather. Where have you been all my life, Heath Jefferson?" Miss Brick batted one false eyelashed eye at him, cocking her shoulder flirtatiously.

"I think you mean, where has *Bobbie-Sue* been all your life?" Heath quipped, slapping his newfound friend on the back. "So can I count you in for a starter kit, too?"

Make that twenty-three starter kits.

Oh, the neener, neeners she was in for now.

Both Miss Brick and Miss Egg Harbor nodded their glossy, wigged heads. Miss Brick shimmied her backside against Heath's hip. "Are you kidding me, dahhhhling? Finding Bobbie-Sue is like finding out George Clooney cross-dresses. You bet I want a starter kit, and I can name at least three of my friends who'll want one, too, sugar lips. Hell, we'll have all of the transgendered community buying from you."

Miss Hopatcong slithered up behind Heath, grabbing a handful of his ass-tastic butt and giving it a pinch. "Sweetness? Count me in, too," she purred, draping a black-evening-length-gloved hand over his shoulder while dragging her finger over his cheek. In her three-inch stiletto heels, she loomed over Heath, curling her body into his back. Her long, platinum blonde tresses brushed his cheek with a sway and a swish. "You sure I can't talk you into switching teams, honey? I'd be your tiara-wearin' bitch any day of the week."

Heath unwound a lanky leg and turned, setting Miss Hopatcong away from him, his smile never faltering. "I'm pretty sure I play for the other team. But if I change my mind, you'll be one of the first to get the bulletin on MySpace," he joked.

All of the contestants crowding the dressing room of Dirty Petey's laughed, the round of husky chuckles, a drastic contrast to their very feminine outfits.

The stage manager poked his head inside the door. "Ladies! Line up—it's almost showtime!" Excited, nervous laughter was followed by each contestant taking a place in line.

Miss Hackettstown hiked her gel breasts upward, shifting them into place with a shake and a jiggle, and smiled at Wanda. "Wish me luck, Princess!"

"Luck!" Wanda yelled after her, giving her a thumbs-up. The

sigh she gave as the last of the pageant contestants headed out to the stage consisted of a mixture of things. Regret that the makeover spree was done, and amazement that each and every one of them had not only filled out the Bobbie-Sue order forms, but handed over their credit cards to place their orders.

"So I guess you can say it now, and we'll get it out of the way." Heath was still behind her, the heat from his tall body reaching out to hers, sending goose bumps willy-nilly along her arms.

Wanda turned to face him, backing away from his close proximity. "Say what?"

"That I was right."

"You were almost right."

"How do you figure?"

"Those aren't really women."

"Ah, but in a dimly lit room, I'd dare you to say they weren't."

"Not the same thing."

"I think I have to disagree with you. If I'm not mistaken, they feel like women, and wasn't that speech you gave me back at your house all about how Bobbie-Sue can make a woman *feel?*"

Point. Sort of. Cocky, but a point she had to concede. "Okay. I think. I don't know. I say we pack it in and save the 'I told you sos'."

"But I did."

"You did what?"

"Tell you so."

Wanda rolled her eyes at him, pushing up the sleeves of her teal calf-length sweater dress, and busied herself scouting the tables for any unopened samples. "Fine, you told me. Okay? Now how 'bout you stop getting a hernia over patting yourself on the back and help me clean up this stuff."

He scooped a bunch of lipstick samples up in his palms and dumped them into a basket. "You're mad."

So? "Why would I be mad?"

"Because I was right."

Right is as right does. "This is the part where I remind you what a man you are. If you're so secure in that manhood of yours, you wouldn't need me to tell you you're right."

He hovered close behind her, trailing her as she gathered product. "Question?"

Christ. "Go."

"I don't get why you're mad. It seems counterproductive to me. I did just sell a bunch of makeup—and that makes you money—you should have your happy on. Instead, your mouth is all pinched, and I think I might see fire shooting from your nostrils. This was a coup for both of us, wasn't it?"

Yes, it'd been a coup, but in her experience, all good coups were like an adrenaline rush. They went down as quickly as they went up. She was still skeptical this would all pan out the way he thought it would. The real killer was, Heath had actually managed to rope some of the contestants into not just buying the makeup, but the starter kits, too. "I hate to be the glaring fluorescent lightbulb of reality, but you do realize they have five business days to back out. Not only that, statistically speaking, when those who bought the starter kits realize they have to actually work to find clients, more than half of them will turn tail and run."

He tossed the last of the foundation packets into the heavy suitcase she'd brought. "Yep. I know the statistics. I read them, and if that's the case, then I guess we'll be spending more time together. But if even half of them stay in the Bobbie-Sue program, I've already sold what, ten starter kits? Don't be such a naysayer."

"Eleven and a half." But really, who's counting?

He nodded, raising one eyebrow. "Exactly."

She turned to find him gazing down at her, his eyes full of the look of triumph. The Marty look—glowing with the victory of the kill. "Question?"

Heath shoved his hands in his pants pockets. "Hit me."

Because she just had to know. "What, in all of creation, made you think to scope a venue like this? I mean, never in my wildest dreams would I have ever thought something like a pageant of this nature would drum up so much business."

"That's because you're a woman."

Her face instantly hardened. "Pardon?" She was a little tired of the knuckle-dragging comments.

But that didn't thwart his honesty. "I said, you're a woman, and you think only other women wear makeup. It's a natural conclusion. It was kind of an outside-of-the-box thing for me. It's not a fault on your part, just a gender thing, I guess. I happened to see the flyer for the pageant in a paper I was reading, and it dawned on me that this would be the perfect place to sell makeup. Even if it's unconventional."

"It was genius," she mumbled, unwilling to admit too loudly that he'd just set some kind of Bobbie-Sue sell-a-thon record.

"Say again?" he prompted, sucking his cheeks in, clearly fighting off a grin.

Wanda planted her hands on her hips and sighed out loud. "Okay, fine. It was genius. The thought never occurred to me. In a million, bazillion years, I'd have never thought to sell makeup to transvestites."

"Transgenders."

"Right, and on the way home, I'd really like the full explanation on the difference between the two. Because it seems, you're the go-to guy and all. So kudos to thinking outside the box, if there is one," she added dryly. "Now I have another question. How'd you know the foundation would do such a bang-up job of covering their facial hairlines?" She paused, then shook her head with a lift of her lips. "Wait, do I want to know?"

He smiled, all cat-like and secretive. "Nope. You don't want to know."

Wanda nodded her head and held up a hand. "That's all you need to say. So do we have everything? Or are you interested in maybe sticking around to see if Miss Hopatcong brings the house down with her rendition of 'Don't Cry Out Loud'?"

Heath's laughter was gruff, but full and hearty. He ran a hand over his chin thoughtfully. "I liked Miss Hopatcong, but I think my money's on Miss Aberdeen. Did you see her legs? They go on and on." He held his hand up to his neck for emphasis.

Wanda finally laughed, too, and it held a girly, giggly tone Nina'd crack on her about for days. But she couldn't help it. There was just something about this man, something wildly sexy, something hotly secure about who and what he was that made her feel giddy. He'd had not a single qualm about coming here, a place most straight men would run out of slicker than snot runs out of a nose in winter. He'd waved tubes of makeup around, applied eyeshadow, glossed the lips of *men*, and never once batted a single, judgmental, mocking eye.

That he hadn't said word one about the fact that in reality, these were men who were dressed like women, was so—so—sooooo . . . just so. She hadn't quite found the right adjectives to apply to Heath, but that he hadn't had a field day with what some would consider out of their comfort zone left Wanda feeling some serious respect for him. Whether she wanted to or not.

Wanda picked up her Bobbie-Sue case and shot him a half smile. "You know, if I were less secure in my womanhood, I'd be caaaar-aaaazy jealous of Miss Aberdeen and those legs, but, Jesus, did you see Miss Allamuchy's butt? Holy crack a walnut on it."

Heath took the suitcase from her, taking the lead out of the dressing room and down the long hall to the back exit. "I avoided butts. Sorry, there are just some places even I, secure in my manhood, can't go. Legs couldn't be helped when they're wrapped around your waist."

Yeah, the contestants had all thought Heath was cute, too, and he'd pleasantly removed limbs and stray hands from his person like he'd been dealing with grabby toddlers in a candy store. "Okay, I just gotta know. How did you keep a straight face? You didn't look at all uncomfortable when they came on to you, and you were more than a gentleman when Miss Hopatcong all but gave you a lap dance. Most men I know would have been embarrassed at the very least. In fact, I'm sorry to say it, but most of the men I know would have said some pretty cruel things to them."

Heath pushed open the heavy exit door, sunlight pouring over his sharp, handsome features. "Well, don't you think they thought it was kind of strange that I, a straight guy, was selling makeup?"

"Uh, yeah, but you already know how I feel about that. Remember, open mouth insert both feet?"

"Yep, but here's the thing. They didn't judge me, did they?"

"No. On the contrary, I think they all fell in love with you."

"Maybe so, but they were willing to give me a chance—a straight guy with color wheel charts and some lip gloss—why wouldn't I do the same in return?"

Touché.

WANDA'S stomach growled, howling furiously as they left Dirty Petey's. The smell of hot dogs from a nearby vendor called to her. She hadn't been this hungry in a long time, especially after eating breakfast. Maybe the thrill of Heath's triumph had stirred her appetite. She would, after all, be getting a serious paycheck even if half of the men bailed. But that thought came and went. She'd been so caught up in absorbing what a decent guy he was, in how accepting he was of men he claimed were so different than him, that in the end the money had never entered her mind.

That's 'cause you like him, Wanda. Despite the fact that he's got no explanations for his designer suit and crappy car—you think he's killa dreamy.

She swept those thoughts away, instead focusing on the hot dog vendor. She'd begun to stray toward the hot dog cart instead of Heath's car. "C'mon, I feel like a hot dog with everything on it. My treat," she said, casting him a suddenly carefree smile. Wending along the sidewalk, she stopped in front of the cart.

The vendor tightened his scarf around his neck, ducking from the sudden wind that had struck up. The tops of his cheeks were bright red, poking out from beneath, and his eyes watered. "What'll ya have?"

"One with everything, please. Heath?" She motioned for him to give his order.

He stood behind her, sheltering her from the blast of cold air. "Sounds good to me. I'll have the same."

Just his presence behind her made her knees quiver and her toes, which should be frozen, do that tingle thing again.

"Here's one for you, and one for your lady," The vendor plopped two hot dogs in Heath's hands, dripping with sauerkraut and mustard, but Wanda wasn't paying attention to the food, she was staving off the soooo inappropriate twinge of schoolgirl silliness that had followed the hot dog vendor's statement. The one Heath wasn't correcting him about.

She handed the vendor his money and took her hot dog from Heath. He paused before biting into his. A small peek of the sun filtered through the heavy gray and purple clouds, and Heath lifted his face upward as if he were basking in it. It was weak with little or no warmth to it, but he didn't seem to notice. More clouds zoomed in to quickly cover it, but for that one moment, the serene calm that had flitted over his sharp features stole her breath away.

Not that nearly everything this man did didn't steal her breath. Or make her behave like what Nina called a fucktard.

Heath took a healthy bite of his hot dog and grunted. "This," he said, grabbing a napkin from the cart and wiping the side of his mouth with it, "is pretty damn great." He winked, shoving another bite into his mouth as quickly as he'd chewed and swallowed the last.

Wanda munched on hers thoughtfully. Yeah, it was a good hot dog, but it clearly didn't leave her feeling as euphoric as it seemed to leave Heath. "Hmm-mmm," she agreed, following his lead back down the sidewalk.

Another gust of air swirled around them, lifting the scattered debris along the curb and making her shiver with a violent shake. Heath threw an arm around her, and although it appeared it meant nothing to him other than a way to brace themselves against the chill, it was way too close to leaving her breathless again. "It's freeeeezing! And you have nothing more than a suit coat on."

His chuckle sent skitters of heat from her head to her toes. "It's damned cold, but it's good for you. Reminds you you're alive."

"You're going to get sick if you don't wear something warmer." She flicked at the breast of his coat with an icy finger.

"The flu . . . also something to remind you you're alive. All good things."

Alive.

Yeah.

What a fucking irony. It was at this very moment that she wanted to rail against the unfairness of her terminal illness. She wanted to scream her rage, throw things, out-swear Nina, stomp and rant. But she wouldn't, because she just didn't do public hissy fits. Not only was it un-Bobbie-Sue-like, it was in bad form. And Heath couldn't possibly know how close to home his words were.

She stopped when they got to his car, cocking a grin at him as he opened the door. "Well, if you get the flu, you won't be in any condition to hit the transgendered pageant circuit. Ooooh, hurry up and start this thing. It's flippin' cold."

Heath walked around the car and got in, cranking up the heat, and reaching behind to the backseat to pull out a blanket. "Here, this'll help until the heat kicks in."

Grateful, Wanda threw it over her legs and leaned her head against the window, closing her eyes, and letting go a small sigh because he wasn't just hot, he was considerate.

"Wanda?"

She struggled to open her eyes, the low vibration of Heath's voice seeping into her pores. It was warm where she was, warm and cozy, and Heath was interrupting a perfectly good catnap.

He placed a hand on her shoulder and gave it a gentle shake. "Wanda, wake up. You're home."

Her eyes popped open, but she couldn't see much but whorls of blinding white snowflakes. They battered the car and danced across the beams of Heath's headlights.

Her heart clenched. She loved the snow. What if this was the last snowstorm she ever saw? A moment of regret shadowed her face, but she shook it off. "Ohhhhh. It's snowing. Isn't it beautiful? I love the snow. Love it. I know most people hate it. Hate to shovel it, hate to drive in it, but it makes me smile."

He nodded his head, a small smile tilting his lips upward. "I like the snow, too. Used to love to ski, but I have a long drive home, and if the temp is any indication, it's probably going to freeze. So I'd better get going."

Impulse, something she wasn't terribly prone to, made her speak without aid of her brain. "Oh, nooo. You can't drive in this. It's a blizzard out there. Why don't you come in, and we'll get some of this paperwork done while we wait it out. Maybe it's just a squall and it'll blow over, but for now, I wouldn't drive anywhere." Had that sounded overeager? Had the mere idea of him alone in her small house with just her and Menusha sent a chill of anticipation versus fear up her spine?

Why yes, yes it had.

Jesus and all twelve apostles.

She tried to clear her brain of the cobwebs that crowded it after such a peaceful nap and think of a way to save her pride. "I mean, especially seeing as you're officially my best new recruit ever. We can't have you all jacked up in the hospital." He looked torn, as if there was something else he had to do. She could see the wheels of his razor-sharp mind turning. He was hiding something.

What? A girlfriend? A wife? Kids? Bodies?

Wouldn't that just fucking figure. Of course someone as brick shithouse as Heath would have at least a girlfriend. One he could go home to and make color wheels for while they lounged their perfectly honed bodies on sheets of silk while sipping champagne from fluted glasses. If he had a wife, his application hadn't indicated as much. He'd checked off single. But that still didn't mean he didn't have a friend of the female persuasion whom he belonged at home with.

Heath's face took a sudden turn in expression, brightening, as if he'd cleared up whatever mental war he was having. "Sounds like a plan."

Wanda hopped out of the car without saying anything else, yet there was that ridiculous flutter in her stomach again. She placed a hand over her belly and clicked her garage door opener, pushing open the door that led to the kitchen.

Menusha hurled herself at Wanda, winding her tail around her ankles and meowing with a loud whine. Just as she stooped to gather her up, a sharp pain assaulted her lower abdomen, piercing and hot. The very same sharp jab that had sent her to the doctor to begin with. Wanda stumbled, dropping Menusha and biting her lip to keep from gasping. She clutched the countertop for support until the pang eased.

Heath was right behind her, his warm palm on her lower back. "You okay?"

Wanda immediately popped upward, grimacing at the tug to her belly when she tried to stand erect. "Yeah, too many sit-ups, I guess. Must have pulled something. I'm fine, just give me a sec to catch my breath."

Menusha howled again, stalking the kitchen floor as Heath flipped the lights on. He bent and picked her up, his long arms encompassing her dark body. She burrowed against his chest, and he scratched her under the chin. "Ya hungry?" he asked her. "Where's the food? I'll feed her." He dropped a hungry, howling Menusha to the floor with a gentle plop and headed for the pantry.

Jesus Christ in a miniskirt he was getting harder and harder to stay irritated with when he was so thoughtful. "Pantry," she gritted out, tugging her coat off and reaching beneath the sink for her hot water bottle. Lately, that seemed to offer a modicum of relief.

A lightly bronzed hand grabbed the bottle from her while the other sprinkled some dry cat food into Menusha's bowl and plunked it down in front of her. His confident hands flipped the tap on, testing the water to see if it was hot enough. "Go sit," he ordered.

"I can get it."

"Sit." His order was like that of the first time she'd spoken with him on the phone—commanding in a sit up and take notice kind of way.

Wanda was too tired to protest, too embarrassed to say much at all. Instead, she plunked down in the kitchen chair, sliding her heels off and wiggling her toes.

Heath handed her the water bottle without a word, but his face held questions she had no intention of answering. Especially when he stared at her like that. It alternately unnerved her and sent rushes of heat on an APB throughout her body. Taking it from him, she smiled her thanks and laid the warmth across her belly.

He dragged a chair out and sat down beside her. "That must've been some workout." His comment rang skeptical to her ears.

Wanda looked down at her feet, grateful that even in the dead of winter she'd thought to have a pedicure. "Yeah, I forget which one it was. Tae Bo, hip-hop, break dance your way to a flatter belly, or something along those lines. It was brutal. Really brutal." Heath hadn't stopped staring her down. In fact, if it were possible, his intent gaze had become more concentrated. God, she was the crappiest liar.

He was clearly unconvinced. "I see."

No. He would never see. Not if she had anything to say about it. "I'm okay now. Let's hit that paperwork, huh?"

Heath leaned back in the chair, crossing his long legs at the ankles, the muscles of his thighs bulging, clenching, and unclenching as he did. He was so at ease with his body, so comfortable in his skin, making him so much sexier. "Why don't you go lie on the couch, and I'll make you some tea or something?"

"Because really, I'm fine, and we have a ton of paperwork to do."

His face grew stern, the hard planes freezing in place. "You know, Wanda, I'm not buying that you're fine, but I won't meddle in your business."

She shot him an ironic smile. "Unlike me, all prying and getting personal, you mean?"

A chuckle slithered from his lips at the truth in her words. "Very much unlike you. And I can take care of the paperwork. All I need is your sign-off on the sales receipts. Should be easy enough. Now, just point me in the direction of the stuff I need, and I'll make you that pot of tea."

She rose, sorry she'd done it so quickly for the gnawing ache in her belly that grabbed her intestines, leaving her skin clammy and her head swimming. "Above the cabinet, and thanks." Plodding off to the couch, she slid onto it, wincing as she settled in and repositioned the water bottle.

Heath followed behind her, flipping the TV on to the news. "You rest, I just want to see how much snow they're predicting." Heath took the knitted afghan her mother had made her from the back of her couch and draped it over her.

The dim light from the kitchen left her face in the shadows, but the bright glare of the TV allowed her enough light to watch him undetected.

No matter how condescending, how utterly, unashamedly confident he was, no matter how much it tweaked her, seeing him standing over the back of her couch, engrossed in the news, made her heart do backflips.

Goddamn, he was sexy. Hard, and lean, and . . .

This absolutely, in no uncertain terms, had to stop. Why he had this effect on her left her uncomfortable.

It would only make this strange working relationship more difficult, if she let thoughts like the naughty ones she was having overrule her better judgment.

Not to mention, she shouldn't be pursuing anything but an attorney and a will. She could only attribute this odd pull to him to her vulnerable state. No man had affected her like this—not ever. Not even the dick she'd married and been dumped by.

Her lashes fell to her cheeks while she forced herself to take a deep breath and relax. Maybe she could pawn Heath off on that bitch Linda Fisher. Linda had never minded stealing recruits or accounts. She'd once stolen Marty's accounts, and she'd been punished for it, but Marty's good heart, and Linda's divorce, had made Marty give her a second chance. Linda was good at what she did— even if she was a viper.

Heath would be better served by someone who wasn't going to up and bite the dust on him. She should have never taken on the task of training him, knowing what she knew about her own personal affairs. But her curiosity, his strange determination, and okay, his hunkiness, had gotten the better of her. If today were any indication, Linda Fisher'd put flowers on her grave every week, once she realized how gifted Heath was at selling Bobbie-Sue.

Yeah. That's what she'd do. She'd call Linda and offer her up a piece of man-cake.

"HEY, Wanda. Why don't you go to bed?"

Ahh, that delicious voice, coming from those lickable lips. Like the ice cream in à la mode, melting over warm pie. The last sinful dollop of calories. She stretched, still not fully awake. The sag of the couch beside her and the scent of Heath filled her nose. But she didn't want to open her eyes. This was nice—very nice. Her stomach didn't ache, and she was fabulously warm beneath the blanket.

"C'mon, wake up," he cajoled, silky and smooth.

Her eyes opened in slow increments, Heath's face filling her vision up with its rigid planes and taut skin. "You can't be comfortable here. I just wanted to be sure you were okay before I left."

"Did I fall asleep again?"

He nodded, his gaze still concerned. "I think I've worn you out."

Oh, if only that statement had to do with designer sheets and a box—no wait, maybe two boxes of condoms. "What time is it?" she whispered, sleep still enticing her back to its haven.

"Eleven, and I have to hit the road."

Shit. It was late. She'd slept nearly four hours. Oh, God. Her fingers went instantly to her mouth. Had she drooled?

Wanda sat up, turning to catch what the weatherman said. Pictures of the highways and outlying roads covered in a thick blanket of snow flashed on the screen. "You can't drive in this. Look, just stay here tonight. You can have the couch. I'd never forgive myself if something happened to my brand-new selling machine or your—your Yugo."

He was close—she'd hadn't realized how close until she sat up. When his mouth, enticing, lip-smacking good, was only an inch from hers. "Are you sure? I don't want to impose." His voice held an odd, husky quality to it, but it wasn't the normal range of husky it usually had.

And was she sure? *Don't be silly. You can't let the man go out in this. Just get up off your wanton ass and go to yon room, then lock the door and handcuff yourself to the bed. No worries.* His virtue was safe with her. "Of-of course I'm sure. It's terrible out there . . ."

"It's pretty bad," he agreed, still not moving, the air between them becoming less easy for her to intake.

"Bad . . . very bad." She should get right up off this couch now and run screaming to her bedroom, but his breath on her face, his eyes piercing hers, was killa mesmerizing.

Who leaned in first, eliminating the tiniest of space between them, she couldn't say. In retrospect, though, she knew she'd hope it wasn't her. Because desperation was sooo not attractive.

One minute they were talking about the weather, the next, their lips were connected, and a white-hot bolt of sizzle snapped and crackled, wending along every nerve ending she owned. Her nipples tightened, and the space between her thighs had a jolt it hadn't felt in a long time. Longer than she cared to admit. Some sappy Barbra Streisand song that sounded like "Evergreen" began to play in her head, and behind her eyelids, unicorns were jumping over a bright rainbow.

His mouth, warm, inviting, as demanding as he was, caught the edge of her lower lip and then covered hers, evoking a breathy sigh from Wanda. That brief connection came and went, when Heath broke the spell. "Not a good idea," he said, and again, she couldn't tell if the regret she heard was because he didn't find her attractive or because he regretted it had to end.

In one swift motion even her vampire friend would find impressive, Wanda shoved the blanket off her and jumped up off the couch. Her voice shook, as did her legs. "Absolutely not. So let's add something else to our list of things we should just forget. Like you forget I'm a nosy *B* word—"

Heath remained on the couch. His stoic presence when she felt so out of control jarred her. "What's a *B* word?"

Her sigh was ragged, her cheeks uncomfortably hot. "Bitch— you know? I try not to swear. Forget it. Anyway, you forget I don't know how to shut my yap, and I'll forget . . . well, I'll just forget. How's that?" She didn't wait for an answer, fully aware she was rambling. Wanda waved a hand in his general direction. "You go ahead and take the couch. There's another blanket in the hall closet if you need it, and I'm going to bed. I'll see you in the morning. Night," she tacked on with as much cheer as she could muster, so he'd think that mere moment—so brief it didn't even count as a real kiss—was no big thang.

On feet that wasted no time getting from point A to point B, she flew into her bedroom, closing the door behind her. Her eyes slid closed, bright lights and color flashed behind her eyelids.

Hell's bells.

Tracing a finger over the outline of her lips, she trembled, squeezing her eyes shut to fend off the visual of Heath's face just before they'd kissed.

It was the best almost, sorta kiss she could ever remember. He'd elicited all sorts of raging emotions by what most would consider absolutely nothing. He'd made her libido sing a chorus of hallelujahs with just a brush to her lips.

And that brought to mind another pathetic notion.

She was going to die, and she'd do it having experienced only her ex-husband's less-than-expert attempts at lovemaking. That meant she'd never get to experience all the stuff Nina and Marty talked about all the time. Like multiple orgasms and whatever the hell riding cowgirl was.

She'd never experience the "You just haven't had sex with the right man, Wanda" deal. Because she was never going to find the right man.

Ever.

She was going to die and not have wonked in over three and a half years.

Jesus. What a rip-off.

Who was in charge of this life stuff anyway? She deserved a word with them. You should get like a last request or something.

And what in all of fuck was she doing thinking about sex when she was going to kick the bucket? Despite the severity of her situation, she smiled in irony at her last thought. Kicking the bucket . . . Last night she couldn't begin to even acknowledge the words—tonight reminded her, she had no choice. She *would* die, and if she didn't take care of all of the things that needed doing, who would? Her mother? She couldn't leave all of that to her—especially when she was so far away in Florida, and her mother was no good at organizing anything. That left her sister. Hardly. She and Casey hadn't physically seen each other in two years, and she only lived in Manhattan. They were as different as night and day, and though she loved Casey, she'd never leave what needed to be done to her younger sister, who was a carbon copy of her mother.

A list. She needed to make a list of what had to be taken care of. First on it was Heath.

While throwing on her pink, fuzzy, bunny-bedecked nightgown, she searched for the pad she kept in her bedroom. A pocket-sized spiral bound pad. Dragging it out of her nightstand drawer, she dug around for a pen and scribbled—"Things To Do Tomorrow."

Number one on her list—call Linda fucking-account-stealing Fisher.

Like the moment day breaks.

FUCK. Archibald was probably shitting drunks and meth users at the shelter, wondering where the hell he was, but there wasn't any way to get in touch with him. And Wanda was in the next room.

Sleeping.

Maybe in that crazy pink, fuzzy nightgown with the rabbit on it that she thought she'd hidden beneath her robe.

Definitely had a hot factor to it—even with the bunny's googly eyes.

He cracked his jaw to stop from thinking about his nether regions. Or to stop them from thinking about Wanda. All day he'd fought the impulse to run a finger against the softness of her cheek, averted his eyes to keep himself from eyeballing the curve of her breasts every time she lifted her arms to touch up one contestant or another's makeup.

And now he was on her couch—the smell of her perfume all over the blanket she'd used, enveloping him in her light, floral scent.

Fuck again. He was in no position to be chasing after a woman. He, for all intents and purposes, was what some in society today would label a loser. Involving himself with anyone at this point was fucking crazy. He and Archibald needed to get on their feet before he considered even acknowledging there still was an opposite sex.

But what the hell would he do when he was on his feet?

How would he explain his unlikely circumstances anyway?

This wasn't like the days of old where he could play whenever he chose to, do whatever he wanted to do—with whomever he wanted to do it with. He couldn't erase their memories of any entanglements with him if things got sticky. Those days were gone.

Heath hunkered down under the blanket, massaging the throb at his temple. He'd forgotten how irritating a headache could be. Life affirming, but nonetheless, irritating.

No more fast moves on the answer to all things cosmetically profitable, dumb ass, he resolved.

But her lips, all wet and soft—kinda like pillows—plump and . . .

He halted his thoughts, envisioning them like he was slamming on the brakes of a car to avoid hitting a tree. She was kind of his boss—in a weird, color-wheeled kind of way. Besides, he had no business being interested in anything but getting his life together.

So focus, fuckwit.

He fluffed the throw pillow behind his head, which made him think of Wanda's lips again, and that they reminded him of pill—

Cut it the fuck out.

No more pillows, and no more Wanda.

No more.

CHAPTER
5

She'd weep if she had the energy.

Would it be too much to ask that Heath not only be unsightly, but have vacated her house so she wasn't forced to like look him in the eye after last night? Why, why, whyyyyyy did he have to still be in her immediate vicinity, and why did he have to look so scrumptious while he was there? There just wasn't an unattractive thing about him, even after a night on the couch, for Christ's sake. His clothes were as flawless as they'd been yesterday. Crisp and looking like they'd been freshly laundered. Bet he didn't have morning breath either.

Stupidhead.

Damn, damn, damn.

Heath's back was to her when Wanda traipsed into the kitchen, and she was thankful, because she didn't know if she could face him after last night. Oh, just the memory evoked a new shade of red on her cheeks Bobbie-Sue could make a mint off of.

And he'd made coffee. Tendrils of the black, rich scent wafted to her nose.

If he weren't so damned sure of himself, he'd be just this shy of perfect.

Heath's hand went immediately to her cabinet, pulling out a mug and pouring some coffee into it. He swung around, holding it out to her, his mouth forming a crooked grin. It made her knees feel weak, and her mouth dry.

"Morning. Feeling better?"

Define better. Was it making her feel better that he wasn't even acknowledging what happened last night? Then, yeah, she was better. But wait, had it been that unforgettable? "I am, thanks." She took the cup he offered, snatching it from him to avoid touching his fingers.

He backed away instantly, pulling his jacket from the chair and slipping into it. The ripple of muscle that followed made her mouth water. Her eyes immediately went to the floor to avoid getting caught up in his beefcakey-ness again.

"I gotta get going, but I'll call you tomorrow so we can work on my cold call techniques."

"About those tech—"

He was halfway to the front door when he turned to say, "I really have to go, Wanda. I just wanted to be sure you were really okay after last night. You looked pretty pale. Whatever you need to talk about, we'll take care of it tomorrow. Thanks for the loan of your couch. Oh, and someone named Nina called. I probably shouldn't have answered the phone, but it happened out of habit. I apologize. I took her number down. It's there on the pad by the phone. See you tomorrow." With that, he was gone, followed by a cold rush of air as he pulled the door shut.

Well. That was that, wasn't it? He hadn't even given her the chance to tell him she was going to send him to Linda. She'd at least wanted to do it in person, but now it would have to wait for something as impersonal as a phone call.

Her throat tightened. This was the last time she'd see him. Why that made her so sad made no sense. She'd known him less than two days. Sipping her coffee, she sank to her couch, noting how he'd folded the blankets in a neat stack. She tugged at them, dragging them to her nose and inhaling his lingering scent.

Menusha hopped up along the back of the sofa, rubbing against her cheek. "You slept out here with him, didn't you? Is there anyone, animal or mineral, who doesn't have lust in their loins for him? And yes, that includes me. I'm chalking it up to where I'm at in my life—I'm fragile, Nusha, verrrry fragile. So I think I should get a hall pass for lusting after this man who's essentially my employee. I'm not in my right mind."

When her phone rang, it reminded her that Nina had called, and she was probably calling back now. And she'd want answers. Lifting the phone from its base, Wanda checked the caller ID.

Yep. It was time to produce some answers. She squared her shoulders. "Hey, Nina."

There was silence for a moment, and if Wanda didn't know Nina like she did, including that she no longer breathed, she'd have thought no one was on the line. Oh, but she knew Nina, and the kind of momentary silence she was displaying meant she was winding up her tongue for the fastball. "Don't answer your phone like you're all innocent, Wanda. Who in the fuck was that man, and what in the fuck was he doing at your house on a Saturday morning at eight a.m.?"

"He was Heath, and he spent the night," she offered casually.

More silence—dripping through the earpiece while she grabbed another metaphoric baseball to hurl. "Ooookay, explain, and do it *now*. This is not like you. Not even a little. And honestly, you've been doing a lot of weird shit lately that I don't get. No one spends the night at your house but Marty and me. No man has walked through those doors since I've known you. Not even the hint of a man."

"That's totally not true. I had you and Greg and Marty and Keegan over just last month for fondue and blood-sicles—or whatever that was you brought. Greg and Keegan are men, in case you've forgotten about how often you've both told me of their manliness—their manhoods, too, for that matter."

"Wanda?"

"Uh-huh?"

"Knock off the smart-ass shit with me, okay? You know exactly what I mean. No man that Marty and I don't know or bump uglies with has ever been in your house."

"How do you know no men, strange or otherwise, have been in my house? I might have men here all the time. Maybe you've just never seen them." *Men, men, men, men, manly, men, men, men.*

Wanda heard Nina cluck her tongue. Hoo boy. Now she was pissed. When she cracked her knuckles or clucked her tongue— shit would surely fly. "Wanda—cut it out. Like now. Who was the guy who answered your phone? If you're doing some guy—cool. You deserve to get laid more than anyone I know. In fact, we'll yuck it up over at Hogan's, if you want. You can tell us all about it. Every naughty detail. I'm all in. But if he was like the plumber, and I got in my fucking car in broad daylight to come check on you for nothing, I'm gonna beat you like a redheaded stepchild. You know what it's like for me to come out during the day. It's an—"

Wanda yawned, pulling a pillow to her lap. "Event. I know. You remind me with startling frequency. What was the last count? Ten?"

"Wanda—spill."

"Are you really on your way over?"

Nina's snort held her usual sarcasm. "When do I ever joke

about shit this important? When do I ever joke about slapping on a pound of zinc oxide just to get out the door? Never. I'm halfway to your house, because I was worried. Greg said I was being an idiot, and if you wanted to boink—even if it was the plumber you were slamming—I should mind my own business. But Greg doesn't know you like I know you, Wanda, now does he? He doesn't know what lurks behind that pretty smile and those—what the fuck do you and Marty call them? Come—"

"Come-hither eyes." Wanda closed her come-hithers to thwart the headache she felt developing.

"Yeah, those. My man doesn't know that you're about as pure as the fucking snow I plowed through in my driveway to get to you. So I panicked, okay? You've been bizarre lately, and while I can't put my finger on it—I will put my finger in your eye if you don't tell me what's going on."

A ripple of irritation skittered along the surface of her skin. What if she did have a man here? Why was that like the Geneva Convention? "How come you didn't just fly here, Elvira? It would've saved you a ton of trouble. And what were you doing up at eight in the morning?" That Nina could literally transport herself from one place to the other was just one of those magical, mystical, freaky-deaky things about being a vampire Wanda couldn't dwell too long on. It made her head swirl.

"I was up because I had an attack of insomnia, and I called because I wanted to see if you wanted to go do karaoke later this week. I didn't fly because it's daylight, nimrod. Remember the whole burn to a crisp thing? I'm still not as good as I want to be at this mind-over-matter crap—so I'm not taking a chance I'll stall, lose my concentration, and end up a pile of ashes in the middle of Hackensack because I lingered too long over the Island—worrying about *you*."

Nina so loved her, Wanda mused. She hated it. She'd never say it out loud, but she loved Wanda. Nina loved Marty, too. It frosted her Wheaties, but it was true, and that made Wanda gulp back a watery response. "Okay, I'm sorry. You can go home now. I'm fine."

"You know, lately, I hear a lot of that statement. 'I'm fine, Nina. Stop treating me like a baby, Nina,' " she mocked, taking on the higher-pitched tone of Wanda's voice. "Now stop yutzing around with me. The man, Wanda. Speak."

"He's a recruit."

"Hah! The hell he is. Weak, pal. Very weak. No man sells Bobbi-Sue. No *real* man."

Wanda bristled at that. She'd dare anyone to say Heath wasn't a real man after that almost-kiss last night. Double dog dare them. But she held her tongue. "No, I'm serious. He's a new recruit."

"Shut. Up. A dude who wants to sell makeup?" Wanda could understand Nina's astonishment. Been there.

"Yeahhhhhhhh."

"Was that the breathy, dreamy crap you and Marty call the big girly sigh I just heard in your voice?"

"There was nothing breathy or dreamy in my sigh." Was there?

"Bullshit. I heard it, and we both know if I can do nothing else, I can hear a pine tree fucking fall in Trenton. So explain. And hurry up. All of a sudden, I'm beat."

"There's nothing to explain. I was as shocked as anyone when he answered the ad, because as you well know, it's only women who answer it. He showed up here two nights ago, ate a bunch of weenies in a blanket like they were caviar, snarfed almost all of my cheese log down with a side of crackers, wowed everyone with his mad color skills, sold twenty-three starter kits yesterday, and spent the night last night. But not because of what your dirty little mind is creating. Because it was snowing and I didn't want him to drive."

"Twenty-three starter kits?"

"Yep. And no one has backed out yet. But the day is still young."

"Dude, doesn't that beat your record? Shit, that beats Marty's, too."

Yeah, whatever. It still rubbed salt in her wound that Heath had come up with the idea of selling at the transgender pageant in the first place. The salt had a sprinkle of admiration, but it still stung. "It beats *everyone's* record. It's a Bobbie-Sue jackpot. No one's ever sold that many kits in one day. Not that I ever remember seeing on that board they have in the lobby, anyway."

"Okay, so he's a guy who actually wants to sell Bobbie-Sue? There's only one conclusion—he's gay."

Wanda's cheeks instantly lit up with her former guilt about the latter. "Nope."

"Nope? You know this how, Wanda? He's a guy. A guy—selling makeup. Isn't that like a man-sin or something? So if you know he's not gay, that must mean you found out through carnal knowledge. Oh, fuck. Tell me you protected yourself."

This was only making things worse. Had Heath not yanked the rug out from under her, the last thing she'd have done was sleep last night. "Nina—cut it out! We didn't sleep together, and I know enough to use protection if we had. There was no sex." None. Absolutely none. How grim.

"Okay, fine. What the hell does a guy know about makeup?"

Wanda had to laugh. "What did you know about makeup, Nina?"

Nina laughed, too—tension free. "Okay, true that. But still, I'm a woman. I know what it feels like to be a woman—don't you have to be all relatable and shit to your client? That's like the cult of Bobbie-Sue's rule number one. How can he relate to a woman?"

Oh, he related. "I don't know. I only know the women at the party didn't seem to mind. In fact, they loved him."

"He's scammin'." Nina's voice said her mind was made up. "And you're a prime target, because you're so damned Holly Hobby. And I swear to Christ, if he touched you, talked you into anything, I'll fucking kill him."

"Oh, Nina, knock it off! Does anyone think I can actually take care of myself? What makes you think I can't take care of myself? What makes you, and Marty, for that matter, think I can't see a guy who just wants to get in my pants from a mile off?" Jesus. She wasn't a total social tard. It wasn't like she hadn't had the very same thoughts about Heath that Nina was so worried about anyway.

"Hah! How quickly we forget, Wanda. How quickly we forget the freak at the House of Hwang who was trying to get your phone number while his wife was in the fucking bathroom! Remember that, oh worldly one?"

Okay. There *was* that, but he had been really cute. "How was I supposed to know he was married, Nina? Osmosis? Jesus!"

"Um, because he had a wedding ring on?"

Okay, there was that, too. "Fine. So sometimes I don't look closely enough but—"

"Just hold on a sec—that's Marty clicking in."

Wonderful. Marvelous. Tag team. Wanda rolled her eyes and twirled the length of her hair around her finger in exasperation.

"Wanda?"

"Marty . . ."

"You bet, and what the hell is going on here? Nina texted me about some guy and something about spending the night at your house."

Wanda's sigh was ragged and fed up. "Yes. A *man* spent the night at Chez Schwartz. Big deal."

"And he claims he wants to sell Bobbie-Sue," Nina interjected pointedly. "I dunno 'bout you, Marty, but dude seems fishy, and our fair Wanda says he isn't gay. If he's not gay and he wants to sell chick-shit, I say he's scammin' to get in her knickers—especially after she did the girly sigh crap—that's if he hasn't already. So you wanna knock the crap out of him, or should I?"

Wanda huffed into the phone. "Oh, Nina, S-T-F-U!"

"Ohhhhhhh, harsh, Wanda. Very fucking harsh—what the fuck is S-T-F-U?"

Marty cut in. "Um, shut the fuck up."

Wanda could visualize Nina's nostrils flaring. Another sure sign her temper had peaked on her anger thermometer. "You did not just tell me to shut the fuck up. You *did not*."

Wanda stuck her chin out as if Nina could see her. "Yeah, super-vamp. Yeah, I did. What in God's name is it going to take to get you to understand not everyone has malice on their mind and murder in their heart? All this yelling and threatening to beat people up will end. Seriously, why can't the two of you once, just once, trust that I'm a big girl, and I can take care of myself? How do you suppose I managed before I met the two of you? Did you think I just limped through life, broken and battered until you two knuckle-heads rode in on your white horses and saved innocent, little ole me? I often ask myself what the two of you would do if I weren't here to order around—or referee your fights!" Oh, God. The gut clench that created held her stomach in an iron grip. But her sense that they'd drift apart if she wasn't in the picture tore her up.

Yeah, they fought. Yeah, they lobbed threats at one another all the doggone time, but Wanda couldn't bear it if they didn't continue their friendship because she wasn't around to see to it they didn't chew each other's heads off. If she had to leave this world, she'd darn well do it knowing her two best friends would still do all the things they'd once loved to do as a threesome.

One of the two women whistled. "Wow, honey." Marty—it was Marty. "We were just looking out for you. It's only done out of love. We worry. You haven't even looked at a man with any interest since we've known you, and that was almost hot off the heels of your divorce. You don't date, you read romance novels like they're going out of print any day now, and then I get a text message from Nina that says a man—unknown, mind you—slept at your house. So can you see where we're coming from? All I'm saying is, we've been exposed to more than you, and we don't want you falling for some guy's line of shit and getting hurt. Capice?"

The guilt. There was always the guilt trip when she called them on treating her like she was their kid sister. And it always worked. She hung her head. "Yes, I capice, okay? I'm sorry I jumped down your throats."

"You're way edgy lately, Wanda. Way. Neither Marty nor me get it, but what the canine says is true. We just want you to be happy, and we don't want some guy taking advantage of you."

Wanda let her head fall to her knees. "He didn't take advantage, I promise. And, Marty, when I tell you how many starter kits he sold, you'll flip."

"Tell me."

"Twenty-three. Yes, you heard me right. Twenty-*three*."

"No way! That puts our sales history to shame. In fact, that's the best ever. It's like a record. And he's a guy . . ." was Marty's dry response filled with suspicion.

Wanda closed her eyes, a vision of Heath still behind them. "Yeahhhhhhhh."

"See!" Nina yelped. "There it is again. That dreamy sigh shit you two do when you talk about Keegan or Wanda talks about those crazy romance novel heroes named stupid things like Hunter and Colton."

"Omigod! Do you like him, Wanda? Is he cute?" Marty prodded.

She shrugged her shoulders as if she were trying to prove her indifference. "He's okay, I guess."

"Noooooo. No, no, no," Nina clucked. "That dreamy sigh wasn't a 'he's just okay' sigh, Wanda. I'm not fallin' for it. So what I'm hearing here is that this guy is cute, and he spent the night at your house. Wanna tell me if anything happened? Like did you get all crazy and celebrate those twenty-three starter kits by doing him?"

Hah! If only. As if. Oh. Jesus. "No! You saw how bad the weather was last night, didn't you? I couldn't let him drive home in that."

Nina's response was oozing with her cynicism. "Where's home?"

"That's kind of none of your business, Nina," Wanda said tartly. "But if you just can't stand the suspense—it's on Dunlap. At least that's what he put on his application."

Marty scoffed. "You do realize this makes no sense, don't you, Wanda? No man wants to sell Bobbie-Sue."

"I do, but after yesterday, what should I tell him, Marty? No, please don't sell any more starter kits for me, because I don't want all that lovely money?" That'd shut her up.

"Point. Okay, I concede. But if this man does anything suspicious, I'd *better* hear about it. I'll have him taken out so fast, he'll break the time-space continuum."

"But wait," Nina interrupted again. "You still haven't told us if you like him, you know, in *that* way."

She liked him in all ways—except for the way he'd outsold her. But she couldn't forget, this was the worst time in her life for even thinking such things. She had a duty to hand him over to someone who was going to live. That that someone was Linda Fisher, as much as it chapped her ass, was neither here nor there. Taking on a new recruit, especially one as compelling and skilled as Heath, man or not, had been wrong, knowing what she knew about her own fate.

But she couldn't afford to tell Marty and Nina that, or they'd become suspicious. Especially seeing as Wanda'd often said how much she despised Linda. So she was going to lie. Like big. "He's nice enough, and yes, he's cute, but not so cute I'm losing my panties over it. Besides, wouldn't that be like poor management on my part if I did one of my reps? Either way, the way I see it is, he's a moneymaker and I'd be stupid to ignore his potential." There. Very casual, very nonchalant—all about the business.

"Okay. So look, that he's a guy makes me nervous because you have to spend so much alone time with him—keep your cell with you at all times. All you have to do is speed dial me, and I'll fly to wherever the fuck you are and yank his balls up through his throat. 'K?"

"Yes, Nina," Wanda drawled. "And now I'm going. I have stuff to do, errands to run, and lists to make. You know, my typical OCD Saturday? I'm fine, but I appreciate your concern. Marty? I'm hanging up. I'll talk to you guys later. Byeeeeee."

Wanda clicked the phone off before they had a chance to protest.

Though she had shopping to do and a house to clean, she sat on the couch, Menusha curled up in her lap while she stroked her silky fur. Staring at nothing.

"I warn you, sir. If you ever leave me in this hellhole alone again, I fear you may find me employed elsewhere."

"I'm sorry, Arch. It was a long day yesterday—we got back pretty late—but I sold twenty-three starter kits." Heath rubbed his fingers together. "That means money, and better I stay at Wanda's during that snowstorm than risk trashing the only tangible thing we have—the car."

Archibald swiped at imaginary dust on Heath's shoulder. "Oh, sir. Surely you don't think I'm given to falling for such tall tales,

do you? You got your, as they say in this new millennium, freak on
with the cosmetics maiden. And by all means, Heathcliff, far be it
from me to interfere. When have I ever interfered in your personal
matters? Your freak is yours to get on or not—and you've gotten
plenty in your time here on Earth. However, when my well-being
is at stake, I must take steps to prevent my person from injury.
Sadly, and without reservation, I hesitate not at all in saying your
rather imposing figure keeps the"—he leaned in, pointing to the
surrounding cots, and whispered—"heathens at bay."

Heath gave him a knowing nod. "Ah, were you worried
somebody'd kick your ass for the Happy Meal toys you've collected or something?" Because lesser valuables had certainly been
fought over in their time here.

Arch nodded solemnly. "So worried, I didn't sleep a wink." He
circled his eyes with two fingers. "These are my tired eyes, sir. And
in future, whilst you go freaking, please think of me, your faithful
manservant, who, I might add, has followed you to hell and back
with nary a question when you chose to, ah, cavort."

Heath slapped him on the back, giving his manservant a direct
stare. "I didn't cavort or freak, old man. I slept on the couch—
with the cat."

Archibald's snort was loud as he straightened the short ends of
his jacket over his stomach. "Of course you did."

Heath raised his right hand. "No, Arch, it wasn't like that. Swear
on a Reese's Peanut Butter Cup."

"Oh, my. A Reese's Peanut Butter Cup, you say? This *is*
serious."

"I like Wanda, and I respect her as my regional supervisor."

"Of course you do. You've respected all the women you've
bedded."

"Arch, you're not listening. I can't afford to screw this up, and
making a move on Wanda could have my ass deep-fried. She seems

pretty uptight—no matter how good looking. She makes lists—
they're all over her kitchen. She writes everything down, and
when she's done writing one list, she makes another for the first
list. She's a rule follower, and I don't know if there's a rule about
fraternization at Bobbie-Sue, but I ain't breakin' it to see. We need
to play this right, or we're right back where we started. Remember that place, pal? You know, the one where we have nothing? At
least for now we have something. It isn't a lot, but it beats the shit
out of where we were four months ago. Now we just need to save
some cash and get a place of our own. That means I can't make a
move on my boss." No matter how kissable she was. No matter
how . . . no matter. End of.

Arch clucked his tongue. "Ah, but do I see the twinkle of interest in your eyes, young Heathcliff? Were circumstances different,
would you set about casting your net of charm and capturing the
fair cosmetics maiden?"

Heath didn't answer, and apparently that was enough for Archibald to draw his own conclusions. "Your silence says it all. I
sense regret in it. Never you worry, sir. It won't be long before
you have the means to stalk your prey properly."

"I don't want to stalk anything, Arch. I just want us to survive
and live out the rest of our lives in semi-comfort. Be able to afford
to have a beer every now and then. Watch football and eat chicken
wings, ya know?"

"And that life will never involve a woman again? I believe you
protest too much, young man. And don't you miss the finer things,
sir? Your mansion, for instance . . ."

Heath's face broke into a smile. "You know what? Not even a
little. We had some good times, lots of nice shit, but there were
lots of things we didn't have, in case you've forgotten. We can get
the material things back. We can't get our lives back—but we can
get Reese's Peanut Butter Cups whenever we want 'em."

"True, true, sir, and I can promise you, if you leave me here alone again, I wouldn't count on keeping this new life of yours much longer."

Heath snickered. "Okay, I get it. I won't leave you alone again."

"Sir?"

"Yep?"

"She's pretty, this Wanda?"

"Yeah, and?"

Archibald gave him a curt nod, but his eyes held mischief. "Oh, and no matter how fair our Wanda is, she's off limits, sir. Completely, totally, irrevocably so."

"And don't you forget it."

"Never, young Heathcliff. In fact, I shall write it down and repeat it thrice daily. It will be my mantra. Words to live by—"

"Archibald?"

"Sir?"

"Knock it off."

CHAPTER
6

Wanda brushed the finishing powder over her makeup, wrinkling her nose. Her lightly lined eyes looked glassy to her tonight. She turned away from her bathroom mirror and put her makeup bag in her purse with a careless toss. Squaring her shoulders, she went to the living room and pulled on her knee-length coat, digging her car keys from the pocket.

Tonight wasn't going to be easy.

In fact, tonight sucked.

And Linda Fisher was going to experience a coup de grâce bar none in her small, petty world.

The bitch.

But it had to be done, Wanda reminded herself for the thousandth time as she drove the familiar route to Bobbie-Sue corporate. She was going to hand Heath over to Linda on a silver platter. Lock stock and starter kits—all twenty-three.

She wasn't sure if she was doing him a favor by literally offering him up to the huntress of all things dangly, but she was hoping in the end—her end—he'd see she'd just done what she thought was fair. Wanda'd battled all weekend long over whether she should try to contact him, but that was impossible since he didn't have a cell phone. Corporate would contact him, and she'd be relieved of ever having to see him again. Which made her feel that twinge of sorrow for the nine-millionth time. That she'd never see his killa buns again was surely reason to go into mourning.

She'd decided late last night, the coming months would be spent preparing instead of working. She had enough in her savings account to last her at least a year—which was six months more than her doctor had given her. Her savings might just allow her to do a couple of the things she'd always wanted to do, too. She'd also decided last night to make a list of those things—ASAP.

And she wasn't just handing over Heath. She was handing over all of her reps and clients, resigning from Bobbie-Sue with a request that Marty be left out of the loop for the time being. Hopefully, corporate would honor that. She just wanted a little time for herself before she had to tell Marty and Nina . . . her sister . . . her mother.

Pulling into the underground parking garage, she selected a spot and turned the ignition off, double-checking her makeup one last time in her rearview mirror. She threw her keys into her purse and headed up in the elevator to the massive room where they held their weekly meetings. The meetings Nina had always said were like attending a Jim Jones fest.

Perfume floated in the air, tinged with the scent of hunger for a sky blue convertible. A smell all too familiar, and it brought a smile to her lips for a brief moment. When she wrote her list, she could check that off as something accomplished. By God, she'd gotten the coveted Bobbie-Sue sky blue convertible—and she'd done it without the aid of her prick of an ex-husband and his money.

When she'd earned the car, it had become a symbol to her. A symbol of her independence—a sign she could take care of herself. And although she collected alimony, she didn't need it to survive. So she wrote a check to one charity or another every month with the money George dutifully paid her. The pride she'd felt when she was able to do that had been big.

She made her way past the throng of women gathered in small groups. Brightly colored business suits, reflecting the level of Bobbie-Sue success, were worn by women who bobbed their heads in animation, their hands flying about in lively conversation.

Her eyes scanned the room for her target. And how apropos, Linda Fisher, said target, held court in the midst of all the hubbub. Wanda brushed a hand over her sky blue suit, tugging at the ends of her jacket to straighten it—lest Linda forget who held color court in this joint, at least for now. She pressed between the swarm of bodies and signaled Linda with a wave of her finger. "May I speak to you?" Wanda fought to keep her teeth from clenching.

Linda straightened her shoulders, smoothing the skirt of her yellow suit. Nina was right. Hell really was the color yellow. No one should ever wear it unless absolutely forced. Wanda'd skipped right over the yellow level and had shot right to red—much to Linda's dismay. Linda gave Wanda one of her patented fake smiles. "Of course." She pivoted on her heel and shook her scrawny yellow ass off to a nearby corner, turning back to Wanda and crossing her arms over her chest. Her stance was defensive, and well it should be. Linda'd done some shitty stuff to Marty, and since then, Wanda dealt with her as little as possible. "So what can I do for you, Wanda?"

"I have a favor to ask."

Linda narrowed her beady eyes, running her tongue over her lips, but she remained silent, merely cocking her head, the flipped-up ends of her Marlo Thomas hairdo shivering.

Wanda decided there was no point in fucking around. "I need you to take on a rep for me."

Linda's look screamed dumbfounded. "You're giving up a rep?"

"Yesssss, Linda," she hissed. "I'm giving up a new rep. As you know, I have *many*—and right now, I'm on overload."

"You're giving a new rep to me—willingly?"

Wanda sighed, knowing full well Linda'd look for some dirty ulterior motive. Because that was just Linda—because she was a skank, she suspected everyone else was, too. "Yes. I'm giving a new rep to you."

Ah. There it was. The look. The familiar glitter of a potential kill glistening in her eyes. Wanda knew that look. She'd seen it once before when Linda had stolen a huge account from Marty just after she'd been bitten. "Realllly," she drawled long and windy, biting the tip of her clear polished nail. "The curiosity is killing me. Why would you"—she pointed her finger at Wanda's chest—"want me"—then pointed it back at her own much bonier one—"to take on one of *your* reps? As I recall, there's no love lost between us."

Uh, no. She wasn't going to let the heifer get 'tude with her. She didn't have to be nice to her anymore. In fact, she didn't have to ever be nice to her again. That thought brought a sense of freedom Wanda planned to run with—like a quarterback. "Because I like to watch you salivate. When you get that little drop of drool on the side of your mouth, it invigorates me."

Linda pinched her Rousing Red lips together. "How about you just get to the point. I never thought I'd see the day you'd offer me up one of your reps. Is she a bitch? Is that why you want me to take her? It would be just like you and Marty to conspire against me and ask me to take on some loser."

Wanda hovered over Linda, her eyes narrowed, her jaw stiff. "If it weren't for Marty, you'd have no job, Linda—so back off, you client-stealing whore," she growled. "And you leave my friend out of this—one of my best friends—oh, and your *boss*." Nah-nah-nah-nah-nah-nah.

Linda gasped at the reminder that she'd once stolen clients from Marty, and in the end, Marty'd ended up owning Linda Fisher. "How crass of you."

Wanda shot her a look of surprise with the raise of her eyebrows. She planted her hands on her hips, moving in on Linda. "Me? Crass? Oh, no, sistah. That was you, you weasel. You stole Marty's clients, not me. She let you stay here at Bobbie-Sue because she's a good person. Now shut that yap of yours and pay attention. I have a new rep. A very *special* rep. I'm only offering this new rep to you because, while you're not exactly beyond reproach, you're good at what you do. Even if it makes me want to gag just saying so. And this newbie is no loser. This rep could outsell you limbless and mute."

"And what's so *special* about this rep, Wanda?" She spat the words at her.

Wanda rolled her tongue along the inside of her cheek. "This rep is special because this rep is a *man* . . ." She let the gravity of that statement sink in, watching Linda chew on the information from behind hooded lashes.

"Wanda?" a low, gravelly voice called from over her shoulder. "Are you bragging about me to the girls?" The tone was teasing.

Wanda's eyes went wide.

Oh. Good. It was the man.

She spun around to find Heath smiling down at her, casting a quick glance at Linda before returning his gaze to hers. His grin, playful and charming, made her want to drag him out of there by his ear. Shitshitshit. "What are you doing here?" Looking so good—smelling so good—flashing perfect teeth and wearing that damned suit again and holding a handful of shortbread cookies.

He popped one in his mouth and smiled before replying, "Attending the Bobbie-Sue weekly meeting. Just like it says in the—"

Aggravation sizzled along her spine. Wanda snapped a closed-fingered hand in his face, signaling him to shut it. "Pffftt! I know what it says in the Bobbie-Sue handbook. I'm not a sky blue for nothing." She sent Linda a pointed, glaring reminder.

He leaned down to her ear, letting his lips almost brush the shell of it, his breath, cookie scented, made her cheeks flush, hot and an angry red. "Touchy, touchy. I'm just doing what I'm supposed to, according to the booklet you gave me. Page eighty-four, paragraph sixteen says in order to fully appreciate the joys of selling Bobbie-Sue and properly reap the benefits of your skilled senior representative's wisdom, you must attend the weekly meetings." He threw the last of the cookies into his mouth, swallowing them with that odd look of euphoria, then held out his arms with pride. "So here I am. Because you know, I'm just like that—a good employee and all." He held out his hand to Linda. "I'm Heath Jefferson, by the way."

Linda took his hand, then used it for leverage to push her way between Wanda and Heath, blessing Heath with one of her cattiest smiles. "Linda Fisher," she introduced herself, then swung back to Wanda. "A man, you say, Wanda? Is *this* the man?" Her eyes glazed over as she took in every delicious inch of Heath while he pried his hand loose from hers.

Heath looked over Linda's head to Wanda, a question in his eyes. "This man, what?"

Linda's hair quivered again. "The man she wants to give to me to"—she paused momentarily, licking her thin lips in anticipation—"to tutor." Her tongue rolled the R.

Heath ran a hand over his cleanly shaven jaw, shooting Wanda a question not just with his eyes. "Tutor? For what?"

Wanda planted her hands on Linda's yellow shoulders and spun her around. "Linda—slink on off to your hole now. When I'm done, I'll send Heath to you."

Heath held up a hand, palm forward. "Why are you sending me to her?"

"Wait a minute!" Linda interrupted, moving back to face them both. "You're really a Bobbie-Sue rep? But you're a man! And what's wrong with me?"

"Yeah, I hear that a lot lately," Heath agreed, offering a congenial chuckle. "And nothing's wrong with you. It's just that I've grown attached to Wanda . . ." He winked in Wanda's general direction, sending another wave of red along her cheeks.

Linda popped her lips. "Wait a minute. Is this a joke, Wanda? Is this some kind of payback for what happened with Marty?"

"Who's Marty?"

Wanda, out of exasperation, placed a hand over Heath's mouth. "Quiet." Her gaze returned to Linda's. "No, this isn't a joke, Linda, and it's not payback. Heath signed up to sell Bobbie-Sue. He's sold twenty-three starter kits in a day, and so far, no one's even backed out yet. I'll just bet that makes your zest for cash sha-wing, huh? Now if you'd just give me a minute to talk to Heath, I'll send him your way."

Linda kept her feet firmly planted in front of them. "Twenty-three starter kits—in a day? A *day*?" Wanda could feel Linda's astonishment—like totally. She'd felt the same way about Heath's amazing selling spree.

Heath nodded his head and smiled, puffing Wanda's hand outward when he said, low and muffled, "Uh-huh. Good, right?"

Linda's mouth fell open before she regained her composure. "Are—you—kidding—me? That's stellar. Incredible. So what's the catch, Wanda? Is he wanted for murder?"

Heath nodded his head in sympathetic understanding, finally removing Wanda's hand from his lips. "You know, I've heard that a lot lately, too."

"What?" Linda asked.

"The murderer thing. You women are pretty suspicious, and I guess I can't blame you for protecting yourselves, so I'm just going to clear a couple of things up. I'm just a guy who really needs a job. I'm not a murderer. I'm not here to pick up women, though all of you are very attractive. I'm not into women's clothing or fetishes, and I'm not gay. I think that covers everything, right, Wanda?" He grinned in Wanda's direction, looking for affirmation with hazel eyes full of innocence.

Linda took a deep breath. The rise and fall of her chest made the pearls at her neck bounce. "You're not gay." Her statement was flat.

"You say that like you're disappointed," Heath pointed out.

Linda was all atwitter, her face changing with the recognition that this beautiful specimen of man-cake was heterosexual. Which meant fair game. "You seriously want to sell Bobbie-Sue, and you're not gay?"

Heath sighed while people meandered around them, gathering at the sound of the commotion to form a loose circle a few yards away. "I've already sold Bobbie-Sue, and may I just make mention of something? This skepticism among you ladies is beginning to beat me down, if I'm being honest. I don't get the big deal about me being a straight man, wanting to sell cosmetics, but all this astonishment—the gasping and the outright shock—will it pass soon? Because I'm feeling sorta like no matter what I do—no matter how much I sell—you'll all always treat me differently. I'm just as good at this as you are—despite the fact that I'm a man." He gave Linda a feigned look of pathetic-ness—so put upon, so beautifully executed, Wanda might have fallen for it if she didn't know Heath didn't give a crap what anyone else thought. He was many things, but insecure wasn't one of them.

Nice. That was very nice. Way to tug at Linda's equal-rights-amendment heart. Hook, line, and sinker, he'd reeled Linda in. A roll of her eyes and the flick of her wrist at him were all Wanda had.

Linda shuffled nearer to Heath, letting her breast graze his arm. "So are you telling me that Wanda's treated you differently because you're a man? Made you feel like less than an equal. Because the Bobbie-Sue creed does say every Bobbie-Sue representative is created equally—"

"And each one is as unique as a snowflake," Heath finished for her. "No, I'm not saying that exactly. I'm saying she had the same reservations as you, Ms. Fisher, and I was simply wondering out loud if everyone would question my mad color skills each time they realize I'm in this to win this—even if I'm just a mere man."

Wanda sent him a silent bravo. He really was good, playing the man card the way he had. She'd almost venture to say he was better at this than Marty.

"Sold," Linda said to Wanda, shooting her a smile of sly delight.

"Sold?" Both she and Heath repeated.

"Yep," Linda answered as fast as her lips could move. "You don't need to say another word. I'll be glad to take Heath off your hands, Wanda. Just send me the paperwork for transference of a rep. And you," she cooed to Heath, "can come with me. I'll be over by the punch bowl with the lavender juice in it." She winked before she sauntered her saggy yellow-clad ass off into the melee of women who had questions written all over their brightly painted faces.

"They have *lavender* juice? For real?"

Wanda would have chuckled if she didn't feel so miserable. Linda was going to glom onto Heath like the cellulite that riddled her thighs, and it incited Wanda for some ungodly reason. Heath wasn't hers in that way. He was her recruit, er, ex-recruit. "And lavender cups and lavender napkins and all things lavender," she offered dejectedly.

Heath rounded on her, forcing her to move back against the wall, the tall length of him but an inch away from her smaller frame. Shivers wended across her arms and along her scalp—the same reaction she had whenever he was near. Which was one of many reasons why he could no longer be near. She found it hard to focus on his words when he was in such close proximity, the heat he emanated, his size, his flippin' yummy lips made her grit her teeth. "Forget the juice. Are we breaking up?"

Wanda pursed her lips while trying to keep her face expressionless. "Yup."

"After we've come so far? I thought we'd finally bonded over color wheels and the transgender guys. Forgive me if I feel just a little blindsided."

"I'm sorry."

"Explanation?"

Wanda tilted her chin upward, sending him a hard, determined stare. "Linda's going to be your new regional rep."

"And the reason for that is?"

"I'm resigning from Bobbie-Sue."

"Because?"

"That's my business."

"Is it the man thing again?"

God, he was so arrogant. What made him think she'd up and leave a perfectly good income because of him? "Not everything's about you. This is about me."

"You can't believe the relief I feel knowing this isn't about all about me," he said with sarcasm. "So when did you plan to tell me you were giving me to whatsherface, who, by the way, should never wear yellow."

Wanda came close to giggling, but she had to keep this as impersonal as she could. "I didn't. I was going to let corporate notify you."

He mocked a hurt look, running a hand through his hair. "Is that any way to treat a new recruit? Just dump them without a word? I feel so snubbed."

She snorted up at him. "Oh, puuulease. Save the pity boloney for Linda. She fell for it. Me? Not so much. You've got it goin' on, Heath Jefferson, and you know it. You don't need me or anyone else to tell you so. My guidance wouldn't be any different than Linda's, it just probably would have been minus the goo-goo eyes she's going to be flashing at you."

"Why would you subject me to goo-goo eyes? Isn't that cruel and unusual punishment of a new recruit?"

Wanda thinned her lips to keep another giggle in check. "Maybe, but it's the way it has to be—unless you have a better alternative. I'm handing you over to the best—next to me, that is."

"Can I ask you something else?"

"Go."

"You're clearly very successful at what you do. Why would you give up a career like this?"

Because the afterlife has no color wheels. "It's a personal matter." Jesus, with all the questions. He couldn't be that attached to her. They'd only known each other a few days. Why was he being so difficult?

"So personal you can afford to give up your primary source of income?"

"I have alimony." She slapped a hand over her mouth before she could stop it. Jesus. TMI. She didn't need to defend what she was doing, or why. And that kind of info was hardly keeping things impersonal.

He raised an eyebrow at her. A scathing one. "I see."

Wanda skirted out from the corner he'd backed her into and said, "N-no. You don't see, and it doesn't matter whether you do anyway. I-I have to go," she stuttered. Squaring her shoulders, she fought to keep her shit together. "And do me a favor, please—keep the resignation thing between you and me for the time being. I didn't tell Linda because she'd just find a reason to gloat, and I'm not up to that tonight. Now go find Linda. She'll be the one holding court because she's bested Wanda Schwartz. In fact"—Wanda tilted her head to the left—"I think I hear her cackling to the west now. Good luck, Heath." She zipped around him, trotting past the group of women Linda had gathered, with feet she almost couldn't keep up with in their haste to blow this joint. She had to, or she'd fall apart in front of everyone. She was eggshell fragile; telling Heath she was handing him over to Linda had scrambled her eggs.

"Byyyyyyeeeee, Wanda, and thanks for the new rep. I think we'll make a beautiful team," Linda cooed sweetly.

Linda's tone, sticky and bubbling sugar, burned a hole in Wanda's gut. It made her fume. It made her stop in her tracks, her heels screeching to a halt.

What made her turn around and saunter up to Linda, parting the crowd of women, probably had a little something to do with retribution, and the fact that she'd never have to atone for her un-Bobbie-Sue-like behavior, because she wasn't coming back.

Which made her next words that much more satisfying. Popping her face in Linda's line of vision, she grinned, letting her eyes flash some crazy Linda's way. "Do me a favor, would ya, Linda? First, you remember who nailed the first ever male Bobbie-Sue recruit. That was me, honey—not you. And second, when you teach Heath all about how to build his clientele—avoid the territory encroachment part of it, will ya? Because we both know—you're aces at that." Wanda winked and wiggled her fingers at the flabbergasted crowd of women. "TTFN, ladies!"

She hightailed it out of Bobbie-Sue corporate, biting the inside of her cheek to keep from crying. The last glance over her shoulder was of Heath, surrounded by hordes of women doing what they did best where he was concerned, making googly eyes and tripping over their multicolored high heels to get near him.

Wanda paused for a moment when she stepped out of the elevator doors in the parking garage and took several shuddering breaths. She dug around in her purse to find the list she'd made just this morning and crossed off Give Heath to Linda with a firm scratch of her pen, but she didn't feel the typical sense of accomplishment in doing so.

Tears stung her eyes.

The problem with those tears? She wasn't sure if they were all because she was leaving Bobbie-Sue—her livelihood, her recruits, the place where she'd sprouted wings—or if one or two involved the fact that she'd just sent Heath packing.

Her heart clenched and then let go, leaving behind a hollow, empty ache.

The chilled air of the parking garage finally hit her, making her move with speed to her car. Wanda ran a hand over the smooth surface of the door before clicking the key fob to open it. She'd never regret being a part of Bobbie-Sue, no matter how rabid Nina thought the company and its reps were. It had given her her self-esteem back, her sense of self-worth, and it had also facilitated her friendship with Marty and Nina.

Convertibles aside, for that, she'd always be grateful.

WANDA pulled her bathrobe tighter around her chest and ripped a sheet of paper from the spiral bound notebook, poising her pen over it. She sat at her kitchen table with only the light from her stove on, doing what calmed her, brought order to her world—a world that felt very chaotic right now.

She was making a list.

Of all the lists she'd ever made—this was the most important. Of all the things she'd wanted to do in her lifetime, she'd never expected they'd have to be crammed into such a short span of time. And there was no telling how long that time would be. Four months—maybe six . . .

For now, except for the occasional twinges, aches, and pains, she felt okay. Dead tired sometimes, but okay. In fact, she'd never know her prognosis was so bleak if she hadn't seen the test results with her own eyes.

Yet, her resignation from Bobbie-Sue tonight, leaving Heath in Linda's care, had made her fate abundantly clear—final. She'd quit her job—it didn't get much more terminal than that.

Over the weekend, she'd given far more thought to Heath than she should have. But after the day they'd spent together at the Miss TransAmerica pageant, and its aftermath, she'd found herself going over their time together. There were things he'd done—maybe unnoticeable to most who didn't have a defined time frame for the rest of their existence on Earth. Those things might appear subtle to someone who wasn't clinging to life—but they were definitely clear to her, knowing now how fragile life was.

His exuberance for one. She'd literally felt his love of life. It'd seeped beneath her skin and burrowed in her consciousness, leaving her incredibly aware in its wake. The vibes he gave off pulsed in life-affirming waves, washing over her. He was jobless—which couldn't be pleasant in this day and age. Yet he'd found great pleasure in such simple things.

Heath had an uncommon zest for living, and it showed in the way he'd eaten the hot dog with extra relish, eyes closed, his lightly tanned throat exposed when he swallowed, head thrown back while he grunted in pleasure.

It was in the way even the coldest day of the year didn't make him mutter that he wished he were somewhere warm. She'd caught him lifting his face to the weak sun more than once.

And it had taken her breath away when she'd reflected on it. Not just because he was a hottie, and he made her twitch with awareness when he was near her, but because he seemed to take such unadulterated joy in the smallest of things. She'd forgotten what it was to do that—and as cliché as it was, as often as she'd heard it said, noted it, planned to practice the theory, she'd lost sight of the little things.

It was what inspired her to savor every last nanosecond left, and why she was writing this list.

The "Fuck It" list.

The title represented exactly how she felt about what was going to happen to her. Fuck this shit called dying. Fuck this being forced to leave her friends and family before she was good and ready. Fuck Linda Fisher for snatching Heath up like he was an ice cream sundae, and that Linda'd spend endless hours with him. Fuck this notion that she was going to let it all slip away before she at least tried to grab what was left of her life by the horns, before she had the chance to take care of some old hurts, heal some old wounds, cleanse the ones that remained open.

Wanda hovered for a moment, the pen in midair, before she wrote the number one, filling in the blank space with a crazy desire she knew she'd never fulfill. But if wish lists required honesty with yourself, number one on her list, while now elusive, had become a ridiculous yearning. If she were to ever experience that one act again, it'd be with number one on her list.

So it was time to live like she was dying.

Because she was.

Entries two through ten had been easy—writing number one,

actually putting it on paper, seeing the words in black and white, made her heart skip a beat.

A knock on her door startled her. Her eyes flew to the microwave's clock. It was almost eleven. Who the frig was banging on her door at this hour? Stuffing her list in her bathrobe pocket, Wanda made her way to the door, grabbing the bat she kept in the umbrella stand, just in case. The way she saw it, only *she* could be murdered when she was due to bite the big one anyway, and right when she was in the middle of making her list of things to do before she bit it. "Who is it?"

"It's Heath, Wanda. I know it's late, but we need to talk." His silky voice was muted by the heavy front door, but it didn't thwart the effect it had on her.

She looked down at her bathrobe and fuzzy matching slippers, and let her head fall back on her neck. She was a far cry from the composed woman of this evening at Bobbie-Sue. "Aren't you all talked out from Linda and gang?"

"Open the door, Wanda—please," he tacked on for obvious courtesy's sake.

She put the bat back and turned the heavy locks on her door, pulling it open to a very haggard, oddly ruffled looking Heath. "What's wrong?"

He made a face at her. "Can I come in? I'll explain everything." Wanda waved a hand, motioning him inside. "Have a seat."

Heath plopped on her couch, grunting, his long legs crossing at the ankles. "Do you have any idea what you've done?"

Wanda slumped down in the chair opposite him. "Me?"

"Yeah, you, Wanda. That Linda—that Linda's a—hold on"—he held up a hand—"let me think. I'm going to try and remain a gentleman here." He sighed as though gathering his words, the deep release of breath drawing her eyes to his hard chest, his expression playfully pained. "That woman's not interested in teaching me anything, Wanda. How could you leave me with *her?*" He said the word *her* on a high-pitched keen.

Hoo boy. "Oh, c'mon. You're kidding, right? Big, bad you can't handle scrawny Linda Fisher? I'm sad to hear I underestimated you," she joked.

He shook a finger at her and boomed, "Oh, no, no, no. Don't even go there. Don't start attacking my manhood—no one's safe with her. She's a piranha. That woman's like an octopus—an *octopus*—all tentacles. After the meeting, where everyone kept petting me and treating me like I was the well-oiled pool boy, I offered to walk Linda to her car. It's what any gentleman would do. It was late, and dark, and okay, so she mentioned about a hundred times it was late and dark. I can take a hint. But, Jesus, she's grabby. It was all I could do to fend her off. She's my superior—I didn't want to insult her. But she was babbling about divorce and being lonely and something I can't remember and then wham—she went in for the kill. Laid one right on me." He narrowed his hazel eyes at her. "And you knew she was man hungry. I feel so cheap so dirty, so—so—thrown to the she-wolves. This is on you, Wanda Schwartz."

Wanda's snort burst from her open lips, and she had to clamp down on her knuckle to avoid rolling around on the floor in a fit of laughter at his woeful expression. "You're kidding me? Okay, yeah, I knew she was man hungry because she's recently divorced, and it seems us divorcées go one way or the other after the end to a long marriage. You know—totally swearing off men or chasing after them like we're still in high school and it's cool to make a list of the guys you bedded down. But I swear, I never thought she'd behave like that at Bobbie-Sue. Linda's done some unscrupulous things in her time as a rep, but this was totally unexpected. I really was only joking about the goo-goo eyes . . ."

His mood went from dark to light in a half a second. "You made a list of the guys you—you know . . . in high school?"

Yeah. Cause there were soooo many. There'd just been one. George, and he was hardly worth noting on a list. "Um, no. I wasn't referring to me. I just meant in general."

"So you went the other way after your divorce?"

Oy. She squirmed uncomfortably, folding and unfolding her hands. "I—I didn't go any way. Look, I'm really sorry—do you want to file a complaint? I don't know that the reps have any harassment rules that involve men and women, because we're all women. But I'm sure corporate has some. Corporate's run by a lot of men."

"How long have you been divorced?"

Her eyes strayed to her hands. "How many more personal questions do you have?"

Heath gave his broad shoulders a lift and followed it with one of those confident grins. "I dunno. I figure, seeing as you're not my supervisor anymore, you're fair game. Now we're just acquaintances, and acquaintances make small talk, don't they?"

Oh, this man with his answer for everything. "Almost two and a half years." Two and a half blissful, glorious years.

"Why'd you get divorced?"

Because he forgot his dick belonged to me when he said "I do"? She fought an outward cringe. Even though she was glad to be rid of George, it still didn't sting any less that he'd called her unexciting, accusing her of not making him feel like a man and only after informing her he'd had an affair. Because naturally, his new wife with the foot fetish made him feel all male all the time. Bleh.

Wanda looked down at her feet. She knew damned well she had nothing to be ashamed of, but every once in awhile, being left for another woman still left her with a twinge of inadequacy. "He was unfaithful." She gulped, swallowing the words like shards of glass.

The wrinkles on Heath's forehead stood out when he cocked an eyebrow at her. "To you?" His surprise rang genuine.

"Last time I checked."

"Sucks."

"Yeah, that was my reaction, too."

He chuckled, letting it ripple from deep within his thickly corded throat. "Are you over it?"

How could she not be over George? There'd been a time, shortly after she'd found out about his affair with Darcy, Darcy, Darcy, that she'd thought she'd never survive without him—no matter how much she longed for something more. She'd never been alone in almost her entire adult life. She'd been in high school, and a year after graduation, she'd been married. She'd been forced to make her own way since the end of her marriage, and in the process, she'd discovered how much of her life had been all about George. Eventually, that had really hacked her off. "Yeah. Way over him. I'm not without scars, but if you're wondering whether they involve men in general versus the act of infidelity some commit—it's just the act of infidelity. I don't think all men are lying, bottom-feeding pigs." Christ. Why was she telling him something so personal? Shut. Up.

"I'm sorry."

Now her surprise was genuine. "Why are you sorry?"

"Sometimes my gender makes me feel like I have to apologize for all of them."

Warmth flooded her belly, unnerving her. "It's over now. My life is better for it."

"And your life is better with no job?"

Wanda immediately clammed up, stirring in her seat, then re-positioning herself to respond with as much nonchalance as she could muster. "My life is fine. It's not my life we have to worry about. It's yours."

"And that hand-happy woman with the wayward lips, Linda . . ." His words trailed off. "But I have an idea. How about we make another deal?"

Wanda sucked in her cheeks. "Look, Monty. I'm all outta doors here. I'm resigning from Bobbie-Sue. I'm in no position to make deals."

Heath held a palm up. "Just hear me out. The only time I really need to be in Linda's presence is on cold calls, and we'll be with other recruits, so I'm safe. But she did make it clear I have to be certified by my supervisor on my makeup applying techniques. She also mentioned we could practice those techniques at her swinging bachelorette pad—at night—after dinner and drinks." He gave her that "poor me" look again.

Wanda silently fumed. That fucking woman would hump a lamppost if she could get her legs around it. She was like a yippy, snippy terrier, shaking and rabid half the time, looking to mount someone's leg the other half. Heath didn't need any help with his technique. Wherever he'd learned to apply cosmetics, from whomever, he was pretty good at it. Linda was looking to hook up, and Wanda could hold herself fully responsible for his misery.

"So here's my deal. Hold off for just a little bit on your resignation. Maybe a week. Teach me how to apply the makeup properly, certify me, and then I can begin to branch out on my own—without sticky lips Linda. I'm already the subject of gossip because I'm a man selling makeup, but I don't need more, and that's just what'll happen if I ask to leave Linda's group. I mean, I've been shuffled around enough, don't you think?" He gave her his best sad face.

She wasn't buying it, despite her guilt for fobbing him off on Linda. "But you don't need help with your technique. You know exactly what you're doing. I watched you glide over Miss Allamuchy's face like it was a sheet of ice."

He shook his head, leaning forward with his elbows on his knees, his expression serious. "Nah. I'm still iffy about the eyeliner, and I have trouble shading the foundation under the jaw. You know, so I have that seamless flow from face to neck? I figure, I could practice on you. We'll be like girlfriends or something." He gave her a lopsided grin.

Sure. That's exactly what she needed. His hands. On her. Pretending they were girlfriends. Rad. She didn't want to do with her girlfriends the kind of things she wanted to do with him. It just wouldn't work. "I have a lot on my plate right now, Heath . . ."

He grunted. "Like what? You're at loose ends. You don't have a job, remember? Besides, everyone at Bobbie-Sue, aside from Linda, that is, says you're the best. In fact, they all had a lot to say about you giving me up like I was being sold at auction on eBay."

Her mouth became a thin line. God, those women and their gossip. "Yeah, I'll just bet they did." Haters.

"All I'm asking is a few hours of your time—and I think you owe me after handing me over to that viper without warning. You were going to send me some cold, sterile form letter from corporate. You weren't even going to tell me in *person* that you were breaking up with me."

Wanda rolled her eyes at him, clucking her tongue while fighting a grin. "We didn't have anything to break."

"Says you. You're not the one who was broken—by *Liiinda*." He drew her name out with a mock shudder on a hushed, ominous whisper.

A giggle bubbled up in her throat. "Oh, stop being so dramatic. You're trying to make me feel guilty for something I had no idea would happen."

"Is it working?"

Wanda blew a breath out in admission, letting her chin fall to her shoulder to hide her smile. "Yeah. Kinda."

He rose from her couch and winked at her. It was obvious he'd gotten what he came for. "Awesome. So tomorrow, say two or so?"

Wanda narrowed her eyes, keeping her face gravely serious. "You have one week—that's it. After that, I resign, and you're on your own."

He leaned over her chair, bracing his hands on either arm, and smiled that smile that made her heart tremble in her chest and her toes tingle. His breath smelled of mint and shortbread cookies; his eyes glittered with the satisfaction of once more getting what he wanted. "That's more than enough, and I really gotta run. Night, Wanda," he rumbled, gravelly and self-assured, whistling on his way out, and reminding her to lock the door as he left.

Wanda pulled the overstuffed pillow from behind her and pressed it to her midsection. Now she'd have to wait to resign or her certification of Heath would be no good. This was a bad idea. This was an überbad idea. She shouldn't be spending any more time with him.

But it sure would piss off that makeup whoring Linda Fisher to see her signature on Heath's certification, now wouldn't it?

She smiled—wide. Ah. Good times. Good times.

Her mind forcibly turned off her thoughts about Heath and focused on what she'd been doing before he'd arrived. The Fuck It list and entry number ten. She dug it out of her bathrobe pocket, running her finger over the words she'd written.

Some might say entry number ten was overboard grudging and that very grudge was long past its prime, but it had stalked her since seventh grade—still made her squirm in embarrassment twenty years later. Though it might have seemed minor to most even in hindsight now, it had been the most humiliating moment of her school career. An event so degradingly memorable no one had forgotten it—as was evident at her fifteenth high school reunion when her whole table, including the perp of said degrading event, still making no apologies, quite kindly reminded her while they chuckled on their stroll down Humiliation Lane.

She'd hoped since they were adults he'd at least offer an apology. Surely at their age, her nemesis now understood the kind of impact it had on a thirteen-year-old girl. But nothing had changed—not if the guffawing laughter he'd opened wide and spewed out of his mealy mouth was any indication.

So in the spirit of cleansing and mondo regret she hadn't picked up that spine Nina joked about much sooner in her life—this particular item seemed like a niiiice way to begin clicking off the more easily doable Fuck It list entries.

Glancing at the clock, Wanda decided she didn't care that it was almost midnight. Entry number ten probably had a lot longer to live than she did. Thus, he'd get plenty of sleep to make up for her interrupting one measly night of it. Besides, he owed her for all the nights she'd tossed and turned—cried herself to sleep from the torment she'd received throughout her entire school career and even long after.

So payback was the bitch that was about to slap him.

Yeah. Rage against the machine and all.

But in the most adult of ways. Well, at least semi-adult.

Wanda grabbed the phone, running strictly on adrenaline with a side order of impulse, hoping this was the right number. According to her mother, the person responsible for making her seventh and eighth grade years a virtual hell on Earth had inherited his mother's house in the town they'd grown up in. Which didn't seem terribly upwardly mobile.

"Hello?" a sleepy, much less squeaky than seventh grade voice answered.

"Is this Warren Snelling?" her voice quivered just a smidge.

"Yes?"

"The Warren Snelling who attended Our Lady of Perpetual Aid Catholic School in Point Pleasant?"

"Uh, yeah," was the gruff answer. "Who the hell is this?"

"This is Wanda Schwartz, and I know it's late. I mean, you're probably all comfy in your bed with your wife at this time of night, huh? That is, if you have a wife. Do you, Warren? Have a wife, that is?"

There was a pause, as if he wasn't sure he should answer, and then with hesitance, he said, "Um, yeah, yeah I do."

Her smile was sly and growing more confident by the second. "And were you all warm and comfy in your bed with her, sleeping the sleep of the guiltless?" *You fucking reject.* She bit her lip. There was nothing about thinking Warren Snelling was a fucking reject that was even remotely adult-ish.

"*Who* the hell are you again?" Ohhhhh, Warren was getting pissy, if the boom in his voice was any indication.

"Tsk-tsk. I'm so sad you don't remember me, *Warren*—because I remember youuuuuuu," she sing-songed, vaguely aware that she sounded like some crazy phone stalker. "I'm Wanda Schwartz. You remember, the 'Schwartz has warts' Wanda from Sister Angeline's class? You know the one. The Wanda you terrorized every damn day at lunch for almost two years and then, in a stunning culmination of brain-cell-less shithead-dom, ripped my shirt up in front of the entire class while I was swinging across the monkey bars." Thus, dumping half a box of the tissues she'd used to stuff her bra, because at thirteen, she hadn't graduated from a training bra. She'd never, ever forget how awful it had been to see those white, crumpled wads of paper lying at her feet. Some must have come loose while she'd swung from the bars, and Warren had picked them up, juggling them in his pudgy hands while he'd danced around. "You remember those monkey bars, don't you? You know, the ones you couldn't manage to get your mean butt up on?" At thirteen, she was way past playing on the monkey bars. She'd only been swinging around on them because as part of a school program, she'd mentored some sixth graders with learning disabilities, and on that day, she'd been their "lunch pal."

"Are you friggin' serious? That was like twenty years ago, you dumb bitch!" Ahhh, so Warren did remember. How fun. "Are you kidding me?" His high-pitched tone of disbelief made her smile. She could almost picture him sitting up in his warm, cozy bed, scratching his big, red blockhead in confusion, his pudgy freckled face all scrunched up while he called her a dumb bitch—which Wanda knew after spending so much time with Nina wasn't terribly creative.

Novice.

"Well, well," was her snide response. "I see you haven't changed much, Warren, and you're damn right I'm friggin' serious. Would I joke about something as awful as having boxes of tissue left on my desk in homeroom for over a year? Would I joke about the notes attached to those boxes that said horrible things like, 'Here's my contribution to the itty-bitty-titty committee'? You were a real doody head way back when."

Doody head? Christ. How inspired. Did calling Warren a doody head really properly represent how much she'd hated him after he'd shown her—her boobless-ness to her classmates? It wasn't nearly mean enough. What she needed to do here was channel Nina. But that wasn't what this was about.

"A doody head, huh?" he growled, chuckling.

Wanda's eyes narrowed, her temperature rising with a hard shot, but then she paused—this was about closure, settling old scores like a mature adult. "Yes. An *über* doody head, and I just want to say one thing. Okay, well, maybe a couple. The couple of things I should have told you when you did something so heinous to me the kids in class made fun of me for years afterward. And then, when I'm done being very unladyike, getting this monkey off my back, so to speak, you can go right back to bed. You game?"

"Game on," he said with a tone that screamed he was daring her. Like he didn't believe she actually had a set and never in a million would she, pathetic, meek Wanda Schwartz, take on the challenge that was Warren Snelling.

She didn't hang around Nina just for the sport of it.

Wanda gripped the phone with a tight fist, closing her eyes and remembering every last ounce of humiliation he'd bestowed upon her, like it'd been just yesterday. "What you did to me was disgusting and degrading, Warren Snelling, you spineless, weak, mean-spirited fucktard! But despite the fact that you have the syndrome known as peanut dick, I just wanted you to know I *forgive* you, Warren. I forgive you for being so horrible to me I cried for nearly a year. Because people like you, bullies like you, only pick on other people because they're insecure fuckwits. And I just wanted you to know that." Wanda pressed the Off button on her phone and hurled it to her couch, roaring in triumph.

She was actually gasping for breath when she plunked back down on the couch. A bead of sweat had formed on her upper lip. She wiped a thumb over the corner of her mouth to remove the spittle, pressing a hand to her flaming hot cheek.

Omigod—she'd just told Warren Snelling he had a little dick and she felt not an ounce of remorse digging her pen out of her bathrobe pocket and crossing off entry number ten with zeal.

Wee doggie—she outghta let the power of Nina compel her far more often.

Wanda grabbed Heath's hand—a hand that held the square sponge applicator—and buffed it under her jawline, using a light, circular motion. "See?"

His fingers tilted her chin upward under the light. Their light stroke made her nipples tighten ridiculously beneath her bra. "I think I see, but I don't know. I think this must be a man deficit."

She crossed her arms over her chest to hide her traitorous nipples poking from beneath her teal silk shirt and scoffed, "Ohhh, don't even play the man card now, Mister. That's tired. You can do it if you just relax a little bit. I think the problem is you had to use a heavier hand on the Miss TransAmerica contestants. They had distinct shadows on their faces because of the facial hair. Women need less foundation. And your subject this afternoon is a woman." She brushed his hand away and took the applicator from him, sitting up straight on the edge of the closed toilet seat. "Now watch," she instructed, placing the square sponge at her jaw and brushing downward. "We're blending—we're blending," she muttered the technique she'd repeated a thousand times since she'd begun at Bobbie-Sue.

Heath sighed his exasperation. It bounced off the tiles in her small bathroom. "Yeah, yeah. We're blending; we're blending," he mimicked her tone of voice. "Except when I blend, it doesn't blend." Heath glanced at his watch—something he did quite often in the few hours a day they spent together.

"In a hurry?" she asked as casually as she could, when in reality, she'd kill to know where he needed to be.

"Not really. Just have some stuff I need to do today."

"Like?"

"Like stuff." His face remained unreadable and blank, his attitude kinda jiggy, his lips a stiff line, his jaw set in a stubborn lock.

"Like house stuff? You know, scrubbing the toilets? All those annoying things we hate, but have to do?"

"No."

Just no. Jesus, it was like pulling teeth to get him to tell her anything about himself. "Got a roast in the Crock-Pot?"

He made a face at her. "What's a Crock-Pot?"

Hookay, then. She wasn't getting anywhere—she was no further along than she'd been five days ago when she'd agreed to help him with his technique. No matter how casual she kept her questions, no matter how average-everyday-normal-conversation-like they were, he wasn't biting. He kept his personal life just that—personal. Wanda slapped her hands against her knees. "How about we take a break from foundation and move on to lip liner? We only have one more day as part of our deal, ya know."

His look was skeptical. "Do you women really do all of this every day?"

"Again, it's what makes some of us feel pretty. I wear it almost every day. You really need to remember that when you deal with clients—Bobbie-Sue *enhances* your beauty. It breathes life into your skin, making it glow and allowing your best features to shine to their fullest potential while downplaying your worst. I know you're a man, but you're going to have to really get in touch with the sensitive side of yourself in order to pull this off. It's like being girlfriends when you woo a client, you know? You have to treat your client as if she were your best friend in the whole world. Remember the girlfriend thing you mentioned?"

Heath rolled his eyes, furrowing his brow. "I've decided I think you look just fine without makeup—and so does every other woman on the planet."

Really? He could see past her blotchy, sometimes dry skin and see "fine"? Fancy that. "And that's lovely—but if I didn't wear makeup, you'd have no job. So pay attention. Now, hold the lip liner like this." Wanda put the pencil between her thumb and forefinger as an example. "Then you follow the outline of my lips— like this." She did it without looking in the mirror.

"What if the woman you're putting it on has no lips—like say, Linda? Your lips are really full. Not all women are so lucky."

Wanda fought a raspy breath. That he thought her lips were full and that made her lucky, made her hormones do the Mexican hat dance. For the past five days they'd been in this small, small guest bathroom, going over his application techniques. Having him use her as his model, hovering over her while she caught glimpses of his well-muscled chest as his shirt gaped open, was killing her. His hands on her chin, the way he stuck the tip of his tongue out of the corner of his mouth when he was concentrating, would be the death of her. "You just have to work with what you're presented with, and never make them feel anything less than beautiful for it. I did say this wouldn't be easy, didn't I? But you thought you had it all figured out. It was just selling goop, according to you. But it involves far more than you think. It isn't just how much you can sell, it's about making women feel good about themselves, and that takes a special kind of patience. So man up." She wiped off the liner with a tissue and handed him the pencil, smiling. "Your turn."

Heath leaned forward, his face directly aligned with hers, concentration written all over it. He placed a thumb by the corner of her lip and began to stroke the pencil over her mouth. His breath fanned her face, his white teeth gleamed under the large bulbs over her medicine cabinet, his tongue did that thing it did when he focused. Wanda found herself closing her eyes, luxuriating in the calloused touch of his thumb, swallowing hard when he brushed it over her lip to wipe away the excess lip liner. Her nostrils flared at the musky scent of his cologne, her lips parted of their own volition, memories of their one and only almost kiss flashed in vivid Technicolor in her mind.

When he used the brush applicator to blend the lipstick with the liner, his knuckles grazed her cheek, and a groan, unbidden and totally unavoidable, escaped her lips. "Am I hurting you?"

Hurt-schmurt. "Nuh-uh," she managed to squeak from the back of her throat. Wanda clenched her eyes shut, fighting the rising heat in her chest that always seemed to make her heart jump whenever Heath was near her.

She felt rather than saw him take a step back. Her eyes popped open to find him doing the stare thing. "How do I look?"

He cleared his throat. "Good. You look really, really good," he responded with a strange, husky quality to his voice. Instantly, he looked away, his eyes straying to his Rolex. "I'd better go—it's almost three thirty. I have some things I have to do."

Wanda cocked her head at him, but didn't ask the question that had been burning on the tip of her tongue every single day for five days. Where the hell did he have to be and why was he always in such a rush to get there? He left every day at four thirty on the dot with the exception of today. He must have a girlfriend. But she didn't want to think about that.

Wanda rose, tripping on the bath mat at her feet. In the small space of her guest bathroom, she fell right into the hard wall of Heath's chest. Her fingers immediately gripped at him to keep herself from falling, but when her hands fell palms flat on his chest, her breasts crushed against the solid muscle, her legs gave way. His arms, strong, supportive, bloody hard as a rock, encircled her, bracing her against him as they fell into the wall. Wanda's fingers curled into his shirt, allowing her to feel the merest hint of what was beneath.

The press of his hips to hers through her thin pencil skirt told her he felt the same chemistry she'd thought was only something she was experiencing.

'Cause it was all right there between those hard thighs—waving hello from all parts tropical.

Holy way bigger than anything George had ever packed.

She could feel every nuance of the rigid outline, and while it wasn't going to make her run screaming from the room, it definitely had more impact . . .

Did they really come bigger than George's? She'd often wondered if he'd been full of shit when he'd told her size didn't matter. Maybe it didn't, but it sure felt like it just might. Her sexual experience only extended to George, and clearly, she'd been on the short bus.

Literally.

Heath hauled her upward by her upper arms, because it would seem she was sinking. Her head fell back so she could begin to apologize, but his eyes, filled with emotions she was unsure of, halted her words. His breathing became uneven, their chests bouncing against one another's in a rhythm Wanda could actually hear.

"It's three thirty. I have to go," he said, but didn't move. The stillness between them mesmerized her into remaining immobile.

She stammered. "O-okay. Then go."

"I'm going."

"No, you're still here," she whispered. Believe it—he hadn't *gone* anywhere.

"Now I'm really going." Again, he didn't move, but then, neither did she.

Wanda gulped audibly. "Bye."

"Bye."

Neither of them let go. "When y-you say good-bye, that means you follow it up with l-leaving."

"And I'm going to do that. Soon."

"Define soon," she said, hating the squeak in her voice.

"Right now." He dropped her abruptly, righting her with hands that barely touched her, then he slipped out of the bathroom on steady feet. "I'll see you tomorrow," he called from the living room.

She stood there for a moment, makeup scattered everywhere, her pulse skittering unevenly, her body flush with zinging heat, gathering her wits. She just didn't know if she had it in her to see him tomorrow.

But there was only one tomorrow left—and then she wouldn't see him anymore.

He'd be certified, and she could resign from Bobbie-Sue.

And right now, she just didn't want to think about it.

So there.

Her phone rang, sharp and jarring. She managed to uproot her feet and make a dash for it just in time to see on the caller ID it was from her doctor's office. Her hand shook when she reached for it, then pulled back, coming to rest at a tight fist by her side.

She knew what they wanted. She knew what they wanted each

time they'd called in the past weeks. Tears began to swim in her eyes, but she swiped them with an angry finger.

They wanted to help her prepare to die. To make her comfortable—maybe try and talk her into some end-stage hocus-pocus like chemo or surgery to prolong the inevitable.

She didn't want to prolong her death.

She just wanted to live.

"OH, sir. Please say this is all a nightmare I'll soon find myself awakened from."

Heath and Archibald stood on the curb. The cold early evening air grew chillier as Arch gave him a scathing look.

Heath slapped him on the back uttering a good-natured chuckle. "Don't be so negative, Arch. It's cash, my friend. This means to-morrow, instead of waiting in line at the soup kitchen for lunch, you're getting a Happy Meal, and you know as well as I do, even if you call it 'food designed for primates' out loud, you secretly love a good Chicken McNugget—with honey mustard sauce—and don't tell me you don't. Now tell me that's not livin' large."

"Sir?"

"Uh-huh?"

"If I'm seeing this correctly, your car has a rather large feminine protection product, with wings—*wings?*—sprawled across its side with the logo *'The Best Ever . . . Period'* on it in massive, neon letters. Might I ask what led you to this newest level of degradation?"

Heath rubbed his fingers together under Arch's hawk-like nose. "Money, Arch. Cold, hard cash. Almost a grand. Until my first Bobbie-Sue paycheck comes in, it'll help feed us. Maybe we'll even buy some clothes so we don't have to keep finding creative ways to wash what we have on our backs. It's not enough to rent a place to live, but it's definitely better than what we had before—

which was squat. This here"—he spread his arms wide—"is called wrapping. The company wraps the car, and I advertise the product. Advertising feminine protection products pays higher than say, an energy drink." Heath slapped the hood of the car with pride. That the feminine protection pad on the side of his car looked like a big, white bird taking flight, and took up half the driver and passenger side doors, didn't trouble him in the least.

Archibald's face, lined with wrinkles in the waning sunlight, was thoughtful. "A thousand dollars, you say? To advertise feminine protection products on your vehicle. The world has gone mad and taken you with it."

"Aw, c'mon, old man—it means you can have *whatever* you want for dinner tonight. I bet you won't mind the wings so much when you can have a cheesy stuffed gordita."

Archibald perked. "It's a gordita supreme, Heathcliff, and really? Whatever I want?"

"Yep. You're warming to it, aren't you?"

"Does it mean I have to actually get into the car with wings to go get whatever I want?"

Heath popped open the passenger side door, sweeping his arm wide. "Yep. After you."

Archibald slid into the car with a stoic expression and a slump of his defeated shoulders. Several people passing along the sidewalk stopped to stare for a moment, making him slide farther down the seat. "Oh, Heathcliff," he groaned.

Heath fought the impulse to flip these gawkers the bird as he, too, got into the car. He wasn't ashamed to do what he had to do. A grand was a grand. Then the paycheck from Bobbie-Sue, and it meant a deposit on an apartment. Okay, so it wouldn't be in the best neighborhood, but it would be theirs, and they wouldn't have to show up at the shelter by five every night to ensure they had a cot.

Now that was livin' large.

He looked over at Archibald and grinned, hoping his optimism pierced Archibald's pessimism. "Look, Arch, I'm our only hope at this point, and you damned well know it. You've had no luck finding a job—nowadays, you're past retirement age, and I hate to say it, but it's working against you. You shouldn't have to find a job, anyway—you should be playing golf and chess with your buddies in a retirement village. But now, I've got one. It may not be what I'd have chosen if I had my way, but it's making us some money. If Wanda can live off her Bobbie-Sue paycheck, so can we."

Heath shifted positions, facing Arch head on. "I mean, do you really think I want to sell makeup? I don't think I can tell you how sick to death I am of color wheels and auras and all the other crazy shit these women do to earn a living. I really, really don't give one whit about what color lipstick these women wear or whether it matches their outfits. Call me a slug for saying that, but it's true. I'm a man—we don't care how you wrap the package, just that we get to unwrap it. I'm doing my best to be sensitive and open to these women and their makeup crises so I won't be labeled a Neanderthal, but it isn't easy. It's just friggin' makeup as far as I'm concerned. I will say, I admire them. Most of them. Some of them? Not so much. Some of them, like that batshit crazy Linda, are vipers."

"All but the fair Wanda, sir? You've been very creative in keeping yourself in her presence. You speak fondly of her oft. I take it she's not, ahem, batshit crazy."

Heath shot him a warning glance. That moment in Wanda's bathroom was seared into his brain. Her almost too slender body pressed so close to his you couldn't have gotten a paper clip between them played back in his memory. Yeah, he hadn't been thrilled being left with Linda, but he was even less thrilled that he wouldn't see Wanda anymore. A week ago he didn't think he wanted to be involved with anyone because he was in no position to wine and dine. This week had brought hope.

He didn't plan on Wanda dumping him like she had, but the dumping had brought an odd feeling of losing something he couldn't explain why he needed.

So he'd hatched the plan to pretend he needed help with his technique. It'd happened somewhere between seeing Wanda's sweet, round ass leave Bobbie-Sue and sticky lips Linda laying one on him. He got the technique—totally. He could blend at a hundred paces—he just dug doing it in Wanda's bathroom where she didn't have a choice but to be close to him.

But right now, he wanted to keep this bizarre desire to be near her to himself and plan how he was going to add getting her to go out with him to his roster of things to accomplish. "She's not up for discussion—what is, is our situation. It's the only job I could find, because neither of us are skilled at any twenty-first-century work, and we sat around on our asses way too long, thinking we had an eternity of riches before us. If we have to supplement with crazy crap like wrapping the old Yugo, well, I'm not ashamed to do what needs to be done to get us out of this hole." Heath thumbed his finger over his shoulder at the brick building behind them.

Arch reached up and slapped Heath on the back. "I know you've made sacrifices for the greater good, Heathcliff. After what's happened, I'll always be grateful that you've kept me by your side— degradation and humiliating ordeals aside. But I have a question. Will you always sell cosmetics? Surely there are other things you'd enjoy doing for work."

Heath nodded. "I have a plan, Arch. I want to get a degree, go to night school, but degrees cost money, and for now, hawking lip gloss is what will give us the helping hand we need. I can't even think about much else until we at least have a place to live."

Archibald gave him a curt nod, erecting himself in the seat to find more people staring at him curbside. He rolled down the window, sticking the upper half of his body through it. "What? Have you never seen a feminine protection product? Young woman over there, do put your eyes back in your head. Surely *you're* familiar with such products!"

Heath leaned over him, sending an apologetic look to the poor woman Archibald had verbally attacked. Heath grabbed the older man's collar and dragged him back inside. "Chill, Arch," he commanded, rolling the window back up.

Archibald sniffed, harrumphing as he brushed at his formal black jacket with a brisk hand, his round cheeks flushed. "Gawkers!" he yelled through the closed window, flipping his middle finger at them, spittle flying from his lips to land on the windshield.

Heath had to fight to keep from roaring his laughter. "Archibald Crane. Did you just flip that lady the bird?"

"I did, sir, and I'd do it again given the chance. Where has all the class in the world gone, I ask you? To stare is rude!"

"I hate to tell ya this, Arch, but I think, at least for the time being, we're going to be subjected to a lot of staring. We do have a feminine protection pad with wings on the side of our car. So get over it and think about the cheesy gordita instead."

Archibald cleared his throat and breathed deeply, his composure returning. "You're right, sir. I've completely forgotten my manners. Carry on." He rolled his hand in the familiar way he'd always done when he departed a room.

Heath turned on the ignition and headed down the street toward the nearest Taco Bell. "Life doesn't get any better than this, Arch. We have a ride, and now we have money to buy food. It can only be downhill from here."

"I will admit, it beats the slop they call food at the soup kitchen."

Heath's chuckle filled the small car. "That's the spirit, Arch.

Won't be long now before we have a place to hang our hats." *And maybe a place to bring Wanda*, his dark side said.

Yeah. Maybe.

He was beginning to see a future—it was dim, it definitely wasn't stable, but a flickering light at the end of the tunnel had begun to come into view. In that light, he saw himself spending more time with Wanda.

If she'd just let him.

He knew she was hesitant whenever she was around him, but the why of it wasn't clear to him. She was divorced, and the asshole had cheated on her—that made for gun-shy. Totally understand-able, but according to her, she was over it. No matter how many times they'd been in close proximity this week while he applied that dumb makeup she didn't need anyway, she'd firmly slapped up a wall between them, bringing a screeching halt to his lustful thoughts.

Each time he figured he'd just come out and ask her about her personal life, if she was dating anyone, she got that sort of freaked look in her eyes—almost like she knew he was going to move in for the kill. So he'd eased off, but today was enough for him to decide in this new life he'd been given, he wasn't going to waste a moment of it, and he wanted to get to know Wanda. Time wasn't an eternal thing for him anymore. His nature was to be direct in all situations, but he felt the necessity to use kid gloves with Wanda.

Whatever was up with Wanda, it wasn't because she wasn't at-tracted to him. He had some residual perceptions left over from his old life, and he felt her awareness of him. Loud and clear. She wasn't his superior anymore, if that had ever made a difference anyway. She was fair game—and he wanted his playing piece.

But you'll have a lot of splainin' to do if you get involved with the pretty lady, Heath, his conscience reminded him.

Yeah. There was that. That's exactly why he'd halted what

he'd come close to making happen in the bathroom. Because she needed to know about him and his circumstances before they went any further.

He'd have a lot of explaining to do even if it weren't Wanda he wanted to be involved with.

He'd have a lot of explaining to do, period.

CHAPTER
8

"So before we go anywhere, I have an announcement to make." Marty smiled coquettishly, perching herself on the arm of Wanda's cream-colored sofa. Her face had a healthy glow to it, and her eyes were sparkling a deeper blue tonight. "And in no way do I want this to detract from our mission—which is to find out about this Heath guy. But I have to tell you guys or I might explode—literally and potentially, figuratively." She plopped Muffin, decked out in her fuzzy pink sweater with the words *Bitch In Heat* written in rhinestones, on the floor. Muff took off after Menusha, yapping and snarling.

Nina shoved her hands into her trench coat pockets, knocking shoulders with Wanda. "You sure you wanna do this, Wanda?"

She nodded her head, her brown hair falling over her shoulder, sticking to her glossed lips. Irritated, she flipped the strands out of her face. Yep. She wanted to know what was up with Heath. That she was spying, sneaking around, and dragging her friends into this venture with her was shitty. In light of the fact that her time to find out anything about him was limited, she'd decided last night—she wanted answers. "I'm more than sure. But let Marty tell us her news first."

"So what's up, dawg?" Nina snickered.

Marty smiled again, the smile of a woman with a secret. "More dogs."

"Say again?" Nina replied, her almond eyes showing she was clearly puzzled.

Marty said nothing. Instead, she cradled her arms together, swinging them back and forth in front of her.

Nina groaned. "We don't have time for fucking charades, you German shepherd. Get on with it."

Wanda inhaled sharply, placing a quieting hand on Nina's arm. She knew exactly what Marty meant. "A baby?" she squeaked.

Marty grinned, then snorted. "Yeah—me—with a baby. Whoever thought I should be responsible for anything other than Muffin is probably crazy, but I'm three and a half months along and scared and excited and scared." She rubbed the very small mound of her abdomen beneath her oversized red sweater, pulling it tight so they could see the evidence.

Wanda threw her arms around Marty's neck and hugged her hard, clenching her eyes shut and biting her lip to keep from crying. A sharp stab in the region of her heart—because more than likely, she wouldn't live to see Marty and Keegan's baby born—came and then dissipated. Life would go on without her—that it would go on with Marty giving birth could only make her smile. She refused to let it be any other way. "I'm sooooo happy for you and Keegan! How is the dad-to-be?"

A wave of Marty's hand showed off the engagement ring Keegan had given her, a time that seemed like so long ago now. "He's grumpy, and overprotective, and in general a pain in my ass.

Which, by the way, is spreading." She slapped her back end for emphasis. "You'd think he was the one having this baby. I've had some morning sickness—I've had some around the clock sickness, too," she said, with a tinkle of laughter. "I didn't want to freak you out if I yarked all over the place while we hunt down this Heath. So I figured it was time to fess up."

Wanda's smile was wide, her heart full of bittersweet joy for Marty. "So Keegan's happy about the baby? Forget I asked that. Of course he's happy. There isn't anything that man wouldn't do or endure for you."

Marty snorted. "Happy? Puulllease—he's beyond happy. It means he'll carry on his line in the pack, and that makes any werewolf proud."

"So are you having humans or puppies?" Nina snarked, but before Marty could threaten her with the usual WWE fare, she grabbed Marty's hand and squeezed it. "Very, very cool. I'm gonna be an aunt. I love babies."

Wanda was skeptical. "What do you know about babies?"

Nina held up her keys, motioning them out the front door. "Not a fucking thing. I just love the way they smell, and I know I don't want any, but I'm happy to spoil the shit out of whatever Marty ends up having. I can buy a leash or a baby blanket." She paused in the doorway. "Let's take my car, we'll stop for your dinner on the way home. Marty's eating for two—or is that six, you know, like a litter?"

"It's one baby, smart-ass. I had an ultrasound and all that fun va-jay-jay doctor stuff," Marty assured her, flicking her fingers on Nina's arm.

Wanda got into the front of the car with Nina, tightening the belt on her coat. "God, it's cold."

Nina pulled out of Wanda's driveway, glancing at her briefly. "So, you wanna tell us what made you decide to spy on this Heath guy?"

"Nope." She made a firm line of her lips.

Nina gripped the steering wheel tighter. "Why the hell not?"

Wanda covered her face with her gloved hands in shame. "Because I'm being a nosy busybody, and I hate it, but where he lives and maybe even with who is killing me. Okay? So don't snark on me for it. Just get me there."

Nina must have sensed her determination, because she didn't pick. "He's on Dunlap, right?"

"That's what his Bobbie-Sue application said. It isn't far—just not in the best of neighborhoods." Wanda flipped the dials on Nina's dashboard, turning up the heat.

Nina swatted at her hands. "It's too fucking hot in here. Leave the damn thing alone, and the last thing you have to worry about is the hood he lives in. Me and Marty can take care of whatever might go down."

Wanda nodded knowingly. "That's exactly why I asked you to come. But don't put up those dukes unless asked, got that, Sugar Ray?" Wanda warned. "I want to be as inconspicuous as I can. In and out."

Nina grunted. "Yeah, yeah. I'm gonna park a street over, and we'll walk so we can hide and all that stupid Mystery Channel shit. Marty? You okay with walking—your ass looks like it could use the exercise, but I don't want you to blow a gasket on account of the baby."

Marty reached from behind and slapped Nina on the top of her head. "Just drive, Elvira. I'm fine walking. I'm also fine with a good smack down if you don't shut up."

Wanda couldn't take commotion or the usual chaos between them tonight. She was already on edge for being so sneaky, and instead of just asking Heath where he lived and if he lived with anyone else, she was finding out the hard way—the *Get Smart* way. It was ludicrous. "Both of you knock it off! Can't you see I'm fragile here?" she yelped, hearing her raw tone, then cringing because of it.

"Sorry," Nina mumbled in contrition.

Marty reached a hand around the seat and rubbed Wanda's arm. "Yeah, me, too, honey. I don't think you have any reason to feel guilty. It's your right to know about who works for you. Especially if you question his character."

Wanda's sigh was ragged. "That's not why I'm doing this. I think his character's just fine. I'd almost feel better if that was why I was doing this."

"Well, whatever your reasons are, we're here," Nina announced in her no-nonsense way, pulling into a free underground parking garage.

Wanda hopped out before they could prod her anymore. She tightened her scarf and sucked in her cheeks.

"If we go down this alleyway, it cuts across to Dunlap." Nina pointed to her left as they climbed the small hill to exit the lot. "It puts us right at the number of the building you gave me, according to my GPS." She rubbed a hand against her thigh, clad in faded jeans with a huge hole in the knee. "And when we get to said destination, I'd like some more concrete answers about this little mission we're on. Let's roll." Nina latched onto Marty to help her around some bags of trash that had spilled over from the smelly Dumpster in the narrow passage between the streets.

The three women came to a stop at the corner of the path, huddled in the alley behind the faded red brick building, allowing each of them an unobstructed view of the entire street Heath claimed was his address. If Heath happened along, and Wanda couldn't see him from this far away, Nina and Marty, in all their paranormal glory, sure could.

"Got a question, Wanda," Nina said, her dark eyes glittering in the shadows.

"Question me."

"What makes you think we'll even see him outside? Wouldn't it make more sense to just go knock on his door than to hang around back here with the stench of garbage?"

Of course that'd make more sense, but nothing about Heath made sense. So why should this sojourn make sense? "Just give me a minute, okay? Let me work up to this. I'm already freaked out enough because I feel dirty for lurking around back here. I'm hoping he'll miraculously walk out of his building and I won't have to go banging on his door. But if he doesn't, then I'll go knock on his door, all right?"

"We're doing this again, why, Wanda? Details, pronto," Marty demanded.

Wanda pinched the bridge of her nose. "Fine, I'll tell you. Because I want to know what the hell this guy's gig is, okay? I mean, he has a designer suit, he speaks in full sentences, and his manners are impeccable. Why would a guy like that want to sell makeup? Something's very, very fishy. So just call me curious."

Marty nodded her head. "Okay, that's a perfectly logical explanation. However, I do want to point out something. Why do you give a shit if, in the long run, he's making you money? Who cares where he lives and how?"

Her guilt over spying on Heath gave way to a rare display of frustration. "Because I fucking want to know! Now would you be quiet, Marty, and just stay still? Jesus, you two suck at this!"

Nina tugged on the hem of Wanda's jacket.

"What *now*, Nina? I can't watch the front of the building if you're distracting me like a two-year-old."

"You're swearing again. While I gotta admit, it's totally cool by me, you've been doing it a lot lately, and it's just not you. So what gives?"

Wanda shrugged her shoulders, feigning indifference. "Nothing gives. I just decided I'd subscribe to your way of thinking. What harm can using the word *fuck* cause? It's almost cleansing— refreshing. Now leave me the fuck alone and shut the fuck up."

Nina's hand landed firmly on Wanda's shoulder, pulling her backward so Nina's lips were near Wanda's ear. "Okay, first rule of swearing. Never, *ever* tell me to shut the fuck up, 'cause I will fuck you up. You can swear at anyone you'd like but me. Practice on Marty. And you make the word *fuck* sound like it came from Florence Henderson's mouth—so work on that, would ya?"

Wanda reached behind her, pinching Nina's lower lip between her forefinger and thumb. "Get off of me, vampire, and don't tell me what to do. You two are always telling me what to do, and when you're not telling me what to do, you're fighting over who should be the one to tell me what to do. So knock it off and shut your mouth. This is about me. *Me, me, me.* Okay?"

Nina laughed, flicking at Wanda's fingers. "Okay, already. You know, you so rock lately, Wanda, I can't even get jacked up enough to be pissed at you. I kinda dig this feisty, mouthy version of you."

"Good, then you won't mind when I tell you one more time, shut it. I'm trying to concentrate here."

Marty laid her chin on Wanda's shoulder, her perfume filling Wanda's nostrils, and for a moment, Wanda savored it, closing her eyes and inhaling. The scent was the essence of Marty, and she never wanted to forget it. Marty nudged her arm. "This guy Heath—why the interest if he's nothing more than a measly rep? I mean, weren't you the one who played like he wasn't all that interesting? Why, just a little while ago you were telling us he was just okay. So I get that he's a guy, and no guy I know wants to sell makeup, but again, honey, why do you care if he's making you money and he's not that big of a deal?"

"Uh, Marty?" Nina leaned over Wanda's other available shoulder.

Marty shooed her with a twist of her wrist and the clink of her gold bangle bracelets. "Didn't Wanda tell you to shut it?"

"Yeah, and if she does it, it's almost okay. When you do it, it just pisses me the fuck off. But in light of the fact that I may have the answer to your question, and you're preggers with puppies, I'm going to forgo whipping your ass."

"Whaaat question, for God's sake?" Marty asked with exasperation.

"The one about why Wanda wants to know more about Heath."

Wanda craned her neck to look over her shoulder at Nina. "Why does Wanda want to know about Heath, Nina? Do tell, because me, being the Wanda in question, is giving you her full attention."

"Because if that's Heath"—Nina pointed her finger to the left, directly at a man who was indeed Heath, who was standing with another man in a black suit on the curb by a mailbox—"dude can rock a suit. He's hot, Wanda, if my supersonic eyesight's in working order. Oh, and I'm betting a year supply of Bobbie-Sue blush, you liiiiike him. That's why you want to know about him. So you were full of shit when you told us otherwise, and I hate to say I knew it, but I knew it. In fact, I told Marty on the way over here that that was why you wanted to find out more about him. We just wanted you to admit it—get it out in the open—feel comfortable about owning your, what the hell did you call that, Marty?"

Marty clucked her tongue. "Her womanly desires."

"Yeah, that was it. We're all about our womanly bullshit. We want you to be, too."

Wanda's breathing paused for a moment, stopped by the sight of Heath, heartbreakingly, unconventionally gorgeous. She closed her eyes and forced herself to slow her heartbeat. She ignored comments about womanly desires and comfort. "How'd you know it was him?" she asked Nina.

"The blue suit. You said he always wears a navy blue suit in one of our conversations this past week, and he's all you've talked about since you met him. It didn't take a degree in rocket science. Plus, and I don't want to be remiss in adding, he's fucktacular. If it wasn't for Greg, I'd definitely tap that shit."

Wanda could only nod. She was guilty of thinking the same thing. All day. All night.

Marty whistled softly, blowing the hair that peeked out of Wanda's knit cap against her face. "Wow. He's really cute in a way I never thought I'd find cute. There's nothing pretty about him, huh, Wanda? He's kinda all—"

"Man," Wanda finished on a sigh. "Yeah, that's what I think, too, and it's why I don't get what his deal is. He's such a guy, well, minus the burping and leaving the toilet seat up, and he's selling makeup. There's not a feminine bone in his body—not that that would necessarily mean anything, but still . . . and he's got an answer for everyyything. Yet, he claims he just needed a job, but that still makes no sense to me. Wouldn't you think a guy who dresses like that and hangs around another guy who dresses equally as well would have like an Ivy League education—or at least something more manly he wants to do for work? But I'm telling you, he sold those starter kits at the Miss TransAmerica contest like he was giving free prosthetics to the limbless, and that was only after he came to my in-home party and wowed every woman who attended. It was incredible."

"The Miss Trans who contest?" Nina asked.

"Miss TransAmerica," Wanda corrected. "And here's the rub. He was smart enough to consider all those men who were competing would want makeup with some serious, long-lasting coverage, and that their friends might want some, too. Balk all you like about Bobbie-Sue, Nina, but you can't deny their foundation is awesome. I mean, seriously, Marty, did it ever occur to you when you sold Bobbie-Sue to contemplate trying to sell makeup to transvestites?

It's a whole untapped market. Even you, in all your creative glory, never thought something like that up."

"So another question," Nina poked her arm.

Wanda sighed, blowing a chilly breath out of her mouth. "Knock yourself out."

"Is that Yugo he's running a hand over like it's his lover his car?"

Wanda peered more closely. Nooooooo—he didn't. Oh, but he had, in all its feminine protection glory. "Uh, yeah. I think so."

"Is it me, or am I the only one who finds those wings a lot on the eyes. Why would he do that?"

Marty shrugged. "Money? He is out of a job, Nina. I've read about this type of advertising. It's called wrapping or something. I'd bet advertising *that* pays some pretty good cash."

Wanda had nothing to offer. He'd been so broke he'd wrapped his car? In a freakin' feminine protection product?

"Okay, last question," Nina said to Wanda.

"By all means," she responded.

"Why not just *ask* the guy what his deal is? I don't get the problem."

No, Nina wouldn't get the problem because her direct nature wouldn't let her. She'd just beat it out of him. "Because he seems to clam up whenever I ask him anything personal, yet he has no problem asking me all sorts of stuff."

"Oh! Look, they're going up the stairs." Marty jabbed at Wanda's arm.

Nina's brow furrowed. "What the hell is this place anyway? And why is there a line of people as long as a supermodel's legs outside of it?"

Wanda grabbed their hands, pulling them out into the open, once Heath and his friend had gone inside. "I don't know, but I say we find out."

Wanda's footsteps came to a sudden, abrupt halt when she had a clearer view of the tall brick building.

Nina linked her arm with Wanda's. "Uh, you readin' what I'm readin', Wanda?"

She gulped, shoving her free hand into the jacket of her coat. "Uh-huh."

"Well, hell," Marty muttered, slipping her hand through Wanda's other arm.

Hell indeed. So here was the question thrumming through her brain.

How in the frig did a classy guy like Heath Jefferson end up in Atman's Homeless Shelter for Men?

CHAPTER
9

Wanda threaded her way through the rows of flimsy cots. How she'd slipped past Attila the homeless shelter coordinator had been an act of God. And Nina and Marty's help in distracting her.

Her nose filled with the smell of antiseptic cleansers that did little or nothing to cover the scent of men who, sadly, spent a good portion of the day on the streets without the benefit of a place to wash their laundry, or even their hands.

Suspicious eyes cast their glances her way, some even moved protectively toward the shopping carts that contained their possessions.

Wanda scanned the room, spotting Heath, who stood out with his tailored suit in the sea of men in tattered clothing. She sauntered up behind him, lingering before she said anything.

The man who'd been with him outside cleared his throat. "Ah, sir? I believe you have a visitor."

Heath whipped around, the rush of air he created swelling and filling her nostrils with his cologne. "Wanda." He said nothing more than her name—like he was making a statement, not like he was wondering why the fuck she was here. His gaze penetrated hers.

And all of a sudden, she felt like a total ass—a complete idiot. Who the hell did she think she was, barging in on his personal life like he owed her an explanation? She was his supervisor and loosely at that—supervising him didn't mean she could stalk his ass, demanding answers about his unusual personal circumstances.

"Um, sir?" the man in the black, also impeccable suit crossed his arms over his chest. He had a distinguished presence to him, as though he was far above the clutches of the shelter. His British accent was cultured in just the few words he spoke, his face unreadable.

"Yeah, Arch?"

"I believe curiosity has arrived in the form of the lovely Ms. Schwartz. And indeed, sir, she *is* lovely. Just as you said." This Arch guy nudged Heath. "And introductions can only be appropriate on such a festive occasion as a visit to our lair."

Heath stood silent. The room around Wanda swelled with the noise of the other men and their chatter. The neutral colors of the walls were dull against the vivid image of Heath. And all she could hear was that Heath had told this man she was lovely . . .

He waved an impatient hand under Heath's nose. "Never mind, Heathcliff. Clearly I'm the only one capable of retaining his manners. Ms. Schwartz—I'm Archibald Crane. Heathcliff's manservant. It's a pleasure. I would have wished we'd met under any other circumstances but these. However, as you're here, and this hellish place is our setting, do pull up a cot and sit down. I promise I've aired the linens personally and to the best of my ability, given our crude, rudimentary accommodations. I'd offer you refreshment, but again, do forgive our rather rustic backdrop." He gave a slight bow in her direction.

Heathcliff? His name was really *Heathcliff*? And he had a manservant. A *manservant*? Like one of those guys that catered to your every need way back when?

She spewed the word before she could stop herself. *"Manservant . . ."*

He nodded affirmation, the coarse, sparse gray hairs on his head ruffling when he did. "Indeed, miss."

"Hookay." It was all she had in the way of sparkling conversation.

When Heath spoke for the first time, not a shred of embarrassment for his surroundings tainted his words. "So what brings you to my crib, Wanda?" His grin was devilish, laced with a mocking, amused glint in his eyes.

"I-I . . ." She remembered her oath to keep things as real as possible until she was gone. However, she hadn't factored in the utter assholish-ness it would require. Nor had she accounted for how humiliated she'd be by it. "Okay, so I'm just going to be honest here. Um, Archibald, here, well, he's right. I was curious. I mean, wouldn't you be curious if I showed up at your house every day, dressed in the same suit—a suit that sports a designer label, mind you—not to mention the fact that you're smart, and you're a whiz at selling units of foundation." Archibald's snicker cut into her speech. Amusement lit up his face. "Yet you never mention where you live, if you're married, have children, and you have a car that's a complete dichotomy to your clothing," she lowered her voice with the last phrase. "It's a Yugo, for God's sake. So okay, I'm here, admitting I couldn't stand it anymore. I was subtle, I tried not to pry, and then I couldn't take it anymore. I had to know what your deal was. And now I do. Sort of."

Heath still said nothing. His gaze neither condemned her nor offered any clue as to what this was all about.

She'd been dissed in the most silent, painfully obvious of ways. "So, Archibald"—she tugged her glove off and held out her hand to him—"it was nice meeting you. Heath. I'll see you tomorrow for the Bobbie-Sue weekly meeting. I'm totally stoked you're getting your level-two red suit—sash, whatever you'll end up getting, being a man and all. And so soon, too. It sometimes takes weeks, even months for new recruits to get where you are. You'll be a lavender in no time flat. You should be proud. Very proud. Now, I'm going to slink on out of here with my tail between my legs, which seems to be becoming a habit with me. I'm sorry I interfered in your private . . . um, in your business. It was crass and nosy and very, very un-Bobbie-Sue-like. In fact, if you lodged a complaint about me, I wouldn't blame you one itsy-bitsy bit." She'd never live to see it come to fruition, and she found herself saving face over that thought.

Wanda grimaced, pivoting on her toe, prepared to fly out on the heels of humiliation. But Heath stopped her, grabbing onto her arm and turning her back around. "You talk a lot sometimes."

Guilty. "Especially when I feel like an idiot."

His gaze remained just as steely, but his eyes were warm. "It's appealing in a rambling sorta way."

Her cheeks instantly grew hot. "No, it's intrusive and rude. And stop staring at me like that."

"But still, oddly appealing. Plus, I figure if I just stare you down, you'll let the cat out of the bag without me even having to try and figure out what you want to know."

Wanda's stomach clenched. "Kudos are definitely in order for the 'stare.' You rock at it, in case anyone ever asks."

"Years of perfecting the craft, I guess."

"It makes me spill my guts without compunction."

"Noted."

"Right. Okay, so like I said, I'm going to go now. I don't think I can handle any more of the 'stare' tonight. It's really unnerving; looking you in the eye is getting about as easy as liposuction minus the anesthesia."

"Can I walk you out?" He glanced Archibald's way, as if seeking confirmation for something.

Archibald waved him off with a dismissive hand. "I'll hold your cot, Heathcliff."

As he ushered Wanda out, her disbelief made her ask, "Didn't you just hear what I said? I want to run away and hide now, and you want to walk me out? What is wrong with you? Are you looking to bask in the glow of my humiliation? And what does 'hold your cot' mean?"

"If we aren't here by five, we lose our spot. You have to wait in line every night for a bed. Archibald's older. The younger, more streetwise guys won't let him save one for me if they can stop it."

Ohhhhh, how awful. Her heart constricted. All this time she'd thought he was going home to some woman, when he was really leaving so he had a place to sleep at night. How demeaning. Shit. She was scum. "And that makes you feel how?"

"I dunno, *Oprah*—grateful to have a place to sleep?"

The flush of her cheeks deepened. "Sorry. This is me shutting up." But it explained why he had to leave her house at four thirty every day. To secure a cot—at the homeless shelter, so he and his manservant wouldn't be sleeping on the sidewalk.

Jesus.

Of all the scenarios she'd put together in her mind about Heath, this had never been one of them. Now she'd gone and pried into his business and exposed something that had to be very humiliating for a man who was as confident as Heath.

Way. To. Go.

When they entered the shelter's foyer, Nina and Marty exchanged confused looks, then focused in on Wanda. "Ya all right, Wanda?" Nina asked, coming to stand beside her and place a protective arm around her shoulder.

She slapped on a cheerful half smile and nodded her head with vigor. "Yep. Right as rain. Fine as the day is long. Good, good, good."

Heath leaned in next to her ear as he stuck a hand out to Nina. "You're rambling again," he whispered, then turned his attention to Nina and Marty. "I'm Heath Jefferson. Good to meet you."

Nina gave him the killa glare before finally accepting his hand with reluctance. "Nina Statleon, and this is Marty Flaherty."

Marty smiled, smoothing a hand over her blonde hair. "*Heath*. Nice name. So you ready, Wanda?"

Heath looked to both Marty and Nina. "I'd like a moment alone with Wanda."

"Uh-huh, and I wouldn't like you to have that moment," Nina, immediately on the defensive, spoke up abruptly.

"I understand your hesitation. Nina's your name, right? But I promise, she's safe here with me."

Nina crossed her arms over her chest, planting her feet wide. The rustle of her trench coat echoed in the cold, sterile foyer. "Yep, that's my name, and look, man—this place is creepy. Sucks to be you, being so down on your luck and having to live here and all. I can totally relate in ways you'll never understand, but there are some seriously unsavory types hanging around here—and we have no proof you aren't one of the gang. So, have your moment, or whatever, but keep one thing in mind, if Wanda comes back with a solitary hair on her head missing, I'll know. And then, I'll fuck you up for it."

Marty looked to Wanda helplessly. "Jesus, Nina! How rude, but really, should we expect anything less of you? Stop being such a potty mouth and knock it off. I'm sorry, Heath. Nina's . . . well, Nina's Nina . . ."

Nina waved a finger under Marty's pert nose. "Don't you tell me what to do, Marty Flaherty, and don't apologize for me. We don't know this guy from jack shit. He's been hanging around Wanda for nigh on three weeks now, and we know squat about him. Then we find out he lives in a homeless shelter with another guy who dresses like he's from one of those History Channel shows, and his car's got some crazy feminine protection product with wings all over the side of it. *Wings*, Marty. Forgive me for being suspicious, but I'm just lookin' out for my own."

"Ladies," Heath's commanding voice made them both stop and take note. "I understand where you're coming from. I do have a car advertising a feminine protection product. With wings. As you can see, I'm in no position to say no to some cash. Having your car wrapped is good cash," he said unapologetically, upping Wanda's respect for him another level. "It's not like I don't know where I live and yes, it can be dangerous—especially after five p.m. when some very questionable characters are all vying for space here in the shelter. You want to reassure yourselves I'm not out to harm Wanda, and that makes you good friends. I promise to stay in your line of vision while I talk to her, but I *will* talk to her."

Wanda shivered, voiceless. Mostly because Nina had shut up, and partly because when Heath made a demand, there was no mistaking his intent.

And still, he grows hotter.

Nina sidled up to Heath, standing just below his chin. She'd gotten over her obvious surprise and reverted back to what she was such a master at. Threats. "You make sure that happens, bud. If I lose sight of her—you're meat."

Wanda watched Heath fight a grin. "You have my word." He pointed to a wall that wasn't so littered with people. "We'll be right over there."

Wanda followed him, mortified, stupefied, horrified—all sorts of fied. "I'm sorry. Nina's a long story, and I love her like family, but she's kind of overprotective."

"An understatement if I ever heard one. But she's right to be careful. You shouldn't be here, Wanda. It really can be dangerous—especially at this time of night."

What could she say? He was right. "Again, I'm sorry. This was sooo wrong of me."

"Yep."

"Okay, then. Is that all you wanted to say? Or are you into public humiliation, too? I wouldn't blame you if you ripped me a new one. Go ahead. I can take it. Forget I'm still sort of your supervisor—lay into me. I have no business being here, but once I was, my feet and my curiosity wouldn't let me leave without talking to you. It was impulsive and intrusive."

His face held not a trace of anger—instead it displayed his amusement. "Yep. But I know why you came here, Wanda, and it isn't just about wondering where I live."

She opened her eyes wide, feigning innocence. "It isn't?" *Oh, Wanda . . .*

"Nope."

"Okay, so if it isn't about my insatiable curiosity, what's it about?"

"It's about me."

"Do tell."

"You like me, Wanda." There was no mistaking his words. They were a statement of fact, not a question.

Her legs trembled. "Like you? You mean, like you as an employer likes an employee? Definitely. I definitely like you that way." Definitely. And if employers were allowed to demand that their employees wonk them until their eyeballs rolled to the backs of their heads, she'd be all in—in *like*, that is.

He ran a finger under her chin. "No, Wanda. That's not what I mean, and that isn't what you mean, either."

She let her eyes go wide. "Really? If that's not what I mean and it's not what you mean, then what do you mean? Because I don't know what you mean. In fact, I forget what I mean, too." *Oh, you have not. You know exactly what he means because it's exactly what you mean . . . or something like that.*

"Wanda?"

"Yeah?"

"I have no idea what you just said, but I'll tell you exactly what I mean. I'm just going to be as straightforward as I can—so forgive me if this sounds blunt. You like me. You find me attractive, and that's the other part of the reason you're here."

How fucking arrogant—egotistical—true. So? "You know what? You're pretty damned sure of yourself, aren't you? You're sure of yourself all the time, in fact. Well, let me tell you a little something, Mr. You Know You Like Me. You might be able to sell a starter kit at a hundred paces, but that doesn't mean that *every* woman you come across is going to throw herself at you because you seem to have this magical, mystical aura about you. I'm the exception to the rule, I'll have you know. I don't think you're magical or mystical. So I don't know where you get off thinking you're Fabio or something."

That eyebrow of condescension rose. "Who's Fabio?"

"Forget it. Just get a grip on your big, fat ego and stop reading something into absolutely nothing."

"Wanda?"

"Now what?"

"I saw your, and excuse my language, Fuck It list."

Oh.

Delightful.

"So that means you were snooping in my stuff, too." She realized her voice had risen an octave in panic, she just couldn't stop it from happening.

"No, that means you left it on the kitchen counter where anyone could see it. If you remember, Tuesday I think it was, I made the coffee, because you said I made better coffee than you."

Oh again. That was true. He did make better coffee. And apparently, he read well, too. She'd pray for death at this point, but it would seem her prayer had been prematurely answered.

Thankfully, Nina strolled up behind them, tapping Heath on the shoulder just in the nick of time. "Uh, Heath? According to my watch, your time's up. It's getting late, and I don't much like the way I'm hearing raised voices. It means you've upset my friend, and I did say if you upset her, I'd kick your ass."

Heath swung around, eyeing Nina. "You could hear raised voices over this ruckus?" Loud voices surrounded them. Clearly the men who hadn't managed to make the five o'clock cutoff for a cot weren't happy. Wanda had been aware of only the pinpoint of sound their conversation had become. Everything else was muted and dull.

But it was time to intervene before Nina gave herself up as a night dweller with ears like the Bionic Woman. "Stop, Nina. I'm fine. Let's go. Heath? First, wherever we go from now on, we're taking *my* car. Second, I'll see you tomorrow at Bobbie-Sue." She grabbed Nina by the arm and dragged her to Marty, who was leaning against someone's abandoned shopping cart. "Marty—let's go."

Wanda flew out of the shelter and down the steps, taking big gulps of air, clinging to the railing once she hit the bottom.

Nina stepped in front of her. "Wanna tell me what that was about?"

Wanda let her head fall back on her shoulders, but Marty came up behind her and tilted it back up so she could gaze directly into Nina's eyes. "No. I don't want to tell you what that was about, and you'd better be more careful. You were pretty far away from the two of us, but you told Heath you could hear us. For a human, that'd be impossible in all that noise."

"Never mind that now. What's this list, Wanda?" Marty asked, jumping down a step to stand beside Nina, planting her hands on her hips.

Her stomach flopped, but she was quick to reply, hoping her face didn't betray her and praying Nina hadn't heard what she'd titled the list. "It's like a life list. Things I want to do before I die kind of thing. You know, like see Paris in the spring or parachute out of an airplane—maybe get a tattoo." None of which she wanted to do.

Nina nodded. "And Heath was on this list?"

"You heard?"

Nina's dark eyes glittered in the harsh glow of the streetlamp. "I swear, I tried to block you out, but it was kinda hard when you were all wide-eyed and doing that thing you do with your hands when you talk and you're excited. I only heard a little. Wanna tell us why Heath was on the list?"

"Not particularly."

Nina's face was sympathetic. "Okay, then I'll say it for you. You wanna do him. Why's that such a big deal?"

Wanda groaned. "Because he wasn't supposed to know I wanted to do him."

Nina playfully punched her in the arm. "You left the list on your counter, numbskull."

Her face flushed with humiliation. "Like I need to be reminded?"

Marty chucked her under the chin. "So you like him. It's not that big a thing."

"It is when he reads it off some stupid list of things I want to do before I die." Christ, there was that word again. *Die*.

Nina grinned. "Um, yeah. I see your point. Lust can be a powerful thing—especially if you put the lustee on your list. So you gonna do him?"

"You're so black and white, Nina! No, I'm not going to do

him." She didn't do people. There'd be no doing of anything or anyone. Especially now that Heath knew she wanted to do him. To do him would prove his point, and that was just too humiliating to ponder.

Marty tilted her head at Wanda. "How many things to do did ya have on the list?"

Ten . . . and? "I don't know. Why does it matter?"

Marty snorted. "I was just wondering what number he was on the list."

Wanda let her chin drop to her chest, her eyes scouring the bottom step.

"Shit. He was number one, wasn't he?" Nina guessed, punctuating it with with an amused laugh.

Wanda rolled her eyes at Nina. "What-ever, vampire."

Marty grabbed Wanda's hand, giving it a squeeze. "So he knows now, and it didn't look like he was running away in terror. It really is okay if you take your womanly needs into your own hands, Wanda. You're allowed to be the aggressor."

Wanda's response was dry. "Thanks, Dr. Ruth. I'll keep that in mind, and I can't take my womanly needs into my own hands. I'm his regional supervisor." *For now*, an unbidden voice reminded her . . . "It's unethical." Problem solved.

Marty shook her head, the soft blonde curls of her hair ruffling down over her shoulders. "First of all, there is no rule about something like this for regional color reps, because Heath's the first ever *male* color rep. They're just a bunch of chicks who have to treat each other equally. The color reps mostly don't deal with anyone in corporate except via a liaison, and she's a woman. The rules in place do, however, apply to upper management. Harassment of any kind, be it verbal or physical, is strictly forbidden. Second, I own a portion of Bobbie-Sue, and I say it's fine. There. Permission granted. Go get yon man and do him till your eyeballs wobble."

"No."

Nina looked confused. "Why the hell not? I mean, I'd understand if you're hesitant. He does live in a homeless shelter, so it's not like he'll be buying you expensive meals and taking you sailing on his yacht, but he seems like a decent enough guy, and you don't care about material shit anyway. You don't have to have a lifelong relationship with the dude. Bag him and tag him. Be fuck buddies or something."

Lifelong . . . Wanda swatted Nina on the shoulder with the glove she'd dug out of her jacket pocket. "I don't want to get involved." And just the phrase *fuck buddies* made her cringe.

Nina nodded her understanding. "Right. No involvement. I get that. That's why you're called fuck buddies. You just fuck—then he goes away to his cot at the homeless shelter, and you flip on the WE channel then sleep like a baby."

This was so frustrating. How did you tell your friends you weren't a candidate for a fuck buddy of any kind because you had more important things to take care of? Like the kind of wood your casket would be made of. "That's not what I mean, Nina. I just mean, I can't get involved right now."

Marty made a face at Nina. "Nina, stop making it sound so tawdry. Wanda's not that kind of girl."

"And I am?" Nina's question was haughty.

"You were," Marty reminded her.

"Shut the fuck up, Marty. You make it sound like I was some cheap ho. I just wasn't afraid to get my freak on."

Marty nodded her head in the affirmative, clucking her tongue. "Or get a freak—"

Wanda whipped a hand up. "Both of you shut up. I don't want a—a fuck friend or buddy, or . . . I don't want anything. I want to go have that dinner we talked about. End of discussion." Wanda stomped down the steps and along the sidewalk, heading for Nina's car.

Nina caught up with her in the time it took to blink her eye. "Maybe it's better that way. He smells funny, Wanda."

"I dunno, Nina. I think he smells pretty damned good, especially considering his, uh, his circumstances." Marty thumbed a finger over her shoulder at the shelter, sandwiching herself between the two women.

"No, Marty, that's not what I mean. Look, when you're a vampire, you can smell humans versus paranormals. I told you that. For instance, I can smell the dog in you." She pointed at Marty.

Marty reached across Wanda and popped Nina on the arm with her palm. "Nina, I swear on all things fucking olfactory, I'm going to offer you up a good right hook if you call me a dog again. I'm not a dog, nor am I a canine, nor am I having puppies. I'm a shapeshifter, all right? Now knock off the insults and explain the smell thing."

Nina flipped Marty the bird before shrugging her slender shoulders encased in a black trench coat. "I can't. I just know he's got a distinctive scent. It's not his cologne. It's not his natural scent, but whatever it is, it's very vague. Like every time I get a whiff of it, it slips away."

Wanda stopped walking toward the car and grabbed at the side of the building so she wouldn't lose her footing, her hand going instinctively to her belly. Marty was right behind her, placing a protective hand on her shoulder. "Honey? What's wrong?"

Sometimes the sharp zing of pain took her breath away. She held up a finger, silently asking for a moment.

Nina brushed Wanda's hair out of her face. "I'll go get the car, Wanda. You stay with her, Marty." Nina took off in a blur of silent motion while Marty held her hand until Wanda could stand upright.

"Sweetie—you're pale. Maybe you're coming down with something. The flu's been going around. This is when I'm glad I'm a werewolf—I'm flu-free forever." Marty put the back of her hand to Wanda's forehead. "No fever."

Wanda shrugged her off, averting her eyes to the hard pavement beneath her red heels. "I think you're right. I might be coming down with something. I think I might have to beg off dinner tonight."

Nina pulled up to the sidewalk, rolling down the passenger side window. "C'mon, Wanda. Get in, and we'll take you home."

Wanda slipped into the backseat, grateful for the cover of darkness.

Soon she'd have a secret to share just like Marty.

Soon sucked.

CHAPTER
10

"About that Fuck It list."

Flames fought to lick at her cheeks, but Wanda refused to allow it. Marty and Nina had dropped her off, tucked her in after giving her some aspirin and tea, then left to get Marty something to eat. By the time they'd gotten her home, the cramping had passed and she'd felt much better. After throwing on her fuzzy bunny nightgown, she'd promptly plopped down on her couch, and it was where she'd been ever since—humiliated and mortified—until her doorbell rang. She'd found Heath, his rugged features sharply defined by the weak light of her front porch. The chilling wind whipped his jacket around his waist, and a vein in his temple throbbed.

The list, the list, the list.

Whatever had she been thinking when she'd left the goddamned thing on the counter? Whatever had she been thinking when she'd simply written it? Of all the lists she'd ever written—this was the humdinger of them all.

Her fingers went to the bridge of her nose, massaging it. "Can't we just forget that list? Because we're so good at forgetting things and all. Hell, most of our relationship I've already forgotten. In fact, do I know you?" She let her eyes scan his face as if he looked only vaguely familiar.

Heath shoved his hands into his pockets and rocked back on his heels. "No, we can't forget, Wanda. Haven't been able to think of anything else since I saw that list."

"Well, try."

"Don't want to."

"You have to."

"I was number one on the list, Wanda."

She fought to maintain a cool, disinterested facade. "Yeah, well number two on my list was doing John Cusack at a Tom Jones concert while he sings 'She's a Lady.' I think it's obvious, that probably won't happen."

"You like Tom Jones?"

"Who doesn't?"

"He's the guy chicks throw panties at, right?"

"That's him. So you can see how far out my dumb list was."

"And this John Cusack?"

"Longtime crush—he's a movie star. Since I was a kid. Again, something else that won't happen."

His face went dark. "How about that tattoo, you know, on your—?"

Wanda's face went red. "Another thing that probably won't happen. It's just a stupid list. It's what I do. I make them all the time. You've seen them—they're everywhere. On my refrigerator—on the counter. Just because I made a list doesn't mean I'm going to do everything on it . . ." Some of the list would take a travel agent and a bit of time she might not have to plan.

"Was it like a life list or something?"

Her eyes went to his shoulder. "Or something," she mumbled.

"Well, big dreams of Tom Jones and John Cusack aside, number one on your list *can* happen."

"No. It can't. I can't get involved right now."

Heath lifted his sharp jaw. "I *shouldn't* get involved right now. Not with my life in such a friggin' mess. But here I am."

The question was, why was it in such a friggin' mess? But she didn't ask. She wasn't sure what had been worse, exposing Heath's living arrangements or the fact that he'd seen her Fuck It list. "Then go home and you won't be *here* anymore."

"In case you've forgotten, I don't have a home."

"Then go shelter."

His laughter was gruff, yet melted-chocolate smooth. "I'd much rather be here. Helping with that list."

She ran a hand over her face, resting it on her cheek to thwart the flush that would inevitably happen. As long as she maintained her cool, everything would be okay. "Look, that was just—just me, sounding off. I won't lie and tell you you're not attractive. You seem to know that already all on your own, and if you didn't, half of Bobbie-Sue can confirm it. But that list meant little to nothing in the way of serious. So go back to Archibald and your shelter before you lose your cot."

"Arch is fine. I put him at the Motel 6 for the night. So no go, Wanda. That list meant more than what you're admitting."

Her bottom lip trembled, followed by her knees. "Really? Wow—conceited much?"

Heath jammed his hands into his pockets while shaking his head. His confidence bled through in his words. "It isn't conceit, Wanda, and you know it. We have chemistry, you and I. You can deny it, you can try and hide it—but it's there."

"Nothing exists but your imagination."

He moved closer, standing to loom above her, his cologne heady and intoxicating, his chest wide and inviting. "That's not true."

"Is."

"Not."

"Look, even if it were true. Even if I were attracted to you, it makes no difference. I can't get involved right now."

"And the reason for that is?"

"I don't have to tell you why. I just can't." She clamped her jaw tight to keep her expression hard and unyielding. She'd practiced it in the mirror earlier tonight before going to the shelter, in case Heath balked at being given back to Linda tomorrow. Apparently, she needed more practice, 'cause he wasn't going away.

"Boyfriend?"

"No."

"I didn't think so. No one ever calls but your friends Nina and Marty."

She bristled. So she wasn't going to be Miss Match.com 2009. Yet it was the perfect opener to find out why he skipped off every night like he was going to be grounded if he missed the dinner bell. "Girlfriend?"

"Nope."

"Then why can't you do house calls after five?"

"I told you, I have to be back to the shelter by five to get in line or risk losing my cot. Archibald gets nervous when he has to hold one for me. He's pushing seventy, and some of the shelter residents take advantage of that. I won't let that happen."

That's right. He had told her. She'd just been so busy stewing in her own guilt juice, she'd forgotten. Okay, so he had to be at the shelter by five to get a place to sleep for the night. That soooo sucked. Christ. He was such a decent guy, looking out for Archibald. Egomaniacal, but decent. Which brought her to her next question. "Care to tell me about Archibald? He calls himself a *manservant*. Does anyone use that term when referring to their hired help anymore? I don't think so. And who lives in a homeless shelter and has hired help?"

His face went unreadable again, the shift of his hard jaw made it crack. "It's a long story. Suffice it to say, Archibald comes from a family of British descent, most of whom served royalty in one way or another."

Well, that explained absolutely nothing. How come he could ask her questions, and she couldn't ask him any? "And you ended up with him in a homeless shelter, how?"

"Another long story," he replied, clamping his lips shut.

"What about your clothes and your car and that Rolex? Thoughts?"

His eyes never left her face. "The Rolex is really old and not very valuable, but it has sentimental value. It was from a close friend who was like family."

Avoid, avoid, avoid. "Speaking of family—got one?"

"No—"

Wanda ran a hand over her forehead wearily. "It doesn't matter. I don't care. It's your business. And now, you have to go." She shoved at the door, but he planted a broad hand on it. Menusha heard the activity and came running, skidding to a halt at Heath's feet and winding her tail around his ankles.

"But you don't really want me to."

Her insides churned. Hell no she didn't want him to go, but if he stayed, it couldn't be anything more than physical, and she just didn't know if she had that kind of relationship in her. "This is me shutting the door on your big ego. Be careful not to let it get caught—we might pop a hole in it."

Heath braced his hand on the door frame, spreading his fingers wide to keep it open, using little leverage to keep it in place. His gaze was direct, intense, and serious as a heart attack. "I'm going to say this once more, and if you send me packing, it'll be the last time I say it. You want me, Wanda. I definitely want you. I've had some serious uncertainty in my life lately, but I know when I want something—and I want you. Are you ready to admit you want me, too?"

What if she did admit she wanted him? Would it be such a bad thing? Who would it hurt? "And if I do?"

"We'll just have to see what happens after that."

Her heart crashed a tidal wave of sound in her ears. If she said no, he'd go away and never come back. She knew he meant it. Arrogant jokes and lighthearted banter aside, Wanda knew Heath took everything he did and said very seriously. It was just implied. Which made this choice she was about to make do or die. *Speaking of, Wanda . . . you* are *going to die. I call fuck like bunnies while you can. It'll be one less thing you'll go to your grave wishing you hadn't missed. You're on the short bus of life, toots. Do this man. Do him now!* Her conscience shouted—loud and without compunction.

Even if it were just this once, she knew without a shadow of a doubt, she wanted Heath. To hear he wanted her, too, even if it was just purely on a physical level, made every nerve ending in her body come alive, scream with lust. But she wasn't the kind of woman who could have a purely physical relationship.

Have you ever tried? her conscience poked at her.

No, she'd never even wanted to try. No one had interested her enough since her divorce to make her want to try.

But Heath does . . .

He did.

The silence between them probably only lasted seconds as her mind raced—and then her brain shut off. A black void of nothing occurred with the exception of one very clear desire. To have Heath. Wanda didn't trust herself to speak. Her lips probably wouldn't have formed cohesive sentences, anyway.

Blue eyes met hazel.

One pair riddled with hesitance—the other dark with anticipation.

The cold air blew in swishes of icy gusts.

The hush between them became palpable.

Wanda knew she should say something, but she opted to do something totally non-Wanda.

Instead, she breached the distance between them by winding her arms around his neck, letting her lips whisper against his before she melted into his hard, sculpted frame.

Heath's arms were around her in an instant, dragging her inside, and he slammed the door with his foot. He walked her backward to the couch, setting her on the arm of it, spreading her thighs wide to stand between them.

When his lips touched hers—full-on for the first time—she grew dizzy. Heath didn't just kiss her, he devoured her mouth, making love to it with hot strokes of his tongue, sipping at her lower lip. Their tongues touched, and she heard him hiss his satisfaction, his groan becoming hers as their mouths entwined. Heath's hands, forceful and sure, roamed over her spine, pulling her flush to his groin. Her belly rubbed against the rigid outline of his cock, encased in his blue trousers.

Need pulsed in her, throbbing an endless ache of hot lust. His fingers skimmed her jaw, his knuckle ran along the side of her neck down to her collarbone. When he dipped two fingers into the top of her V-neck nightgown, she had to clench her eyes shut to keep from whimpering. Her heart hammered out an uncontrollable rhythm, hot lava flowed through her veins, her gasp when he grazed her nipple was sharp.

Wanda found her thighs had a mind of their own, wrapping themselves around Heath's waist, until she'd hooked her ankles together around his lower back. His hips thrust against hers, the thin wisp of material that was her panties twisted when he ground against her. He yanked upward on the hem of her nightgown, tearing it over her head, leaving her in nothing but the small triangle of her underwear.

His hands caressed her hot skin, roaming over her shoulders, kneading her back, trailing along her abdomen, skimming the top of her panties. Wanda's hips jutted upward, silently begging him to touch her, but he didn't comply.

He taunted. He teased. He let his fingers explore every inch of her flesh but the most intimate parts of her, circling them, coming so close to touching her, then pulling away. Her nipples were hard, taut, needy, scraping against the crisp white shirt he'd worn every day since she'd met him, and then she decided to take matters into her own hands.

With a grace she didn't know she possessed, Wanda popped each button open, spreading his shirt wide, planting her palms on the smooth skin of his chest, massaging his pecs, reveling in their firmness. She plucked at his nipple, gratified by the groan he moaned into her mouth. Her hands strayed to the crisp hair just below his belly button, tracing a pattern that went lower with each pass.

He dropped his hands from her waist, yanking off his belt, then lowering the zipper of his pants, letting them slide off his thighs, and catching them to throw them on the coffee table beside the couch. His shoes were next, kicked off in two thunks of muted sound.

Wanda became shy—suddenly and without warning. Hands that had roamed freely over Heath's hard planes stilled. Lips that had met his hot, hard kiss, trembled.

She'd only been with one man her entire life, and he'd claimed she wasn't winning any Kama Sutra contests.

Oh, this was a mistake.

Big, big, big.

"Wanda?" Heath said her name in the form of a question against her lips.

But she couldn't answer.

"Say the word, and I'll stop."

Finally she found her voice. Weak and raw, but found. "There's a word?"

He chuckled, his breathing ragged, his cock insistent and hard between her legs. "Yeah. You say, 'Stop, Heath.' "

"That's two words."

"Do you want me to stop?"

"No—yes—no—it's just that, well . . ."

He kissed the tip of her nose. "You weren't one of the girls who had one of those lists you mentioned in high school."

At least he knew she didn't sleep around, and he'd even supplied an answer for this situation—an awkward one at best. Her eyes fixed on his collarbone. "Of all the lists I've made in my lifetime—that wasn't one of them."

Heath tipped her head upward with a finger, forcing her to look into his eyes. "Good."

"Good?"

His lips curved into a smile. "Yeah, it means I might know a thing or two you don't—which could be enlightening."

A shiver slid along her spine as he stroked her cheek, relief sped down to her toes and back up again. She blew out a shaky breath. "Okay, then. Enlighten me."

When his mouth found hers again, his lips were just as demanding, yet gentler at the same time. "Take my underwear off, Wanda," he rasped, sipping at her lower lip, nipping the full flesh with lazy nibbles.

It was the last piece of his clothing that stood between her and his total nudity. She hooked her fingers in the band of his boxer briefs and slid them down along his hard thighs, feeling the crisp hair on them. Heath kicked the boxers aside, but kept a small amount of space between them. "Touch me, Wanda," he demanded, low, husky, taking her hand from his forearm and putting it between them. Her fingers wisped tentatively over the sharp indentation along his hipbone, skimming it before delving shaky fingers into the pubic hair a few inches below his belly button.

When she wisped over his cock, hard, hot, pulsing with life, she took a startled breath. Unbidden came the conversations she'd had with her friends, and Nina and Marty hadn't lied, but George had.

They *did* come in different sizes, and clasping Heath's was definitely laying claim to the size matters theory.

She fumbled before she found the right grip, and what had in the past always been such an unsure act became surer as she stroked the satiny smooth skin. Each raspy groan Heath made emboldened her, each rush of his hips to meet the push of her hand left her empowered.

This sexy, hot, deliciously hard man enjoyed her touch, had asked for it with encouraging words, and moans of pleasure. She ran her finger over the swollen head of his shaft, lingering at the slick bead of pre-come.

Heath tugged at her panties, and Wanda found she no longer had any inhibitions about him seeing her naked.

She didn't care about anything but being as close as humanly possible to him. She didn't care that her hipbones were now painfully noticeable. She didn't care that her ribs were probably more visible with each harsh breath she took. She didn't care that her breasts weren't what the old girls used to be ten years ago.

She didn't care.

And that, unto itself, was sinfully freeing.

When Heath found the undersides of her breasts, caressing

them with his index fingers, heat pooled between her legs, moist, hot. He circled each of her nipples with thumb and forefinger, bringing them to stiff peaks. Heath planted hot kisses along the side of her neck, dragging his lips down, down until his head rested between the two mounds of flesh. The first lick of his silky tongue made her jump, making her let go of his rigid shaft. White-hot heat flashed, sizzling in a wave of lust when he took her nipple into his mouth and tugged on it, enveloping it with the heated cavern of his mouth.

Her hands wound into his hair, thick and soft as she strained toward him. He flicked each nipple, cupping her breasts, pushing them upward, bringing tears to her eyes.

And then he was sliding her off the low arm of the couch and onto its soft cushions, kneeling between her legs, fanning the most intimate part of her with his hot breath. Her thighs trembled when he spread her soft, inner flesh, slick with need. She found herself clinging to the top of the couch with frantic fingers, her heels braced against his shoulders until he put her legs over them. He cupped her ass with his hands, kneading it, bringing her closer to his lips.

What he was about to do was foreign to her. Something Nina and Marty talked about with a bunch of oohing and ahhing and their eyes glazing over. Wanda could never participate in those conversations, because they teased her about being a virgin to all things oral.

And that all changed with the first lava-hot stroke of Heath's tongue. The bolt of electricity that jolted her was like nothing she'd ever experienced before. It struck with a quick hand, leaving the most intense need Wanda had ever felt in its wake.

Heath's fingers slid between the wet lips of her flesh, finding the swollen nub of her clit, before he lightly sucked it between his lips. Her hips rose, her chest tightened, flickering light danced behind her clenched eyelids, a whimper of carnal delight slipped from her throat.

A thick finger, deliciously calloused, slid into her with ease, the glide of it wet as Heath continued to lick her. Waves of tingling pleasure darted to all points intimate on her body, the slow burn that had begun with the first touch of Heath's mouth increased, simmered, pushing her to find release.

A sweet, sharp sting began low in her belly, making her clench her thighs around his neck, seek the rounded muscle of his shoulders with fingers that dug into his skin. The sudden crest of climax made her muscles tighten like a bow preparing its launch; her teeth gritted; her breath, raspy and intermittent, sat heavy in her ears.

The hot rise drove her to seek fulfillment. Heath's mouth flush against her clit suckled, his finger glided in and out of her passage, and the combination of the two tipped her over the edge to a place that swirled with no sound and myriad colors.

Wanda shuddered hard, clamping down on her bottom lip to keep from screaming, as her hips pumped against Heath's lips, frantic and urgent. How long her orgasm lasted, she was unaware, she only knew it had come from somewhere deep within, yanking at the core of her and refusing to let go until it was ready.

Her harsh intakes of breath were soothed when Heath slid up along her body, kissing her belly and reaching toward the coffee table to drag his pants into his hand. She watched him from the slits her eyes had become, realizing he had a condom, and not caring even a little that he'd been presumptuous enough to bring one.

He held himself over her, pushing her back to cover the length of the couch, then settled once more between her legs.

His eyes held hers, they grew darker, more glazed when he positioned himself at her passage. His lightly tanned throat worked, the few veins there pulsing, the strong column bulging with what she pinpointed as restraint.

Just before Heath entered her, he used two fingers to brush aside her sweat-dampened hair. The gesture so intimate, so tender, Wanda couldn't hold his gaze any longer, so she buried her head in his neck and hooked her legs around his waist once more.

His entry wasn't in the least hurried, burying each inch of his shaft into her with slow, subtle increments. As he stretched her, filled her, Wanda took a deep breath to accommodate him, focusing on the widening of her legs.

Heath's cock, finally imbedded deep within her, brought with it an uncomfortable pleasure. Uncomfortable because she hadn't had any sexual activity in so long it was foreign, pleasurable because he remained almost still inside her, but for the grind of his hips against hers.

She felt his restraint in each corded muscle, reveled in their skin melded together, luxuriated in the crisp pubic hair that made a delicious friction against her clit. Heath didn't drive into her, he ground against her, letting her adjust to his thick width.

He clasped her wrists together in one hand, pulling them from around his neck, and yanking them upward over her head, maximizing the press of their bodies, making her arch upward against him. Heath circled his hips instead of thrusting into her, the sensual rotation of their bodies so tightly wound together making her dig her heels into his lower back.

A white-hot pulse of heat threaded along her veins, beckoning her, leaving her fingers clenched in tight fists. Heath's breathing became harsh, his bare chest scraping her nipples, taut and needy. When he finally lifted his hips up and away from hers, the cool air on her sweat-slickened body became a delicious whisper.

His first thrust, a slow glide of his cock, made her lungs inflate, filling them until they threatened to explode. Heath drew back once more, sliding into her with sure precision. He let her wrists go, giving her the opportunity to grip his shoulders, pull him to her until their bodies absorbed one another's.

With each slick glide of his cock, steely within her, he brought her closer to orgasm. Thrust after silken thrust Heath pushed her. Her heart crashed against her ribs, her groin tightened with electric heat, his moans of pleasure as he sank deep within her were sinful, erotic to her ears.

The first wave of orgasm crept up on her with stealthy fingers, clinging to her, slithering along every muscle, every nerve ending until it consumed her, made her rock her hips upward to have all of Heath's cock.

Her hands reached down to the hard globes of his ass, clenching them, pushing him hard against her, begging him silently to bring her to satisfaction. The aching, yearning need superseded everything else.

Heath seemed to know instinctively what she needed. His final plunge into her was heated and driven. But the strain of his muscles suggested he was holding back, until she lifted her hips a final time to milk his cock.

Wanda drove upward, her breath harsh against Heath's ear, signaling her climax. She was suspended in a haze of breathtaking lust, and just as she reached the height of her orgasm, it enveloped her, left her shuddering, gulping for air. Raw waves of heat crashed against her skin, her stomach muscles tightened, the heated place between her thighs contracted, then let go, catapulting her over the edge.

Heath roared his release, the growl of it coming from deep in his throat, blotting out everything but the complete bliss Wanda experienced knowing she'd satisfied him.

Nestled beneath him, Wanda luxuriated in the command he'd taken, reveled in the stick of their skin and his heavy weight, sinking into her. Clenching her eyes shut, she fought the onslaught of what surely had to be the fuck-buddy syndrome.

How lovely.

Wanda clung to Heath's neck while her thoughts swirled and her insecurities began to creep up on her. And goddamn it, why was she just *now* finding out sex could be so frickin' amazing? She'd spent thirteen years of her life having mediocre sex with a podiatrist, when she could have been wonking a homeless guy that sold cosmetics who was red-hot. Jesus—how unfair.

And multiple orgasms really did exist. She'd just had two.

Two.

That was almost more than she'd had in an entire marriage to George.

Crazy that.

It was all like information overload. Thoughts of all those steamy passages in the romance novels she read came to mind. Heath was like Erik in *The Highlander's Lust* and Esteban in *Master of Ecstasy* all rolled into one.

Wanda Schwartz had hit the sexual jackpot. Imagine that.

Bingo, bitch!

She was overwhelmed, breathless, confused. "I'm not sure what this all means." The words escaped before she'd meant them to—if she'd meant them to at all. They should have remained a silent question.

Heath trailed a finger down to the tip of her nose, following it with a kiss. "It means we'll take this slow and see what happens."

That wasn't what she'd meant at all. She meant she didn't know why in the hell of all hells, whoever was in charge of all things living would choose now to bring her the man of her darkest sexual fantasies. After her divorce would have been plenty fine, thank you very much. Why now? It was grossly unfair. Wanda didn't say anything more—it was too risky to respond at this point. She'd just

had the best sex evah, as Nina called it, and that left a girl vulnerable. Never show your hand, Nina always said.

And really. Where would she be without all of the crap Nina'd
fed her during their friendship? She and Nina were poles apart
in how they defined what should be involved in a sexual encounter. She didn't fuck just to fuck, there had to be more than just a
physical attraction there—but in this instance, because her life was
coming to a screeching halt, she couldn't afford to show Heath her
hand.

Or anything, for that matter.

As much as she wanted to understand what had just happened
between them, as much as she wanted to tell him she felt selfish
for letting him into her life without telling him he was doing an
almost dead chick—she just couldn't.

Or wouldn't.

Heath dragged her mother's afghan off the top of the couch,
nestling them in it. Pulling the blanket to her chin, she burrowed
underneath it, letting Heath cradle her from behind. Shutting up
was the best thing she could do right now. She'd only find herself
in too deep. She had to keep this as easygoing and unencumbered
as she could. Even if she didn't know the first damned thing about
having a fuck buddy.

"Tomorrow we should talk, Wanda," he whispered against the
top of her head.

No. No talking. Talking led to involvement and somehow she
had to convey where her intentions for this lie. Wherever they
lay . . . lie . . . whatever. "About?"

His broad hand stroked the curve between her waist and hip.
"I dunno. I thought maybe I'd give you some answers to some of
those questions you have."

Wanda's gut clenched. Maybe she didn't want those answers

anymore. Because if he gave her answers, then she'd owe him some, too . . . "You don't owe me any explanations."

"Nope."

"Okay, then, so no explanations." Good. That was that.

"Tomorrow, Wanda," he said, as though it was a command. When she didn't push any further, he asked, "You wanna do dinner?"

Wait—didn't Nina always say if you were going to remain emotionally unattached, you should never eat a meal with the guy you only planned to bag and tag? Nina, Nina, Nina, all up in her head. Her advice during the course of their friendship kept ringing in Wanda's ears. She kept her response light. "You can't afford dinner."

"I thought maybe I'd cook. I'll bring the stuff."

And if eating with the guy was off-limits in emotional detachment, surely him cooking for her was waayyy off-limits, but the stir of her heart, warming to his words, made her ask, "You cook? Will it be scrambled eggs again? You didn't even know what a Crock-Pot was."

"And I still don't. I'm no Iron Chef, but I can make a couple of things. So I'll cook. How's six tomorrow night? You can tell me what a Crock-Pot is."

Tears stung her eyes. Just the thought of sitting down and having dinner—like a real date—with Heath made her heart ache. That was normal—healthy—relationship-y shit she should be doing at this point in her life instead of making a list of things to do before she died.

Heath gave her a gentle nudge. "So dinner tomorrow?"

She squeezed her eyes shut. "Sure."

He burrowed closer to her, letting his chin rest on her shoulder.

And it felt so good to be held.

It felt so nice to have Heath's warm body close, his defined abdomen pressed to her back, his arm securely around her waist.

And it felt new, but at the same time like she'd been doing this with him for a lifetime.

And that shit had to stop.

CHAPTER
11

Heath knocked on her door at six sharp. She yelled that it was unlocked before turning back to her hall mirror to check her makeup. Like it would matter if her eyeliner was perfect when she told him they could either keep this strictly about the sex—or it was ovah.

Yeah.

Last night had been incredible, insightful, enlightening on levels she didn't even know existed, but while Heath had held her long into the wee hours of the morning, she'd battled every possible scenario in her head—and they all led to the same conclusion.

She was going to kick the proverbial bucket.

Which made for major suckage.

How did you tell someone you just wanted to wonk? Uh, by the way, in case you were thinking you're valuable to me for any other reason than your dangly bits—don't be all full of yourself. If time were something she had, that's not what she'd want at all. She'd want to do things the traditional way—the way her sappy, sentimental, old-fashioned heart always dreamed it would be if she ever found anyone she liked enough to date after her divorce.

What had happened last night wasn't like the conservative Wanda she'd always been—the Wanda whose skin she was so comfortable in. This new Wanda was someone who was afraid not to take her one last chance at throwing caution to the wind—it was a desperate attempt to act without writing a list of pros and cons—without hemming and hawing until she'd turned it into something far bigger than it had to be. This was impetuous and unorganized—totally unplanned—and very, very scary.

But she consoled herself with the idea that maybe Heath felt the same way, and it'd all be happy clappy. Maybe he wasn't interested in anything more than sex, and just because that made her heart clench and her teeth grind together, and that it hurt more than she was willing to admit, was neither here nor there. Last night, while Heath had slept, his even breathing rhythmically mesmerizing her, she'd decided fair was fair. She had nothing to offer but the here and now. And she wanted to enjoy the here and now, but not at someone else's expense—so clarity was in order.

So, yeah. She was going to clarify—like she'd done this a million times before. Okay, maybe not a million, because that'd just be hootch-ified—but at least a couple. Which was just stupid because Heath knew better after she'd waxed and waned last night during their encounter.

Squaring her shoulders, she decided she'd just figure it out as she went along.

Her nervous fingers gave a final fluff to her hair before she made her way into the kitchen to find Heath dropping a brown paper bag on her counter. He had on a pair of jeans and a button-down, dark blue fitted shirt. It enhanced every good attribute he had and then some, and it left her surprised to see him in something other than his suit.

"Hey," she called softly without looking up, going to the fridge to offer him something to drink. "Do you want something to drink? I have Pepsi and water and milk. I'm sorry I don't have any alcohol. I'm not much of a drinker."

Heath slid up behind her, snaking an arm out to pull her to his chest. She fought the sigh she wanted to shudder at the contact between them. The warmth of him made her want to curl into his solid frame and stay there. Instead, she stiffened, but he turned her in his arms and smiled that smile that every dentist in the land would be proud to claim ownership of. "I don't want anything to drink. I want a kiss. You know, that crazy thing people who did what we did last night do when they've been apart for a few hours?" Heath didn't wait for an answer, he swooped down, claiming her lips, leaving Wanda unable to protest—and unwilling, too.

He parted her mouth, slipping his tongue in to stroke hers. That same rush of heat—the one that made her nether parts hotter than lava, began working its way up the length of her body.

Heath molded her to him, cupping her ass to bring her hips as close to his as he could. She wrapped her arms around his waist without thinking, the demand of his hot mouth making her forget everything but him naked—inside her, above her.

Their breathing grew harsh when Heath tore his mouth from hers. He took her hand, planting it on the rigid line of his cock. "You feel that?"

"I do," she rasped.

"I bought a big box of condoms. I say we make use of them and this." He ran her hand along his shaft again.

Condoms . . . she hadn't given that much thought—even after last night. She and George hadn't been able to conceive, and her disease wasn't of the STD variety. But he was protecting himself—them—and that was sensible. "But dinner . . ."

"It was just hot dogs."

"You said you could cook," she playfully accused.

"I can. They *were* chili dogs."

"Ahhhh—well, then, the chili part makes you a real chef."

Heath hauled her closer, unbuttoning her top with skilled fingers. "Hey, I have chips, too. With ridges."

She giggled. "Sweet. I like ridges."

"I like you," were the last words he rumbled before he grabbed the brown paper bag, then took her hand and led her to her bedroom.

Just like the night before, her legs were weak, her pulse racing in fiery threads of need. It took but seconds for Heath to have the backs of her knees pressed to the edge of the bed and her longing to have him burning like a brush fire. He threw the bag on the bed, then captured her mouth once more.

His lips absorbed hers, demanding she return his urgent request. Clothes flew, buttons popped, and then they were flesh upon flesh, thighs pressing together, chests hard pressed. "Don't move," he ordered, splaying his hand over her ass until they were connected by every inch of their skin. "You feel goddamned good, Wanda Schwartz. I figured I'd better say that before I ravish you."

A thrill of anticipation skittered from the soles of her feet to the top of her head. Her shiver made her nipples harden, boring into Heath's chest. But Heath didn't move, he took her hands from around his neck, placing them around his waist.

They began an easy sway, melting into one another with a gentle rocking motion. As though music played that no one could hear but them. Heath's hands skimmed her skin, now on fire from his mere touch. He roamed the planes of her body, the slope of her hip, the curve of her spine.

And Wanda returned the favor, trailing small paths over the rung of each of his abdomen muscles, molding her fingers into the firm skin of his back, burying her head in the broad shelter of his chest.

Heath bent her back over his forearm, leaning her into the bed, covering her body with his before pulling her to lie on her side, her thigh straddling his leg, the rough hairs tickling her freshly shaven legs. His large hands cupped her breasts, and she found herself arching into them, placing her palms flat on his chest to push against the calloused surface.

Heath's lips were at her neck, teasing the flesh, running his teeth with light nips over her skin, moving down to her breasts, hissing an intake of breath when his tongue found her nipple.

Her sigh came out in a raspy, ragged breath of completion, her fingers threading through his hair, pulling him closer. Heath hiked her leg higher over his thigh, pushing her upward, letting his hand stroke her spine, caress each vertebrae. He let his fingers slide down along one cheek of her ass, then slip behind her and between the folds of her sex.

He parted the swollen flesh with care, using two fingers to spread her wide. Her whimper was audible, a soft cry for more when he dragged a digit over her clit, thumbing the nub until it swelled beneath his touch. His leisurely, seductive exploration had her hips gyrating, rising up to meet each stroke of his finger.

The blistering sizzle from the night before returned, upped a notch by the fact that she knew only hot release awaited her. Wanda found her hand had a mind of its own. She cupped the top of Heath's hand, covering his knuckles, lifting her breasts so he could lavish more attention on them as he stroked her sex.

Slick with moisture, the light glide of his hands grew more insistent, demanding she find her pleasure. Her hand on his, show- ing him the spot she found pleased her the most, was almost too erotic, too bold for someone who'd known so little about finding her own erogenous zones. Yet he didn't brush her aside, he encouraged her with wicked words, husky and deep. "Show me what you like, Wanda." The words he spoke against her breast clung to her ears—hot and sinful.

Her muscles clenched almost painfully, she positioned his hand, following his lead as he caressed her, until the scintillating fingers of orgasm overwhelmed her in sweet rushes of blessed release.

Her breathing was choppy, her hands shaky while they clung to his shoulders, letting the shudders wrack her body. Heath's breath was hot at her breasts, fanning them, patiently waiting for her breathing to even out.

Wanda pulled him up to lie beside her again. Heath dragged her length close to him, his cock between them, resting on her belly, rigid, hard, heated. She smoothed her hands down over his chest, grasping his shaft to the tune of his satisfied hiss.

She slid along his body, luxuriating in his smooth skin, flush to her own, stopping at his thigh, letting her lips move over the thick muscles until her mouth rested near his cock. The dim light in her room allowed her her first real glimpse of it, thick, lightly veined, and pulsing when she took him in her hand.

Wanda hoped her nervousness didn't show, skilled at this she definitely wasn't, but Heath gave without reserve, and she wanted to do the same. She let her mouth come to rest along the length of his shaft, his groan above her making her stomach muscles clench. She ran her tongue with a tentative swipe over his cock, lashing out, then slithering it over the tight skin.

Heath's hands went to her hair, gripping the long strands, running his fingers through it, lifting his hips. When she enveloped him, he bucked upward, the hard planes of his stomach visibly contracting. Her heart hammered in her chest when he wrapped a thigh around her, straining against the heat of her mouth. She took slow passes, gripping his shaft with two hands, dragging her wet lips and tongue over the smooth flesh.

Heath's breathing pumped in and out, harsh, rasping on each intake, and then he tugged at her. "Stop, Wanda. Stop *now*." His demand was urgent, drawing her back up into his arms, setting her atop him with firm hands.

She planted her palms on his chest and blushed when he asked, "Do you like to be on top, Wanda?"

Her tongue became too thick to speak, and she lowered her eyes, the curtain of her hair covering her flaming cheeks. She knew what she wanted to like . . .

His powerful body sprawled beneath her left her winded, unable to voice her desires.

Heath slid up to the head of the bed, grabbing the bag of condoms, then bracing his back against her ornate, cherry headboard. She saw the tinfoil wrapper flutter to the floor out of the corner of her eye. Then he pulled her along with him, taking her face in his hands and slanting his mouth over hers to give her a kiss. "Don't ever be embarrassed to tell me what you want, Wanda—or to *show* me what you want. How about you take the reins," he said with a playful wink, spreading his thick arms wide. "Do with me what you will."

How uncanny that he should care that she even had needs. She couldn't recall George ever asking her what she wanted. George hadn't been a horrible person, he just wasn't terribly interested in much but himself.

A shuddering, nervous breath later and she'd repositioned herself on his lap. With her back facing him, her hands gripping the strong width of his thighs. Heath lifted her hips, settling her on the tip of his cock. Wanda sank down on his shaft in slow increments, smiling to herself when she heard his deep growl of pleasure. The instant he was inside her she leaned back against the warmth of his chest. The shelter she found there felt like completion. A dangerous emotion she had to set aside in favor of living in the moment.

Heath's hands cupped her breasts, plucking her nipples to hard nubs. Heat, white-hot and prickling her skin, traveled to every intimate place on her body. Her hips had ideas of their own as they picked up the gentle rhythm Heath had begun, rolling in tune with his thrusts. The slick glide of his cock, his hands at her breasts, being in control of her own climax brought with it yet another level of intimacy she'd never experienced.

Her thighs trembled with each plunge she took, her clit swelled when he found it, rolling it between his fingers. Her womb clenched with a sharp tug, her knees ached from sitting on her haunches, but the ache was a pleasure/pain, a necessary evil to explore this newfound sexual paradise.

She knew the familiar clench of her stomach muscles, the shiver of goose bumps that slithered along her exposed skin. Wanda's arms went up behind her to wrap around Heath's neck, bringing his mouth to her ear, his ragged breathing a sure sign he was ready to come.

The hard jerk of his cock deeply imbedded within her slick channel, the forceful, upward thrust of his hips thrilled her. He spread the lips of her sex to stroke her, while his forearm held her tight to him, sending her toppling over into the vortex of her orgasm.

This time, there was no hiding her cry of ecstasy. It came from deep in her throat with abandon, bursting from her lips freely. Heath's grip on her tightened, the hiss of his moan through clenched teeth, ringing in her ears.

She fell back against him, boneless, sated, breathless, fulfilled. Heath's arms remained around her, strong and secure, and she clung to them, swallowing hard when he nuzzled her neck and teased, "I think you should be in charge more often, Ms. Schwartz. I like."

Wanda closed her eyes, savoring this moment, savoring Heath's embrace, the intimate whisper of pillow talk.

But that wasn't the only kind of talk Heath seemed to want to indulge in. He lifted her from him, settling her beside him. "So about that talk."

"What talk?" For real, she was getting almost too good for her own comfort with this playing dumb thing.

Heath dragged the comforter up over her. "You know exactly what talk I mean."

She kept her face blank. "I told you, we don't have to talk. We can keep this, you know—just like this." She spread her arms wide to indicate the rumpled bed—and their nakedness in the bed. Wow. Very expressive, Wanda. Way to make yourself clear.

"And what's this, Wanda?"

Wanda bit the inside of her cheek. It was now or never. If she didn't tell him her intentions this second, she'd lose her nerve. *May the power of Nina compel me.* "It's—it's . . . sex."

"Yeaahhh," he said, then smiled. "Good, right?"

Maybe he was getting the picture, and she wouldn't have to actually say the words. "Very. And that's all it has to be." Score. A whole sentence and not one sign her tongue was thick and her stomach was a mess of knots a Boy Scout couldn't untie.

His smile never faltered while he adjusted the pillows behind his head, thwacking them with his hand. Her stark white sheets against his lightly tanned chest made a mouthwatering picture. "Oh, really?"

Wanda looked down, keeping him a vague blur in her peripheral vision, twisting the sheet between her fingers. "R-really."

He grinned, infuriatingly. "I say bullshit."

"Sorry?"

His smile was typically cocky. "Don't be sorry that it's bullshit."

And then again, maybe he wasn't getting the picture. So she'd paint him one with as little stroking of her brush as possible. "It's not . . . bullshit, I mean."

"Yeah, yeah it is—but forget that for now. I have to explain some stuff to you."

Wanda averted her eyes to her wrinkled comforter. "No you don't. It's okay. I told you—"

He placed a finger to her lips. "You can tell me all about how what happens between us is just sex after I talk."

"But—"

He pressed her lips more firmly. "Shhhh. Now I need you to really listen to me. What I'm going to tell you is probably going to leave you pretty disturbed—but I just need you to hear me out, and then you can ask as many questions as you want."

Her stomach fell. Jesus. Christ. He was married. He was cheating on his wife. That was probably the only thing he could tell her that would *disturb* her. That's what she got for taking her stupid, immoral womanly desires into her own hands. She deserved this because she was selfish. That made her officially a tart or, as Nina would say, a ho. Puuurfect. It was exactly as she wanted to be remembered when she left this world—aiding and a-bedding an infidel.

"I'm not married."

Wanda let out a rush of air with only a little surprise he'd read her mind. "So why am I going to be disturbed?"

"Because what I'm going to tell you is going to sound crazy, but it's who I am—who I was—and in the interest of my new lease on life, I want to be as honest as I can with the people in my new life. First, I live in a homeless shelter, and there's a reason for that—it has nothing to do with the fact that I lost my job, or that I ran my credit cards up, or even that my home was repossessed.

Second, I have no past that you can trace, and that might seem fishy to someone like you who has all these roots in the way of family pictures and memories." He pointed to the pictures of her parents and Casey, sitting on her dresser and hanging on her walls.

But she didn't need to know if he didn't have roots. Not if they were just going to . . . to just . . . wait—why didn't he have roots? Omigod—he was part of the witness protection program or something. Her mind raced with possible scenarios. He'd witnessed something horrible, something heinous, like a mob hit and now was in hiding—in a homeless shelter. What kind of people were running the government these days that they'd allow a man and his elderly manservant to live in a homeless shelter?

He stopped all of her crazy notions with his next words. "It's not whatever you're thinking, Wanda. It's probably not even close."

Oh. "Okay," she offered with a tentative drawl. "So what is it?"

"I've been around a long, long time."

"Haven't we all," she joked, totally on shaky ground.

"That's not what I mean. I mean that literally."

"Yeah. Me, too. Or at least it feels that way some days." Especially lately.

"No, I mean I've been around for a hundred and ninety-nine years."

Wanda cocked her head at him in question, focusing on keeping her jaw from swinging on its hinges. But she kept silent. His age, and the absurdity of it, sounded verrryyy familiar.

No. Nuh-uh. For the love of all things winged and furry.

Heath took her hand, massaging her knuckles, obviously ignoring the fact that she'd said nothing about his lifespan. "I guess there's no other way to do this but to just say it, and let you commence with the freaking out. Just know, when you're done flipping, I promise not to let you sit in the fetal position in the corner, rocking for long." His tone was light, his words not so much.

Yet Wanda didn't speak. She was afraid to, because she had this sinking feeling . . .

"So here we go. I'm a vampire, or I *was* a vampire." Heath paused, clearly waiting for the supposed oncoming freak.

Which she just didn't have in her. But she guessed Heath probably took her ongoing silence as shock-related. And she wished she could summon up some surprise so he'd feel some measure of justification for the buildup to this big reveal. It just wasn't happenin'. She was all tapped out on shock, dismay, incredulity. Her fear factor account was officially dry. This conversation *was* familiar. Like twice familiar. Like this past year's paranormal-palooza familiar. It wasn't that she didn't want to boost his ego by losing it—she just couldn't summon the will.

Actually, she had to stifle a yawn.

Heath had wonked the life out of her—and it had been beyond better than even last night. She was whooped.

And he was an ex-vampire.

Booyah.

CHAPTER 12

So Heath continued with a strange glance of what some might label the reverse freak. "Okay, so here's how this went down. Like I said, I'm a *vampire*," he reiterated as though Helen Keller had possessed her momentarily, and she hadn't heard him the first time. "You know, Dracula, fangs, blood drinking, mind control kind of vampire?"

Uh-huh. She knew.

He waited.

Silence became that golden thing.

"My sire, one of only five of the original vampires, or creators as they're called, in the world, was killed in a logging accident. He was a logger in Oregon, driving a truck when it happened. Staked through the heart by an oncoming log in another truck and decapitated."

Oh, ow. Total and complete bummer. Still, she had nothing. Her eyes sought his, waiting patiently for more.

"And that turned everyone he'd ever turned, and everyone

they'd ever turned, and so on, back into humans. It was like a domino effect."

How bloody ironic. A tragic logging incident . . . a logger vampire. Who knew vampires did mundane things like log? Did Greg now knit? Had Keegan taken up quilting or maybe barrel rolling? An odd, fleeting thought occurred to her then. "And how do these vampires get Social Security cards to work jobs like being a logger—or a Bobbie-Sue representative, for that matter? You have one—I know you do, it's on your Bobbie-Sue application. I thought vampires were off plotting world domination, not driving trucks in Oregon, selling makeup, and applying for Social Security." And while she knew that was totally untrue—not all vampires wanted to wreak havoc—it sounded way good. It sounded like something someone would ask if she didn't have a best friend for a vampire. At least that was her hope.

Heath's face turned bleak as he traced a pattern between her fingers. "Yeah, when I say it out loud, even I think it sounds like bullshit. And, yep, some vampires I'm sure want world domination, but most of us just wanted to live out our eternities in peace. As to the Social Security card—well, you meet some real characters in a homeless shelter. Ask around, and you'll find there's someone who can get you almost anything."

Her hand twitched in his. "And this turning into a human thing happened when?"

"Just over six months ago. Woke up one morning in broad daylight—if you know even a little about vampires, you know the sun can be like death to us. Arch was with me in what used to be our driveway."

Now that did leave her puzzled. What an interesting imagination he had. "What *used* to be?"

"Most of what our clan had accumulated in the way of monetary gain over the centuries wasn't created in a way of physical, or real-world work. It was via magic—I've always considered that particular gift compensation for stealing my mortality. We—Arch and I—had a mini-mansion in the suburbs of Manalapan for many, many years. Then one morning, we didn't."

Wanda continued to keep the serene facade, but her heart sped up. Nina had said the same thing about Greg and all the stuff he had—like his castle on Long Island. In fact, Heath felt the same way about his David Copperfield abilities that Nina said Greg did. Huh. Maybe Heath read romance novels, too? It's where she'd gotten most of her information when Nina'd been bitten—he could have done the same. Right?

Yet her silence didn't daunt him even a little. He appeared determined to stick to this new life vow he'd made and cleanse himself of his secrets. "When we were all returned our mortality, we were left with the clothes on our back—and Arch's car—which still baffles the shit out of me, but I wasn't up to looking a gift horse in the mouth. I think it was because it was one of the few possessions we didn't conjure up. Arch actually cashed in some old coins and physically bought the Yugo. Wheels are pretty important in this day and age—though you tend to forget that, living the lifestyle we did. And Arch, if you're wondering about him, has been with my family forever. He was my father's valet—or manservant, then mine since my birth."

"For almost two hundred years now," she rebutted flatly. That would have put him in the Regency era. Ohhhh, she knew tons about that time in history—she'd spent plenty of late nights with rakes and noblemen. How festive—or insane—but considering what she'd been through with her friends, he wasn't wowing her. In fact, his tale was comparatively average. Well, except for the human part of it—now that *was* impressive.

"So you had *nothing*? You really believed you'd never have to worry about human things like money—like ever?"

"Well, when you've been a vampire as long as I had and nothing ever changes, you tend to become pretty complacent. However, I did have money that had nothing to do with my magic—real money I'd invested with someone I trusted—or thought I did. But it seems when it rains it pours. Three days after Arch and I were reverted, we went to my bank and what I did have was almost completely gone—so was the person I trusted. Somewhere in the Cayman Islands, I hear."

What a shit wreck of bad luck. "But what about your vampire friends? Surely you couldn't have been the only one who was smart enough to have some kind of tie to the human world—couldn't you contact them? Ask for help?"

"I guess I could have if I'd made many friends in my clan. There were very few people I associated with on many levels, Wanda. Unlike some, I was pretty resentful for a long time about being a vampire to begin with."

"And now you're a human . . ."

Nina was going to shit bats when she told her Heath's tale. A whole flock of them.

Heath's granite face remained impassive, yet curious. He was clearly still waiting for her to flip. "Right." His voice was hesitant while he eyed her with that infamous stare.

"And you found out this sire guy was knocked off from who?" Because a thought had just occurred to her—if what Heath said was true, Nina was going to be soooo pissed when she found out there really was a way to get your mortality back. Oh, the fuck-tards that would zing over that.

"It took about a month or so, but we eventually ran into a clan-mate who'd fared better than us. His life ma—er, wife is human, and he'd had word from some distant clan members in Oregon. Several of us, those of us without real-world attachments, anyway, are pretty much in the same predicament—sort of wandering around with no roots, no money, no homes.

"Anyway, getting to where we are now is a long, drawn-out story, but that's why we've been living at the shelter. We couldn't get jobs anywhere, because we don't exactly have current job skills or people just weren't hiring—so when I saw the Bobbie-Sue ad, admittedly I was pretty unsure when I found out what I'd be doing for that three to five K per month, because it was makeup, but we had nothing left to lose. I didn't care about anything but the cash. It motivated me to get my color wheels in gear."

Well, that definitely explained his drive to sell Bobbie-Sue. The strange urgency in his tone when he'd insisted he could pay her back the money for the starter kit—the deal he'd thought up to do it.

More silence, eerie and still, fanned out between them.

But it wasn't because she was in shock, or freaked out—she wanted to know who'd turned him and why. With Nina it'd been an accident, her life mate, Greg, had a much different story about his turning, and it wasn't pretty—or an accident. "So how exactly did you become a *vampire*?" Wanda wasn't sure if she should come off like she was mocking him for his tale, or if she should allow him to see her genuine interest. She had to be careful with her terminology here. She was way more in the know about the paranormal, and sometimes it bled through in her conversations with humans.

His expression grew hangdog, but his eyes never left hers. "I wasn't exactly what you'd call a gentleman back then. I had a reputation with women I'm not particularly proud of—but there it is. I'd left a dinner party in London, where supposedly I'd flirted with a vampire's mistress. Apparently, a big no-no. I don't remember it, because I was hammered. I'd had way too much to drink, and Arch was with me. Being the good servant he's always been, he wanted to make sure I made it back home safely. Horatio, the vampire who turned me, attacked from out of nowhere, bit me, and drained me almost dry. If you drain a human, you can turn them into—"

"Zombies—soulless creatures."

He cocked his head, clearly wondering how she could finish his statement.

Crap, crap, crap. "Romance novels," she offered in the way of explanation. "I read a lot of them. Especially paranormals. Ya know, vampires, werewolves, et cetera. Some of the stuff you're talking about is in the books I read—you'd be surprised how much, in fact. Sorry." She cast her eyes back down to the sheet. "Please, finish."

"Arch interfered to protect me, scuffled with Horatio and wound up bitten, too. If not for Arch, I'd have ended up really dead instead of undead."

Now she could see the reason for the attachment between the two. Or could she? Better still, *should* she? "So how old were you when you were, uh, bitten?"

"Thirty-six."

"Wasn't that old to be single back then?"

"I made single an art form back then, yeah." He didn't look proud of it, but when she looked back up, his eyes held a sincerity she could almost touch.

"And what about your family?"

"Dead."

This was the part she always wondered about with Nina and Marty. How did you go on and on and watch the people you love die one after the other? Anyone you ever become involved with outside of your paranormal-ness you'd outlive. She put a sympathetic hand on his arm. "I'm sorry. That much I assumed—you being alive for almost two hundred years. What I meant was, what did they have to say about this vampire stuff?"

His jaw stiffened, tension formed in the way of the bulge and twitch of his pecs. "They disowned me. They'd been on me for a long time to marry, lay off the booze, settle down. Had I stayed and anyone human found out what happened to Arch and me, they'd not only have hunted me and Arch down, but they'd have killed my family, too. Can't say as I blame my parents much. I mean, back in the day, vampires weren't what they are today."

She had to be very, very careful here. "And what are they today, Heath?" She let the tone of her voice take on a sarcastic lilt.

But he surprised her with a grin. "No one believes in them with the kind of connotation they did back in my day—which means no one is hunting you down with torches and ropes of garlic, followed by a good dousing of holy water and a stake through the heart." He grinned wider when he finished.

She really shouldn't be encouraging this conversation, but she had to know. "Are you happy being all human again?" She kept the hint of sarcasm in her tone for good measure, but if what he said was true—what a mind fuck.

His chuckle was hearty, carefree—like now that he'd told her something most people would find absurd, he'd been left absolved, cleansed. "Yeah. Yeah, I do. Despite the hardships of the homeless shelter and my job situation. I can eat again. I'd forgotten how much I like a good meal. When I tell you food is much better nowadays than it ever was back then, you can trust me. I found I like Reese's Peanut Butter Cups at Christmas when there were free samples on a counter of some store in the mall. I could eat bagfuls at a time. Beer—Christ, beer is much better in this day and age, and I knew how much I missed the sun, I just didn't know how much I missed the sun until I could go out in it without protective measures, you know?"

Oh, she knew. Nina bitched about it all the time, with colorful words and lewd gestures.

If she had any other women for friends but Marty and Nina, she probably would've called him a lunatic and told him to shove his craziness right up his ass. But it explained a whole lot about Heath. His fancy suit—the *only* suit he owned. It explained his living arrangements, his complete joy at eating a stupid cheese log or a hot dog, and the Rolex he wore on his wrist. So nope, no explanation required. "Oh, well, then, okay," she offered with as much no big deal as she could mix into her voice.

His eyes, wide open now, said it all. "That's it?"

"That's what?"

"That's all you have to say?"

She pretended to be confuzzled, twisting a piece of her hair around her finger. "Well, what else do you want me to say?"

He rolled his tongue along the inside of his cheek, his eyes growing skeptical. "Shouldn't you be pitching a full-on hissy fit and calling me crazy?"

She threw him a nonchalant glance. "Shouldn't you just be glad I'm all easygoing and accept your explanation minus the histrionics?"

Heath ruffled his hair. "I just have to ask."

"Hit me."

"Do you take some kind of medication? That you not only accept my explanation, but haven't freaked out on me, has me worried."

"No meds. I just get it. Isn't that enough?"

"No. I don't think it is."

"Why not?"

"Because that I'm sitting in your bed, telling you I was once a vampire, should make you very afraid that I'm either psychotic or delusional, or at the very least, *crazy*. Oh, and I live in a homeless shelter—with my *manservant*."

"I'm sorry to disappoint you."

He gawked at her. Full-on, eyes round, mouth slightly ajar. God, he had a nice mouth. Great teeth. Fresh breath. Big, girly sigh. In fact, he looked much the way she was sure she had when Marty had revealed she'd been turned into a werewolf. She couldn't begrudge him the astonished thing—it happened, but by now, after this kind of revelation not once, but twice in her life, it was soooo passé.

But he deserved an explanation. Here's where her prior community acting abilities would have to come into play. She couldn't afford to let him get even a hint that she knew just as much if not more about the vampire lifestyle than he did. "Look, here's the thing. You shouldn't have had to tell me anything. I had no business messing in your personal life when I went to the shelter. And when we got, well, involved, intimately last night, I decided I'd just go along for the ride—we enjoyed each other's company. That's enough for me. And if you think you were a vampire, but you aren't anymore, who am I to say you weren't?" *How blasé, Wanda. Who knew you had it in you?*

Heath shook his head, chuckling deep in his throat, as if he were shaking off his disbelief. His dark blond hair wisped over his forehead, his eyes screamed a thousand questions. "If only all humans had been as easy as you—I'd have told everyone I've ever known over the past almost two hundred years."

She thought about that number for a moment. He was a young vampire—Greg was over five hundred now. "Wow. You were a young one, huh? I think the oldest vampire I've ever read about was like almost seven hundred years old. Damn, what was the name of that book . . . *Love's Eternal Bite*. Yes! That was it. I think after seven hundred years I'd get tired of drinking blood, too."

"Love's what?"

"Forget it. It's a romance novel. I told you I read them, and you can keep your smart remarks to yourself about it," she said, giving him a teasing smile.

He put a hand to her very cool cheeks. "Do you hear yourself?"

"Uh-huh. Do you hear *yourself*?"

"I do, and this is crazy. You're crazy."

Wanda made a face at him. "Ahem. *I'm crazy?* Oh, I dunno about that. I mean, aren't you the one who's telling me he was once a vampire? How does my being crazy fit into that equation?"

"Because you *believe* me. That's crazy."

"Well, welcome to crazy, then."

"Care to explain?"

Now that she'd processed some of his story, she wasn't one hundred percent convinced his explanation was fact. While everything fit in his story, that didn't necessarily mean it was true. He enjoyed the simplest of foods like no other. Faint sunlight made him lift that rugged face to the sun almost immediately, but it didn't mean he wasn't lying.

However, was it a totally off the wall coincidence that for the third time in her life someone was telling her they were paranormal? Yeah, it sure the hell was. But he had no proof he was once a vampire. He could call vampire all he liked now, as a supposed human, but she knew paranormal. Hell, she shopped with the real thing—she'd even seen the evidence in the form of a tail on Marty's ass of the real thing.

But no one knew better than she that the knowledge she had about Marty and Nina was something you just didn't talk about to anyone but them and those you *knew* were like them, and she'd never risk endangering two of the people she loved most in the world to prove to anyone she was a believer in the paranormal. So no, she didn't care to explain. Maybe she should have behaved more surprised, but her sense of "no fucking way" had been dulled by her friends' experiences. There wasn't much left that could rock her world. This confession was no exception. "Nope. Not any more than you cared to explain things to me."

He nodded like he suddenly got it. "Was that like a nah-nah-nah on you sort of thing? Like backsies?"

"Nope."

"So you're just going to skip right along as if I didn't tell you I was once a *vampire*? Let me repeat, blood drinking, Dracula-like, night dweller."

"That's the plan."

"C'mon. You don't really believe me."

"Oh, no. I assure you, I believe."

"Do not."

"Do."

"Seriously?"

Wanda finally giggled. "What do you want? An ovary?" For all the good it would do him. "Maybe something in writing?"

He barked a laugh. "Nope. I just want to understand."

Wanda tugged the comforter tighter around her. "Let's look at this rationally. Even if I didn't believe you, is there any way you can prove to me you were once a vampire?"

He chewed on that statement for a minute. "Nope. I guess there isn't."

"Then I think we've hit a wall. You can be whatever you want to be as long as you keep the numbers you've been keeping while I'm still your regional rep. Vampire, ghost, werewolf, ballerina. It's all the same to me."

He had the audacity to grin and chuck her under the chin. "So now I'm just a number?"

She threw on the hat she wore often when Nina and Marty sparred. Her hard-ass hat. She had to if she hoped to come off sounding even remotely like someone's fuck buddy. "Um, stop me if my memory's failed me, but wasn't it you who said, and I quote, 'I shouldn't get involved. Let's just see what happens' after our mattress stomp last night?"

"Nope. I said I shouldn't get involved, yet here I was, and then I said let's just see what happens. I didn't say a thing about a mattress," he added smartly, giving her another cocky grin that made the deep grooves on either side of his mouth stand out.

"Right. So you could get me into bed. Now I remember. Sorry." Oh, she was all about the cold and callous. That these words were even coming from her mouth was a testament to how afraid she was to get any closer to Heath than she was at this moment. This wasn't very Wanda-ish. She didn't do noncommittal sex, and she totally sucked at dissing anyone, but if she hoped to maintain a careful distance from Heath and his fabulousness, his incredible charisma, she had to.

Heath crossed his arms over his chest. "Uh, no, Wanda. That wasn't it at all. If you'll recall, you were the one who just moments ago was giving me the 'this is just sex' speech. I wasn't the *only* one who said they shouldn't get involved."

"Which must have made it that much easier for your conscience. It meant you didn't have to worry about any pressure from me for sticky stuff like relationships and commitment and all the other emotionally draining crap clingy females seem to want these days." Who the fuck was she? Spouting stuff she'd read in *Cosmo* like she lived it. She loved emotionally draining crap . . . she lived for it—breathed it.

That smile wasn't leaving his face. It'd begun to reek smug. "While that was true when we first met, it doesn't mean that's how I feel now—even after the sticky stuff. I didn't want to get involved with anyone because of the situation I'm in, but my situation is improving. You're well aware I just collected a fairly decent paycheck from Bobbie-Sue, and Arch and I found an apartment today, and I got a cell phone. So consider my mind changed." His look was pleased.

Her chest tightened, as did her hands on the sheets. "Well,

nothing's changed for me. I still don't want to get involved be-yond . . . this . . ." Those words—so simple, so direct—left her mouth because they had to, not because she meant them. If time weren't a factor, she'd beat off color wheel whores for miles with her high heels just to spend all of it with Heath—to have the time to find out if they could have something more than a passing fling.

"Okay," he said, smiling and rising from the bed to throw on his jeans.

Tears stung her eyes. He'd leave now because she'd treated him like so much meat. And it was nothing less than she deserved. *But you got what you wanted, didn't you, Wanda? A nice toss in the sack with a few eyeball-rolling orgasms to top it off. You're officially a bitch. Good on you.*

Heath threw her bathrobe at her. "Put that on. I can't prom-ise I won't jump those pretty bones of yours if you eat hot dogs naked."

"But—"

"No buts," he said, grinning with that cocky half tilt to it. "Naked and hot dogs just won't work," he said over his shoulder on his way out of the bedroom.

Wanda slid to the end of the bed. She should be tweaked he hadn't up and left. That's what any woman who really just wanted to keep things uninvolved would be, but instead she found herself smiling, too.

Stupidly—from ear to ear.

Heath wasn't leaving. He was in her kitchen preparing to cook hot dogs.

With chili.

The relief of that left her shaking and weak. However, she shouldn't be relieved—she should want him gone, just like all good fuck buddies would when the naughty was over. Yet here she was—glad he was still around.

Maybe he was just being nice . . .

He had just confessed to once being a playa—he clearly understood the uninvolved game far better than she ever could. But did men who agreed to be uninvolved stick around after the boffing was over to cook hot dogs? And, if she was going to keep this a sex-only kind of thing, why was it making her batshit that he hadn't protested when she'd laid the rules of the game on the table?

She should just make him go whether he cooperated or not. It was selfish of her not to push the issue.

So here she was not pushing, and it didn't soothe her conscience one itsy-bitsy bit that she'd been as honest as she possibly could be with him, and he was still here.

And he was still in the kitchen.

And she was still smiling.

CHAPTER
13

"So Wanda doesn't want to get"—Heath swiped his fingers in the air to make quotation marks—"involved. I got the 'let's keep this just about the sex' speech."

Arch's sagging jaw quivered when he chuckled. "Bully for you, sir."

"No. Not bully for me," Heath said, sticking a fork into the potpie he'd pulled from the oven in their new apartment to see if the crust was done.

"Isn't that exactly how you like your women, Heathcliff— with no involvements? I'd daresay you should be jumping up and down."

"Not this time, Arch."

"Has there ever been a different kind of time?"

His smile was rueful. "No. I guess there hasn't. Our lifestyle didn't really allow for it, though."

Arch shook a gnarled, wrinkled finger at him in admonishment.

"Ahhh, no, young Heathcliff. 'Twas *your* lifestyle that didn't allow for it. There wasn't any reason you couldn't have had a committed relationship with another vampire—you simply chose not to."

His grin was purposefully sheepish. "All right. That's true. I wasn't ever interested enough for anything serious, but getting involved with anyone other than a vampire when I was one, too, just didn't work for me. I'd live forever, and they wouldn't. I did take that into consideration, you know. However, I just never met the right vampire, and we all know I only had so many years to do that before I met my demise or became lunch for a dust cloth. It's been freeing knowing I'm not tied to that kind of clan rule anymore. I like knowing there's no time limit for me to find a mate—er, life partner. I just never expected to meet someone like Wanda so early in the human game. And, yes, Arch, you're right, I didn't exactly want anything permanent either."

"Precisely. And Miss Wanda has changed that, how?"

Heath didn't have words to explain why he found Wanda more attractive than any other woman he'd ever met. One minute he'd just thought she was hot, a little overzealous about color auras and Bobbie-Sue, the next he was peeling back layers of her personality like an onion, and liking her more the deeper he went. Getting much from her was like pulling teeth, even after he'd told her he was once a vampire. At first he'd thought she wouldn't talk about even the most noncommittal things because he wouldn't. Then he figured she was just in shock about what he'd told her. Now, the vestiges of his leftover vampirism told him something else.

Heath leaned against the rusted metal sink. "I got nuthin'. She just is. She just works. She makes sense. She rambles when she's nervous—her eyes light up when she talks about some volunteer work she does for cancer patients, and bingo night at the senior citizens' home. Her smile makes me smile. The more she pushes me away, the closer she drags me in." His shoulders heaved upward.

"Does anyone ever have a logical explanation for what makes one woman stand out from all the rest?"

Arch pulled the new dishtowels they'd purchased from the Wal-Mart bag, folding them into a neat stack on the cracked kitchen counter. "Could it be that she's elusive, sir? That she doesn't want any of these involvements you speak of? Surely that would make her more of a challenge—more exciting to a man such as yourself who once enjoyed the bed sport like some men enjoy say, hunting or fishing."

Heath closed the oven door and crossed his arms over his chest, licking the fork while he thought. "Nope. That's not it. I decided I wanted her *before* she told me no involvements."

Archibald threw a dramatic hand over his forehead. "How crushing to your ego, Heathcliff." He cocked a gray eyebrow at Heath, clearly reminding him he'd said what Wanda'd said to him at least a hundred times. "Payback was a bitch" was the message. But Heath wasn't buying it.

"Nah, I'm not crushed."

Arch pursed his lips. "I don't understand."

"I'm not crushed, because I know she doesn't really mean the crap she spews."

Archibald snorted as he put the towels into a drawer that was crooked and misaligned. "Could you possibly be pulling the pro- verbial wool over your own eyes, young man?"

"Nope. She wants more—I just can't figure out what's holding her back. But I will."

"And how will you do that if she won't let you?"

"I'll wear her the fuck down, Arch. I'll wear her down till she screams uncle."

"Oh, I'm ever so positive that will go over well, sir. By all means, wear away. As for me, I believe I'm going to make use of the shower. Our very *own* shower. Forgive my fit of unbelievable joy as I do—while you plot the winning of the fair Wanda, that is." Arch grabbed the new package of underwear they'd bought at Wal-Mart, then looked over his shoulder directly at Heath. "I do have a question, if you don't mind me prying."

As if Archibald had ever had a problem sticking his cultured nose where it didn't belong. "Pry on, old man."

"Does the fair Wanda not wonder why you're selling cosmetics and were, as early as two days ago, living in a homeless shelter?"

"She does."

"And your explanation?"

"I told her the truth."

"Everything?"

Heath's nod was sober. "Everything."

Archibald's face distorted in horror. "And you wonder why she doesn't want to become involved with you? I'm certain she's in the process of notifying the local authorities as we speak. Authorities who will certainly come and haul you away to one of those seedy clinics where they drug you into a stupor and leave you to pickle in your own filth. How could you, Heathcliff?"

Heath held up a hand to stave off Arch's misgivings. "It wasn't like that at all, Arch. In fact, I think I'm more freaked out because she wasn't more freaked out." And he was. Freaked out. He'd told her what most would consider a tale so wild he should be in the nuthouse—but she hadn't batted an eye. Not one pretty hair on her head had moved. Even if her real deal was that she didn't want to get involved—she still should have had a far bigger reaction than she'd offered. Which left him suspicious and intrigued at the same time.

Arch's voice took on a low tone, almost a whisper. "She didn't freak out? Sir!" he hissed. "You told her we were once vampires, and she didn't become the least distressed? I hate to be the bearer of bad news, but I have to believe she really is in this strictly for the bedroom sport. No sane woman would believe you—let alone accept such an outrageous explanation!"

"Yep. Something's just not right about that. But it isn't because she's only in it for the bedroom sport. I may not have most of my typical vampire qualities anymore, but I have some residual abilities—and I get a glimpse into her mind from time to time. You have them, too, Arch. You know exactly what I mean."

Arch's nod was sharp. "I do indeed, and they're fading fast. But need I remind you, the mind is a very tricky thing—you can convince yourself of almost anything if you want it badly enough. And it's evident the fair Wanda is something you want enough to make yourself believe almost anything. Like the idea that she returns your affections in a deeper manner than the sport of the bed." His smile was rueful. "I never thought I'd see the day, Heathcliff. The day you'd find yourself wishing for more than just the physical pleasures of a woman. I find myself misty over it, in fact. So misty I'm taking my leave and showering before I embarrass myself with my delight." Arch took sure steps down the very short hallway to their antiquated shower without looking back.

Heath glanced around at this place they'd now call home. Paint peeled from the walls, the cabinets in the kitchen were crooked and splintered, the floors were warped and rippled.

It was a far cry from their former home filled with luxuries in Manalapan.

But it was cheap—and it beat the shit out of a cot at the homeless shelter with a bunch of drunks and drug users.

And it was a place to bring Wanda.

Whether she wanted to be brought or not.

He didn't get what her bullshit speech about fuck buddies was about—it wasn't how she really felt. Wanda didn't have it in her to have that kind of relationship. He'd had plenty over his long lifetime with women who'd wanted the same—Wanda just wasn't like those women.

And he had no intention of letting her get away with trying to feed him that crap. He'd watched her struggle with her attempt at remaining detached last night, in word and thought, but her pretty face held a million different emotions, all emotions even someone who wasn't a vampire could read if they tried hard enough.

However, he did intend to find out what she was hiding from him, and why the hell she'd listened to what he'd told her without blinking an eye.

Something was up.

He was officially on the hunt for whatever that something was.

"So I need you to do me a favor, Nina." Wanda sat across from Nina and Marty at their favorite diner, Hogan's, pushing her fries into a pile.

Nina gave her the eye. "First, stop playing with your food. If anyone could use a good meal, it's you, and, Wanda, I swear to Christ, if you want me to go to that dumb-assed community production of *Cats*, I'll just scream. I swear. I'm not up to hearing amateurs trash a perfectly good song like 'Memories.' And don't give me that bullshit that the money's for the senior citizens' home. You secretly like it—it has nothing to do with building those horny toads a conjugal visit room, and you know it."

Wanda raised a hand, palm forward. "It's nothing like that. Honest. No more *Cats*."

"So what's up?" Marty inquired, tearing into her heaping plate of rare steak and eggs.

Her look was secretive. "I need Nina to talk to Greg."

"About?"

"About Heath."

Nina eyed her from across the diner's scarred and yellowed Formica table. "What about him?"

"I have something to tell you guys, but you have to promise you'll look into it for me. Because you have all those vampiric connections and all."

"Could we get where we're going with this, Wanda?" Nina's look went from curious to suspicious.

Wanda leaned into them and whispered, "He says he was once a vampire."

Nina laughed derisively. "Yeah, and I was once Mother Theresa."

Marty's derisive snort made her choke on a piece of her steak. Nina thwacked her on the back.

"Nina!" Wanda snapped her fingers together to quiet her. "I'm serious, and I need you to ask Greg about him. I mean, I figure he'd maybe know someone who could verify it, right?"

Nina flicked the napkin Wanda held. "Wanda? He couldn't have been a vampire because he's a human. He's off his rocker. Time for Heath to go, and I can take care of that." Nina began to wiggle out of their booth, but Wanda grabbed her arm, pushing her back down into the red vinyl booth with a hard shove.

She looked around to see if anyone else had heard them. "Will you just wait! God, Nina. Gimme a chance to explain here. Now stop rushing off to beat people up and listen to me, please."

Nina's look was impatient, but she waved a hand in Wanda's direction. "Fine. Speak."

Wanda huffed back at Nina, while Marty continued to shovel food between her lips, occasionally swiping delicately at her mouth with a napkin. Wanda settled back in the booth and looked them both in the eye. "I have to say, it all makes sense. It explains why he's living in a homeless shelter with his manservant, of all things.

If you knew anything about *manservants*, you'd know that term was practically extinct in this day and age. It explains why he acts like my cheese log is lobster tails—"

"Well," Marty said with a full mouth, "it *is* a rockin' cheese log."

"Shit, dude. I so remember. It was all kinds of awesomeness," Nina agreed with a regretful tinge to her tone.

"It's good, *dude*," Wanda mocked Nina. "But it isn't worthy of the eye rolls and groans of delight he spews. Either way, what he told me last night explains a lot."

"Last night?" Nina perked up.

"Yes. Last night."

"Uh, don't cold calls end at like three on Fridays so you crazy Bobbie-Sue bitches can begin the animal sacrifice at sundown?"

Wanda leaned forward, narrowing her eyes at Nina. "One more snide remark, Nina, and I'm going to pop you. There are no animal sacrifices."

"*Riiiight,*" Nina dragged the word out. "It's a cult without the animal sacrifices. Still doesn't explain why you were with him at night."

She shrugged her shoulders in her denim jacket. "I don't have to explain."

Marty dropped her fork, swallowing her food with a hard gulp. "You-did-him!"

Nina cackled. "My, sistah! Gimme one." She held up her hand for a high five.

Wanda threw a french fry at her. "Could we not share that with all of Hackensack?"

"So was it goooood?" Nina cooed. She watched Wanda's face change. "Never mind. I can see it written all over your face."

Marty smiled, reaching across the table to grasp Wanda's hand. "Aw, honey. It was good, huh? So tell us, did you—you know?"

Yeah, she knew. Yeah, she had. Wow, she had. Multiple good-ness. "That's not why I asked you guys to meet me."

"Don't be shy, Wanda. We tell you details." Nina looked offended.

"For which I'll be forever grateful during my long, dry, sexless season," she drawled back.

"So you're doing the homeless guy. Did you give him the speech?" Nina asked.

Her face instantly caught fire with shame. She'd tried again after dinner—failed—and had another date with him tonight. "Could we just get to the point here?"

"Okay, okay. Sorry," Nina apologized. "Go ahead. Tell me all about the guy who says he was a vampire and who's now human—which is impossible, but whatever."

Finally. "Okay, this is what he said. Heath says he was turned back in London almost two hundred years ago by a vampire who he'd pissed off at some party. He'd made a pass at the vampire's mistress or something. This guy, Horatio, jumped him when he and Archibald, the guy who was with Heath in the homeless shel-ter, were walking home. Heath had had too much to drink. This Horatio bit Heath, and when Archibald interfered, he bit him, too. Anyway, Horatio's sire, one of five original vampires left from the beginning of the world as we know it, and the people responsible for creating vampire clans, was killed recently." She dragged a fin-ger across her neck.

Nina tilted her jaw defensively upward. "Killed how, Wanda?"

"He was a logger in Oregon. His truck was hit head-on by another truck carrying logs. The log staked him, Horatio's sire, and by proxy, Heath's sire, too, in the heart, and in the accident, his head was severed as well. We've both done enough reading to know what that means." She shuddered, as did Nina.

But Nina's eyebrows furrowed. "Okay. So? How does that make Heath and the manservice guy a human?"

"Man*servant*," Wanda corrected, pushing up the sleeves of her cropped jacket. "This is the part I think will really hack you off, Nina, and in advance, I'm crazy sorry, but save the screaming hissy fit for later. Heath said it's like the domino effect. When their original—*original* being the key word here—sire was offed, it turned Heath and anyone else turned via this sire back into humans. But it totally explains so much about him. Heath says he still doesn't understand why they were left with only the clothes on their back, and that crazy Yugo of Archibald's. One morning they woke up in what was once their driveway with the clothes on their backs and nothing else."

Nina jabbed a finger into the hard surface of the table. "Hold the fuck on. What you're telling me is Greg's sire, that whacked bitch Lisanne, once had a sire who turned her, too, and this person, whoever it was, can turn me back into a human if I kick the wings off him?"

Wanda nodded, wincing. "If what Heath says is true . . ."

Nina sat for a good, long while—stunned.

Marty broke the silence. "But hold on there, Mohammad Ali. If you kill Lisanne's sire, technically also Greg's and yours, as well, if what Heath says is true—you'd be screwing a lot of vampires. So don't go there. That'd be like mass vampiricide. And this isn't about you—it's about Wanda and that nut she's sleeping with."

Wanda gasped in outrage. "Wait a freakin' second. Why is he a nut? Are you two nuts? You're both super-paranormal. Why couldn't Heath have been, too? And, Nina, I'm sorrrry. I really didn't know the stuff about the first vampires roaming the planet. I guess if there's only four now, finding the original sire to your clan might not be so hard."

Nina cracked her knuckles and her jaw simultaneously. She'd obviously thought about the repercussions Marty mentioned. "Actually, I gotta tell you the truth—I'm okay as a vampire. If I'd known this a few months ago, it might be different, but now I'm okay. Shocked as all hell, but in a good space. I do have to wonder what my man will have to say about this—or if he even knew it was possible. That's what would hack me off more than anything else—if he knew something like this was possible and just never told me." She shook her silky, dark head as if she knew that was impossible. "So why did Heath end up in a homeless shelter, Wanda? If he was vamp and for as long as you say, he'd have a lot of shit."

"Because much like you and your mind-over-matter craziness, almost everything he owned was created via mind control and that vampire magic you haven't mastered yet. He did have some investments, but he claims the guy took off with his money, and he didn't find out about it until three days after he was reverted. In light of this particular revelation, if it has even a grain of truth, I'd say that's something you and Greg might want to think about— like securing investments in the real world—building a *real* castle. If, by some fluke, something like this should go down—you guys would need a really big cardboard box." A good portion of Greg's, and now Nina's, wealth had been acquired via this vampire magic—much like the means Heath had described. Some crazy conjuring up of monetary things with their minds—which almost freaked her out as much as Nina's flying did.

"Holy. Jesus," Nina muttered.

Wanda's nod was grave. "Yeah. Precisely."

Nina flipped open her cell phone. "What's his clan's name again? Is it Jefferson like him?"

"I don't know. I didn't ask, because if I got too involved in that conversation we had, I might give away what I know. It was hard enough as it was."

"Did you tell him about us?" Marty asked.

Wanda was almost offended. "Don't be silly. Of course not. But do you have any idea how hard it was to cover up my lack of surprise? I mean, hearing a tale like that is kinda so five minutes ago for me, after you two."

Nina held up a hand, sliding out from the booth to head outside. "Okay, let me see what I can find out from Greg—then we'll decide what to do."

"There's nothing to decide, Nina, because we're just—just—" Wanda stumbled on her words.

Nina and Marty exchanged glances. "Doing each other—yeah, we know. I guess a guy would share something as killa huge like that because he was just *doing* you. Or maybe he thought it'd be crazy cool to try and impress a chick with the notion he was once a vampire. That'd be a new and refreshing take on making an impact on someone."

Wanda feigned indifference in Nina's direction, and she was getting damned good at it, keeping her face as unreadable as possible. "Well, that's all it is to me."

"You keep telling yourself that, Wanda—I'll be right back." Nina strode out the silver door of the diner.

"Sure that's all it is to you, honey," Marty chimed in. "That's why you give a rat's ass if he's telling the truth," she said sarcastically.

Wanda became thin-lipped. "I'm just curious."

"Yeaaahhhhh."

Wanda stuck her tongue out at Marty. "Stop mocking me."

"Me, mock? Nope. I'm a believer. You're just doing this guy. That's cool by me."

How in all things carnal did women do this? Remain so casual about the man they were giving their bodies to? She liked Heath far too much out of bed to treat what they'd done in bed so informally. Never in a million years, when he'd come to her door that night after she'd been to the shelter, had she ever thought he'd want something—anything more than a sexual relationship. Now he implied it left and right, and she didn't quite know how to deal with that. But she couldn't stop the tingle she felt when she thought about him. There was no thwarting the erratic beat of her heart when she heard his voice on the new cell phone he'd bought.

And it all had to end.

"Wanda?"

She clenched her eyes once before opening them to look into Marty's. "Yeah?"

Marty's voice was filled with concern. "Do you wanna tell me what's really going on? If what Heath says is true, then he told you because he's doing that open and honest new millennium relationship stuff. That means this is more than just sex to him. If it were just sex, he'd boink you, go home, come back and boink you again. He wouldn't give a shit if you cared whether he was homeless or not. All you need is a bed when you're just slamming each other, honey."

Marty cupped her chin in her hand and gave Wanda a thoughtful gaze. "I know you, Wanda Schwartz. You don't casually have sex. George, the putz, was the only man you'd ever slept with. If casual sex were your thing—you'd have been doing it long before now. What are you afraid of where Heath's concerned? That if you get involved he'll steal your independence the way George did? That he'll control you the way he did? You're a different woman now, honey. So much different than even six months ago. You won't let that happen, because you're empowered. Nina and I wouldn't let that happen either. So why not just fall, sweetie? Nothing would make Nina and me happier than to see you happy. We want you to have what we have. You know, your HEA."

Yeah . . . happily ever after didn't look likely at this point. If only she could just explain to them why she couldn't fall, but she wasn't ready yet. "I'm just not ready to fall, Marty. I'm not ready. My divorce was ugly—I'm just getting back on my feet. Isn't playing the field all part of being divorced these days?" Because truly, she was such a playa.

"It is—but a player, you're not." Marty bowed her head for a moment; when she looked back up at Wanda, her eyes couldn't hide the fact that she just didn't understand this Wanda. "Okay. I won't pressure you. Just hear what I've said, all right?"

Nina bustled back in, slipping into the booth once more, taking the pressure off Wanda to say anything more. "Well, a liar he ain't."

Wanda's eyes widened, her hands suddenly clammy and cold. "It's true? He really was once a vampire?"

Nina gave her a thumbs-up. "Yep. This Horatio dude was some badass mutha, too. Greg knew exactly who I meant. Horatio's sire was some guy named something I can't even pronounce. Greg made a couple of calls, called me back, and bam. Heath's telling the truth. He was well known in certain vampiric circles."

Wanda was astounded. "Then why didn't you guys know about this? Don't you vampires keep in touch with emails or something? How could something this big have happened without you knowing about it? It's basically a cure for you. Remember that little thing you were looking for a few months ago, and threatening bodily harm if someone didn't give you back your mortality?"

"Yeah, I remember, but not all of the clan feel like I do—did. It's like Marty said, it wouldn't just be me I turned back if I hunted down one of these sires. And Greg and I are in the honeymoon stage of things—you know, we're doing each other all the time—kind of the way you and Heath are . . ." Nina let her words sit with Wanda. When she refused to react, Nina added, "I guess we were out of the vampire loop, but Greg says maybe some vampire rescue is in order. I don't know how he'll locate thousands of clan members turned human if there are no records of them in the human world, but we can't just let them piss in the wind." Nina's face had sympathetic written all over it.

God, Nina had grown so much over the past year. She took other people into consideration with regularity, and she was getting better at showing it, too. Nina was growing, changing, being with Greg and his mother, Svetlanna, and that made Wanda smile. Nina would be well taken care of if anything ever happened to her grandmother Lou. She wouldn't be alone, and Wanda let that comfort her.

Marty flagged the waitress down to get more water. "So what are you going to do, Wanda?"

Her composure would surely slip if she let them hammer her any more. She grabbed her purse and pushed out of the booth. "There's nothing to do. So he was a vampire—now he's a human. Human, vampire, it's all the same to me."

She only caught a glimpse of Marty and Nina's surprise before she made a conscious effort to leave in a calm, orderly fashion.

It took every last ounce of effort she had not to run from the diner, run from her friends, but most especially—run from Heath.

CHAPTER
14

"Miss Schwartz, again, the pleasure is all mine." Archibald, Heath's manservant—*manservant*—opened the door and waved her in with a formal hand.

Wanda couldn't help but smile. Seeing Archibald in this setting, dressed as though he'd just opened the door to royalty, was surreal. The smell that greeted her nose was heavenly—clearly hot dogs weren't on the menu. "Hi, Archibald. It's good to see you again, too." The apartment was drab, and that was being kind. The paint was peeling, the floors were warped, and they had not a stick of furniture—but neither of them showed an ounce of shame or apology.

And it made Wanda admire Heath that much more—which she shouldn't be doing, but in light of the fact that that's all she'd been doing lately, she accepted it.

Heath, big and sculpted, was in the kitchen. He wore a black, tight-fitting sweater and jeans that made her gulp because her mouth was so dry. "Hey," he called, the indentations on either side of his mouth deepening.

The warmth in her belly spread up and directly to her cheeks. "So what's for dinner tonight? Is it hot dogs—or maybe mac and cheese from a box?" she teased.

"Bah!" Archibald scoffed, raising an eyebrow and pushing past the folding chair in the nearly empty living room to shoo Heath from the kitchen. "I'm in charge of your dining pleasure this evening, Miss Schwartz. And you can thank the heavens above for such. There will be no boxes or processed pork products involved. Of this I can assure you. Now if you'll excuse me, I'm off to tend to the duck and fingerling potatoes. You two go get comfortable on—on the *floor*." He rolled his eyes at that, gliding off to the kitchen to handle the duck in the oven that smelled so good.

Wanda's gaze toward Heath was hesitant. "Duck, huh? Did that like kill your budget, or what?"

He held out his hand, and she slid hers into it like she'd always been doing it. "You're worth the Ramen Noodles we'll eat for the next two weeks. Arch can be very creative when he has to. It was actually him who insisted on cooking."

"I think I know why."

"Why's that?"

"Because aside from your eggs and coffee, your cooking sucks."

He chuckled, the deep rumble from his throat sending goose bumps along her arms. "Well, it's not your cheese log, that's for sure."

"Oh, I forgot. I brought you something." She dug around in her purse, pulling out a lumpy package.

"For me? Wow, Ms. Schwartz—you know what that means, don't you?"

She peered at him with cautious eyes. "What?"

He pulled her closer, tucking her under his arm and running a hand along her hip. "It means you've been thinking about me. Not very *uninvolved* of you, eh? So whad'ja bring me?"

Okay, so she'd been thinking about him. Okay, so she'd thought of nothing else. Big whoop. She held up the bag, now with reluctance. If he'd pinned her for thinking about him before, for sure he'd have her pegged now. "These. And it's just like bringing wine to a dinner party. Nothing more, nothing less." Humph. *And no, Wanda, that didn't sound petty or churlish at all.*

He snatched the bag from her fingers and held it up to the light that hung in the middle of the living room. Heath's grin was smug. "Well, well. How very *uninvolved* of you." He popped the bag open, unwrapping the wrapper that surrounded his favorite candy, and popped one into his mouth. His eyes instantly closed, his delicious mouth formed a smile of satisfaction. He took another out, unwrapped it with nimble fingers, and popped it into her mouth. The gesture, his fingertips against her lips, so intimate it made her bones melt, made her accept the candy, attempt to revel in it the way he did.

"There's nothing like a Reese's Peanut Butter Cup, huh?"

"Heathcliff," Archibald called from the kitchen, leaning over the small breakfast bar and giving Heath a stern look. "Do not spoil the dining treasure I'm creating with hedonistic cooking ware from Wal-Mart. This duck cost the earth, not to mention I've been preparing it all afternoon so the fair Wanda wouldn't have to suffer through that ghastly block of meat you called Spam. Which, I might add, was Heath's intention." He wagged a wooden spoon at Heath.

Wanda giggled and found herself leaning her head against the hard nub of Heath's shoulder.

Heath's chin rested on the top of her head. "You want a beer?"

"No, thanks. Not much of a drinker. It makes me stupid."

"You mind if I have one?"

"I'd never deny you something you couldn't have for two hundred years."

"About that—"

Shit. No more personal stuff. If you must eat with the man, then chow down, but no more delving into his life. No more comments about where he came from—if he was a vampire or a fireman. The less said the better, dipshit. "No—don't say a word. You don't have to explain anything else."

His eyes held amusement. "Right, 'cause that would be a sort of a couple thing and all—and we don't want to do couple things, because we're not *invoooolved*," he drew out the last word, then grinned.

Once more, he joked a lot about her desire to remain uninvolved, but hadn't ever seriously stated his desires. And he had confessed to once being the ultimate in playas, she reminded herself for the umpteenth time. Though lately, she wondered if it wasn't just a convenient tactic to soothe her conscience. "About that—"

"No—don't say a word. You don't have to explain anything else," he repeated her words verbatim. "I say we venture out to my fancy verandah and stargaze. That's very uninvolved, don'tcha think?" He pointed to the glass door that led outside.

Wanda grabbed her coat and scarf. "It's a fire escape, funny man."

"Well, it's the closest thing to a verandah I've got. You wanna?" He held out his hand to her once more and wiggled his eyebrows.

Taking it, letting the warmth of his flesh sear hers, stabbed at her heart. "I guess that's not such a couple thing. Lot's of uninvolved people look at stars together," she said, keeping her tone breezy and light.

The air was heavy and moist with the possibility of another snowfall. The sky dark streaks of purple and slashes of lighter grays. Archibald knocked on the glass, holding up a Styrofoam cup with steam pouring out of the top. "Hot cocoa, miss." He looked up at the sky and sniffed. "I believe more snow is on tap. This will keep you warm." He bowed his way out of the sliding glass door after Wanda thanked him.

"It's really raw out here tonight," she commented, wrapping her fingers around the cup Arch had given her.

Heath took a deep breath, blowing it out in a frosty stream. "Yep, and I can feel it. Means I'm alive."

She stood next to him against the black railing of the fire escape, their elbows touching, watching as he took a long pull of his beer. "I'm going to take a wild stab here, but I'm guessing you like being human again a whole lot more than you thought you would."

He looked surprised and amused that she'd brought something personal up again, but he didn't snark her for it this time. "I do. I'd forgotten how much until I ate a chicken wing and a whole bag of Reese's Peanut Butter Cups. I didn't realize how many things I missed about being human."

Wanda cocked her head, her hair ruffling as the breeze picked up, the shoulder-length strands blurring her vision. "But all of your stuff . . ."

Heath shrugged his wide shoulders with disinterest. "It was just stuff. You can always get more stuff. I just bought some stuff today." He cocked his head toward Archibald in the kitchen.

His incredibly well-adjusted attitude about losing everything made her heart shift in her chest. Yeah. It *was* just stuff, and the saying that you can't take it with you was crazy true. "So you don't miss anything about being a vampire? Nothing?"

Heath's expression was contemplative. It was almost as if being a vampire had been a weird-assed dream he'd just woken up from. "Not a whole lot, no. Sometimes I miss not having to struggle, but I didn't ask to be a vampire. Though Arch and I joke a lot about it and how I became one. I tend to think it was a wake-up call for me. I lived a life of excess, and Arch was always bailing me out for it. I didn't just pay by way of hangovers and angry husbands, so did he—because one of the angry husbands I pissed off ended up biting him, and I always regretted that he had something stolen from him, too. Arch didn't ask to be a vampire. He became one defending my honor and saving my ass. I was long past the point in my life where I should have been boozing and womanizing."

"Womanizing?" Yes, dumb ass. You know sort of what you're doing to Heath, only in reverse? Don't play ignorant—it isn't in your color wheel. It's like manizing or something.

He swallowed a gulp of his beer and held her gaze. "Yep. I took advantage a lot more than I care to admit. So I kinda get your push to be uninvolved—no strings thing. I've done that more times than I can count. I just don't want to do it anymore." He let his last words sit between them—they hung in the air like helium balloons, hovering, floating.

When she didn't respond, because defending her position would only make things worse, he said, "I think having eternity handed to you is a lot like that divorce you spoke of. You go one way or the other. Either you behave as though you're untouchable and wreak havoc, or you become more guarded—cautious. I became more cautious."

Her hair blew in her face again, and Heath brushed the strands away with cold fingers. "Being a vampire kinda breeds caution, no?"

"It breeds a lot of things. Things I wasn't prepared for. Some things I miss. I tend to forget that I can't just conjure something up in my mind anymore. If I think it, it won't necessarily materialize.

But I kinda like knowing I earned the cup you're drinking from right now."

She sipped the rich, frothy chocolate from her cup while she pondered materializing things. Nina couldn't do that . . . "You could make things materialize?" It was out before she could stop it. She was at home with conversations like these. Flying, shifting, friggin' drinking blood. Even though she had confirmation from Nina that what Heath said was true—that he'd really been a vampire—she found herself more than hesitant to reveal why she was so comfortable. It was personal—her friends and their paranormal-palooza experiences weren't supposed to be his business if they were just . . . God, she couldn't even think it, let alone say it. The phrase *fuck buddies* was such an ugly description—not just about how she was coming to feel, but it negated the conversations they'd shared late into the night, the arm she'd tucked under his possessively when they'd napped the other day.

"Some things, yep."

Wanda flashed him a grin. "That's a pretty cool gig to have. My friend Nina can . . ." Oh, snap. Christ and a sidecar. Next time she was with Heath, she was bringing the duct tape and wrapping it around her head and over her big, freakin' mouth.

"What about her?"

"Uh—I bet she'd love to make stuff materialize. She's very, very materialistic. *Very*," she added for good measure. Nina was the last person on the planet who cared about anything remotely materialistic. Now Marty . . .

His forehead creased, and he jammed a hand into the pocket of his jeans. "You know, I just have to say this once more. I haven't said anything for a while now because I'm still not sure what to say. But I don't get it."

"What don't you get?"

"That you don't think I'm crazy—or at the very least, a liar."

Wanda let her head hang for fear he'd read her thoughts. She fought to keep her voice impersonal and carefree. "I think you can think you were once whatever you want to. I'm a firm believer in the power of the mind."

"It's not like I told you I was once a doctor or a lawyer, Wanda. I told you I was once a vampire. *A vampire.*"

"Uh-huh. I heard you last night, and I still hear you tonight."

He nudged her shoulder with his. "I guess I should just be glad you accept my explanation—but it's definitely been the cause of some deep thought."

"I say you should just call yourself lucky and shut up before reality sets in and I wake up from this fugue-like state and really freak out on you," she joked, nudging his shoulder back.

He caught her with one hand around the waist and pulled her under his arm. The shelter he provided, the broad width of his chest pressed to her side made her bite the inside of her cheek. She found herself just wanting to spill her guts. Right at his feet. She wanted to tell him she knew he wasn't lying. Why she couldn't let this thing between them get too deep. Why she kept herself at arm's length. But what would that do? Ruin it. Who wanted to wonk a dying chick?

No one.

Heath wouldn't be so eager to get involved if he knew she had one foot in the grave. He'd probably do some of that freaking out he worried she'd do. Telling someone you were dying beat telling them you were a vampire probably every time.

"Penny for them," he whispered against her cheek.

She smiled, closing her eyes and letting his cologne penetrate her senses. "You don't have a penny."

His laughter vibrated against her cheek. "Not after that damned meal Arch is cooking in there, I don't."

Her laughter tinkled on the frosty air totally uninhibited. "We could have had hot dogs and Reese's Peanut Butter Cups. I would have been okay with that."

Arch waved to them from the big glass window, signaling dinner was ready.

"No one eats my Reese's Peanut Butter Cups without my permission. It's the one thing I don't share well." He kissed her on the tip of her nose before dragging open the stiff, creaky glass door. The delicious scent of dinner invaded her nostrils, but when they entered the kitchen, her chest felt empty. Keeping their conversation impersonal left her feeling unfulfilled. There was so much she wanted to ask—so much she wanted to share with him.

That's because this kind of relationship just isn't for you, Wanda Schwartz, her conscience nagged.

How long could she keep this up before her guilt ate a hole in her gut?

DINNER was incredible. The duck crisp on the outside, succulent and tender inside. Wanda was still savoring it as she helped Archibald clear the table while Heath began to wash the dishes.

"So do you like the new apartment, Archibald?" Wanda asked, passing him the paper plate of leftover potatoes.

Archibald's smile was broad, crinkling the lines of his already deeply lined face. "I daresay it's better than where we were, miss. I don't need much. I do, however, enjoy not having to hoard my personal belongings like a squirrel hoards acorns to keep those heathens at the shelter at bay."

Wanda chuckled, giving him a warm smile. "I bet there's some big plusses to that."

Archibald rolled his eyes, throwing the kitchen towel over his shoulder. "Oh, miss. If you only knew the things I've seen—been forced to endure for my Heathcliff."

There was genuine tenderness in his words when he said Heath's name. Two hundred years of it, Wanda supposed. "I take it you've done a lot of that for Heath. I bet he's in good hands with you."

"He's in his rightful hands, miss. I served his father and then young Heathcliff."

"So I heard."

He lifted his chin. "And you *believe*, miss. Forgive my forwardness, but I find myself astonished that you haven't refused to see Heathcliff ever again after he's told you of our——our past."

Wanda nodded her head and smiled again. "Yeah." She thumbed a finger over her shoulder. "He says the same thing."

Archibald paused for a moment, sending her a grave look she didn't quite understand. His sage eyes held fire. When he spoke, he kept his voice low, almost a whisper, but his tone was unyielding and no-nonsense. "I don't understand your acceptance of us, Miss Wanda. It makes no earthly sense. And not for a minute do I believe you're the kind of woman you'd like Heathcliff to believe you are. I never interfere in Heathcliff's affairs——or I haven't until now. But do take note. You're not who you wish us to believe you are. I know women like you're pretending to be. I've known *many* in my lifetime. Whatever it is that's keeping you from my Heath is of course your business and I would never meddle. I will, however, take no shame in telling you I have never seen my Heathcliff this way with a woman before. And it would trouble me greatly if he were to be in any way pained by your relationship. Do we understand each other, miss?" His last words were part ominous, part protective, and all kinds of filled with warning.

And now she knew what Heath wanted——or at least what Archibald thought Heath wanted.

Her.

She could no longer dismiss the jokes Heath made about their relationship——she could no longer pretend she was blind to the fact that Heath wanted more. She could no longer fool herself into believing that he was only in it for the wonking, and the snide cracks he made about their not being involved were just that— snide cracks. Because they weren't—not if what Archibald said was true.

And that meant she now officially had mad callous-like skills. Her throat grew so tight she nearly choked.

Heath came up behind Arch, thumping him on the back. "What are we understanding?"

Wanda's stomach sank, but she pasted on a conspiratorial look, sending it in Archibald's direction. "The fine art of roasting a duck as fabulous as Archibald's."

Archibald ever so slightly tipped his head back at her, letting her know he was pleased she'd covered for him.

Heath barked a laugh, making her jump. "You can keep the secret, old man. I'll stick to chili dogs and chicken wings."

Archibald's face instantly lightened. "Thank heaven for chili dogs, sir." He took the rest of the paper plates from the table and swept them away.

Wanda stooped to snatch up a paper napkin that had fluttered to the floor when her stomach clenched. She gritted her teeth to thwart a groan, her hand going to her abdomen to press against it in the hopes that the sharp stab would pass.

Heath kneeled down beside her, curling a lock of her hair around his finger. "Those damned workout DVDs again?" He asked the question, but she wasn't sure if she heard skepticism in his tone, or if he was taunting her.

Her intake of breath shuddered and whistled. "Yeah. It's killa."

Heath's smile was flirtatious, flashing his white teeth. "I don't know if I told you, but I like your abs. Maybe you should lay off the working out thing. I have much more, uh, fun ways to work 'em out."

Her head bent low, tears stung her eyes from the throb in her belly. This past week, she'd experienced them more frequently, and there was nothing she could do to ease it but go home and take the painkillers her doctor had prescribed and she'd finally filled. "I think I have to go," she stuttered. She rose on legs that didn't want to hold her.

"Are you sure you're okay?" Heath's concern, just a flicker in his eyes, made her nod her head harder.

She had a well-practiced answer for just such an occasion. She was a liar—but breaking a commandment didn't seem so bad knowing why she was breaking it. Wanda leaned in to whisper in his ear, pausing for a mere second to let her nose rub against his silky hair. "I think it's, you know, a woman-thing. Some aspirin and a hot bath and all's good."

"I'll grab my coat and walk you out to your car."

"No!" She lowered her voice. "I mean—it's okay. It's cold, and my car's right outside. I'll be fine. You can watch me from the fire escape."

But Heath wasn't deterred. "Nope. I can't. Now stay put for two seconds, and I'll get my coat." He went to the small closet in his entryway and threw on his old, navy blue suit jacket.

Wanda slipped on her own coat and grabbed her purse. "Thanks again, Archibald, for *everything*. It was wonderful. I haven't had a meal like that in forever." Or a warning like that either.

Archibald bowed with a slight bend to his waist. "It was the greatest of pleasures, miss. Please, come back to our humble abode again, and again. Good evening."

Wanda could barely focus on Heath when he opened her car door, turning the key in the ignition for her as he started the car and cranked up the heat. The pain in her gut worsened while she waited. It took everything she had to keep her face placid, her body relaxed. When Heath took her in his arms, planting a light kiss on her lips, Wanda made it a point to memorize the warmth of his mouth—despite the growing pain in her stomach. The taste of him, his scent, the way her fingers fit at his lean, tapered waist.

"So I'll see ya when I see ya," she mumbled the words that had become their mantra each time they parted.

"See ya when I see ya." He kissed her forehead, lingering for a moment, then tucked her in her car.

She pulled away before Heath had the chance to say anything more.

As she drove home, Archibald's words banged around in her head. He was just looking out for Heath. She couldn't expect anything less than that from a man who'd taken care of him for almost two hundred years. She deserved every word of warning he'd given her.

No, she wasn't typically the kind of woman who laid down the kind of rules that implied sex was her only wish, but she was doing her damnedest to win an Academy Award trying.

And she was failing—miserably.

Not only that, she was doing exactly what Archibald had warned her, in his own cultured, well-mannered way, not to.

Setting Heath up to be hurt. If what Archibald said was true, that he'd never seen Heath behave this way with any other woman—and surely there had to have been plenty in almost two hundred years—then she was the worst kind of bottom-feeding scum.

And she'd give almost anything to not have to do what she knew she had to do.

Her hands gripped the steering wheel, and her teeth chattered. The pain that had begun in her stomach flared upward to her chest, now tight and constricting.

The thought of her prescription brought some comfort. It would not only take away the pain, but it would knock her out cold. A deep, dreamless sleep promised no lingering thoughts of Heath.

And death.

It promised eight hours without the guilt that had latched onto her and clung with no hope of letting her go.

TWO hours later, a dose of pain meds, and no such luck in the forget your guilt by passing out gig, Wanda got up from her bed and cocked her head at the TV. First to the right, then to the left. Finally she gave up and lay at the end of her bed, letting her head hang off it upside down to get a better perspective on what she was watching.

And upside down seemed to be the way to do it—at least it made sense of the tangled limbs, gyrating hips, slick, spray tanned bodies, and screams of "Oh, yeahhh, oh, yeahhh, oh yeahhhhh!" in decibels that just might have broken her mother's china.

She popped back up, fighting the head rush, and reached for her ever-growing Fuck It list—considering entry number twenty-two, while yet another easily attained mission was officially ovah.

Wanda clicked the Off button on the remote, ending her foray into blockbuster hits such as *Rodzilla, ET-The Extra Testicle*, and *Ghostbusties.*

She drew a line through entry number twenty-two with a firm pen to paper.

Hookay, so porn sooooo wasn't in her color wheel.

"IS Miss Wanda all right, sir?"

Heath ran a thoughtful hand over his jaw. "You know, I wanna believe she is—but something's just not sitting right with me, Arch. I think she's full of shit. Not just about the no involvement thing. It's more and she sucks at hiding it."

"I couldn't agree more," Archibald clearly wasn't hesitant in saying.

"So I think it's time I do something Wanda's going to shit foundation and lipstick tubes over."

"Or, I, as your manservant could do it for you," Archibald offered dutifully.

"Ya like her, huh, Arch?"

Archibald fought a smile, gave up, and let go. "I do, sir. She's very engaging."

Heath clapped him on the back. "Yeah, that she is and nah, Arch, you know it doesn't work that way anymore. You don't have to handle my shit like you did back in the day. I feel like a heel already for considering doing what I'm going to do—but I'm beginning to—"

"Experience a warmth for the fair Wanda that has nothing to do with southern locales. Yes, sir. I see that. When, if I might ask, did you realize she was the woman for you?"

Heath chuckled. "When she made me sit through a marathon of *America's Next Top Model* and I didn't give a shit, first, that Tyra Banks was half naked, and second, that it was *America's Next Top Model*. I decided then and there I could sit forever and watch scantily clad women with her, but not even notice them. I mean, Arch, it *was* Tyra Banks."

Arch raised an eyebrow. "Oh, sir, I daresay that's sacrifice at its finest. So you're in deep like. What will you do about this concern you have about her noncommittal attitude?"

"I like her enough to want to know what the hell's going on, yeah. And in that like, I'm slicker than I'd given myself credit for."

"Slick, sir?"

Heath dug a piece of paper out of his jeans and held it up with a smug grin. "It's her friends' numbers. I got them off her phone while you two were talking duck. Nina and Marty—very protective of Wanda from what I gather, listening to her side of their conversations, anyway."

"Crafty, indeed, young Heathcliff. Do you expect them to be receptive to you?"

"I don't expect anything, but whatever's going on with Wanda worries me, and if she won't tell me because we're all uninvolved, I really think her friends should know something's not copacetic."

"Then we wait, sir."

"Yeah, we wait."

Wanda's bullshit about womanly issues was feeble. Something was wrong. He felt it, and he wondered if it had something to do with the prescription she had in her medicine cabinet. He hadn't read it, didn't know what it was for, but it bore looking into.

So now he was going to figure out what, if anything, it meant.

Come hell or high water.

CHAPTER 15

"I didn't ask you here today to do anything you don't want to do—if you feel like I'm out of line, I'd totally understand. But I appreciate your both agreeing to meet me," Heath assured both Nina and Marty, who sat across from him at a coffee shop he'd randomly picked. Marty'd taken him up on his offer of coffee, but Nina had refused. The coffee shop was slow for late afternoon; only two or three people littered the many tables and booths.

"So what is it that we might not want to do?" Marty asked, her blue eyes assessing him from across the table. She was suspicious—which made her a good friend in Heath's estimation.

"You might not want to tell me what's going on with Wanda."

Nina sat back in her chair, crossing her arms defensively across her torn-T-shirt-clad chest. "Whaddaya mean? What's going on with Wanda?"

"Something's wrong." He didn't know how else to put it—or

how to use the kind of finesse it took to tell two virtual strangers he was beyond concerned.

"What's wrong with her?" Nina's voice rose, her tone filled with menace. "Did you do something to her that'd make her wrong, 'cause I gotta tell ya, I'll kick your ass. Don't think because I'm a girl that I won't either. Don't let my gender fool you. I'm a badass—ask Marty."

Marty swatted Nina on her arm with the back of her hand, frowning. "Yes, yes, Nina's a badass—even for a girl—and you'll soon learn, she'll tell anyone she is, too, whether you care to hear it or not. Just hush, Nina. Let Heath explain." Marty sat back in her chair, folding her hands in her lap. "So what do you think is wrong with Wanda?"

Heath sat stoically, prepared to take whatever backlash might come from him sticking his nose somewhere he knew Wanda'd think it didn't belong. He didn't give a shit if she liked it or not—he knew his gut was telling him something was fucked up. He'd never denied or ignored his gut. Not in almost two hundred years. Yet he chose his words carefully because he didn't want her friends to worry unnecessarily. "Maybe she's not feeling well? I dunno. I just know she's always got stomach cramps. She says it's from working out, but it's happened at least twice in the time I've known her."

"Wanda doesn't work out . . ." Nina mumbled, looking bewildered.

And he'd have known that if she'd just let him be "involved" with her. Goddamn it. What he knew about her to this point came from observations, and the minimal info she'd let slip. He wanted more. Much more. "I figured as much. Look, I asked you here because I hoped you two knew something I didn't. You're her friends. You're closer to her . . . it could be any number of things."

"And why would we tell you if we did know something?" Nina asked suspiciously. Her dark, almond-shaped eyes narrowed.

He held up his hands. "You don't have to tell me anything, Nina. I just hoped you would." Jesus, she was a prickly one. If you didn't have a set of steely balls, she'd likely scare the man out of you. Marty, on the other hand, seemed far more reasonable. Meeting them now, he decided they were like an odd combination of Wanda. Nina was over the top loud and mouthy. Wanda was quick, but never loud, and she definitely didn't swear like Nina. Marty was as feminine as they came, but still a softer version of Nina. Wanda was somewhere in between them both. He decided to appeal to Marty with a reverse method. "If you're not aware of what's going on with Wanda, I'll leave you two to your afternoon." He began to rise, but Marty stopped him.

She gave Nina a dirty look. Heath watched the two send each other messages with their eyes in a matter of seconds. "Wait! Please, sit down. Ignore Nina. Communicate with me. I'm the only one of Wanda's friends who can do that in full syllables and complete sentences. And Nina"—she pointed a finger at her—"not another damned word. Now please, tell me what you know."

Heath resituated himself in the chair, folding his arms on the table. "I don't know anything, Marty, that's why I contacted you. Maybe, for the record, you should just know that I really think something's wrong, and it has me worried."

Nina looked at Marty with concern streaking her pale face. Her very pale face, he noted. He knew that kind of pale. "She's gotten so skinny in the past few months, Marty—skinny and mouthy. She used to be so kinda mousy, timid and shit, but since the thing with you and then me and Greg, she's changed."

"What thing with you and Marty?" He probably shouldn't have asked, but he'd take whatever snippets he could get about Wanda—and he didn't care how or from whom.

Marty gave Nina a sharp, unmistakable warning glance before waving a hand in the air. "Oh, you know, love-life stuff." Her answer was as vague as she could make it without being obviously vague. Quite frankly, she sucked at it. He might not have the ability to tap into her mind anymore, but he could tell she was avoiding something.

Nina shook her head, twisting a strand of hair that was caught up in her ponytail. "I seriously thought it was just the freedom of being divorced from that pig that had made her so quick with a comeback—"

"You know her ex-husband?" Heath cut her off. Maybe whatever the problem was did have to do with the asshole. But it didn't make sense with what he knew at this point.

"No, and damned good thing I don't. I'd have ripped the prick's balls up into his throat and out of his mouth if I'd known her when she was married to him—but I didn't. She was divorced when we all met. Anyway, we both just figured her weight loss was because she was working a lot and her mouthy 'tude was a good toughening up, because divorce and life do that to you. And if I'm honest, we do that to her, too," Nina said on a chuckle.

Marty nodded her agreement. "It's true. We, Nina and me, we argue a lot. It's mostly out of love, but Wanda's the peacemaker in our friendship—in order to shut us up, she has to go the extra mile." She gave a sidelong glance to Nina, then caught Heath's gaze again. "If you know what I mean. Anyway, we're always teasing her about how she's going to be the ultimate negative size zero if she doesn't eat a sandwich or something. Do you think she's dieting—doing something crazy like one of those cleanses?"

Nina's hands now fiddled with the ties on her hooded jacket. "No, Marty—that's not Wanda. She's the sensible one of us three. She's the smartest one of all of us. She's the one who keeps us together. She's like Mother Earth. I tend to agree with Heath, and it isn't like we haven't been asking her what's wrong for months. I think maybe something's really wrong." Heath heard the admiration for Wanda in Nina's voice—felt it from Marty—was glad she had friends like this. Even if the dark-haired one was mouthy.

Marty's lower lip trembled. "That's true. We have been worried about her, but she always brushes us off. If it's not just all that work she's doing, and not eating properly, then what could it be?"

"I dunno, but I say we find out." Nina whipped out her cell phone.

Marty rolled her eyes, yanking the phone from Nina. "Just hold on for two seconds. Don't go off half-cocked, Nina. If something is wrong, wouldn't she just tell us? We do almost *everything* together. Maybe she's just having a midlife crisis? She was married a long time to that fuckhead—he controlled everything she did—maybe it's just a little thing called freedom."

Nina took her cell phone back. "And that's what's making her so skinny and tired all the time, Marty? Sometimes you're a moron."

He could see where Wanda's role in their friendship came in now, clear as day. "Maybe it's freedom, maybe it's something else," Heath added. "But there's more to this, and I wasn't sure if I should tell you, because my intention isn't to stir you up without real cause, but it bears mentioning. Wanda asked me to get something from her medicine cabinet last week—a Band-Aid. She'd nicked herself on a glass she'd broken in the kitchen. Neanderthal that I am, I knocked half the medicine cabinet over and into the sink. As I was cleaning stuff up, a piece of paper floated out—a prescription to be exact. I don't know what it was for because I felt guilty enough for finding it in the first place—but it's been bugging the hell out of me since I saw it."

Marty's face flashed Nina a perplexed glance. "Wanda hates to take even aspirin. We had to make her that night we brought her home from—from the shelter." She cast her eyes down. "Sorry to bring up a tough time in your life," she said to Heath before her eyes lit up. "Omigod! Do you remember that night, Nina? She said she thought maybe she was coming down with the flu, but she was holding her *stomach*." Marty reached out to Nina, taking her hand, her face becoming a mask of worry. "We need to talk to her, Nina. I don't want to jump to conclusions, but I have to admit, I'm worried now, too. Will you tell her you talked to us, Heath?"

Heath gave her a stiff nod. "If you want me to, absolutely. But in my case, it'll just piss her off—I don't know if she's told you much about me and our not really a relationship—"

"She did, and just for the record, 'cause I think you're a stand-up guy for even bothering to get in touch with us, we think she's full of shit when it comes to you," Nina replied.

Marty slapped a hand over Nina's mouth. "Nina! Zip. It. Our impressions are no one's business, and Wanda'd kill us if she knew you were shooting off that mouth of yours again." She turned to Heath, her eyes filled with what he clearly read as sympathy. "Look, it's evident you really like Wanda. That you'd get our phone numbers and call us here is proof of that. Thank you. Thank you for giving us a heads-up. I guess we've been so involved with our own lives—my pregnancy, Nina's recent marriage—that we stopped paying attention as closely as we should have. Don't say anything to her about our meeting. We'll take care of it."

"Will you tell me if you find something out?" Heath knew what the answer would be—their fierce loyalty wouldn't allow it, but he figured what the fuck, it couldn't hurt to ask.

Marty reached across the table, grazing his hand with hers for just a moment before returning it to her lap. "You know we can't do that. Wanda's our friend. If something's wrong and she chooses to tell us, we can't betray her by telling you—no matter how much I would have it differently. Can you understand that?"

Heath hitched his jaw at them, clenching his teeth to keep from demanding they call him—whatever the outcome was. "I do. I don't like it, but I do understand. But if I find anything out—

though I wouldn't count on it—I'll definitely tell you. She'll need you, if in fact we're not making mountains out of molehills. For all we know, it could just be something as simple as an ulcer."

Nina rocked back on her chair, clutching the edge of the table as she did. "You two have me pretty freaked out. I wanna call her right now and go beat whatever she's not telling us out of her. And, dude, you got it pretty bad for her. It's written all over your face, and that's way cool. Which makes you all right by me. I can tell it's for real."

Heath cocked an eyebrow. "Can you?"

"Yeah, yeah I can," Nina assured him.

He might as well let the cat out of the bag. "Know why you can tell?"

"'Cause I've gone all Dionne Warwick on you? You know, the psychic hotline shit?"

"No. Because you're vampire—and that explains everything. Everything." It was a relief to say it out loud. To let her friends know he knew. A relief to know this was why Wanda had accepted his explanation like he'd told her he once was on the football team.

Marty gasped, spilling some of her coffee.

Nina was immediately on guard—a stance he knew well.

"And you, Marty. You're not vampire, but you're something."

Nina leaned forward on the table, shoving her face in his. "Okay, I take it back. You're a fucking nut. All bets are officially off."

His laughter filled the small café. "Sorry, I don't mean to laugh. I know your kind of pale, Nina. I also know that strip of zinc oxide on your nose, and I know you know about me, too. We may as well cut through the bullshit. Meeting you here cleared up a lot of stuff for me as far as Wanda's concerned."

"Like?" Nina's head moved back and forth in a half circle on her neck.

Marty sighed, putting a hand between Nina and Heath. "Oh,

Nina—give it up. Like the fact that Wanda wasn't at all surprised when he told her he was once a vampire. And no, I'm not vampire. I'm a werewolf. Don't ask—it's too caa-razy for even us to believe. But we get where you are—just in reverse."

It all made sense now. Wanda's dulled reaction to his confession—her understanding about zombies that she said she'd gotten out of some romance novel. She'd seen it, done it, been there with these women. And that was just too much of a coincidence for him to spend a whole lot of time thinking on. "It's true. I was once a vampire."

Nina scoffed, shaking a finger at Marty. "I told you and Wanda he smelled funny—and, yeah, I know you were once vamp. You have no fucking idea how much that pisses me off."

Heath's look conveyed his confusion.

"Long story again. Suffice it to say, Nina wasn't happy about being turned. It was an accident. But now she's happy clappy, aren't you, sunshine?" Marty tweaked her cheeks.

Nina batted her hands away. "Get the fuck off me, Marty. Yeah. I'm happy. How 'bout you, Heath? You like being human again?"

He grinned. "Yeah. I'm pretty okay with it. It's had some bleak moments, but things are rapidly improving." He looked at his watch. "I'm sorry, but I gotta go. I'm meeting Wanda. Anyway, thanks, ladies. I hope someday you'll tell me all about how you came to this point in your lives."

"We'd like that," Marty said, casting him a warm smile.

"Can I ask just one more favor of the two of you?"

"Sure," Marty offered.

"I think you both know Wanda feels something for me that runs a whole lot deeper than she's letting on. That may sound arrogant—it may sound egotistical, but it *is*. And she isn't alone in that. That said, I'd appreciate it if you'd just mention to her that whatever's going on, I'd like to know, too."

Marty and Nina grew solemn again, both brought back to the reason he'd asked them here.

Wanda.

"I'll definitely do that, Heath. Promise," Marty whispered.

"Yeah, me, too," Nina piped up, her voice softer than he'd heard it their entire conversation. "Promise."

THEY lay in her bed, Wanda snuggled against Heath's smooth chest. Menusha curled at Heath's feet, the slight rise and fall of her back a sure sign she was out cold. The TV played low in the background. Humphrey Bogart was bidding Ingrid Berman adieu, and just like every time she'd ever watched it, Wanda began to tear up. A salty fat bubble escaped her eye, landing on Heath's chest.

"Need a tissue?"

She smiled a watery smile. "I'm okay. I always cry at the end of this. Just call me girl."

Heath ran a toe along her calf, rubbing it seductively up to her thigh. "I like my women girly."

"Your women . . ."

His lips whispered along her cheek, slipping down over her neck to her shoulder. "Oh, right. Sorry. That was definitely an involved label. And we're anything but involved, even if we spend almost all of our free time together."

Wanda squirmed beneath him, arching into his hard embrace, gripping his shoulders as he let his lips trail hot kisses over her chest. "We spend most of our time in bed."

He slid beneath the covers, capturing a nipple between his teeth, stroking it between words. "Right. Not counting lunch every day this week, dinner, too. Oh, and the *Top Model* repeats I sat through for nearly four hours just last night while we ate popcorn and I ogled Tyra Banks."

A twinge of jealousy skittered along her spine—irrational and pathetic, but there it was. Like she could evah compete with Tyra Banks. "You ogled Tyra?"

"Uh, yeah. Sorry. But see, here's the thing. I can do that because we're *uninvolved*. Said half of the uninvolved couple is allowed to ogle others who are uninvolved with other halves of uninvolved parties or otherwise. It's in the uninvolved contract." He lifted himself over her, parting her thighs and giving her his infamous smug grin.

Heath was doing his best to get a rise out of her, but he made her giggle girlishly anyway. He made her laugh. He made her smile to herself when she was alone—when she least expected it. He made her heart race when he smiled and even when he gave her that penetrating stare.

Heath slipped his hard length into her, slow, lazy, meeting her hips when they rose upward in anticipation. A sigh slipped from her lips—a sigh of contentment, a sigh of completion. Her nipples beaded, tight, stiff, scraping against his smooth chest as he skillfully made slow drives of his cock into her.

Wanda's hands sought his hair, silky soft between her fingers, her thighs wrapped tighter around his waist as he ground against her, making that delicious friction with his pubic hair against her clit. Swells of heat rose and fell with each plunge he took, forceful, growing in speed until sweat broke out on her forehead. Her heart throbbed in time with his. Her legs grew weak from the tension in her muscles created by clinging to him, their bodies slid against each other's in a slow, seductive dance.

Her orgasm gripped at her gut, contracting the place between her thighs, growing with each thrust of Heath's cock until the leisurely burn turned into a whimpered plea for satisfaction.

Heath reared up, his chest muscles tight, corded, tense beneath her fingers. Sweat trickled between his pecs in enticing droplets.

Her nails dug into his firm flesh, raking over them, gritting her teeth when she felt his cock pulse, then jerk inside her.

They found relief together, in the tumble from scorching flames of heat, in the sweet, blessed respite of satisfaction.

Heath collapsed on her, the heavy weight of him delicious, every inch of him glued to her. She was boneless beneath him, but her fingers stroked his hair, cradling him to her, savoring the scent of their lovemaking. Loving his heavy weight, spent on top of her.

He kissed the sensitive flesh just under her ear. "I'm starving," he mumbled when he'd caught his breath.

"When aren't you hungry?" she teased.

"Never it seems," he said, rising up on his arms. "And if I'm not careful, me and Jenny Craig are gonna be like this." He crossed two fingers together.

"You're making up for all those years of not being able to eat."

Heath slid off her, slipping from the bed and wandering over to her dresser as she watched with sleepy eyes. He grabbed the plastic bag of Reese's Peanut Butter Cups and unwrapped one. "I think you're right, but as a vampire, I didn't have to worry about gaining weight. As an almost thirty-seven-year-old human, I do." He popped the chocolaty goodness into his mouth, once more closing his eyes, licking his lips while he savored his favorite candy.

He was utterly unashamed of his nakedness—in the dim glow of the television, his silhouette was sharply defined. The rough cut of his jaw as he chewed, the bulge of his thigh muscles clenching and unclenching while he rocked from foot to foot, the way he ran his strong, sure hands through his blond hair made her pause and think, she could watch him eat Reese's Peanut Butter Cups forever.

And then her heart began to pound erratically from her place on the bed, watching him indulge in his favorite chocolate, her throat tightened, her hands curled against the sheet.

If lightning bolts and crashing thunder were how falling in love was announced—that's not how it happened for Wanda Schwartz.

It happened watching Heath Jefferson do something as stupid as consume nine bazillion calories like it was a meal cooked by Emeril himself. It stole the breath from her lungs. It made her intestines twist and shake. It made her gulp for air.

It made her reconsider asking Marty or Nina to turn her so she could watch Heath forever.

Oh. Fuck.

Heath came to her side of the bed, tugging the sheets from her. "Hey, I said I'm starving, woman—I say we go get a Whopper. All the uninvolved people are doing it these days." He winked and chuckled, grabbing her hand and giving it a yank.

For the briefest of moments, she clung to his fingers, letting his warmth suffuse her hand, hoping to fend off the tremble of what had just hit her upside her stubborn, foolish head.

Her laughter was unsteady, her legs like soft butter when she let him drag her out of the warmth of the bed. She needed a moment to herself—a moment to adjust—maybe a lot of moments. "Why is it that I have to go with, Mr. Jefferson? You know where the Burger King is. It's two blocks from here."

He dragged his jeans over his bulky thighs. "Because it's almost eight, you haven't had dinner yet, and I know I'll have to lug something back here for you. It's only fair you should help. I'm only one man, and I don't know if I can carry two Whoppers alone. It can be a burden. So come on. Get dressed, and let's go before it snows again or something."

Wanda bent forward at the waist, grabbing her own jeans and panties, pulling them on with thick, fumbling fingers. Heath held her sweatshirt out to her, kissing the tip of her nose when her head poked through the neck. "Why do we have to walk? We could just take the car."

Heath sauntered out to the living room to get his coat. "Because it's good for you to walk."

"But it's cold," she protested, smiling and looking for the gloves she'd thrown off when she'd gotten home.

"Yes, but that lets you know that—"

"You're alive. Yeah, yeah." She pulled on her cap and jacket, smiling up at him. She reached up on tippy-toe and kissed the corner of his mouth. "I know how important that is to you ex-immortals." Wanda pulled the door open with a tug, taking the stairs down to the curb in front of her house with light feet.

Heath was right behind her, catching her hand, but Wanda stopped. "Damn. I forgot my purse, and if you're a nice ex-vampire, you'll go get it for me," she teased. "It's on the counter in the kitchen."

He mock-sighed, his face teasing in the light of the streetlamp. "Heath, do this. Heath, do that. Heath, can I have some of your Whopper? Even after I asked you if you wanted one, too, and you said no. Heath, watch *America's Next Top Model* with me, but don't eyeball Tyra with lust. You're a pushy broad." He smiled over his shoulder, heading back up the stairs at a trot.

Wanda watched his retreating back, broad, filling out the new jacket he'd gotten at a thrift shop like it had been his from the start. And she loved watching him. She loved talking to him.

She loved.

End of.

And she should feel horrible right now. She had no right to love Heath—not at this point in her life. She'd had no right to even get a little involved with him. This was exactly what she'd been trying to avoid in her quest for no strings attached. But he was like crack, and she hadn't tried to stop injecting herself with huge doses of him. Oh, she'd done a lot of talking about how uninvolved they should be—but her heart clearly hadn't had its listening ears on. And now this. Allowing it to go this far had been selfish, self-serving, wrong, wrong, wrong.

But she didn't feel horrible.

She felt giddy.

And cold.

What the hell was he doing, searching for the Holy Grail? It was just like a man, she thought with a smile, taking the steps back up to her house. Whatever they were looking for could be right in front of their faces, and they'd still need a GPS system to find it.

She found Heath standing in her doorway—unmoving.

Wanda placed a hand on his solid back, and he jumped. "Hey, are you blind now? My purse is right there on the counter," she teased then ducked around him and strode to the kitchen to re-trieve it from the counter, stopping short when she saw his face.

A face that had a million flashes of different emotions happen-ing all at once. His jaw clenched, unclenched, his tongue rolled along the inside of his cheek. His eyes grew dark with what could only be defined as rage in all its many facets.

Alarm, fear, uncertainty made her voice quiver. "Heath? What's wrong?"

"You're dying." He didn't coat his words. He didn't ask a question—he said it with a tone that implied he couldn't believe what he'd just said.

Her stomach sank like lead. Yeah. There was that.

He slammed the door behind him, striding across the floor to rear up in front of her, his big body shedding waves of pal-pitating fury, his fists making large balls on either side of him. *"You're—dying."*

There was no use denying it. She hadn't planned to tell him when this began, but after what she'd discovered tonight, Wanda knew she probably wouldn't have let things go much further with-out telling him. She just didn't want it to be now. Not now when she just wanted to be in love with him. Just for a few days—without her imminent departure hovering over them like some big ax of doom. "Y-yes. I am. How'd you find out?"

His eyes searched hers with a gaze that left her cold. "Call me an interfering son of a bitch, but when you asked me to come back and get your purse, your doctor was leaving a message it sounded like you've heard before. Something like, 'Miss Schwartz, please call my office. We've been unsuccessful in our attempts to reach you, and it's imperative that you call us so that we can at least secure your comfort in the last stages of your *life*.' He sounded a little like he was at his wits' end, Wanda. Like maybe you'd gotten a message like that before." His words were tight, his mouth a thin line of anger.

Yeah, Dr. Eckert had called a time or two—or eight since this began, and she'd promptly ignored every call, filling only the one prescription he'd given her just last week. A thousand words stuck in her throat, like she'd swallowed a mouthful of honey and her well-rounded vocabulary was all glued to the stickiness of it. "I see."

His eyes went wide, then narrowed with yet more disbelief, outrage, simmering, ready to boil over into anger. He looked like he was barely holding on to his temper, and it would have frightened her if she didn't know it was only out of shock. "You see? You *see*? Do you see, Wanda? It's pretty fucking clear you've been ignoring the doctor's calls. Why the fuck would you do that?"

Because she didn't want *this* to happen. Call it foolish. Call it the dumbest fucking thing she'd ever done in her life—but she didn't want to spend a single second mourning, and that's what people did when you were dying. They sent silent messages over your head, behind your back, with their eyes. They called each other privately to talk about you—they avoided making simple plans like next summer's vacation, because no one fucking wanted you to be upset by them.

She had nothing to say. No defense. There wasn't anything a doctor could do for her. If he didn't have the magic fucking death cure, then what good did answering his phone calls do? She knew how to make a list of things that needed taking care of—she didn't need a doctor for that.

Heath gripped her shoulders, his hands barely contained in his grip. "You planned to tell me this when, Wanda?"

Did never count as when? Her shoulders lifted in a guilt-ridden shrug, and her eyes found the ground beneath her feet. "I-I guess there was no specific plan."

"Right," he said tightly. "And can you see where that might piss me off?"

"I can."

"And can you see how fucking unfair that is?"

She winced at his barely contained rage. "I can."

He stared at her long, hard, and she couldn't look away. She wanted to hide her eyes in shame, but she couldn't. She deserved his heated glare. "Good. Because I'm so fucking furious with you right now for not just telling me the truth, for letting me find out this way, I could—" He cut himself off, stopping as fast as he'd begun.

When she found her voice, it was stilted, wooden—a practiced speech she'd given her reflection in her mirror almost every time she was near one. "It was selfish of me, and I know it. I do. I didn't tell you because I didn't want you to feel sorry for me. But it's why I didn't want to get involved . . . why I was resigning from Bobbie-Sue. I—didn't want things to be awkward between us."

"And you don't think a little thing like dying would be awkward, Wanda?" he roared, so loud, with such force, the loose strands of hair ruffled beneath her cap.

She licked her dry lips, searching for something to say. "I don't know . . ."

But Heath wasn't accepting her lame answers. "So you were just going to die. Die, and leave me to piss in the wind? What was going to happen to uninvolved us, Wanda? Would you just not pick up the phone one day when I called, and I'd come over here and land in the middle of your funeral? I didn't deserve to know? Is that how *uninvolved* we are?" He spat the words, venomous, hateful truths.

He was hurting, and it made her heart ache with sadness. Yet as heart wrenching as that was for her, the smallest bit of happiness crept into her tumultuous emotions, too. It meant Heath cared. How much, or even if anymore, was something she knew she shouldn't ask. Not now. "I don't know what I was going to do. I was still trying to figure it out. I—"

His face was a mask of fury, hard as granite, enraged hacked off. "Yes you do, Wanda. You know exactly what you were going to do. You're not the kind of woman who doesn't think things through. You have a list for your lists. That's what the Fuck It list was about. Don't try and bullshit me."

She'd managed to move her hands to his arms just as he let go of her shoulders, letting his body go slack. "I was wrong. What I did was wrong. I should have made you go a long time ago—before that first night, but . . ."

"But I'm good in the sack—so why pass up a good fuck?"

This emotion she understood. It was one Nina displayed often when she wanted to hurt the person who'd hurt her—but it didn't cut any less deep, and sadly, was nothing less than she deserved. Her fingers dug into his arms, frantic, urgent. "You're angry. Please, please let's not leave things like this. I don't want things to end like this."

His response was cold—as hard as he could sometimes be. "No, you just want them to end."

No, no, no. She didn't want them to end. But they had to. Had.

To. How did you ask someone to stick around and watch you die when their life was just beginning? How did you explain the self-ishness involved in inviting someone into a life that was going to end?

In this very moment, she found herself waffling over her stern resolve to never ask Marty or Nina to turn her.

Wanda wrung her hands, folding them and unfolding them. "Yes—no—I . . . I'm not ever going to get any better, Heath. But you have all these great things happening now. You're doing really terrific at Bobbie-Sue. You have an apartment—a job. You can have a family someday. You said it might be nice to have children some-day. You did. Just the other night. I swear I never thought you'd be interested in anything more than the—the sex, even with all the jokes about how we weren't involved. I didn't think, especially after what you told me about your past, that you would ever be serious about someone like me!"

Heath's eyes glittered, cold and dark.

How could she possibly explain the kind of fucked-up logic she'd applied to this whole mess she'd made? "Everything is just beginning for you. You have a new life ahead of you. Go live it."

Heath turned on his heel, leaning forward, letting his dark blond head hang between his shoulders, gripping the edge of the table until it shook. His fist hit the table with a sudden, thundering clap. His words, when they came, were measured, filled with his absolute fury. "What you've done—or planned to do— explains a lot of things about whatever we have going on, but it doesn't ex-plain why you didn't give me just a little fucking credit for being a decent guy. Despite my past. Did you think I was the kind of guy who'd figure the hell with it, why bother fucking a chick who's halfway to the grave? But then maybe telling me would have been just a little too involved for you, Wanda, huh? Uninvolved couples don't share deep, dark secrets, right? Fuck buddies just fuck." He took a deep breath. She heard him fight for control. Saw it in his stance. Felt the ripe thickness of it in the air.

Tears, hot, unwelcome, slid from her eyes, pooling to the white tile on her kitchen floor. The pain that lanced every nerve in her body made more unbearable by Heath's next words.

"I can't stay here and listen to this, and if I don't haul my ass out of here, I can't promise I won't lose it. So I'm gonna go do something stupid and selfish—like get drunk, beat the shit out of some asshole—and then I'm coming back." He turned to face her finally, and she wanted to throw herself at him, beg him to forgive her, but she knew now wasn't the time. His body was rigid, his face a hot red. Everyone handled grief differently—anger was common, the need for space was, too, but it didn't make Wanda want to shelter herself with his warmth any less.

Yet she had to let him go, and hope—pray—that he'd come back and try to understand what she'd done. She silently prayed that he'd want her even if their days together had numbers attached. Or if nothing else, he'd just come back to make peace with her.

Heath went to the door—clamping a fist around the knob, shrugging it open. Menusha ran to it, twisting herself around his legs. She loved Heath—loved to curl up on his big chest—hated when he left. He stooped to run a quick hand over her back before rising, his voice low, "This isn't over by a long shot, Wanda. Not even."

Silence, in all its deafening sounds, crashed in her ears, beating like a distant drum when he closed the door.

A million thoughts raced through her mind while she stood rooted to her kitchen floor—a crazy fucking list of things she could do to make this better. But she couldn't focus on any one task. They became jumbled, semi-thoughts that came and went, and between those thoughts, there was only one that was clear.

Now that she'd gone and fucked up a really potentially great thing, she needed a cigarette.

CHAPTER
16

"What in the fuck are you doing, Wanda?"

Wanda held up the cigarette, letting the plume of gray smoke drift toward Nina and Marty, who'd called a hundred times tonight, apparently had gotten fed up, and decided to ambush her, no longer caring what they thought—or if they knew she'd once been a dirty smoker. "I think it's obvious. I'm devising a plan for world peace. It's a big job—stressful, but someone has to do it—I figured I deserved a cigarette while I pondered." She took a long drag. God, that was good. There was a freedom in this dying game to be had. She already had cancer—she couldn't get more cancered.

Nina grabbed it from her fingers, by the lit end. "Wow, you're one mouthy chick lately. Enough with your snark—don't be offhand with me. Give me that fucking thing and knock it off. You don't smoke." She flicked it into the kitchen sink and flipped on the tap.

No. Not for some time now. But she had, and tonight, after

Heath had left, the craving for one, something she'd fallen back on hundreds of times in the past due to stress, had grown. In the midst of sobbing uncontrollable tears of self-pity, tears for the hurt she'd caused the man she'd ridiculously, unexpectedly found herself in love with, she'd driven to the deli and bought first a pack, then two—because she could. "Oh, but I did. I smoked nearly two packs a day—it was before you guys knew me. I gave it up after I got a divorce from the puke."

Marty waved her hands in the air to rid the kitchen of the acrid smell. "So? Last we checked you were still divorced, and you've decided to begin smoking again? Why, Wanda?" Marty asked.

"Because I forgot just how much I loved it. I quit so I could be healthier. Now that's not so important." Because she was dying, dying, dying, for the love of Christ!

Nina rounded on her, yanking a chair out from the table and sitting in it with an abrupt drop. "Okay, enough of the bullshit, Wanda. We're here, and you're going to spill. I told Marty tonight that if you don't fucking tell us what's going on once and for all, I'm going to beat it out of you. Stop playing stupid with us. Stop acting as if we're the ones who're nuts and overreacting. I don't need a degree in Oprah to see something just ain't kosher. I'm tired of worrying about you. I'm tired of Marty telling me to shut it when I'm all set to make you give me an answer. You've lost a lot of weight since I met you. Mostly in the last five or six months. I know what size you are, because I've held the clothes you yank off the rack when we do that stupid designer clothes-shopping shit, and it isn't the same as it was six months ago. And you always look tired. Even when you have on makeup, you look beat down. Now, tell me, or things get freaky."

"Ovarian cancer." Bam—just like that. She dumped the filth of that word at their unsuspecting, unwarned feet. Terror, cold, clammy, heart-thumping grabbed her with fists of iron and clung—tight.

Nina averted her gaze away from Wanda's, stilled instantly by Wanda's words. "Christ . . ."

Wanda inhaled on a shaky breath. "There's more. I'm in stage four. It's terminal."

Marty's head, a moment ago hanging low, popped up, her eyes rimmed with disbelief. "What? Says *who?*"

"My doctor. The tests. It's true."

Nina gripped the edge of the table. "And how long have you known about this?"

"Almost a month now."

Marty's face contorted. "A month? You've known for a flippin' month, and you didn't say anything to us? Why, Wanda?" She held up her hand to stop Wanda from speaking, her incredulous expression giving way to more disbelief. "Wait, you mean all this time we've been asking if you were okay, why you were losing so much weight and look so tired all the time, and you've known what was wrong *all along?*"

Wanda's head dipped low, tears rimming her eyes. She nodded. "Yes. But please, please let me explain, okay. I didn't know anything was seriously wrong. I really didn't. I told you guys about my partial hysterectomy, right? They took everything but my ovaries and after that, I never wanted to see another doctor again. I did all the right things, went for checkups and all that jazz post-op. But I guess, well, I guess time just got away from me once it was over. All of a sudden I was getting divorced, and then I found you guys and Bobbie-Sue . . . I was working and getting out and learning to make my own way and going to see the va-jay-jay doctor just wasn't on my list of things to do. Until I started to lose weight and sometimes I felt bloated—I guess I just felt like *something* was wrong. I didn't feel bad, just not right, ya know?" She looked at Marty and Nina for understanding, both silent, both so still.

She pulled in another deep breath, her eyes burned, her head throbbed, but it felt so good to just say it. Out loud. "I still don't feel horrible. I've only had a couple of really bad days since I found out. Anyway I went and saw my gynecologist who suspected it, then he sent me to another doctor. Dr. Eckert did a biopsy, and the day I found out the results of the biopsy was the day I was supposed to go shopping with you guys. It's why I forgot our date. I feel like such an idiot. I mean, I watch TV, for God's sake. I've seen a million commercials and enough talk shows about it to know that I should have seen the gynecologist a long time ago. I'm not an idiot—but I sure as hell feel like one now. And I also know early detection is crucial. But it just never occurred to me when I went in for a checkup that the diagnosis would be something this—this—"

"Bad, Wanda?" Nina cut her off with a fierce whisper-yell. "Because this *is* bad. Very bad and for all the times I fucking asked you if you were okay and you dismissed me like so much aggravation, I want to wrap my hands around your scrawny neck and squeeze the life right the fuck out of you. But I don't have to, do I, Wanda? And why is that? Know why, *Wanda*?" Nina had risen from the table, her face rigid and angry, her fury one you could almost taste. "I don't have to squeeze the life out of you, because ovarian cancer's doing it for me!" she roared, shoving the table and its contents so hard, everything scattered, tumbling to the edge of the table.

Both Wanda and Marty jerked backward in their chairs in surprise when the ashtray crashed to the floor, scattering into plastic pieces and black ashes.

Nina turned her back to them, her finger twisting a piece of her long, dark hair with a hand that shook. "Goddamn you, Wanda Schwartz," her voice broke then, wobbling with a weak tremor. *"God-damn-you."*

Marty was the first to jump to her feet, straightening the mess on the table with fumbling hands. "Okay, wait. Both of you just wait and get a friggin' grip." She placed a hand on Nina's shoulder, holding out the other to Wanda. "Let's go into the living room and sit down. Just give me a minute to think clearly, and we'll talk this out."

They traipsed into the living room, each taking a place on the couch. Marty sat on the loveseat, facing them, folding her hands together to form a steeple. She brought them to her mouth and took a long, shuddering breath of air. "Okay, first, isn't there any kind of treatment, chemo, radiation, whatever to—to—pro—"

"Prolong my life?" Wanda finished for her. She'd become really good at facing the reality of her situation as of late, and there was just no mincing words anymore.

"Yes, *anything*," Marty said on a stifled sob.

"There is, but I'll be miserable, and that's really all treatment will do—prolong my misery. Why live yarking my brains up after chemo and losing all my hair, needing someone to take care of me day and night, when I can just live in semicomfort until . . ."

Nina'd apparently caught her second wind. "Until you die, Wanda."

Marty grabbed at Nina's knee, giving it a white-knuckled squeeze. "Stop, Nina. Just shut the hell up for one minute. How—how long?"

Wanda let her head fall back on her shoulders, rolling it from side to side. Her chest expanded. She hated the number of days she'd been granted. She hated that she knew them. Hated that she could mentally tick each one off as it passed. "Maybe as long as six months."

Marty's harsh gasp, followed by Nina's choked, dry heave made the conversation she was having starkly vivid. She was dying. She was sitting in her living room, telling her two best friends in the whole world she was dying. That she had six months to get her affairs in order, tie up loose ends, find a home for Menusha, check off the stupid entries on her Fuck It list—was drastically real. "This is exactly why I didn't want to tell you—because you'll spend all your time avoiding it, trying not to hurt my feelings with words like *death*, and *dead*. You won't want to mention plans you'll make with each other, because I might not be around for them. It'll be awkward, and nothing will be the same."

Marty cocked her head, shock written all over her face. "And it was going to be the same if you just suddenly died on us and never even let us know what was coming? Did you think we'd just go off and have brunch at Hogan's, or maybe do a few rounds at the discount designer mall like you'd never existed? I don't want to cast stones here, Wanda, but that's ludicrous. Your ride on the crazy train is officially over."

"You know, Wanda, right now I'm so fucking pissed at you, I wanna jam my fist—no wait, *both* fists, down your skinny throat. Jesus! Did you plan to just slink off and die? Die, Wanda. *Die*. And never tell us a thing. You've known for a month. Were you just going to let us live forever—and we will live forever—knowing these were our last days with you and not speak up? What the fuck kind of friend are you? This is all very dramatic and brave and all that other bullshit. Very Lifetime movie channel valiant."

Nina placed her fist against her eye and rubbed. When she spoke again, her words were soft, but tainted with a harsh revelation. "That you would leave this world without looking back—without ever thinking both me and Marty would spend an eternity mourning you . . . well, I gotta say, if I still had a beating heart, it'd be broken. Seeing as all I have is a dead organ, I'm just going to go with a sadness I can't quite explain, but I can feel it right down to my bones. Dude, that hurts me like almost nothing I've felt since Lou's brush with death." Nina's beloved grandmother, Lou, had come close to dying, and it had torn Nina apart at the time.

And the idea that she'd caused this much pain made Wanda

jump up, steadying herself by clinging to the arm of her couch. "Nina, I—"

Nina's eyes cast downward, but not before she held up a pale palm. "Don't. You being this sick isn't just about you, Wanda. Yeah, to a degree, it's all about you. But your suffering ends when you leave this earth. Ours? Not so much. Maybe it's selfish of me to want to be with you, but for fuck's sake, Wanda Schwartz, to just keep this all to yourself and want to slink off to some hospital room and die? Fuck you and fuck that! Because there are people you're going to leave behind and this is about them, too. People who need you. *I* need you, okay? I've got but two friends in my life, and losing one who was just gonna leave me some lame-assed good-bye note or whatever you planned to do, sucks." Nina's head bent to her chest, her eyes focused firmly on her shaking fists in her lap, her silence so clearly thick with grief Wanda had to fight to keep from screaming her anguish.

Marty's blue eyes suddenly filled with salty tears, her mouth opened to speak, but only gasping puffs of air came out. Her intake of breath shook and rattled with a wheeze. "Wanda . . . oh, God . . . okay—I . . . I think I can't keep my shit together anymore. I need to cry. I'm a fucking hormonal mess these days as it is. There's no doubt this is definitely about you, but I need a second to catch my breath. For all this time we've suspected something just wasn't right . . . but to have it be this? I just need . . ." Marty paused, gulping and clearly fighting for composure. "Just give me a minute, okay? I'm going to go outside and bawl like the big, honkin' girl I am for you—with you—because I love you, and I know if I don't get this out of the way now, I'll be good for shit. I'm going to scream my fear. I'm going to out-swear Nina like a champion. I'm going to rage at whatever I can get my hands on—at how fucking unfair life is. Then I'm going to come back inside and do whatever you need me to do. I just need a minute—just one."

She rose from the couch with stiff legs, taking jerky steps to the back door that led to Wanda's postage stamp–sized backyard. Opening it, she let herself out, the door closing with a hush.

Wanda slid back down onto the couch beside Nina, who jerkily grabbed for her hand, squeezing it so tight she thought it might break.

But it didn't matter. She clung to the cool flesh of her friend's hand anyway.

And they both listened to Marty howl into the screech of the wind. Scream her pain, curse the injustice of Wanda's dying with huge gulping sobs. Her gut-wrenching tears, torn from her throat, slammed against Wanda's kitchen windows, echoed in her ears, vibrated in her chest.

Nina jammed her free fist back into her eye again, her face a mask of emotion after emotion that Wanda had never witnessed until now. Each gasp of air Marty took into her lungs made Nina cling tighter, each wretched sob of bleating agony made her body jump.

Tears fell freely from Wanda's eyes, streaming to pool in her lap, but she held fast to Nina, welcoming the shooting stabs of pain in her knuckles, for it affirmed the little bit of life she had left.

Menusha hopped on graceful paws to the back of the couch, curling herself around Nina's neck, rubbing her cheek against Nina's hair.

Marty's howl of tears subsided, then grew jarringly silent while the clock in Wanda's kitchen ticked, counting down the moments she had left with painful clarity.

The back door opened with another soft brush to the tile floor. Marty grabbed a roll of paper towels from its holder and swiped at her face, inhaling with a slow rasp, each breath growing steadier. She ran a hand over her hair, windblown and glistening with beads of the misty rain.

When she turned around, her face held obvious resolution and her stride toward them on the couch was confident.

Crossing her sapphire blue silk arms over her chest, she looked down at Wanda. Her first words rasped, as though she'd smoked a thousand cigarettes instead of Wanda. Her eyes were swollen and puffy, her artfully applied Bobbie-Sue makeup all but gone. "So, Wanda Schwartz, what are we going to do about this pansy-ass way you've chosen to leave the world?"

Nina's head popped up, and Wanda was convinced she was going to give Marty hell, but then she grinned.

A sly, encouraging grin.

"You know you don't have to die, Wanda."

Oh, God. Yes, she knew, but no, no, and no. If they were thinking what she thought they were thinking, then no. She'd thought it, too. Christ knew she'd thought about it, too, but . . .

It was wrong—she'd go to Hell and have to spend eternity in a yellow room.

But . . . maybe she could have the life she'd set out to have when she'd married the puke if she . . .

Fear, fear to do something so drastic, live a lifestyle she only knew on the outskirts, was maybe even scarier than dying.

If you lived forever . . . she shook her head. With her luck, some tragic twist of fate like a designer shopping trip gone awry would occur, and she'd end up decapitated by a clothes rack, with like a wooden hanger through her heart, and then she'd definitely go to Hell. "I do. I know, Marty, but to do what you're thinking we should do is interfering with fate. I was meant to die now. I wasn't bitten by accident like the two of you. That was fate. But fate must somehow feel I'm undeserving of, say, a paranormal life mate. Fate sent me a guy who *used* to be a vampire. I have to believe that's some kind of otherworldy message. Now, you can't just go around biting people because you'll miss them when they die.

It's not right. If that were the case, just imagine how many super people would be running all over the planet." She said the words, but did she really still believe them?

Nina vehemently shook her head. "No, Wanda. That's not true. I'd never bite someone just because they wanted to live forever because it might be considered cool. This lifestyle isn't easy, not by a long shot. I'm offering to bite you because yeah, I'll miss you and you already know what you'll be up against if I do bite you. It's not like you'd go into this clueless after what's happened to me and Marty."

Wanda waffled—to take their offer meant she'd live—something she wanted to do more than anything else. It also involved great risk to their well-beings. And then there was the possibility of eternal Hell. After twelve years of Catholic school, you just couldn't beat the notion of fiery pits of darkness out of her overnight. "First, it would risk you two and your standings with your—your paranormal people, and I would never, ever do that. And second, who's to say if you or Marty bite me and I turn into a vampire or a werewolf, that there won't be someone in my life I want to keep alive forever and I'll do the same thing to them—and they'll do the same thing to someone else. It's not right."

Marty stooped down, eye-level with Wanda. "Know what, Wanda?"

"What?"

"I really don't give a shit about what's right. I don't even care if Keegan freaks out on me about it. I'm just not ready to give you up. What's not right is you dying at this age. Before you've had a chance to live your life. Get married again. See what happens with the hunky Heath . . ."

Her stomach somersaulted at the mention of Heath. God, she'd so gone and done it to herself where Heath was concerned. She was falling in love all along, and she knew it. She'd tried to stop it, thought she was all hip and savvy by sending him as many signals as she could that they were just having sex, by using words like *uninvolved* and phrases like *not too personal*. But it had backfired—big. Yet, what Marty proposed—so enticing—so damned enticing, well, it meant involving people she loved who could quite possibly pay a penalty for turning her. "Lots of people die young, Marty, and they die young because that's life. Lots of people die much younger than me because that's the universe's plan. Are you going to go around and chew on everyone who's unfairly dying?"

Marty shook her head with purpose. "Nope. Just you. I don't know those other people who're dying young. I just know you."

Fire burned along Wanda's cheeks—her fear making her react. "Look, if I were meant to live, someone would have accidentally bitten me, too. So lay off!"

Nina rose with menace in her step, circling Wanda and Marty. She jammed her face in Wanda's. "I can make it an accident, Wanda, when I ram my fist down your throat, I'm pretty sure I'll nick some of your teeth on my way down."

Wanda reared up. "Don't you use those tactics with me, Nina Blackman-Statleon! I got nuthin' to lose by popping you in the jaw right now. I'm dying. Not even you, big, scary night dweller that you are, can scare me compared to that!"

All three women went silent again.

Reality had begun to wind its sharp, deadly black tendrils around their brains.

"You're *dying*, Wanda." Nina's throat worked furiously. "I just don't think I can take that. I don't think I can imagine my unlife without you always bitching at me in it. There'll be no one to keep me from stomping Marty's ass. I don't want to seem all self-serving here, but someone has to stick around so World War Three doesn't break out."

"And there'll be no lists," Marty muttered with defeat. "Who's going to write a list of the stuff I need for the baby? Who's going to keep track of where we last had dinner? Who's going to make me laugh because you just put Nina in her place?"

"Yeah, Wanda. You know just when to shut me up. Who's gonna do that when you're not here?" Nina's voice cracked.

Wanda fought to keep from sobbing. "You'll learn to take care of each other. You will, won't you? Promise me you won't drift apart because you fight so much. No, I won't be here to referee, but who knows if I won't be able to watch you from up there?" She pointed to the ceiling. "You do not want me haunting you in the afterlife. Just promise me you'll always look out for each other. Look out for Marty's baby, huh, Nina? You'll be a good auntie. You can teach it that swearing really is an art form."

"Will you at least think about it?" Marty croaked.

She shook her head with a firm back and forth motion. If she didn't, she might falter. "I don't know if I can. Everything I've been taught all my life says it would be wrong to interfere with fate. It seems almost like suicide—because I'd be dead if Nina bit me. And what if you two were caught turning me? Or are we forgetting all that shunning Nina talks about? Never mind—I can't explain my crazy rationale, and I don't have to explain my fears about what could happen to the two of you—you know what could happen. But if it helps at all, I did think about it. I thought really hard about it." And she had, and even if that crazy niggle that kept her up at night with what-ifs was still niggling, she couldn't. She'd done catechism—she knew what Hell and damnation was all about, and she totally didn't want to go there. She sure as hell wasn't taking Nina and Marty with her. "I'm too afraid of what might happen if I let one of you turn me and I do, for some uncanny reason, eventually end up dead—or worse, we get caught."

Nina dragged a hand through her hair. "So this explains the Heath thing."

Wanda was so used to playing dumb, it happened before she could stop it. "What do you mean?"

"I mean both me and Marty knew it isn't in you to do the fuck-buddy thing. You're all about nurturing and home and Martha Stewart shit. It explains why you've been keeping him at arm's length."

Heath. Just the thought that the kind of man she'd always hoped to find, but had given up on after her divorce, had shown up when her life was going downhill at a rapid pace, made her heart ache in her chest. "I should have never let things go even this far."

Marty's next statement was so true. "Because you're in deeper than you thought."

She covered her face with her hands, her voice muffled. "I really thought I could do this. Live for the moment, you know? Because that's really all I have to offer, but I don't think I'm very good at it. I tried . . ." She choked off a sob while the misery in her chest left her feeling like she'd explode.

Marty pulled Wanda to sit between the two of them, situating Wanda's head on her shoulder. "Have you told him, and for that matter, your family?"

Tears fell down her face, but she knew what she wanted where Heath was concerned. "I haven't told my mother or Casey yet. Heath found out in a way I wish he hadn't. Tonight I'd decided I was going to tell him, maybe in a couple of days or so, but my doctor left a message on my machine, and Heath heard it."

Nina eyeballed her with a stern expression. "That was very fair of you, Wanda."

God, this was miserable. "Look, Nina. Don't razz me. Please. He knows where we stand. We have incredible sex. That's all he thinks it is on my end, too—whether he wants it to be something more or not. Now let it be, okay?" They didn't need to know what Archibald had told her—not right now. They didn't need to know the details of what had passed between her and Heath tonight. To go over it now would only pour more salt on her open wound. She wasn't ready to relive that just yet. Not even with Marty and Nina.

But Nina and Marty gave each other glances, glances she'd typically question, yet Wanda didn't have the energy to make them explain.

Nina wasn't ready to let it go just yet—it was obvious in her next statement. "But it isn't just sex, and if you plan to hit the graveyard and it doesn't matter what you say because you won't be here for any backlash—or God forbid, what I think you're most afraid of, rejection—why not just tell him? You'll have no regrets then."

No regrets. None. She could never regret Heath. What surprised her was Nina's attitude. "When did you go all moral, Nina? You were the one who said I should bag and tag him."

Nina squirmed in her seat, letting her hair hang over her face. "That was before I got how much you dig him, and you do dig him, Wanda."

Yeah, she dug. Way dug. "How about we just let me do this my way? You can tell him whatever you want when—when the time comes. After tonight, I may never see him again. He was angrier than I've ever seen anyone—even you, Nina." By God was that ever the truth. She couldn't breathe for his anger.

"So what do you suppose that means? That he was angry with you, Wanda? You don't suppose he was angry because his fuck buddy was going to go and die on him, do you? Do you think that's all you mean to him—if you were just fucking he wouldn't have bothered to get angry!" Nina yelled from between clenched teeth.

"Nina! Stop. Stop now," Marty ordered.

Wanda put a hand on Marty's arm and squeezed. "I don't really know what it means. It all happened so fast. I just know I really screwed up, and I regret the hell out of it, okay? But please, don't beat me down for it—not tonight . . ." she said, her voice quivering and watery. "I only know Heath needs time to do whatever he has to do to cope. I've learned a lot from seeing your anger, Nina, and I know it means he reacted without thought because I caught him off guard. No one knows better than you what that's like. When you're in pain, you act out."

Marty's look was astonished. "Jesus, Wanda. You're way reasonable right now."

Her response was a dry laugh. "Isn't that what I always am? Reasonable, conservative, rational in times of crisis, fucking ridiculously predictable. I was trying to be something I'm not with Heath, and it blew up in my face." Her words hitched on a sob.

Marty's eyes filled again with tears, but it was Nina who spoke. "But that's what I love about you, Wanda. I love that I can count on you to set me straight, no matter how hinky I get. You're not afraid of me—you call me on my shit—you love me anyway. Don't ever, *ever* discount those qualities—because they're who you are, and who you are is all the good things I wanna be. And that's why I wish you'd tell Heath how you feel—be honest. Because that's *who* you are."

And Nina was right. That's who she was—which was why she'd been so troubled all along when it came to Heath. Because she did want more than just the sex. But tonight, who she was just needed some space. "I can't promise you anything—some of this depends on Heath, but for tonight, I just need to—to think, *please*."

"But—" Nina began to protest.

"Deal," Marty intervened, kissing the top of Wanda's head. "We'll do whatever *you* want. So, you wanna have girls' night tonight? I'll call Keegan and Nina can call Dracula so they know where we are, and then we'll watch stupid stuff on TV—eat popcorn, drink blood, yak all night long."

"Cool." Nina's smile was painfully phony. "I'm in."

Wanda shook her head. "I know you guys are worried. I know you love me, but I think I just need some time to myself. Do you mind?"

Marty smiled, her eyes so sad Wanda almost couldn't look at her. "As long as you promise to call us if you need us."

"Yep. Promise. Now go. The paranormal men in your life will worry if you don't."

"I don't want to leave you." Nina looked directly into her eyes. She was telling her without saying out loud that each moment they had left was important to her.

Wanda trailed a finger along Nina's oh-so-beautiful cheekbone, then chucked her under the chin. "Well, Elvira, I need some space, and if anyone knows what that's like, it's you. So fly on home."

Nina got up from the couch, pulling Marty up, too. Marty slid her jacket on, and as they headed for the door, Nina held up her thumb and her pinky to make the sign of a phone, meaning if Wanda needed her, all she had to do was call.

"Promise," she whispered.

Silence followed in their wake—a silence in voices only.

Wanda's head swirled with their conversation. Over and over, she couldn't seem to drown out Marty's sobs. Nina's choked, dry heaves.

Or the thought that she may have ended things with Heath without even trying because she'd been blinded by her own selfishness.

Bright was not in her color wheel today.

Regret, however, was.

"SIR! What are you doing? I'm trying to sleep, and heaven knows, since this human adventure has been thrust upon us, I feel like Methuselah. So do keep it to a dull roar." He peered into the kitchen where Heath stood guzzling a bottle of his favorite beer.

Archibald tightened the belt of his thrift shop robe with a roll of his eyes. "Oh, young Heathcliff. What troubles you that you must drown your sorrows in discount beer?"

He still didn't know if he could say it out loud. "It's Wanda."

"She drove you to cheap beer?"

"No, I drove myself to the store and bought cheap beer. We're on a budget."

Concern lined Arch's face—so crystal clear, Heath almost couldn't look at him for the stark devotion he saw in them. "I know you well, sir—something's very wrong."

Wrong, wrongful, more wrong, wronger. It didn't get any wronger. "I know why she doesn't want to be involved," Heath said so suddenly, he surprised even himself.

"Please tell me it's not because her twin sister carried Wanda's baby for her, all while Wanda innocently thought her husband inseminated her sister via legitimate surrogacy, only to find out he was really, uh, inseminating her personally under the veil of candlelight and fine champagne. It can happen, sir. I've watched it on the daytime channels at the shelter."

"She's dying, Arch. *Dying* . . ." He let the word go—slipping from his mouth in a gruff, harsh whisper. His throat tightened like someone had their hands wrapped around his neck. He couldn't, in all his years, ever remember feeling this helpless, this desolate. Not even after he'd been turned.

Archibald's typically expressionless face instantly filled with concern, sympathy, dread. "Heathcliff . . . I . . . in all my thoughts about our fair Wanda, they never, *ever* . . ."

Fuck did he get the never, ever thing. "Yeah, me either. I suspected she was sick—just not this sick. Not dying sick."

"But what is it? Is there treatment? Something we can do—

a doctor?" His last word came out squeaky and very unlike Archibald, always so composed.

"I don't know the specifics. I didn't stick around to ask." And he'd been mentally kicking himself in the gut since he'd left her because of it.

"You broke it off with her, Heathcliff?" Archibald let disappointment mingle with the astonishment in his tone. "I'd have thought better of you—"

Heath rolled his head on his neck, moving it up and down to try and ease the tension that just wouldn't let the fuck up. "No, Arch. No. I just felt like I'd been kidney punched when I found out. I could barely ask questions. All I could think of was kicking the shit out of something—someone. I reacted badly, Arch. I said some things I can't take back. But goddamn it, why didn't she tell me?"

"The answer is obvious—she's found deeper feelings for you than she intended. She doesn't want to spend what's left of her time here with people who will mourn her before she's actually departed. This isn't about you, Heathcliff. You'd do well to remember that. Certainly you understand?"

Heath ran a tired hand over his chin, littered with stubble. "Now I do. Four hours ago, I couldn't understand anything—anyone. I saw red. She's known all along and never said a word. That cut deep. I was a shithead, Arch. I yelled, ranted, behaved like a complete fuck."

Archibald took the beer from him, placing it on the counter. He clamped a hand on Heath's shoulder, reassuring, firm. "Grief has many facets, sir. I know you're not proud yours displayed itself in the way it has, but shock, dismay, helplessness are all heady, powerful emotions."

"I just couldn't believe it . . ." He still couldn't believe it. What he really couldn't believe were the words he'd used to demonstrate that disbelief. At this moment, when the possibility of Wanda leaving his life forever was all he could think about, he wished for his immortality. If he were still a vampire, he had to wonder if his fucking heart wouldn't throb painfully quite the way it was now.

Archibald brushed at his shoulder with a swift hand. "And now you have the information, Heathcliff. What will you do with it? Will you continue to let Miss Wanda believe you're a putz, or will you make this right with her? Will you allow your grief to ruin what's left of her life, or do you want your testicles back? I believe I last saw them in the coat closet when I put away that useless contraption called a Dust Eater—or whatever it's called."

Heath couldn't help but laugh, but he sobered immediately. Archibald cupped his jaw, then slapped his cheek with a light hand. "You know what to do, sir. I have every faith."

Heath grabbed Arch's hand for the quickest of moments, gripping it hard—for reassurance, for comfort, for the one person in the world he'd always been able to lean on.

And then he knew what to do.

Just like that.

CHAPTER
17

"Heathcliff isn't at home, Miss Wanda. But do come in—we have a chair now. A whole chair, can you believe that? Come in and sit, wait for Heathcliff." His eyes, lined with wrinkles, kind, and warm, beckoned her into Heath's apartment.

But she shook her head, pulling her coat tighter around her neck. "I can't, Archibald, but thank you. You're very good to Heath. I know he appreciates it. He speaks fondly of you often. I really have to dash, but would you give him something for me?"

"Of course, miss—anything. But I do wish you'd wait for Heathcliff. He only had a brief meeting with, uh, what's her name?" He paused, running a finger over his forehead in thought. "Ah, yes—sticky lips Linda. He said he'd be back in plenty of time for dinner and afterward he had something very important to take care of. In fact, why don't you join us? I'm making something called tuna casserole—yet another dish for heathens everywhere, which makes it of course, budget friendly."

He made her smile even under the circumstances. "I—I can't. I really can't. Just give this to Heath, please, and tell him I'll see him soon." She shoved a small, lumpy package wrapped in blue cellophane at Arch. Blue was Heath's favorite color, he'd claimed in one of their not too personal conversations. She wiped a tear from her eye that had escaped despite her efforts to keep this a Kleenex-free moment.

She'd known Heath wouldn't be home, and she'd come purposely at this time because of it. "I have to go, Archibald, but thank you—you're a good man." She cupped his cheek before turning and heading back down the stairwell, the clomp of her heels echoing against the acoustic ceiling.

Every muscle in her body was tense, tightly wound like a newly strung guitar. Her breathing was shallow—uneven as she got into her car to race home.

She was meeting Nina and Marty there.

Last night had been the kind of hell she was so worried she'd end up in if she let Marty and Nina turn her. She'd lost count of the times she'd picked up the phone to call Heath, only to put it back down as if it had bitten her. He had to come to terms with this on his own—she'd lied to him. Well, okay, maybe she hadn't lied outright, but she'd kept something from him he'd deserved to know from the get-go. Had she been all moral and self-righteous to begin with, instead of letting her infatuation with him cloud her judgment, instead of thinking she deserved some kind of fucking pass because she was dying, she'd have given him the choice to stay or go.

But she hadn't.

She'd taken it upon herself to make Heath's decisions for him.

And that wasn't just presumptuous—it left her disgusted with herself.

Today—well, today was a different story altogether. Today she was going to leave everyone else's lives alone and deal strictly with hers—no matter what the outcome with Heath was after he found out what she was going to do.

And she wasn't going to look back.

Not even once.

She picked up her cell phone and pressed number five.

"Hello?"

"Casey?"

"Wanda?"

Wanda smiled. Her sister always sounded so surprised when she called. "Yeah, it's me."

"What's up? You okay? Mom and Dad?"

Casey always thought something was wrong if Wanda called her, too. She never initiated any phone calls, and sometimes that hurt, but tonight was about something far bigger than who'd called whom first. Tonight was about a revision to her Fuck It list, and Casey and her mother and father were number one on it. "Yeah, everything's fine, honey. I tried to call Mom, but it's Wednesday, and you know they go to that seafood buffet at the Shrimp Shack on Wednesday nights. Anyway, it doesn't matter. I just called to tell you I love you." She bit the inside of her cheek to keep her voice steady.

Casey's sigh was aggravated in the hiss of wind she blew into the phone. "Is this the 'you suck, Casey, you haven't called me in forever' phone call? I've just been busy—"

Wanda's voice was soft to Casey's harassed tone. "Nope. This is just an I love you phone call, Case. I love you, and if you talk to Mom and Dad, tell them the same."

She hung up with a quick click of the Off button, keeping her eyes focused straight ahead.

And never once did she look back.

*   *   *

MARTY and Nina appeared at her door just as she was folding her Fuck It list into a tiny square.

Marty spoke first, her voice tremulous and hesitant. "Ya okay? I mean, I know you're probably not okay-okay, but we're here to help make whatever you need okay."

Nina nodded, her silky, dark hair falling over her shoulder to hang just beneath her breasts. "What she said." She put a hand to Wanda's cheek, her flesh cool, her black eyes burning bright. "So tell me what I can do to make this whatever you want to make it."

Wanda gave them each a curt nod. "Okay. This is what I want. Do me."

"*Do* you?" Nina raised an eyebrow.

"Yeah." Wanda pointed to her neck. "Bite me, here"—then she remembered Marty's biting incident and held up her hand, pointing to the webbed portion between her thumb and forefinger—"or here."

Nina's eyebrows smooshed together. "Did you just say what I thought you said?"

Wanda faced Nina head-on, her lips a thin line of resolution. "I did."

"You didn't."

"I did, too."

"But—"

Wanda flagged a hand upward in an instant. "And I don't care which of you does it either. In fact, surprise me. Just do me this— when I wake up—give me the heads-up on which paranormal way I've gone. 'K?"

Marty and Nina looked at each other, stupefied. "Can I ask what changed your mind?" Marty inquired.

"No."

Nina flicked her arm with a finger. "Don't you tell us no, Wanda.

I want to be sure you're sure. There's no going back. Never, ever. At least not in my case because it would hurt too many people."

Wanda's eyes widened. Who knew better than she there was no going back? Who'd only heard that three bazillion times since Nina and Marty'd been turned? "Ohhh listen to how we're all hesitant now. Just last night you two were going to duct tape me to a chair and make me accept the gift of immortality, and now you want to be sure I'm sure? What difference does it make? Just do it, for fuck's sake!"

Nina's eyes widened. "You swore . . ." she accused, her voice ringing with that same surprise it always held when Wanda actually manned up enough to cuss.

Wanda's face contorted with disbelief, while stabs of fear for what she was about to do needled her gut. She wasn't afraid of her choice to be turned—just that it might hurt. Or that it might hurt her friends. Nina and Marty swore they'd never felt a thing, but she had a fear it'd be like the giving birth metaphor. All that "you forget the pain once you hold the baby in your arms" thing troubled her. "Fuck, yeah, I swore! I'm going to die, Nina. If that doesn't call for a swear word, then I don't know what the hell does. Now quit jabber jawing and friggin' hit me. Riiiiight here, baby." She pointed to the tender flesh of her neck and tried not to wince.

Holy Jesus, she was considering drinking blood for an eternity. When Nina had been turned, the very idea had left her so squicked by what she'd had to do to survive, she'd gagged—often. But it was just a small hurdle compared to leaving Heath forever. She'd battled all night long over which paranormal avenue to take, then she'd decided it didn't matter what freaky road she took, just that the end result landed her on Eternity Lane.

"Wanda," Marty interjected, grabbing her by the hand and leading her to the sofa. "Sit. Shut up. Listen."

She folded her arms over her chest and pursed her lips. "Listening."

Marty's eyes welled with unshed tears when she spoke. "Honey, this is something you have to be more than sure of and, after the way we went at you the other night and your reaction to it, we decided we'd adhere to your last wishes and lay off you. Neither of us liked it, but we were pushing our lifestyle on you, and we were wrong."

"Not that I fucking wanted to lay off you," Nina interrupted, "but Marty went all reasonable on me, and she made some good points that made sense once I was over the shock. We didn't have a choice in our immortality, Wanda. You do and, even if we don't like that choice—even if it's fucking killing me to contemplate it—we don't want to shove our shit down your throat, because that's selfish. Your beliefs are your beliefs, and whether I agree with them or not, I respect them. It isn't always easy to live like this. As much as I love Greg, there are days I'd give my left boob to be human again. If it didn't mean fucking up half a vampire culture, I just might. But I wouldn't want to do it without him. Believe me, I *do* miss my mortality. Hell, I miss stupid fucking things like chicken wings and bleu cheese dressing, but it's still not worth giving Greg up or leaving a bunch of clan members stranded like Heath is."

Marty nodded her blonde head. "Don't do this because we've forced our opinions, our desperation on you. We were impulsive. We just wanted to help and because we have the power to do that, we got pushy."

Well, holy fuck. She never thought she'd see the day. Nina and Wanda agreeing on *anything* meant the apocalypse was surely well on its way.

Wanda brushed her hands together with determination. She wasn't taking no for an answer. Not now. "I know exactly what I'm doing—when do I ever do anything without thinking it through, writing a list, thinking it through some more? I decided going to Hell, even if the possibility is slim, is worth it. Okay? So if you want to help—then freakin' help." Wanda pointed to her neck, cocking her head to the left. "And if you bite me, Nina, do me a favor, don't leave me scarred. God only knows if there's a concealer at Bobbie-Sue that'll disguise it." Wanda pointed to her neck once more. "So go on, hit me right here." But then a thought occurred to her. "Oh, but wait. Promise me if anyone ever finds out—ever—about what happens here tonight, you'll lie like some cheap Persian carpet about how I was turned. I'd never give you up. Never. Now, swear on it," she insisted.

Nina glared at her. "That's the least of my worries, Wanda."

Wanda cracked her knuckles with determination. "Okay, then—hit me."

Both women stayed rooted to their spots on the living room floor.

"Wait—got any booze on you?"

"Booze?" Nina looked perplexed.

Wanda was in take-charge mode, and her sigh of exasperation showed it. "Yeah, Nina. You know, like the stuff you drink when you want to deaden brain cells and turn into a slobbering, crying whiner? That booze." She held her hands wide apart. "Big booze, in fact. Never mind, I think I have an old bottle of Scotch I used to keep for my dad when he came to visit. Daddy loved Scotch." She popped up, heading for her pantry in the kitchen.

Nina, followed by Marty, trailed behind her—nagging. "I don't know if drinking is the way to go here, Wanda. You hardly ever drink. Getting snockered might do something to the effects of the bite. Marty and I were stone cold sober when we were bitten, and I might add, we've never done this turning thing. Which brings me to our big mouths and all our smack talk about turning you."

Wanda grabbed the bottle of Scotch and shoved it under her

arm, whipping around to face them. "Is that chicken-shit I hear in your voice, Nina Blackman-Statleon? Never in all my days did I think I'd hear you pansy-ass out of anything. I've read about plenty of helpless women who were turned because they were too drunk to stop it."

Nina was quick to retort. "You read that in a romance novel, Wanda! Jesus fucking Christ! You've read all that shit in stupid romance novels. You don't know if it's true."

"Oh, puullease. Every stupid thing we read in those books about you when you were whining about not wanting to be a vampire was true. I call pansy-ass, Nina. Whassamatter, vam-pi-re? Are you just good at talking tough? Was all that talk just that? Talk?"

Nina cocked her head at Wanda, her slender face tight, her jaw set hard. She pushed her hair behind her ears. "Did you just call me—*me*—a pansy-ass?"

Wanda bumped chests with her, knocking into her with a hard thud, steadying the bottle under arm when she did. "Yup. What're ya gonna do about it?"

Nina instantly backed off, her expression contrite. "Nothing."

"Sissy," Wanda taunted.

Nina clenched her fists by her side. "Stop, Wanda." Her tone held warning by the growl and sneer that followed.

"Or what? You'll *talk* about kicking my ass?"

"I said, *stop*," Nina growled.

Wanda jammed her face in Nina's. If it took stirring Nina's pot of shit to get her to turn her, just call her spoon. "And I said *no*, wussy!"

Marty was between them so quick, Wanda might not have seen it but for the hand that gripped her shoulder. She placed the other on Nina's, too, parting the two women. "Ding-ding-ding-ding-ding! End round one!" she shouted. "Wanda? I can't believe I'm saying this for the first time in our friendship, but knock it the hell off and leave Nina alone. Now. Nina, if you don't back up, I'll make you back up, and even if you could take me, you won't lay a finger on me because I'm with child. I win, you lose. Back—off." She whisked a hand under Nina's nose, wiggling it in the direction opposite Wanda.

Wanda's chest heaved, her stomach lurched, but she backed away, as did Nina.

Marty dropped, her folded hands in front of her, placing them over the slight swell of her belly. "Now, my very irrational friends, let's get the proverbial grip and talk about this."

Wanda knew her eyes were probably wild, her hair mussed, while she wandered in her pink bunny nightgown with the googly eyes, for the love of God, but she needed to convince them she knew exactly what she was doing. She had no qualms about her decision. She wanted to be with Heath. End of. She was tired of playing it safe. She'd spent a buttload of time married to a fuckwit. Now she wanted a do-over. "That's exactly what I don't want to do, Marty. Talk. I spend all my goddamned time talking, and look where it got me. Halfway to fucking dead. Not to mention all the time I spend talking to the two of you—soothing you—pacifying you. Well, guess the fuck what? It's my turn now. This is about me and what I want, and I don't want to die—okay? I want to live. I don't care how that happens either. I don't care if I'm a vampire or a werewolf or a goddamned fairy. I—want—to—live!" she yelled, gasping for another breath before she continued. "I want to live. I want to see your baby born, Marty. I want to knit stupid booties for it because that's just the kind of girl I am. I want to hear Nina bitch for eternity about what an event it is to shop with us. And Nina, if you call me Holly Hobby once more, I'll yank your fangs out with rusty pliers. Got that?"

Nina nodded, mouth open, but wordless.

Wanda wiped the back of her hand over her forehead and up

into her scalp. "So if it's okay with you both, I'm going to pour myself a drink—maybe I'll even pour myself four or five—I'm going to get stupid-drunk and then, wham! One of the two of you turn me. Okay?"

Marty's pretty face was a mixture of skeptical and sympathetic. "Honey, all of this fire and brimstone isn't helping your cause." She ran a hand over Wanda's messy hair, then smoothed her rumpled nightgown. "In fact, you look a little mental."

Nina nodded. "Yeah. Like maybe we should call the people in charge of butterfly nets and ask them to bring the realllly big one. The one that fits your *entire* body."

Wanda's breathing grew harsh, almost ragged. "Wouldn't you be mental if you were dying, Marty? As a matter of fact, I remember a little mental when you were turned into a werewolf—so cut me some slack." She took the bottle of Scotch and stomped around in the kitchen, yanking open a cabinet door and pulling out a tumbler. She opened the bottle of liquor and poured a healthy shot of it into the glass, taking a whiff of it.

Marty and Nina were right behind her, trailing her like a bad case of the clap. "Wanda, that's not fair. I was already turned by then—this is muuuuch different."

Wanda tilted the glass back, guzzling the acidic liquid. Oh, that was god-awful. She shivered before saying, "Yeah, it is much different. I'm *dying*. You're not, and you never will be, barring tragedies like bullets to your vitals—or decapitation." She swiped the bottle back off the counter and poured twice as much as she had before.

Nina tried to grab the glass from her, but Wanda backed away, raising a finger, shaking it furiously. "Do. Not. Don't even go there."

Marty approached her with hesitance while she downed another double shot of Scotch. "We just want to be absolutely positive you're sure, and we're not sure what would make you change your mind so suddenly after you were so freaked last night."

She threw the plastic tumbler into her sink. Fuck that. She'd just drink from the bottle. Another healthy swig and she had an answer for her change of heart. "Heath. Heath made me change my mind. How's that?"

Nina yanked a chair out from the table and sat, her black almond eyes apprehensive. "How? Did he pressure you? I'll kill him if he did. He has no right."

A bit of the booze dribbled down the side of her mouth. She swiped at it with her thumb, then decided her thumb tasted damned good. "No, he has no idea I know what he told me is true, so how could he pressure me, Nina?"

Nina once more passed Marty a look Wanda couldn't summon the energy to examine. She had some paranormals to convince.

She blew a strand of her hair out of her face. "Okay, here's the deal. I love him—that's why. And know what? As hard as I've tried to keep him at arm's length—do the fuck-buddy crap you talked about, Nina—I sucked at it. Plus, I think he wants more. I couldn't give him that. But I can if you bite me. So . . . yeah . . . so there. That's why I want one of you two lily-livered pansies to change me, because I want to live—with Heath. I want to see if he loves me, too. Or if he doesn't now, that he might given the chance to have me say something other than 'we can't get involved.' "

Marty cocked her head while her eyes darted over Wanda's face. "So tell me this, sweetie. Isn't he going to wonder how the hell you were turned and by who? We're not supposed to turn you according to both pack and clan law. He lived by those rules, too, once. Okay, so he was once a vampire, he'd understand it's possible—which brings up a whole other problem. He's now a human, honey. He won't live forever. If we're successful—you will." Marty placed a hand on her belly and rubbed it with a pro-tective palm.

Yeah, yeah. She'd given that a lot of thought, but she'd rather have the possibility of maybe as much as fifty years with the man of her dreams than none. And she said as much. "I don't care. I'd rather have what time Heath has left on Earth than nothing at all. I want to be able to talk to him about all the stuff that I've kept my mouth shut about because I was foolishly trying to remain nothing but his mattress mate. I love Heath. In fact, I discovered that just last night. It hit me at the craaaa-ziest moment, too. When he was eating, of all things, a Reese's Peanut Butter Cup."

"Love does that," Nina said, her affection for Greg ringing clear in her words. "It sometimes happens in the simplest, most fucked-up of ways."

Wanda's smile was of wistful agreement. "And I knew—it just was. I knew I could watch him eat those stupid chocolates until my eyeballs fell out of my head. I knew I was getting in deep. I knew I wished I had the time for more, I just didn't know it would be this kind of more. I don't know how it happened, or why it hap-pened now, but it did—and I want my shot at happiness, too. If you guys can have one, a shot to live out your HEA, I mean, so can weeee—I mean, I—what-ev-errrr." The effects of the Scotch were hitting her—hard. Before her wits were spirit soaked, she wanted to make her desires clear. "Pleeaassse, do this for me. Please. Oh, and I pomise—don't assssk, don tell. 'K? I won tell nooobody it wassss you guys who did it."

Nina cracked her knuckles, passing Marty a glance Wanda couldn't keep her eyes straight on and might have been left suspi-cious by, 'cept she felt too good to care what all these weird looks between them were about.

"It doesn't matter if you tell him about us or not, Wanda," Nina reminded her. "How the fuck will you explain turning into a vampire or a werewolf? You had the conversation about him being a vampire, but you never said a word about us and what you know. Is he going to think you just found some random asshole paranormal who just happened to be hanging around to turn you?"

Wanda wandered off to the living room, dragging the blanket her mother'd made her off the couch, and followed the path to her bedroom, the bottle tucked under her armpit. Alcohol spilled as she went, but she didn't even care if it stained the carpet. She was too busy focusing on the narrow trail to her bedroom, a path that now seemed kinda warbly and not nearly as easy to follow as it had been yesterday when Heath had playfully chased her into her bedroom. Ahhhh, Heath . . . "I dunno—who caressss. Iss no big deal. I tole you guys that already. I promise I won't say nuffin' about you guuuuys." Ohhhhh, was that her words all smushed together and slurring? Niice. Very nice. Boozer.

Nina looked at Marty.

Wanda watched Nina look at Marty—it was unfocused, definitely blurry, but she watched beneath hooded eyelids.

Wanda slugged back another gulp from the amber-filled bottle, holding out her hand to Nina. "C'mere. Sssssssit wif me." She patted the bed. "Riiiiiggght here."

Nina took her hand and sat with care next to her, grabbing the bottle when Wanda let go of it in favor of planting her two hands on either side of Nina's face. "Yer my frieeennnd. I lub you. Yu got a baaad potty mouf, but I sssstil lubs you. So be a gooood friend and"—she hiccupped—"annnnd bite meeee. 'K? Issseasssssy—just bite." She snapped her teeth at Nina and giggled while trying to find Marty in the swirling vortex her room had become, but it made her stomach lurch to attempt to focus her eyes on anything. So she closed them and called to her instead. "Maaaaaarrrtyy!"

"Yes, sweetie?"

Wanda patted the other side of the bed where Marty came to sit by her. "I lu—lu-luuubs you, toooo, Martyyyy. I didn't alwayssss like you. In the beggiinning when I meet—met you—you were obsess—ob—sess—"

"Obsessed, Wanda," Nina finished for her.

She waved a finger in the air. "Yeaaaaahhhh, thass it. But you got much nicccer. I think the dog is gooood for you. Not Muffff—yoooou know, the head dog."

A tear slid down Marty's cheek. "I think so, too, Wanda." She stroked a hand over Wanda's forehead, light as a feather. "Look, are you really sure? You can't change this if we do it. Well, I guess you can if Nina turns you. According to Heath, anyway."

Nina scoffed. "Don't even remind me, Marty—even if I'd never risk fucking up a whole clan of vampires, don't think there isn't still a part of me that wishes Greg and I could do the human thing together. I'm not sure I'd want to spend any part of my life without my man—even if I could be human again. I love Greg. I love my life. I don't want to hunt down his sire's sire's sire—or whatever the fuck it takes to be turned back."

"But if *I* turn you," Marty said, whispering low in Wanda's ears, "there's definitely no going back."

Wanda'd open her eyes to give Marty the stare she'd learned from Heath, but she was afraid she'd yark if she did. "I'm suuuure. Very, very, very, very, veeee-rr—yyy sure."

Marty's nod was solemn and sure. "Okay, then. Just close your eyes, honey. When you wake up, everything will be okay."

Marty leaned forward while Nina clung to Wanda's hand. Wanda kept thinking she ought to tell Marty to hurry up and get it over with, but her lips just wouldn't cooperate. They were like thick slabs of meat.

And then she was somewhere lovely.

Big, fluffy white clouds drifted into one another like slow motion bumper cars.

The temperature was just right. Not too cold, not too hot.

And Barbra Streisand music played in soft, dulcet tones.

Shiny.

CHAPTER
18

Wanda felt Marty lift the old blanket her mother had made her and look under it, running her hands over her legs. "Nothing. No hair. No outward sign of any even minute changes. It's not working! Oh, holy fuck, what've we done, Nina?"

Wanda drifted, on a soft, puffy cloud of contentment. Yet she could hear Nina and Marty—see them from an almost smoky, sort of out of body haze, doing what they did best. Fight. And what did who do, that required a holy fuck?

Nina's tone was typically gruff and impatient. "We don't know it's not working, you moron. Don't you remember how it was with us? We both woke up the *next day* with symptoms, not two minutes after it happened, dipshit. Jesus, stop panicking. Let it simmer or whatever the fuck it's supposed to do."

"This isn't two minutes, Nina. It's two hours. We should have gotten help from Keegan and Greg. Maybe I did it wrong?"

Nina snorted. "Yeahhhh, that woulda worked out just fine. Greg would shit a bat if he knew what I was doing right now. That strict no biting rule applies to me, too, ya know. I could be shunned from my own man's clan for this. But you know what? I don't give a flip. I'd dare Greg to tell me I can't do what I want to do, and I want to keep Wanda here with me—with us."

Ohhhh, Nina loved her. Wanda's heart tugged at the notion. She'd always known it. Nina had said it, but that she was admitting it so freely as of late made her mentally smile. And then realization swiftly followed. No matter what—if whatever was happening left her alive and kicking—she had this moment to throw back in her face.

Score.

Marty's face softened, big tears welling in her blue eyes. "Oh, Ninnnnnaaaa. You love us. If we weren't sure before, I'd say this cinches the deal."

Exactly, Wanda agreed with soundless approval.

Nina nudged Marty's shoulder with her fist. "Shut the fuck up, Marty. Yeah, I love you and without Wanda as part of this set of sicko triplets we've apparently become, I don't want to get up at night. Okay? Now just be quiet for once in your life and let's see what happens."

Yeah. Some quiet time would be nice, Wanda thought—though she couldn't speak the words. She drifted once more to that dark place, the place where she could shut everyone and everything out and cling to her cloud of calm.

AN hour later, according to the alarm clock on Wanda's nightstand, Nina gave Marty a scathing glance from her seat on the chair beside the bed Wanda lay on, rousing her from the haven of the dark place. "Jesus Christ, Marty. Leave it to you to screw this up.

How hard can it be to bite someone? No wonder you were such a piss-poor werewolf to begin with."

Hoo boy. Now what? Try as she might, Wanda couldn't move her lips, and that meant Nina and Marty were going to have to work on their problem-solving skills alone—together. Again, hoo boy.

She saw Marty instantly pop up from the opposite side of the bed. "You watch yourself, Nina Statleon! I did exactly what I read on the Internet. It isn't like I go around biting people, you heathen. In case you've forgotten, I'm not supposed to sink my canines into anyone according to pack law either. So I didn't get the information booklet that comes with the class on how to turn someone into a werewolf. It's bad enough that if this works we're going to have some splainin' to do to our men, but you're not making it any easier by telling me I've done it wrong." How odd that now Marty's position had become that of Nina's just two hours ago.

"Well, you have, you tard," Nina said plainly.

"We don't know that, you, you, bloodsucker. Stop being so impatient and just wait it out."

Wrong? They'd done something wrong? Leave it to the two of them to wreak havoc when left to their own devices. But once more, Wanda found she didn't care. Wherever she was, it was totally rad. The nag in her belly was completely gone and the worry of her life coming to an end, inconsequential.

TWO more hours later, after the beginning of a marathon of *What Not to Wear*, Nina was clearly eggshell fragile from Wanda's vantage point. "If you don't turn this shit off, Marty, I'll beat you to death with the remote."

But I loooove *What Not to Wear*, Wanda protested in her mind.

"Don't tell me you don't like it, Nina. I saw a flicker of a smile when Clinton threw all that girl's clothes away and Carmindy made her eyes pop with just a little shading of her eyeliner. Besides, I thought it'd be good karma. Wanda loves this show. Maybe if she hears it while the change is happening, it'll lift her spirits."

It has. She's lifted, Wanda confirmed Marty's statement without speaking a word.

"She's not comatose, doofus. She's snockered. Like passed out. We don't even know if the change has happened. All I do know is, I can smell her breath from here, and it's rank."

Wanda watched Marty bite the inside of her cheek from some surreal dreamlike place she could float in and out of at will. Uh-oh. Marty was going to waffle—Wanda knew Marty well enough to know that Nina could create self-doubt in her like Bill Gates had created Microsoft. "Oh, God. It isn't working, is it? Jesus Christ, Nina. What the fuck have we done?"

Waffling complete.

Nina's face went angry. Go figure. "I didn't do a goddamned thing. *You* did it, and frigged it up to boot—which is nothing less than I'd expect."

Marty gasped on a wheeze, her eyes narrowing. "You. Did. Not."

Nina cackled. "Yeah, yeah I did, Princess."

"How dare you accuse me of something so mean, Nina Statleon!"

And it was on, Wanda thought, and she was helpless to stop the two of them from ripping each other apart. Immobile in this odd state of "who gives a shit?"

"Forget it," Nina said with harsh resolve. "I'll fix this."

She decided to return to the dark place in her mind instead of watching her friends fight when there wasn't a bloody thing she could do about it. It was easy to let go, turn away from their bickering—so she did. Wherever she was, it was tres fabu.

But abruptly Wanda felt the bed sag toward her. She felt hair graze her cheek, and then, she felt nothing.

Which was abso-fucking-lutely delightful.

NINA pressed Speed Dial on her phone, clicking the button to put it on speaker, giving Marty the look. "Marty, we are so fucked. Do you know what this means?" The panic was clear in her voice and growing sharper with each ring of Greg's cell. "He's going to kill meeee—" Greg picked up in the middle of her statement.

"Nina? Where the hell are you? I've been trying to call you for hours. In fact, woman, I was just about to tap into that freaky-deaky dark place called your mind and summon you home. Now what's going on?"

"Um, vampire?" Nina's worried eyes looked to Marty, who reached out a hand to her. Nina grabbed it and tightened her grip.

"Yes, dear?"

Marty took a deep breath as Nina spoke into the phone. "We have a problem and before you go getting all hinky with me, let me just explain. It's Wanda. Do you remember what I told you the other day?"

Greg's voice went soft, consoling. "I do, honey. Is that where you've been? Is she okay? Do you need me, babe? Should I be there with you?"

Nina rolled her eyes and then clenched them shut. "Oh, you should be here, punkin'—but not because anything's wrong, per se. Well, wait," she rushed onward, her words stringing together. "I take that back. Something's wrong, but it isn't Wanda's health per se . . ." Marty shook her head vehemently at Nina, giving her the "Omigod, don't even fucking think it" look. "Okay, scratch that. It sort of is about her health—"

A loud crash against the door they'd locked Wanda behind downstairs in her basement made them both whip around and head to the top of the stairs. The wood, old and warped, though thick and heavy, began to bow.

"What the hell was that?" Greg hollered into the room.

Nina shuffled her feet in a nervous dance, her sneakers squeaking on the floor. "You need to come, and you need to come now, honey! I'm at Wanda's. And hurry the fuck up. Get your wings a whirrin'!" Nina clicked the phone off before Greg could respond.

She cast another glance at Marty.

A glance rife with panic.

Marty looked to the door at the bottom of the stairs, leading to the basement.

Nina ran a hand through her long hair. "Dude—we're fucked. You'd better call Keegan, Marty Flaherty—I'll be damned if I'll take the fall for this alone!"

Marty snatched her cell phone from the end table and pressed Speed Dial. Snarling, angry howls in the background made her fingers tremble. Heavy breathing accompanied the wet, slurpy intakes of harsh breaths.

Keegan answered on the second ring. "Marty? Where the hell are you? Jesus, woman! How hard is it to call me and tell me where you are?"

Marty put the phone on speaker. There was no use in hiding the direness of their situation. "Sugarplum?"

"Dumpling . . ." His voice was wary.

"Where—are—you?" she ground the words out.

His voice filled the room, gruff and husky. "On my way to Wanda's. The only thing I could figure was something happened and she needed you. I figured it had to be bad because I haven't heard from you in over eight hours. I didn't want to disturb girl time, but then I began to worry. Is she—Is it time?"

Each woman heard the hesitance in Keegan's voice. The hesitance to say the word *dying*. "Welllll, not exactly." Marty heard the first splinter of the wooden door frame to the basement cracking. "How far away are you?" she yelped.

"About ten minutes and what the hell was *that*?"

"Goood, hubby! That's very, very good. Get here fast—like now!"

"Mar—"

Marty clicked the phone off and threw it on the couch like it was on fire.

Nina ran to the top of the steps and looked down. Marty was right behind her, smacking into her with a thud. Nina clenched her teeth. "Do you see what you've done? Shit, shit, shit!"

"Meeeee?" Marty crowed. "This didn't happen until after you bit her, you pain in my ass. Always yelling at me. Always complaining. If you'd have just left well enough alone. It was *you* who thought I didn't do it right. And don't you forget it, missy!"

The panic on Nina's face was in every pale line—in her dark, dark eyes, in the thin set of her usually full lips. "I just don't get it, Marty! What the fuck did we do to her?"

Marty covered her mouth to keep from gasping her terror. "I don't know. I only know if one of these men don't show up soon, she's going to get out—and if you thought we were fucked before . . ."

Nina puffed her cheeks out. "I don't know if I can hold her off, Marty. We're always bullshittin' about how tough we are, but she's ten times as strong as us. You saw her—she was . . . she was . . ." Nina shook her head, still unable to believe what had happened— what they'd seen. "If you hadn't had that rawhide bone of Muffin's in your purse to distract her, I don't know what the hell we would have done. And you can't help—you're pregnant. If I let something happen to you, Keegan'll rip me apart!"

The snarling stopped for a moment. Blessed silence greeted their ears.

Marty let a breath escape from between her lips.

Nina rolled her head on her neck.

And then Wanda, snarling, hairier than any werewolf either of them had seen during a shift, wild-eyed, and drooling hatred from her canines, shot through the basement door like she'd been hurled from a cannon.

CHAPTER 19

"Oh, sir! Thank the heavens you're home," Archibald exclaimed, his worry evident on his face.

Heath's expression immediately held concern. "What's wrong? Are you okay?"

Archibald held up a blue cellophane-wrapped package. "I will admit, I'm very concerned. Miss Wanda dropped this off earlier for you while you were at that meeting with the man-fiend Linda, and she seemed very distracted. My advice would be to go to her immediately."

He took the lumpy package from Arch, throwing it on the counter and tearing open the cellophane.

Heath paused only for a moment, and then he was a flurry of motion, throwing his jacket back on. "I gotta go, Arch, but I'll call you later. And don't worry. Everything's going to be fine."

He took one last glance at the package.

And then he understood.

Completely.

GREG burst through the front door first, Keegan came up short right behind him to find Nina with one leg securely wrapped around what was once Wanda's human head, her grip white knuckled, on Wanda's now-fuzzy ears. Marty sat on top of her, dangling a raw pork chop over her snarling, dripping teeth.

Greg was the first to speak. "Ladies."

Keegan's eyes narrowed. "So I see we have a problem."

Nina grunted, gripping a snarling, seething Wanda tighter, fighting to keep her in check. "Gregori Statleon, if you don't bring your vampire ass over here this fucking second and help me hold her down, I swear to Christ, there'll be no more 'poor lost maiden in a snowstorm in the Swiss Alps who needs a big, brawny mountain man to save her' night for you, buddy!"

Marty dropped the pork chop to the floor. "You. Do. Not."

Nina's face contorted. "Shut the fuck up, Marty. Greg, help me!"

Greg sauntered over to twist his neck and look down at Nina. "But honey, you look like you have a pretty good grip on things. You're always talking tough—I'd think a little ole thing like whatever the hell this is would be no big deal. So what *is* this?"

"Marty Flaherty!" Keegan thundered, standing beside Greg to give Marty a hard stare. "Your input? Please, punkin'."

Marty sobbed. "I don't know what happened. I swear, Keegan."

"Tell me exactly what you two have been doing. Now, Marty," Keegan ordered.

Wanda struggled beneath Nina. Frothy foam dripped from her mouth. Her eyes, always so calm and sapphire blue, gleamed with wicked, hateful intent.

Marty's chest heaved as Wanda reared up, but Nina managed to pin her back down while Marty repositioned herself on Wanda's back end. "Okay, it went like this. You two know what's going on with Wanda. She's dying—dying, Keegan! Do you know what it's like to know we can save her and not do a damned thing? And Wanda didn't want us to do anything. She said we were messing with fate. She refused to allow us to turn her, but then, well, then she fell in love with Heath, right, honey?" She looked down at Wanda, addressing her as if she were still in her right mind. "Our Wanda fell in love, didn't you?" she cooed as though she were talking to Muffin, reaching out to stroke a hand over her fur until Wanda snapped at her with a succinct chomp of the air. "Stop that right now, Wanda Schwartz!"

"Get on with it, Marty!" Nina growled with a yelp.

"Okay, okay," Marty gasped. "So she asked us to come over tonight and then she asked us to turn her. She said she didn't care which one of us it was either." She took one last, deep breath before rushing onward with, "AndIbitherfirst,butNinasaidIfuckeditup,soshebither,too!"

"Marty, I swear on all things dark and deadly, when I get the fuck up off this floor, I'm going to pull every one of those salon-dyed blonde hairs out of your goddamned head!" Nina roared.

"Nina?"

"Greg?" Nina huffed.

"Is what Marty said true?"

"Would I be rolling around on the floor with this hairy, slobbering version of Wanda gone Cujo if it weren't? Yes, honey—it's *true*. Now help us!"

Greg and Keegan passed each other glances that could only be called ominous.

Then Keegan's face grew harder, his nostrils flared. That meant shit would surely fly. "Do you have any idea what you've done, Marty? Any? We have a strict no biting policy for a reason. This"— he pointed to Wanda—"is one of them!"

Greg knelt down beside Nina, clamping a helping hand on Wanda's writhing, crazed, furry body to keep her from moving. "You've messed her chemistry all up, Nina. Do you know what this means?" He shook his head before Nina could answer. "No, don't speak, or I might have to strangle you myself. Wanda is now rabid—*rabid*, ladies. The wires in her brain are crossed—she's confused—her body is a mass of changes she can't handle. Her senses are on major overload. I've seen this happen once in my five hundred or so years, and I never want to see it again. It's pretty rare, and almost always deadly. Wanda's now a werevamp. All in the space of twenty-four hours. It's too much for her system to handle. But there is a cure."

Marty let a bellowing breath out. "Oh, thank God!"

Greg shook his head again. "Hold on. Know what the cure for a change this magnaimous is, girls? The only cure for this crazed, maniacal reaction is—the blood of an innocent human. Where do you suppose we'll come up with one of those? Who do you suppose is going to give themselves up without a fight to fix what you two disasters waiting to happen have done, snookums?"

Heath flew through the door at just the moment the words left Greg's mouth.

"But look, lov-er," Nina said sweetly on a harsh grunt. "Look what just showed up. A *human* . . ."

GREG and Keegan had managed to get Wanda into the bathroom. It had no window, and while they figured out what to do, it kept her at bay.

For the moment.

Heath's heart sped, his adrenaline level on high. "I know what this is," he stated calmly. Maybe too calmly for even his own ears.

"We did this. Me and Nina. I'm sorry. We just wanted—we

just—" Tears streamed down Marty's face, her eyes swollen and red.

"We just fucking wanted to save her, okay? She's our friend. Thinking about an eternity without her was hell. I won't apologize for wanting her to live it out and die of natural causes—not some ugly disease like ovarian cancer." Nina's contrition was nothing less than defensive and anything but quiet.

Marty flicked Nina's hair. "Stop yelling, Nina. Jesus! Heath didn't do this, we did."

Heath held up a hand, commanding their attention. "No, Marty. It's okay. I know exactly where you two are. I've done nothing but think about it, worry about it—and I came up with what I thought was a solution. That's why I'm here, because I'd do anything to keep Wanda here. With me." He didn't care that it was obvious he had to clench his jaw to keep from fucking shedding some tears. He didn't care that it was in front of two other men who were complete strangers. Tears meant he was still breathing—and he'd savor that for these last few minutes.

Until . . .

Marty wrang her hands together, while Wanda, with sharp talons, tore at the bathroom door. Greg and Keegan were grunting, trying to hold her in. "She told us no at first—she said we were messing with fate. But then—then—"

"She fucking fell in love with you." Nina poked a finger in Heath's chest. "And she wanted to live—for you. So I'll be goddamned if when she came to us and asked us to do this, if I wouldn't do what my friend wanted—so she could be with you." Nina hurled a dirty look in Greg's direction.

It made Heath clamp down on his jaw harder. So he'd managed to get exactly what he'd wanted. If it hadn't been confirmed in the Reese's Peanut Butter Cups she'd left him, what she'd done here was all the confirmation he needed.

Yep, he'd gotten exactly what he'd wanted. Wanda to fall in love with him. He was falling in love with her, too.

Heath cleared his throat. "Originally, I was going to come to you, Nina. To ask you to turn me back, and then I was going to do whatever it took to convince Wanda to let me turn her so neither of you would risk pack or clan retribution. Now, that doesn't look like it'll help. You do both know what has to be done, don't you?"

Marty choked on a sob, reaching for Nina's hand, shooting Keegan a look of pure terror. "Yes."

Heath turned and faced the two men at the door and introduced himself. "Heath Jefferson."

Greg bucked forward as Wanda hurled herself against the door. "Greg Statleon. Culprit number one's life mate."

Keegan thrust his shoulder against the bowing door. "I'd offer my hand, but as you can see . . . Keegan Flaherty, accomplice number two's husband."

Heath looked back once more at Nina and Marty, his face somber. His mind raced like a freed wild mustang, but he fought to keep his head focused on what needed to be taken care of.

Archibald.

He needed to think about where he'd go—who would take care of him. Wanda would—he knew she would. He for sure wasn't coming out of this alive, but if something went wrong with Wanda—he needed backup. "If this doesn't work, and Wanda ends up . . . would you look after my manservant, Archibald? He's got no one—just me—he's old, and older still since we reverted back. I just need to know someone will look out for him if Wanda . . ." There was no fucking way he could say it. To say it out loud was as unthinkable now as it had been two days ago.

Marty nodded, her voice watery and quivering. "He'll never want for a thing."

"Count on it," Nina said between gritted teeth.

Heath swung back to look Greg and Keegan directly in the eye with the stare Wanda had told him unnerved her. *"Open the door,"* he said with a quiet, firm demand.

Marty was at his side instantly, griping his arm, tears running freely down her pretty cheeks. "You can't do this, Heath. We would never ask you to do this. We fucked this up—and it was out of love for Wanda, but she'd never, ever want this. She'll never forgive us if we let you do this. *Please, please* don't do this."

"I'm doing this for Wanda—because I've had my fair share of lifetimes, and having to live another maybe fifty years without her is a no-can-do as far as I'm concerned." He cleared his throat. "Would you two do me a favor?"

Marty gulped, choking off her sobs. Nina dry heaved, but nodded. "Anything . . ." she whispered.

His smile was ironic, filled with everything he'd planned to tell Wanda tonight—he just didn't make it in time. "Tell her—I'd share my Reese's Peanut Butter Cups with her any day of the week."

"Done," Nina gagged out.

The crunch of tile in Wanda's bathroom rang amongst Marty's sobs. "Please, please—don't . . ." she cried.

"Let go, Marty. Let go now."

His stoic command made Marty back off. His tone suggested just how absolute his choice was. There was no thought involved in this. Wanda was suffering. He'd be fucked if he wouldn't do whatever it took to stop it. His life had been far longer than the average male's—he'd used up his life points—and he didn't want to stay here, even if it meant being human, without Wanda. It was just a no-go.

Marty went to stand beside Nina, who put her arm around Marty's back and let her bury her face in her shoulder.

"Open the door," he demanded again.

Greg and Keegan looked like they were about to protest, but

the silent question Heath sent with his eyes to them was clear: If it were Nina or Marty, wouldn't you do the same thing?

Both men nodded curt consent in Heath's direction.

When Greg and Keegan jumped out of the way, it was only seconds before Wanda barreled through the bathroom door, sniffing the air for the briefest of moments before seeing her prey, warm, fresh *human* prey. She lunged in an arc of tangled hair and snarling rage for human blood at Heath, covering him with her huge body.

And then, there was no sound.

Or light.

Or movement.

Not for Heath.

Not anymore.

CHAPTER
20

Wanda woke with a heaviness in her chest and a mouth so dry, she almost couldn't pry it open. Her fingers reached blindly for the first thing she could find, then settled on the blanket her mother had made her—familiar, soothing. Her head throbbed, and her eyes felt like lead. But her roaming hands discovered she no longer had on her pink nightgown.

The filter of the dream-like haze lifted in increments—then accosted her all at once like a sharp smack to the face. She bolted upright, popping her eyes open—color and sound assaulted her senses in blinding clarity. Everything in the room was crystal clear. In fact, she could read the passage in the romance novel she'd been skimming that was way over on a table all the way across the room.

Faaa-reaky.

When she lifted her hand to rub her temple, she almost knocked herself out cold for the speed of the motion. And then, she caught her finger on something sharp in her mouth . . .

Holy fucksticks.

She was a vampire.

Well, hell. Damn, damn, damn. In some beggars can't be choosers way, she'd kinda hoped Marty'd get to her first, so she could still eat. Now she'd have to drink blood—which was squicky.

Or not. Because the thought held appeal right now. It made her stomach rumble. Yet so did the notion of food. Juicy and dripping with blood food.

Tight.

Marty was the first to see she'd awakened. "Oh, thank *God*!"

Wanda pushed the blanket from her and swung her legs off the side of the couch just as Marty gasped. The movement was so quick, she had to let her head hang down to catch her breath.

And that was when she saw it.

The hair on her legs. A buttload of it.

Huh.

And hold on one fucking second—she'd caught her *breath*. Nina didn't breathe . . .

Hookay—explanations were in order.

"Marty?"

"Wanda?"

She peered up at her friend, her eyes swollen and red, her face splotchy. "What gives?"

Marty blanched. "Wellllll, how about if I just say some shit went down, and now you're going to live a long, healthy eternal life?"

"Not cutting it."

Nina knelt down in front of Wanda's knees, grinning up. "You're good to go. Death no longer knocks at your door."

Wanda groaned. "Groovy. What *is* knocking at my door?"

Nina yanked her up, righting her when she stumbled. "A couple of things," she offered evasively, the grin replaced by a darting glance in Marty's direction.

It was then that she saw Heath over Nina's shoulder, sprawled on the floor with Greg and Keegan beside him, and a whole lot of blood. She didn't think, she reacted, knocking Nina out of the way with such force she fell backward onto the couch.

She was on the floor, pushing Greg and Keegan aside with hands that trembled. Instantly male hands were on her shoulders, Marty and Nina on either side of each of the men. "What happened?" she shouted.

"Wanda," Marty had that no-nonsense tone to her voice. "Just listen. We bit you. *Both* of us—"

Nina's eyes narrowed. "Yeah, because genius here didn't do it right the first time."

Marty's eye narrowed, too. "I swear—to—God, Niiina, one more time with the blame game, and I'm going to knock those incisors out of your fricken' vampire head!" she yelled back.

Christ on a cracker—if she was something paranormal, that meant she'd have to listen to their shit for an eternity. For the love of all things fair—what a trade-off. "Nina, Marty?"

"What, honey?" Marty was quick to answer. Too quick.

"Both of you, shut theeee fuck up. Nina—let Marty speak! Okay, so you bit me—what's that have to do with—with—Heath?" her words hitched while her hands roamed over Heath's cool, chiseled features, lifeless and . . . no, she couldn't think it. Oh, Jesus and all twelve apostles.

Marty took a breath before replying. "When we *both* bit you, it didn't turn you quite the way we'd hoped. It's some legend or something. Your body couldn't handle the overload of changes. Because we both bit you in a twenty-four-hour period you became rabid. So the only way to fix that was for you to bite a human, you needed the blood of a human to survive—"

"You *both* bit me? Why the hell would you do that?" Wanda could hear the fear in her cry. What the fuck did this mean?

"Because Nina thought I didn't do it right. You know Nina, Wanda, always with the superior bullshit. It's her way or no way. When we didn't see any changes in you, she panicked—"

"The fuck I panicked, Marty Flaherty! Don't put the blame all on me—"

"Nina, Marty! Shut up, and do it now because I have this crazy urge to clock you both in the mouth," Wanda growled, surprising even herself with the deep resonance to her voice. "So let me be clear here. I bit Heath?"

Both women nodded.

Oh, Jesus, Joseph, and Mary. She'd bitten Heath? Omigod—she'd murdered the man she loved because she didn't want to leave him?

Well, that'd worked out just the way she'd planned.

"You *let* me bite him? What the fuck is wrong with you two? How could you let me hurt the reason I was doing this in the first place?" she sobbed.

"They didn't, Wanda." Greg spoke for the first time—calm, sensible, reasonable in this madness.

"He did," Keegan added, pointing to a prone Heath.

She whirled to face Greg for confirmation. "What?"

Marty worried her bottom lip. "It's true, Wanda. Heath offered himself up for you. He called us the other day and asked to meet with us. He knew something was wrong with you, honey—which was why we finally made you tell us that night. Because we were afraid he was right. And during that conversation, he told us he knew Nina was a vampire. Anyway, when he got here tonight, he said he was going to go to Nina and ask her to turn him back anyway to save you. He also knew what we'd done—because he said he's seen it before. So ask Greg and Keegan—he knew what had to be done, and he sacrificed himself *for you*."

"And then he said to tell you, he'd share Reese's Peanut Butter

Cups with you anytime," Nina said, her own brand of pain written on it.

He'd gotten what she'd left with Archibald. He'd joked he didn't share his candy with anyone . . . hearing he'd share it with her made this a million times more painful. Her heart would shatter in a million pieces if she still had one—did she have one? Now she'd live for eternity, and Heath was dead.

And obviously, upon making the ultimate sacrifice—like his life, for shit's sake—he must have some feelings for her, too.

Oh.

God.

The utter irony.

Only she could find the man of her dreams and jack him up by killing him.

After all this worry, after sending Heath away because she didn't want to hurt him when she died—to have this happen . . . she couldn't. Nope. She couldn't. She should have let fate have its way with her and gone to her death with her big girl panties securely around her hips.

Heath had just gotten his life back, and she'd snatched it from him—only this time he wasn't undead, he was just dead.

Way to show someone ya care.

Wanda rose on heavy, cumbersome legs, looking at Nina and Marty, composing a quick list of things to do in her mind. "Nina, take Menusha home for me, will you? I know Larry the hamster might not appreciate that much, but my choices are few, and Muffin would eat her alive, plus with the baby coming, Marty'll have enough to do. And call my parents—they'll tell Casey. Marty, I have a broom with a wooden handle. Go get it—do it now." Her voice was so calm it might have even unnerved her if she didn't know exactly what she wanted right at this moment.

"A broom? Honey? I think you're just not right yet. You

can't . . . sweep this up." Marty peeked at her through eyes that were strained with worry, swishing her hand in an arc over Heath's lifeless body.

"No shit," she offered flatly.

Nina popped up, her hands in tight fists. "Wanda. We'll take care of everything. It'll be okay. Just go—go—I dunno. Greg, take Wanda out of here. Back to our house—something."

Greg moved to put a comforting arm around Wanda, but she brushed him off. "Marty. *Get—the fucking—broom.*" Her growl, resonant, eerie, deep, low, sounded through the room.

Marty's confusion was clear in the arch of her brows. "For what? We'll clean up. I promise it'll be just like you'd do it. Go with Greg."

Wanda stomped off to her kitchen pantry, yanking the broom from the closet, and returning to the living room. She ripped the green fanned bristles off the long handle, cracking the wood with a loud snap. The green plastic scattered at her feet and flew in the air. She held up the jagged, splintered remains under Marty's nose, her face distorted by rage at what had gone down, but determined—determined to do what must be done. "Do it!" she screamed.

Nina was instantly by her side, pulling at the wood with no success. "Give it to me, goddamn it, Wanda! What the hell are you doing?"

Wanda yanked it back with a force that knocked Nina back a few steps, leaving them both surprised. This—this—whatever paranormal creature she was, had some advantages. Which would be cool if she cared to explore them. But she didn't. Not now that she'd whacked Heath. She didn't deserve to live if Heath couldn't, too. "Marty! Pay attention."

Marty's head swung from Nina back in Wanda's direction. "What? What do you want?" she hollered back.

Wanda thwacked at the air with the handle haphazardly, creating small whooshes of air. "Just dooo it! Get it over with! Stake me!" Wanda screamed. *"Stake me noooow, bitches!"* she roared, spittle flying from her lips in a spray of venom.

"Wanda?"

Now what? She was in the middle of preparing to die—*again*, for fuck's sake, like she hadn't already done this once—and right on cue, someone was calling her name. Could no one get by without her for just one second?

"What!"

"Give me your hand, honey."

Wanda looked down to her feet and nearly collapsed.

It was Heath. Smiling. Holding out his hand. A hand that was moving.

She closed her eyes and sent up a silent prayer of eternal thanks.

Their hands connected, his skin cool and dry. She gave him a good, hard yank upward, throwing her arms around his neck, burying her head there for a moment. She leaned back to look into his face, which no longer had that ruddiness it once had. Ohhhhh, and he had those crazy fangs Nina'd had once upon a time. Not nearly as big as Nina's, but they were there, gleaming at her. She couldn't grasp what had happened. She didn't care what had happened. Heath was alive or dead or undead or whatever. He was talking and smiling and absolutely everything was suddenly right as rain. "I'm sorry. I'm sooooo sorry," she sobbed against his neck. "I thought you were dead! Jesus, don't ever, ever do that to me again!"

Heath cupped her jaw in his hand, running a calloused thumb over her lower lip. "I think I am dead—again—which is okay. I get dead. Human was hard work." He winked down at her.

"What happened? *How* did this happen?" Wanda asked against the front of his now very messy shirt.

Marty and Nina stumbled over each other to explain what they'd done, peering around either side of Heath's body. "You should have seen yourself—you were bigger in Were form than Marty ever was, and your fucking fangs were like elephants tusks," Nina said. "Dude, you were crazed, like some prehistoric, wild fucking animal in a cage. We didn't know what to do—so we locked you in the basement and called Greg and Keegan and that's when we found out that you needed human blood. Then Heath showed up and offered to let you bite him. What the hell that makes him now is beyond me. This paranormal shit gets freakier by the day as far as I'm concerned."

Wanda had grown still, making Marty nudge Nina, shooting her the "shut up" look.

Everyone quieted for a moment, letting Wanda assimilate that information. The air was filled with their hesitant concern—rife with their worry about what they'd done to save her.

But Wanda wasn't even a little upset. Vampire plus werewolf equaled . . . Now she understood exactly what had happened. Exactly what she was—would be eternally.

And she liked.

Instead, she began to laugh, her head thrown back, her mouth wide open. When she could finally speak, she spit the words out. "Marty? Nina? You do know what this means, don't you?" Her question was cocky and held the biggest neener, neener of all.

"You need a new razor?" Nina asked, pointing to her legs.

"It means I'm a *werevamp*—which beats werewolf and vampire every single time."

"Is that true?" Marty asked Keegan.

Keegan nodded his dark head. "Yep, and she's right—she's ten times as powerful as you and Nina put together."

Nina sauntered up to Wanda with that threatening stride she'd perfected, sticking her face in Wanda's. "You know, you've been pretty cocky lately. Don't think because you're paranormal to the max that I can't still take you."

Greg was instantly beside Nina, throwing an arm over her shoulder. "Lambykins?"

Nina's face softened. "What?"

"You and me—we have to talk. You were a bad, bad girl," Greg drawled. "And no matter the outcome of this, shit's gonna fly. So whaddya say we go on home to Castlevania and we conversate about that?"

Wanda instantly regretted teasing Nina. She'd saved her life. Sort of. Okay, so she hadn't saved her life—but good intentions and the paved road to hell and all. "Greg, please don't be angry with Nina. You either, Keegan. I begged them to do it. Nina loooooooves me—so does Marty. Sometimes that's bigger than all these paranormal rules you people have."

Wanda threw her arms around the two of them, pinching Nina's cheek with affection and blowing Greg a kiss. Then she turned to Marty and Keegan.

Keegan had bent-out-of-shape written all over his face, and Marty danced from foot to foot, obviously waiting for the ration of shit Keegan was sure to give her. If Greg wasn't a rule breaker, Keegan wasn't one to the nth degree. "I'm sorry I made Marty go against pack law—I know how much that means to you, Keegan. I promise to stay right here in Jersey, and no one has to know about me, okay?"

Keegan reached out a hand to squeeze her arm, his dark expression going instantly light. "Know what, Wanda? I'm not so sorry the girls did this—broken laws or not. It means you're going to be around a long time, and that makes me damned glad. It also means it won't be up to Greg and me to shut these two up."

Marty made a face at him, nudging him in the ribs.

But Wanda laughed, hugging them both.

Nina gave Wanda another rare hug, her eyes bright when she scanned Wanda's face. "I need to feed, and Marty always needs to feed lately. We'll let you two make nice, and I'll drop some blood back by later tonight. You'll both need to feed soon, I think . . . doesn't matter. I'll bring blood—do with it what you will. And Heath?"

"Nina," he drawled while Wanda watched, fully expecting the "you better take care of my friend" speech.

But Nina surprised her with a grin at Heath. "Dude. You're all right. I'm glad I don't have to kick your ass."

Heath's laugh was a sharp bark. "Well, thanks on both counts."

"Call us," Marty commanded. "Once you've settled and you get used to this—well, just this . . . okay? You'll be going through a lot of changes—you'll need to learn how to shift, and I think I can help. Though I get the feeling you'll handle this better than we ever did, and Heath can help—with at least half of it."

"I will. Now go, and thank you. I love you both." She hugged Marty once more and smiled as the two couples left.

And that was when the reality of what had taken place set in.

Her house was a fucking wreck. Her basement door was trashed. So was her bathroom door.

Thank God for DIY and eternity.

She turned back to Heath and smiled, cocking her head at him with coy eyes and a slight tilt to her lips. "So are you vampire or werewolf—or both?"

His grin widened. "I'm both—just like you."

How could there possibly be a paranormal phenom she didn't know about? She thought she knew them all. "But if I needed the blood of a human, how did you survive me biting you? I don't get it."

Heath scratched his head. "I think I'm going to have to go with the fact that I was once a vampire. I had some very minimal, residual effects leftover. Like I could still read minds—that's how I knew you were full of shit when you said you didn't want to get involved. I guess some of that must've taken over when you bit me. I say we don't question it, we'll just be grateful for what we've been given. Now, there are things you need to know about this werevamp stuff and the combination of the two."

"Yeah, it means I can kick Nina's ass now, and," she said, looking down at her legs, "shaving is going to be an event."

Heath chuckled. "Well, there's that, but there are other things, too. Like dietary restrictions."

Hold on. No fair. "But Marty can eat whatever she wants."

"But Nina can't. The two, vampire and werewolf combined, make our intake restrictive. You can have blood and raw or very rare beef."

"How do you know that?"

"Because I know the legend, and I know a guy it happened to. Name's Ernie. Lives in Oshkosh. Nice guy—shitty diet—bit his ex-mother-in-law to save himself."

The bigger picture had begun to dawn on her, and it had nothing to do with the fact that her weenies in a blanket days were over. "So wait, you gave up Whoppers for me?" God. Heath had loved being human. He'd loved everything about it, and he'd given all that up for her. Which meant, she thought smugly, he crazy-dug her.

"Yep."

"And Resee's Peanut Butter Cups?"

"Those, too."

Still, her disbelief rang clear in her voice. "And—and—beer. How could you give up beer? You love beer. And chicken wings—Buffalo style—with ranch dressing."

"Yep.

She gave him a solemn expression, fighting the sudden urge to discover why his scent was making her nose feel like it was on fire. "Deep. Very deep."

Heath stared at her—those intense hazel eyes refusing to allow her to look away. "That's me—deep. I hope to build up a tolerance again someday. Just takes time."

Wanda trailed a finger along the sharp plane of his cheek. Her chest tightened, and her throat started to clog. The breadth of what he'd done was finally sinking in. "And my cheese log. You can't ever eat my cheese log again. *Why* would you do that?" She was fishing, but she needed to hear it.

His dark blond eyebrow rose. "Because you wouldn't have been here to make me a cheese log. I figured you're the only one who makes a decent one. It was worth keeping you around for."

Wanda's smile was smug. "Is not."

He pulled her closer, setting every available patch of flesh on her to blazing. "Is."

She walked her fingers up his arm and over his pecs. "That's not why you did what you did, Heath Jefferson."

Heath grabbed her hand and kissed the tips of her fingers, giving her a wink. "Huh. I can't think of any other reason. So why did I do what I did, Wanda Schwartz?"

She curled her fingers around his, reveling in the warm reassurance they brought her. "Because you sooooooo love selling Bobbie-Sue and Linda Fisher's your idol. You just couldn't bear going on without her," she teased.

"That definitely has to be what made me do it. Sticky-lips Linda and goop. I don't know if life would have been worth living if I didn't have color wheels and goop. That, and you're aiiight in bed—so all right, I might be willing to break my let's not get involved rule," he joked. His grin was infectious.

But Wanda's face fell. The guilt each time he'd mocked her insistence about not becoming too attached resurfaced, digging a fresh hole in her gut. Her eyes left his to stray to the floor. A floor where she could see every fiber of carpet with startling clarity. A floor that needed the ultimate in vacuuming. "I was so wrong. I don't know what I was thinking. The whole thing—that isn't me. I just couldn't bring myself to tell you, because I thought for sure it would end, and I didn't want it to. I was selfish. I admit it. My potentially dying wasn't just about me, and what I was doing sucked. I swear, I've never, ever been involved in a relationship just for the sex. Not that that's a bad thing—it just isn't *my* thing."

He tipped her chin back up to make her look at him. His eyes were serious, his sharp jaw set. "I know."

"Do you?"

"Why do you think I kept hanging around? I didn't need many of my former vampire skills to tell me something was wrong, honey. I just didn't know what. Which brings me to my next statement. Don't ever fucking do something like that to me again. If something's wrong, whatever it is, I wanna know. Got that?"

Completely, totally, utterly. She sighed in contentment. "Got it."

"So you know what we get to do now, don't you?" Heath's hands roamed over her back, pulling her until her body was flush with his.

"I do. You get the vacuum, and I'll get the mop."

"Uh, no."

Her smile was flirtatious, her eyes lit with anticipation. "So what'd ya have in mind?" She felt empowered, omnipotent, invincible, strong for the first time in a long time. And hairy, very, very hairy.

He tipped her chin up on his finger. "Now we get to be all involved."

"Ahhhhh, and what does *being involved* mean, Mr. Jefferson?"

Heath wiggled his eyebrows, planting a light kiss on her lips. "It means you get to have hot paranormal to the max sex with me."

"Is that different than uninvolved sex? 'Cause I don't know about you, but the uninvolved sex was pretty hot."

"Oh, but it's way hotter than uninvolved sex. Trust me, I know."

Her head came to rest on his shoulder, her next words held the same hint of amusement his eyes did. "So this involved thing— thoughts on it? I haven't been involved since my ex. That didn't work out so well. He did leave me for another woman. I think I might have forgotten what involved is. I do know, if it means having to give up *America's Next Top Model*, you can forget it."

"First, your ex was an asshole who needs a good smack down, and second, don't look at me," he joked, gazing down at her with eyes that glinted amusement. "I haven't ever been involved. I was mostly an uninvolved guy, but I have a plan."

Her arms wound upward around his neck, she locked her fingers behind his head. The thin T-shirt allowed her to feel the press of his hard, hard body against hers. "And that is?"

"I figure, we'll figure it out together."

Her smile was once more smugly playful. "You dig me, Mr. Jefferson."

"You dig me back."

"So I vote we go get involved," she said, her tone light. Her heart, if she still had one—did she still have one?—unburdened by a secret she no longer had to keep, felt free. "Oh, but one question."

He ran his tongue over her lower lip, brushing the undersides of her breasts with his hands. "Ask away."

"This hot, paranormal to the max sex—will my leg hair interfere—it's pretty righteous." She pointed down to her legs again. Jesus, Marty hadn't been exaggerating when she'd told them she'd had to shave twice a day until her body adjusted to the change.

Heath grabbed her around the waist, hauling her even closer. "You know, you're nowhere near as freaked out as you should be about this enormous change you've just gone through. Sometimes it takes months for people to adapt, and here you are only hours into your paranormal state, behaving like you've always been this way."

Wanda grinned. "And you know exactly why I'm not freaked out. Marty told me you met with her and Nina."

"Caught," he admitted, a guilty smile on his face. "I contacted Marty and Nina because I was worried about you, and they told me everything—it all made sense after they explained their backgrounds. And I won't apologize for going behind your back. I was worried. I did what I had to, and I'd do it again. But you're still in for some heavy-duty changes, honey."

Her heart sped up—which was a good sign. It meant she still had one. "I might have done the same, had this situation been reversed," she confessed, raising her head from his chest. "As for the rest, I would have been more honest about Nina and Marty, but you know from experience how secretive their world is. After everything that happened with them and their accidental paranormal mishaps, too many humans found out as it was. I just learned to keep my mouth shut for the sake of their well-being. Believe me when I tell you, I didn't know how to react when you told me. But I'd been there, done that—there isn't much left that can freak me out, I don't think."

His smile was warm, indulgent. "Someday, I want to hear all about how Nina and Marty were bitten. As for freaking out—your not freaking out, freaked me out. It had to rate high on my list of surreal conversations. But I've been here before. Even if you've experienced this with your friends, it's not exactly the same as living it—or not living it." He shook his head. "Whatever it is that we're doing."

"I made a choice. One I understood from the word *paranormal*. I know being friends with Nina and Marty isn't the same thing, but I sort of get what I'm in for. I chose to be in for it because—"

"Of me," he said in all his luscious arrogance. "So I say we go be in it before we have to feed—which will be soon." His grin was lascivious, devilish.

"But shouldn't we wait for blood from Nina?" Her stomach rumbled its agreement. If she didn't feed soon, she'd become weak and turn to dust—or would the werewolf half of her take over and she'd just need a raw steak? Cheerist—what a conundrum.

"I thought you knew all about the paranormal. I guess there's a thing or two I can teach you, and one of those things is feeding from each other—very, very hot perk to the paranormal to the max deal."

Just the thought made her thighs clamp together when heat rushed between them. "I did know that, I'd just forgotten about it—but I do know it means we're not life mates. So you're off the hook."

"I don't know about that," he muttered with a husky whisper against her mouth, scooping her up so her legs automatically wrapped around his waist.

She looked down at him with confusion in her face. "Yes, it does mean that. I know because when Nina and Greg mated it had to be in front of a witness and at midnight on his five hundredth birthday. God, what a mess that night was. There was this vampire—Greg's sire, Lisanne—what a total biotch. She wanted to mate with Greg so she could keep the clan strong, or some such nonsense. Boy, was she pissed when Nina stepped in and decided she wanted to mate with Greg. I also remember she said it didn't hurt—that it was kinda hot. There's never a dull moment with those two, I tell you. Marty, for instance—if you think Nina's turning was a disaster, you should have seen what happened to Marty. Insane, I tell you—"

"Honey?" Heath asked, pressing a finger to her lips.

"Hmm?"

"Rambling. You're doing it. Stop. We have things to take care of." He let her slide down his hard body to the thing that needed taking care of, rubbing against the thin wisp of her underwear.

Sharp rushes of electricity pricked her skin—it was like nothing she'd ever felt before. Each inch of her flesh lit up like a brush fire. Her nipples brushed sensuously against the material of her fuzzy nightgown. Each scrape of them felt like a thousand. "Ohhhh, right. The feeding, hot paranormal sex to the max thing," she mumbled, fully willing to experience whatever that meant—even with legs that were hairier than your average Yeti.

Heath carried her into her bedroom, stepping over the splintered shards of wood from her door with care. "There's that and then there're other things. And they have to happen *now*." He dropped her on the bed and held up two fingers. "Give me two minutes to shower," he grunted, stripping his clothes off with impatient fingers.

Wanda's sigh mirrored his impatient fingers. "Hurry," she grunted back boldly.

And he did hurry. In moments, Heath was back, hooking his thumbs in her panties and tugging them off, his face dark with lust. "I *need* you."

His words made her shiver with an almost violent shake. They were hot with an urgent need threading through them that made having him inside her not just a desire, but a burning necessity.

Heath sank between her thighs, dragging her to the edge of the bed with hands that were insistent and rushed, cupping her ass and bringing her flush to his lips. He wasted no time burying his face between her legs, parting her flesh, now wet and throbbing, opening his mouth over her and swiping her clit with his silken hot tongue.

She reared upward at the contact so sharp and sweet, magnified by whatever this crazy need was that assaulted her every nerve ending. Heath dragged his fingers through the lips of her sex, stroking her, licking her, as her breath became ragged, wheezing in and out of her lungs. Her fingers gripped his hair, tightening their hold with frantic abandon. She came hard when his tongue danced over her swollen clit, clamping her thighs around his head and bucking against his mouth. Colors flashed behind her eyelids, waves of breath stealing, crashing bolts of lightning assaulted her.

Heath gave her no time to recuperate, he rose before her in all his powerful, sculpted glory. His wide chest heaved, his thick thighs moved him toward her, the muscles clenching and tight. He tore her T-shirt over her head and was on top of her in an instant. Their flesh met in a flash of sizzling contact. Heath spread her legs wide, throwing them up over his hips, pressing the tip of his hard cock at her entrance.

He didn't linger, but instead thrust upward into her with a searing plunge of his rock-hard shaft, driving into her with a force that sent them both rocking upward.

Wanda clung to Heath, clenched her teeth at the riveting sensations that washed over her, one after the other. Everything was magnified tenfold, each flaming thrust of his cock intensified as his hips moved against hers.

She caught the flash of his incisors only briefly before he found a place on her neck just below her ear and sunk into it. Her neck arched upward against the smooth enamel, frantically seeking the pleasure his bite brought her. Her body became enflamed, hot, anxious, vividly aware of every square inch of it as he drank from her. Her hands went from his shoulders to his head, gripping his hair, tearing her fingers through it.

Wanda let out a hoarse scream of satisfaction, releasing her pleasure with a howl, while bucking up hard against him. Her hips crashed against his, rocking violently while Heath drove into her.

Heath's growl of completion was feral, reverberating throughout her room, echoing in her ears. He sank into her one last time, his teeth still embedded in her neck, then collapsed on top of her in a heaving, massive tangle of limbs.

Their harsh breathing mingled until Wanda couldn't tell who was gasping harder.

Holy. Paranormal. Wonking.

Hell to the yeah.

If sex as a human with Heath had been awesome, well, there were no words for sex as a werevamp. A werevamp . . . she was a werevamp. Wanda Schwartz was no longer human—or dying. Don't forget the dying.

She wasn't dying, and then, out of the blue a thought occurred to her. She'd told Warren Snelling he had a peanut dick with the idea she was biting the dust.

Hoo boy. Her next high school reunion was going to be very interesting.

Yet warmth spread throughout her limbs anyway, a sense of peace for her choice settled in every pore.

She had time on her side now. Time to learn about Heath. Time to let herself fall all the way for him.

And that was so damned good.

Wanda squirmed beneath him, sighing when her nipples rubbed against his skin. "Wow. I say yay for paranormal sex to the max."

He nuzzled her cheek with his nose. "Yeah, it was worth giving up the Whoppers for."

"Oh, but was it worth giving up the Reese's Peanut Butter Cups for, and beer, too? I dunno, seems like übersacrifice, if you ask me." She kissed his yummy lips and smiled flirtatiously.

He mock-sighed. "Yeah, there is that. Maybe I shouldn't have been so hasty. All this sacrifice was a lot. I mean, we are talking about Reese's Peanut Butter Cups."

She swatted him on his shoulder with a playful nudge. "You can't take it back."

His eyes glittered wolfishly—literally. "Sucks to be me, huh?"

"I guess that all depends on how you look at it. It could be worse."

"There is nothing—nothing, I say—that's worse than giving up Reese's Peanut Butter Cups." He sighed again for good measure. "Somehow, I don't know exactly how, you'll have to make it up to me. It won't be easy. You have a long row to hoe, Miss Schwartz, but it absolutely has to be done."

Wanda wriggled out from beneath him, pushing him back down on the bed, smiling seductively. She straddled his hips, and leaned forward to rest her chin on his. "I promise to work very hard to make saving my life well worth your eternity."

Heath's arms came up around her, pressing her close to him. "That means you have to be all *involved* with me," he joked.

Yeah.

Yeah, it did.

Big, honkin' girly sigh.

Wanda grinned, sliding down to rest her cheek on his chest. "You think you can survive being involved with me? I'm a lot of work. I ramble a lot. I make lists for everything. I read tons of romance novels. I like order. Oh, and I have the caa-raziest friends like evah—"

Heath stopped her words with a kiss. "Before we go any further, you have to feed, young lady." He pointed to his neck with a grin.

A heated rush of anticipation slithered up her spine as she repositioned herself at his neck.

Heath's hand came up to cup her chin. "But wait, this means we jump into the involved pool together. You ready?" He held out his other hand to her.

And Wanda took it, letting him entwine their fingers into one fist. "Yeah," she whispered on a blissful sigh. "I definitely am."

EPILOGUE

Seven Months, a Baby, and Two Werevamps Later ...

"So how's the night dweller relief effort going? Did'ja get any more responses to the ad this week?" Marty asked Wanda as they all sat around Greg and Nina's dining room table, cooing at baby Hollis, now just a couple of weeks old. Marty ran a tender hand over her dark head while she slept in her carrier as only babies can.

Wanda smiled when Heath reached for her hand, still amazed at the myriad emotions he continued to create almost eight months after they'd met. "It's going slow, but sure. With no record of most of the clans created by this logger sire, it's been really difficult, but little by little word's getting out." It had been Nina and Greg's suggestion to try and seek out the remainder of Heath's clan, and subsequent branches, in an attempt to help them adjust to being human again.

Heath suggested they place cryptic personal ads in some of the largest newspapers all over the country reading: *B-Positive. Have you rediscovered fun in the sun? Traded your stake for a steak recently? Finding that leaving the graveyard shift has left you feeling more alive than ever? Don't worry—we have a smorgasbord of volunteers ready and waiting to help you get your blood pumping again.*

They'd all been skeptical anyone would actually reply, but it was the beginnings of a desperate attempt to reach out to stranded ex-vampires and help them acclimate. Find them jobs, help them earn a living in the human world.

Their phone had been silent for a very long month until they'd received their first call. And then another—to date, they had twenty-five ex-vampires working for Greg and Svetlanna at Fango, and with Marty and Keegan at Pack Cosmetics, with the hope there'd be more to come.

Heath had decided, to sticky-lips Linda Fisher's dismay, to leave her as his Bobbie-Sue rep when Marty'd offered him a position in marketing, because he was so in tune with new and innovative ways to sell color wheels in markets corporate had never even considered.

Wanda put her pinky in little Hollis's tiny fist, letting her latch onto it with her firm grip. There wasn't a day that had gone by since she'd been turned that she didn't feel blessed beyond her fair share. Seeing Hollis born was just one of the many blessings bestowed upon her. Her birth had been a typical sicko triplet from hell experience.

Marty'd gone into labor at Hogan's while Nina gagged, because her water had broken in the middle of the diner floor. The ride to the hospital had been a series of Nina screaming at Wanda to hurry the fuck up before Marty spewed baby everywhere, while Marty howled at the top of her lungs that this kind of pain was soooo not in her color wheel.

Little Hollis never made it to the carefully planned birthing room back in Buffalo—she did make it to the parking lot of the Dollar Store in Hackensack, where Wanda pulled to a screeching halt because Marty had declared someone had to help her give birth to the watermelon pushing its way out of her.

Hollis made her entrance in the backseat of Wanda's sky blue convertible, with a paler than usual auntie Nina holding Marty's shoulders from behind while yelling, "Get it the fuck out, Wanda, so she'll stop all this caterwauling!" And take-charge Wanda made a mental list of the medical shows she'd seen in the hopes it would help her to navigate a live birth.

Wanda smiled over at Marty. "I can't believe how beautiful this baby is, and all that dark hair . . ." It stuck up in thick, coarse patches all over Hollis's tiny head.

Nina chucked Hollis under the chin, shaking the rattle she'd just given her today. "She looks like her auntie Nina, don't you, you little carpet clinger?"

Marty swatted Nina's hand. "She does not either look like you. She looks like her daddy."

Keegan grinned, planting a kiss on Hollis's forehead. "Yeah, but she's got her mother's nonstop yap—especially when she's screaming at four in the morning."

Heath's laughter filled Wanda's ears. They did that a lot. Laughed, talked, and had hot, paranormal to the max sex. He planted a warm kiss on her lips before going into the kitchen, probably to check on Archibald and Lou. Nina had finally told her grandmother Lou, with the help of Marty and Wanda, about her and Greg, and she'd taken it far better than even Wanda had expected—despite her deeply rooted Catholic beliefs.

And then, at one of their monthly gatherings at Wanda's, Lou met Archibald—and it'd been on ever since. Lou was teaching Archibald how to cuss and play poker, and Arch was teaching her how to distinguish good caviar with just one whiff.

"Well, my friend, I'd say you got your HEA," Marty said, her genuine happiness for Wanda lilting her words.

"Her what?" Heath called from around the corner of the kitchen doorway, his handsomely chiseled features bemused.

"HEA, Heath," Nina berated him from across the room. "Happily ever after. Jesus, you guys have only been together almost eight months, and Wanda hasn't introduced you to the unrealistic world of romance novels? Oh, wait, sorry, *women's fiction*. An HEA is what happens in all of them at the end. Everyone rides off into the sunset with their duke on a horse or some millionaire in his bad-assed Ken-car."

Wanda chucked her napkin at Nina, rolling of her eyes. "Again, for like the eight hundred millionth time—was there much in those books that wasn't true? No. No, I don't believe there was. If I hadn't done all that reading, you'd still be wandering the streets pissing and moaning about having to drink blood and live forever. And actually, Heath hasn't seen many of them because if you remember, Ms. Negative, I told you I read them because they took me someplace I wouldn't ever be able to go. They let me dream—live out fantasies I'd never be able to live out in my real life. Experience adventures I couldn't possibly squeeze into one lifetime. I don't have to do that anymore. I have many lifetimes to live, and, well, let's just say the fantasy is fulfilled. Plus, I haven't had the *time* to read much." She gave Nina a smug neener neener neener smile.

And that was true. She didn't have time to read much anymore. Between her and Heath's rescue relief efforts and her job with Bobbie-Sue, not to mention her nights were now filled with more romance novelish stuff than you could shake a stick at, top that off with learning to be a werevamp, and it seemed her life had suddenly become a very full, exciting new journey.

But she was happier than she'd ever been. She'd found what she'd missed out on in her one and only relationship with George. What she'd always hoped existed, but hadn't planned on finding while she'd been so busy figuring out who she wanted to be as an individual.

Today, almost eight months since they'd met, and sharing her house for four of those months now, Wanda was more in love with Heath than she ever thought was humanly, er, undeadly possible. He'd even helped her cross a couple of things off her Fuck It list with the promise they'd tick off as many items as they could, and even add more—because they had plenty of time. Heath had enhanced her life—made it richer in tone and quality, encouraged her to express herself physically and mentally, and most importantly, he encouraged her to pursue whatever made her happiest.

And she had.

Just two weeks ago she'd put all of her list-making to good use in a very unusual way—she'd typed "The End" to a romance novel titled *Being Paranormal for Dummies* and had shipped it off to an agent. A week ago that agent had called her and told her she wanted to represent her, and just yesterday, her new agent had called to tell her there was this publisher who apparently liked the crazy in her concept and wanted to buy it.

So that meant there was just one thing left to do.

Wanda rose and planted a kiss on Hollis's head. She grabbed her purse beside the baby carrier and dug out two slips of paper and a pen. Heath came up behind her, wrapping his arms around her waist. "What's that?" he whispered in her ear, his warm breath making her shiver.

Wanda turned in his arms and held up the paper, casting a teasing smile his way. "This"—she held up the first piece of paper—"is an an IOU."

"For?"

"A lifetime supply of Reese's Peanut Butter Cups. You know, for when you build up your tolerance level again."

Heath smiled, reaching for the paper, but Wanda snatched it back, shaking her head. "Nuh-uh. You only get it on one condition."

Marty, Nina, Greg, Keegan, Lou, and Archibald had all gathered in the dining room. Wanda winked at them. "You only get it if you agree to, you know, mate for life with me."

There was a cumulative gasp from their friends.

Heath reached into the pocket of his jeans. "Funny you should say that, Miss Schwartz . . ." He held up the diamond engagement ring, letting it sparkle under the light of the chandelier.

Tears stung Wanda's eyes. Her answer was a kiss, filled with the amazing happiness he'd brought her.

"What's the second piece of paper?" he whispered.

Wanda shook it out and held it up.

He smiled a knowing grin. "Aha! The infamous Fuck It list. Whatcha doin' with that?"

She pointed to her newly revised first entry. It read: spend the rest of her lives with Heath. She'd rewritten some of her list, and during month five with Heath, she'd added her wish to be with him until whatever happened when the end of eternity came.

Just as she was going to cross it off, Heath grabbed the pen and did it for her, winking at her.

Nina came up behind them and thumped Heath on the back. "Nice job, dude. Uh, Wanda? Just a heads-up. I've said it before, and I'll say it again—no fucking yellow bridesmaid dresses."

Marty shook her head in disgust, scooping Hollis up and cradling her in her arms. "Oh, hush, Nina. We'll wear whatever color you like, Wanda—with a smile on our faces and Nina's big yap duct-taped if we have to."

Nina began to protest, but Wanda left Heath's arms to step between the two of them. "You know, you two are like the children

I never had. Knock it off, or I'll show you werevamp beats loser werewolf and lame-assed vampire every time." She followed that up with a wide grin.

Nina tugged a lock of Wanda's hair and snickered. "Cockier and cockier, I tell ya. Every day you get a little feistier. Is this the shit I'm going to have to put up with for an eternity?"

"And then some," Wanda replied, pinching Nina's cheek with a playful tweak.

Plenty of then-somes.

Dakota Cassidy lives for a good laugh in life and in her writing. In fact, she almost loves a good giggle as much as she loves hair products and that's saying something.

Her goals in life are simple (like, really simple): banish the color yellow forever; create world peace via hot rollers and Aqua Net; and finally, nab every tiara in the land by competing in the Miss USA, Miss Universe, and Miss World pageants, then sweeping them in a stunning trifecta of much duct tape and Vaseline usage, all in just under a week's time. All while she writes really fun books!

She loves people, loves to chat, and would love it if you'd come say hello to her on the Yahoo! group of "Accidental Fans." Join Dakota and friends in the chaos by sending an email to dakotacassidy-subscribe@yahoogroups.com, or visit her website at www.dakotacassidy.com.

Dakota lives in Texas with her two sons, her mother, and more cats and dogs than the local animal shelter, and she has a boyfriend who puts the heroes in her books to shame. You can contact her at dakota@dakotacassidy.com. She'd love to hear from you!